THE PIPER'S TUNE

By the same author

THE SPOILED EARTH
THE HIRING FAIR
THE DARK PASTURE
THE DEEP WELL AT NOON
THE BLUE EVENING GONE
THE GATES OF MIDNIGHT
TREASURES ON EARTH
CREATURE COMFORTS
HEARTS OF GOLD
THE GOOD PROVIDER
THE ASKING PRICE
THE WISE CHILD
THE WELCOME LIGHT
A LANTERN FOR THE DARK
SHADOWS ON THE SHORE
THE PENNY WEDDING
THE MARRYING KIND
THE WORKHOUSE GIRL
THE ISLAND WIFE
THE WIND FROM THE HILLS
PRIZED POSSESSIONS

As Caroline Crosby

THE HALDANES

THE PIPER'S TUNE

Jessica Stirling

Hodder & Stoughton

British Library Cataloguing in Publication Data
A CIP catalogue record for this title
is available from the British Library

ISBN 0 340 73865 0

Typeset by Hewer Text Ltd, Edinburgh
Printed and bound in Great Britain by Clays Ltd, St Ives Plc

Hodder and Stoughton
A division of Hodder Headline PLC
338 Euston Road
London NW1 3BH

CONTENTS

Part One – 1898

Part Two – 1901

Part Three — 1906

PART ONE

1898

CHAPTER ONE

The House on the Hill

At one time the Franklins had all lived together in her grand-father's house on Harper's Hill, but wives, babies and that process which Lindsay did not yet understand — growing old rather than growing up — had changed everything. Two by two, like Noah's creatures, Owen Franklin's sons and daughters had left the rambling mansion close to the heart of Glasgow to follow the fashionable trail out of town; not far out of town, however: only a mile or so along the valley of the Clyde to the elegant terraces of Brunswick Park.

The park itself was small and unremarkable. It contained no boating loch or curling pond, no bandstand or bowling green, only three or four drooping shrubs, a flower bed as mysterious as a burial mound and a solitary rustic bench. Above it lay Brunswick Crescent, a handsome piece of architecture with hood-moulds over the first-floor windows, square mullions and pediments that somehow humanised an otherwise austere design. The Franklin brothers had taken to it at once. They were intrigued by the fact that the crescent's apparent curve was made up of subtly angled straight frontages. They were also attracted by the more obvious fact that from the second-floor windows you could look out over the river and observe not only docks and shipyards but a great brooding welter of chimney pots, factory gables and steeples stretching off to the gaunt line of the Renfrewshire hills.

In the last house in Brunswick Crescent Anna Lindsay Franklin had been born and raised. At one time Uncle Donald and Aunt Lilias had resided nearby. And just across the park in a sandstone tenement that even now seemed new, Aunts Kay and Helen had courageously set up residence together.

In the same year that Lindsay's mother had died, though, Aunt Helen had fallen sick and died too. Grieving Aunt Kay had moved across the park to keep house for her widowed brother and care for the newborn infant. Then Kay had found a husband of her own and decamped to Dublin where – so Uncle Donald claimed – she had become more Irish than a field full of leprechauns and more fertile than Macgillicuddy's goat. Ten of Lindsay's cousins, the McCullochs, dwelled near Dublin. But her six Scottish cousins all lived in Grandfather's house where Donald and Lilias had returned after Grandmother had passed away and the big four-storey mansion had proved too forlorn for Owen to occupy on his own.

The Franklins were a close and affectionate family. Lindsay had schooled with the girls, romped at parties and picnics with the boys, and spent almost as much time at Harper's Hill as she had done at home. On that sober Sunday afternoon, however, she felt oddly uneasy as she accompanied her father to her grandfather's house, as if she sensed that some change was about to take place and, whether she liked it or not, she was bound to be affected by it.

She had turned eighteen in February and had shed the Park School's whale-boned bodice, voluminously bunched skirts and the hideous crock-combs that had kept her unruly blonde hair in order. Even cousin Martin, three years her senior and a dreadful tease, treated her with a modicum of respect now. The boys had seen her in more becoming togs, of course, summer dresses and tennis blouses. But it was not until she blossomed into close-fitting skirts and narrow-waisted jackets that Martin, Johnny and young Ross really began to appreciate that Lindsay was not a rough-and-tumble tomboy and could not be flung about like a rugby football.

She was as tall as she would ever be, which was not very tall, alas. She had had her hair coiffed in a style that did not make her seem too coquettish in spite of its coils and carefully nurtured side curls. Papa had also treated her to a halo-brimmed hat and a pair of doeskin shoes with round toes and half heels that Aunt Lilias said added inches to her height, which was just as well, given that she was as small-boned and dainty as her mother had been.

It was a cool, dry April afternoon. Everyone who was anyone was strolling Dumbarton Road or along the paths of the Kelvingrove. Labourers, artisans, wives, sweethearts and children rubbed shoulders with draughtsmen and managers, even with the masters of the factories and shipyards. Those tall-hatted, frock-coated gentlemen and their ornamental wives did not regard it as beneath their dignity to share the Sabbath air and a few hours of leisure with their employees.

Lindsay's father was no exception. He was as brisk and dapper as a redbreast and dressed like 'Sunday' most days of the week. It was not unusual to find him still wearing his morning coat come supper time. He claimed that he did so because he believed in traditional values. Lindsay suspected that he was embarrassed by boyish features upon which, at one time, he had tried to force maturity in the shape of a gigantic moustache until Nanny Cheadle had told him that it made him look like a wanted felon and he had quickly shaved it off.

'Good afternoon, Mr Franklin. Fine day, is it not?'

'Indeed it is.' Hat off, a bow, not too effusive: 'Would this be your good lady wife, by any chance?'

'Well, if it isn't, sur,' the man said, 'Ah'm in trouble.'

'Not a word out of turn then.' Arthur Franklin touched a finger to the side of his nose and winked at the matronly woman whose astonishment at being addressed by such an august person was palpable in her weary brown eyes. 'Good afternoon to you, ma'am.'

'Guid a-a-afternoon, Mr Fr-Fr-Franklin.'

Lindsay smiled too; she could not evade the responsibility of being a Franklin even if she was merely a female. Then her father took her by the arm and with a breeziness that suggested urgency rather than impatience, drew her on towards the fountain and the climb up Harper's Hill.

'Who was that?' Lindsay asked.

'His name's McGregor, I think.'

'One of your employees?' Lindsay said.

'One of our contractors.'

'I'm surprised you remember them.'

'Now, now, Lindsay.'

'I don't mean that they all look the same,' Lindsay explained, 'rather that they all look quite different when they're dressed up.'

They walked rapidly up the sloping gravel path towards the gate. Behind them the university tower soared into a pale grey sky. Ahead, curiously foreshortened, were the mansions of Park Circus and Harper's Hill. Grandfather's house was not visible from the Kelvingrove. It was tucked away on the lee side, a few hundred yards from Lynedoch Street where Lindsay's school was situated. She was so well acquainted with Glasgow's west end that she could have found her way blindfold around the quadrants and terraces that crowned the hills above the leafy banks of the River Kelvin.

'Afternoon, Mr Franklin.'

'Afternoon, afternoon.' Arthur checked his step. 'Calder? Didn't notice you sitting there. Sorry, old chap, can't stop for a chat. Late as it is.'

'Quite all right, sir.' The tall man removed his hat and managed to give Lindsay a little bow – 'Miss Franklin' – before she was whisked away.

'That was very rude, Papa,' Lindsay said. 'Couldn't you have spared him a minute or two?'

'No time.'

'If,' she said, 'we're in such an all-fired hurry to reach Pappy's by three o'clock, why didn't you find us a cab?'

'Soon be there, dear, soon be there.'

'Why won't you tell me what's going on?'

'I can't,' he said.

'You mean you won't.'

'I can't because I don't know. It's your grandfather's surprise.'

'It's not his birthday, is it?'

'No, that's not until next month.'

Papa helped her up the high kerb that separated the cobbles from the pavement. He paused to dab a bead of perspiration from his brow with one of several linen handkerchiefs that Miss Runciman had placed in his pockets. He put the handkerchief away and checked the time on his watch. Then, adopting an air of leisurely decorum that befitted the younger son of a ship-building tycoon, he escorted his pretty daughter around the corner and up the steps to the big, brass-handled front door.

Owen Franklin had no middle name and none of the ancestral debris that perpetuated itself in jaw-breaking monikers. He was lucky to have any sort of name at all, in fact, for he had been abandoned as an infant on the coal-tip at Franklin in the shadow of Penarth Head.

He was by no means ashamed of his humble origins, however. He liked to brag to his grandchildren in the Welsh accent that he had never managed to shake that his father had been a miner, his mother a fishwife and that he had been suckled on salt water in lieu of breast milk and weaned on coal-dust instead of saps. The sad truth was that he had no clue who his parents were. He had been reared in a foundlings' house over-looking the mudflats at the mouth of the Ely until, aged ten, he was put out to work. If you believe in the awkward forces of destiny, which Owen undoubtedly did, it was at this point that fate stepped in and saved him from an undistinguished life of drudgery on the deck of a coastal collier or fishing smack.

He was apprenticed to one Hugh Pemberton who, in a

smoky little forge on the banks of the Glamorganshire canal, was engaged in improving the efficiency of steam valves. In this aspect of mechanics young Owen demonstrated a talent so precocious that it amounted almost to genius. In the course of the next fifteen years he also acquired an aptitude for the management of money. When Cardiff eventually became too small for a man of his talents, he journeyed north to Scotland. He had just enough capital to set up on his own and ensure that his 'bright ideas' earned profits not for some new master but for himself.

It was not until 1874 that Owen plucked up the courage to purchase the sequestrated firm of Patrick Hagen & Hall, a near-derelict little shipyard tucked between Scotstoun and Whiteinch where, aided by a loan from the Bank of Scotland, he set about building river craft, ferries and small, fast steam launches.

Although labouring with metal and money occupied most of his attention, Owen also found time to fall in love. He met Katherine Forbes at a concert given jointly by the Perthshire Choral Union and the Glasgow Tonic Sol Fa Society. Halfway through a composition based on Haydn's 'God is Our Emperor' Owen realised that he had found his soul-mate. He remained smitten with Kath throughout twenty-eight years of married life, rejoiced in the births of five children and mourned one poor little one, Mary, who died when she was eight months old. He was still in love with his dear wife when she fell ill and was finally taken from him early in the morning of a bright and beautiful May day, a tragedy that robbed him, at least for a while, of ambition in all its fiery forms.

'Pappy?'

Lindsay did not have to reach up to kiss her grandfather's cheek; he was hardly much taller than she was now. In the past decade it seemed that age had squeezed him down sinew on sinew so that his grandchildren could look him square in the eye and his sons, Donald and Arthur, appeared at long last like full grown men in his presence.

'Pappy, what is it? What's this surprise you have for us?'

'Patience, child, patience,' Owen Franklin said as Lizzie, the front-hall maid, removed Lindsay's coat and carried it and her father's hat off into the cloakroom beneath the massive staircase. 'What did you tell her, Arthur?'

'How could I tell her anything when you've kept me in the dark too?'

'You don't have to be so peevish,' Owen said. 'It's no more than a bit of indulgence towards an old man that I'm asking for.'

'What old man? You're not an old man.'

'Perhaps not by your lights, Arthur, but I'm rapidly steering that way.'

They were in the great hallway of the mansion, on the huge Indian rug that had been the gift of some foreign shipping agent or other. The rug added cohesion to the oak-floored entrance's job-lots of armour and broadswords and the array of military muskets that Owen had purchased umpteen years ago when he still thought that the best way to please Kath was to turn himself into a duplicate of a Highland laird. In other rooms the decor was more acceptably maritime, with several fine Dutch sea-paintings on the walls, old chronometers, quadrants and sextants laid out in glass cases, and scale models of craft designed and built at the Franklins' yard in Aydon Road.

There was no daylight, save a dusty shaft from the stained-glass window at the bend of the staircase. Lindsay had often wondered if this was what it had felt like to be incarcerated in the hold of an old wooden-walled slaving ship or the engine-room of one of the ironclads that had plied the Atlantic routes thirty years ago, for her grandfather's house reminded her of some sort of vessel beached on the summit of Harper's Hill.

The door to the drawing-room on the right of the hall was closed. She wondered where her aunt, uncle and cousins were, and the manservant, Giles, who as a rule was never very far away.

She studied her grandfather with a degree of apprehension. His wrinkled features and watery blue eyes were not threatening and, indeed, his wispy little smile seemed to hint that the surprise would not be unpleasant or turn out to be some trade matter that didn't concern her.

'Are you ready?' he said.

'Oh, get on with it, Pappy, for heaven's sake,' his son said. 'Open the blessed door, let's see what you're hiding in there.'

Grandfather Franklin allowed himself one more chuckle, then, like a mischievous child, pushed the door open inch by inch.

'What the devil!' Lindsay's father exclaimed. 'It's Kay. Our Kay.'

'Didn't expect that, now did you, Arthur?'

'Why didn't you tell me she was coming home?' Arthur hissed. 'If this is your idea of a joke, Pappy, I must say it's in damned bad taste.'

It had not occurred to Lindsay that there had ever been animosity between her emigrant aunt and her father. She could not recall having heard him say anything detrimental about his sister. Now that she thought of it, though, he had made no effort to visit the McCullochs when business took him to Ireland. Donald had visited Dublin once or twice over the years and kept in touch with Kay by regular exchange of letters, but her father received the Irish news only at second hand. At that moment Lindsay realised that perhaps she didn't know all there was to know about the Franklins' chequered past and that there might be more to this family reunion than first met the eye.

Her father adopted the haughty air that he usually reserved for naval inspectors or agents from foreign governments, a chilly sort of arrogance that Lindsay did not care for. 'Katherine.' He weaved towards his sister. He obviously had no intention of falling into her arms and certainly felt no obligation to kiss her. 'How nice to see you again.'

Allotted pride of place in this pride of Franklins, the woman was seated in a walnut armchair in the centre of the room. The massive gilt-framed mirror above the mantelpiece falsely enlarged the size of the gathering so that the room seemed crowded. In the mirror Lindsay could see the back of her aunt's head and the dark hair of the young man at her aunt's side. His hand was pressed to her shoulder as if to dissuade her from rising too hurriedly or, for that matter, from rising at all.

Aunt Kay remained steadfastly seated. She crossed an arm over her bony bosom, extended her right hand and permitted her brother to take it across his palm like an offering of fish. He dipped his head as if to sniff rather than kiss her ungloved fingers.

'Still no manners, I see,' Kay said.

Lindsay's father stepped back.

'What do you mean?'

'Late as usual,' Aunt Kay answered.

'Minutes,' Arthur Franklin said. 'Mere minutes. *If* a certain party had thought fit to inform me that we were being honoured with your presence I'd have made a point of being on time.'

'Well, you're here now, I suppose,' Kay said.

'I suppose I am,' said Arthur.

He moved away to seek protection from his brother or comfort from Aunt Lilias who, to judge from her expression, was amused by the display of sibling rivalry. Left in the firing line, Lindsay took a deep breath and with all the warmth she could muster presented herself to the lean, untidy woman who, just eighteen years ago, had been – albeit briefly – a mother to her.

'Aunt Kay,' she said. 'I'm so pleased to meet you at last.'

The woman looked up. In her eyes, the pale blue unspeckled eyes common to all Owen Franklin's offspring, Lindsay thought she detected an ember of affection. 'Anna?' her aunt said.

'I prefer to be called Lindsay.'

'So I've been told,' her aunt said. 'By jingo, you've changed. You were such an ugly baby. I thought you were one of Mr Darwin's monkeys when the midwife first brought you out.'

'I'm afraid I don't remember it,' Lindsay said, not seriously.

'I remember it as if it were yesterday,' Kay said. 'You squawking in my arms while she was upstairs breathing her last.'

Lindsay felt her cheeks redden. An embarrassed silence came over her cousins. Uncle Donald cleared his throat. Then the young man said, 'Time enough for reminiscences, Mam. Meanwhile, why don't you introduce me?'

He had a smooth Irish accent, soft but distinct.

The haggard lines vanished from Kay's face when she addressed her son.

'Tell her yourself who you are, Forbes. Give her a hug if that's what you fancy.' She fashioned a scooping gesture to shoo her son out from behind the chair and drive him into the open. 'She's Anna's daughter, her that died along about the same time as my sister Helen. Her father's my second brother.'

Lindsay assumed that he would have heard of her. She had certainly heard of him: Owen Forbes McCulloch: Welsh, Scottish and Irish rolled into one. He had dark hair, brown eyes and the sort of long lashes that a girl might envy. There was nothing remotely feminine about him, however. He was the handsomest man Lindsay had ever met, and he certainly wasn't bashful. In fact, he was possessed of an easy self-assurance that made it difficult to believe that he was younger than she was. When he spoke in that soft lilting accent she could almost smell the lush green meadows of County Meath.

Behind her, cousins Cissie and Mercy giggled, but their mirth seemed faded, almost remote. He did not hug her. He was not so bold, so modern as all that. He leaned across his mother and took Lindsay's hand.

She felt a little shiver go through her, a ripple of awe and something so novel that she did not recognise it as desire, a longing to have him touch her again or, more like the thing, never to let her go.

'Cousin Lindsay,' he said quietly.

And equally quietly, she answered, 'Cousin Forbes.'

✳   ✳   ✳

For twenty minutes after his employer had passed, Tom Calder remained seated on a bench near the Memorial Fountain. The sun had not broken through and soon after three o'clock the air took on a chilly edge. Courting couples abandoned the daffodil slopes and families began to drift away towards the tenements that flanked Finnieston and Dumbarton Road or to catch the halfpenny omnibus that would carry them two or three miles to Whiteinch and Scotstoun. Forearms on knees, Tom observed the gradual exodus.

He was not sly or threatening. He had no designs upon the girls, which was probably just as well, for there was something about the tall man with the weathered complexion that made the lassies who toured the park in search of romance a wee bit wary. At thirty-four, he was probably too old for most of them. His hair was thinning and he had the sort of lean, underfed features that only a desperate spinster would find attractive. His eyes were disconcertingly alert and at the same time unseeing, as if the best you had to offer might not be good enough for him. The impression he gave was not one of moodiness or melancholy but of indifference, and indifference was the one thing with which no girl, young or otherwise, could cope.

Tom Calder, like his employer, was a widower. He had a daughter, Sylvie, who out of necessity he had relinquished into the care of his wife's sister and her husband some years ago. He saw her by arrangement only once or twice a month unless he contrived to encounter her 'by accident' when Florence or Albert brought her to the park between Sabbath school and evening service. He knew that he had lost her and that it would be better to let her go. But some deep paternal instinct prevented it. At eight Sylvie had been 'his little sweetheart'. At ten, after he had returned from Africa, she had still shown him some affection. Now twelve, she was his sweetheart no longer. She wasn't even polite to him and would cling truculently to Florence or Albert whenever their paths crossed.

Motionless as marble, Tom surveyed the Radnor Street gate

and the circular path around the fountain basin. If Albert was Sylvie's escort then the chance of a meeting was remote. Albert was too crafty to follow the same route week after week. If Florence was the guardian of the hour, however, the opportunity was much improved, for Florence, out of habit or lack of imagination, followed an identical path every Sunday.

He heard the university bell call the half-hour. Several clocks in the old burgh steeples lightly answered it.

They were late, or possibly did not intend to come at all. Perhaps his brother-in-law Albert Hartnell had spotted him and had whisked little Sylvie, not unwilling, up the hill to lead her home by the high back ways. He glanced bleakly along the gravel path – and there they were: Florence tall and spare in a costume of smooth-faced Venetian serge with hardly a frill to relieve its severity; Sylvie in the daft countrified style that Florence had foisted on her, in a kilted skirt, a jacket of fawn cloth with a sailor collar, a bonnet with velveteen tassels. Sylvie bore no resemblance to her mother except perhaps in the fine complexion, so pale and silken that it seemed less like flesh than an expensive Eastern fabric.

Tom rose. He could not feign casualness. He was useless at pretence. He stalked towards them, arms swinging. Sylvie deliberately turned her back and surveyed the crenellated rooftops that overlooked the Clyde.

'What are you *doing* here?' Florence asked.

'Taking the air, just taking the air.'

'Have you nothing better to do with yourself?'

'No, nothing. How are you, Sylvie? Are you over your cold?'

In spite of her apparent fragility Sylvie had so far shown no disposition towards the asthmatic condition to which her mother had eventually succumbed. Even so, Tom fretted over every little sniffle and cough and, in years past, had gone almost mad with worry when some epidemic or other swept through the city, scything down children like weeds. These days he was more sanguine about his daughter's ability to survive.

'Sylvie, answer your father.'

'I am very well, thank you.'

'Your cold?'

'That's gone,' said Florence.

'Has it really?' said Tom. 'I mean, really and truly?'

'Yes.'

'No after-effects?'

'Do you think I'd have brought her out if she was ailing?'

'No, Florence, of course you wouldn't.' Tom eyed his daughter in the vain hope that she had found it in her heart to forgive him whatever transgressions had turned her against him. 'Is all well at school, dearest?'

'Yes, thank you.'

No 'Papa', no 'Father', no intimacies graced her reply. He wondered at what point along the way he had lost her.

He had handed her over to Florence and Albert not long after Dorothy had passed on. His sister-in-law had understood the necessity not just of earning a living but of grinding on with a career. He in turn had convinced himself that Sylvie needed a woman's care and a stable home and that all he would be able to provide would be servants and nannies. Florence and Albert had been only too willing to take Sylvie off his hands, for they were childless and Sylvie had seemed like a gift from God. He had no right to feel slighted that she was more attached to Florence and Albert than she was to him.

Florence said, 'I don't know why you do this, Tom.'

'Do what?' he said, still trying vainly to attract Sylvie's attention.

'You are welcome to call at the house at any time, you know.'

'I do not feel welcome,' Tom said. 'Besides, you are out so much these days that I can never be sure . . .' He let the complaint trail off.

'We're never far away,' Florence said. 'Are we, dear?'

Sylvie shook her head.

'Out and about on the Lord's business,' Florence said. 'I take it you haven't sunk so far, Tom, that you would regard that as neglect?' With a certain firmness, his sister-in-law manoeuvred Sylvie round to face him. 'Now you're here, however, there's a certain matter I feel I must mention.'

'Regarding money?' Tom said. 'School fees, by any chance?'

The cost of child-rearing seemed to escalate year by year. At Florence's insistence Sylvie had been put to the Park School and Tom paid the fees, along with everything else on Florence's carefully itemised account.

'I have no intention of conducting monetary business in a public park on the Sabbath,' Florence said. 'I would be obliged if you would call at our house not later than Thursday. We will be at home, I believe, on Tuesday after nine o'clock, and from eight o'clock on Wednesday.'

'I have a choir meeting on Wednesday,' Tom said.

Sylvie gave a huffy little grunt, her first unprompted utterance.

Florence said, 'Is a choir meeting more important than your daughter's welfare?'

'We're joining in a special performance,' Tom interrupted, 'in the cathedral.'

'Oh! That will be *The Messiah*?'

'No, an Easter Cantata. Massed choirs with soloists.' He risked touching his daughter's shoulder. 'Why don't you ask Aunt Florence to bring you along, sweetheart?' he said. 'I'm sure you'll enjoy it.'

Again the grunt, a dainty snort; a flinching, flouncing away.

He looked down at her and, startled, recognised that she was spoiled, a ruined child still capable of cutting through his indifference like a hot knife through butter. It riled him that she should have so much power over him. For a moment he was linked to Sylvie not by love or guilt but by annoyance.

Without quite knowing what he was doing, he bent his long shanks and crouched before her. She tried to sidle off but he would have none of it. He gripped her firmly by the shoulders. His hands looked huge against the rounded velveteen. He squared her, steadied her and peered into her grey petulant eyes.

'Do you not know who I am?' he asked.

She said nothing.

'*Do* you know who I am?'

She nodded.

He felt cruel, but unrepentant. 'Tell me who I am, Sylvie.'

'You're my – you're my – my father.'

'And whether you like it or not I always will be.'

'Tom, please don't chastise . . .'

He ignored Florence. 'I will not be treated like a fool, not by you – especially not by you – or by anyone else. You may not like me, Sylvie, but at least you will do me the honour of being courteous. Do I make myself clear?'

'Yes.'

She pursed her small, sweet, rosebud lips and scowled defiantly. She sensed that she had been exposed, her power diminished, but she would not surrender everything to him, not all at once.

'Yes, what?' he said.

'Yes, Papa.'

Tom grinned a crooked grin, like a crack whispering across ice. It was a small triumph, petty in every respect, but decisiveness gave him a strange thrill, eliminating, if only for a little while, the hollowness within.

He got nimbly to his feet.

'That's better,' he said, then to Florence, 'I'll drop my cheque for the summer term round to the house on Tuesday.'

'After nine o'clock, please,' said Florence.

'After nine o'clock,' said Tom. 'Is there anything else I have to pay for?'

'I think that's all in the meantime.' Florence hesitated. 'Do you wish me to bring her to the cathedral on Wednesday? If it means so much to you . . .'

'It means nothing to me,' Tom said. 'I just thought she might enjoy it.'

'Unfortunately she has no affinity for music,' Florence said.

'And I have a Mission class on Wednesday,' Sylvie said, 'Papa.'

He nodded. 'It would never do to miss a Mission class.'

She was looking up at him, not hiding now. She had adapted quickly to his changed attitude. She had replaced truculence with coyness, a niceness that was entirely self-serving. Perhaps she was not so very different from her mother after all.

'I will come to hear you sing very soon, Papa,' she said, then, to his astonishment, lifted herself on tiptoe and presented her gossamer cheek for a kiss. 'I promise.'

He paused, then brushed his lips against her cold little brow.

'Goodbye, Papa.'

'Goodbye, sweetheart,' he said and, with more relief than regret, watched Florence lead Sylvie away towards the Radnor gate.

Dining in the grand style had never been her grandfather's forte: dining well was quite another matter. Owen Franklin, his sons, daughter and grandchildren were blessed with healthy appetites and a fondness for good food that kept cooks and kitchen hands thoroughly on their mettle. It was not uncommon for a dozen folk to settle around the long table in the dining-room and the entire domestic staff, including the latest fumble-fingered little parlour-maid, to be marshalled to lug tureens, trays and steaming casseroles up from the kitchens.

The dining-table was the family's meeting place. It was also the place where the Franklins' wealth was most obviously displayed in silverware, tableware and fancy linens. Those who fancied themselves in the know – stockbrokers, accountants and lawyers – claimed that the Franklins devoured more in a week than the shipyard earned in a month. That if it hadn't been for its appetite the family would have achieved a higher place on the social scale and that Owen, or possibly Donald, would have been elected to positions of civic responsibility. Although the slander contained more than a grain of truth, it took no account of the fact that Owen and his sons cared less about power than they did about pleasure and devoted themselves to good food and good music with a panache that, in some quarters, was regarded as vulgar.

What the snobs would have made of Kay, who ate scallops with a spoon and chicken breasts with her fingers, was anyone's guess. Safe to say that even the most high and mighty would have been impressed by soft-spoken Forbes whose combination of charm, rapacity and impeccable table manners few aristocratic heirs could match. Lindsay's cousins, Cissie, Mercy and Pansy, were so impressed by Forbes that they neglected their own nutritional requirements and passed him salt cellars, pepper mills and mustard dishes at such a rate of knots that Grandfather Owen eventually had to tap his plate with a steak knife and wag a warning finger just to give the poor lad respite.

Lindsay, too, was impressed by her Irish cousin. She was delighted by his attentions, attentions too discreet to draw sarcastic comment from Martin or Johnny but just obvious enough to confirm that he, Forbes, had also experienced an instantaneous rapport and that of all the girls at table she was the one he found most appealing. They were seated together at the end of the long table, separated from the girl cousins by Uncle Donald and Aunt Lilias. By mischievous coincidence Kay and Lindsay's father had been placed side by side and, with slightly less tact than their offspring, soon fell to bickering and recrimination which, Lindsay guessed, echoed old rivalries between them.

She was unsure just how serious the display of mutual animosity was until Forbes leaned towards her and murmured, 'Mam's bark is a lot worse than her bite, you know. She has a sharp tongue but a kind heart.'

'I have never seen my father so heated,' Lindsay whispered.

'Is it not that he's just enjoying himself?' Forbes said.

'No. I really don't think they're very fond of each other.'

'Oh, now, and I'm sure that they are,' said Forbes. 'It would be a fine thing if they were still enemies after all these years, especially now I'm going to be one of you.'

'What do you mean,' Lindsay said, 'one of us?'

'I'm coming to stay in Glasgow while I study.'

'Are you?' Lindsay tried to hide her excitement. 'What will you study?'

'Engineering.'

'Marine engineering?'

'Well, that will be a part of the course,' he said. 'But it's not on my mind to be going to sea as a regular thing. I'm aiming higher than ship's engineer.'

'What *do* you aim to be?' said Lindsay.

He eased himself away from her, not impolitely.

He speared a final piece of beef from his plate and put it into his mouth. He did not appear to chew, merely to swallow.

Lindsay watched his throat move, a soft undulation.

Everything about him suggested precocious self-assurance, a physicality that she could not equate with a man – a lad – who was twelve or fourteen months younger than she was. She wondered if all young Dubliners were like this or if being the eldest in a family of ten had forced maturity upon him.

He glanced at her, placed knife and fork evenly on his plate, and smiled.

The smile was in lieu of an answer.

She might have put the question again if Cissie, all broad cheeks and freckles, hadn't leaned forward and told her excitedly, 'He's coming to stay here with us. Aren't you, Forbes?'

'I am; for a time at least.'

'Here?' Lindsay's excitement diminished at the prospect of Forbes McCulloch lodging under the same roof as her predatory cousin. 'I mean, here in Pappy's house?'

'In the boys' room,' Cissie said. 'He'll sleep in the boys' room.'

Martin laughed and informed his new-found cousin that he would have to sleep head to toe with Ross since there was no room for another bed. Ross protested. Johnny supported him. Aunt Lilias joined in the teasing. Lindsay stared down at her meat plate, watched the manservant's gloved hand remove it and replace it with a small dish of iced sherbet.

She could feel a tingle in the room, the family's vibrant energy beginning to revolve like one of the new steam turbines that Donald had taken them to see at Spithead last summer. She could feel the energy beginning to flow about her and wondered why she no longer revelled in it, why she felt so cut off and apart. For the first time she felt obliged to acknowledge that Martin was not her brother, Cissie not her sister and that she stood a half-step apart from the others.

She ate the sherbet ice, three small silver spoonfuls, cold and fizzy on her tongue; heard the laughter all about her.

He did not laugh: Forbes did not laugh.

He too had brothers, four of them, five sisters. He knew what to do, what to say, how to take care of himself in the maul. But he didn't laugh, didn't roar, didn't clamour for attention. He smiled and watched, and swallowed the cold confection, his throat undulating as the sherbet slid smoothly down.

He leaned lightly against Lindsay once more.

'I would rather sleep with you,' he said, so quietly that Lindsay could not be sure that he had spoken at all.

'What?' Lindsay said. 'What did you say?'

'In your house. I would rather stay in your house,' Forbes said.

'No, that's not what you—'

'Hush now. Hush,' he told her. 'I think our dear old grandpappy is about to make a speech.'

✻   ✻   ✻

The manservant, Giles, was last to leave the dining-room. He took with him the empty sherbet dishes, decanters and those glasses that did not contain wine. Before lifting the laden tray he carefully swept crumbs from the tablecloth and collected them in a little brass-handled pan. He balanced the pan beneath the tray and used his elbow to open the dining-room door.

Outside, the April sky was tinted brown, not pretty or pastel but flat and sombre and, just before the servant left and Grandfather Owen rose to speak, a few speckles of rain laid themselves against the window panes. At a signal from the old man Donald and Arthur lit the candles and sat down again. Silence in that uproarious room seemed oppressive, almost uncanny, so much so that Pansy, the youngest, turned her face away and clung to brother Johnny as if she feared that she might need protection.

Lindsay too was tense. She might have sought her Irish cousin's arm except that she was no longer sure of him, no longer sure at all.

'First,' Owen began, 'may I bid a special welcome to Kay, who we haven't seen for far too long, and to my grandson Forbes.' He paused, cleared his throat and went on: 'I must say it's grand to have all my children and so many of their children gathered together at last. I wish' — another hesitation — 'I just wish that Helen had been spared to bear children too. That, however, was not the Lord's intention, and we can't go questioning the ways of the Lord.'

With an unusual twinge of resentment Lindsay wondered why her grandfather hadn't mentioned *her* mother, hadn't mourned for the children that *she* had never borne.

'I'm no longer as young as I was,' Owen continued. 'It has been in my mind for some time to clear the decks for the next generation; not a bad generation either, in my biased opinion. Be that as it may, I have decided to retire from—'

'What's this you're saying, Pappy?' Donald blurted out. 'You can't retire. What'll we do without you?'

'Are you ill?' said Kay in that piercing voice of hers. 'Are you a-dying, Daddy, is that why you've brought us from Dublin?'

'No, damn it,' Owen said. 'Don't go getting your hopes up. I am not a-dying. You don't get rid of me as easily as all that. I am, however, just a bit too rusty for many more repairs. I've got to face the fact that my next voyage or the one after might take me to the breaker's yard.'

'Are you giving up the chairmanship?' Lindsay's father asked.

'Yes.'

Out of the corner of her eye Lindsay noticed Aunt Lilias cover Uncle Donald's hand with her own, a gesture not of commiseration but of excitement. Apparently no hint of her grandfather's intentions had reached the Franklins. She suspected that the McCullochs might have guessed what was in the wind, though; that Kay, her husband and possibly Forbes had discussed its implications and made plans in advance.

Grandfather Owen held up his hand. 'Be easy now, be easy. I'm not selling the yard. I'm not leaving you stranded. I've gathered you all together to hear what I've got in mind for the future. First,' he said, 'let me tell you that Forbes will be joining the firm to train as a manager. He will follow the same route of learning as both of you did. Do you remember what that was like, Donald, Arthur?'

'Only too well,' said Lindsay's father.

'Hard, very hard,' said Donald.

'Forbes will start out with a year in Beardmore's, at the Parkhead Forge. I've already arranged it with Mr Peterson. He'll be waged by Franklin's during that period. After he's learned something of forging and casting we'll bring him into the engine shop at Aydon Road while he undertakes a course of night classes at the Maritime Institute.'

'Do you approve of this programme, Kay?' Lindsay's father enquired.

'Indeed, and I do,' Kay replied.

'Was it your idea or the boy's?'

'It was my idea, Uncle Arthur,' Forbes McCulloch said. 'I may be Irish born but I think I've always been a Scot at heart. It wasn't my mother but my father who opposed the notion of my coming across the sea for a career.'

'It may not be so easy as you imagine,' Lindsay's father said. 'We carry no passengers at Franklin's.'

'Forbes will be no passenger, rest assured,' Kay put in. 'He's been taught the value of hard work. Aye, he'll put in more than he takes out.'

'Stop it.' Owen shook his head. 'I won't have this bickering. Forbes is as much your flesh and blood as Martin, say, or Ross. You've nothing against them, Arthur, have you?'

Lindsay watched her father's chest swell. She knew what that lungful of oxygen indicated, how he would hold his breath as if to prepare for singing a long phrase of music or striking out, pure and clear, at a top note in the register. Perhaps, she thought, he's just envious of Kay because he doesn't have a son to put into the business.

'Nothing against any of them,' her father said. 'I'm just a trifle concerned about how many more – ah – apprentices from Dublin we can accommodate?'

'My brothers,' Forbes answered before his mother could open her mouth, 'my brothers, Uncle Arthur, have no interest in shipbuilding. They're all lined up to enter the brewing trade.'

'I see,' said Arthur. 'But you prefer salt water to black stout?'

'I do.'

'Lilias has already agreed to let the lad lodge here,' said Owen.

'Oh, has she?' said Arthur.

'Where are *you* going, Pappy?' said Martin.

'Strathmore, in Perthshire,' Owen answered. 'I've leased a house in that neck of the woods, near Kelkemmit.'

'Perthshire!' Johnny said. 'What the heck will *you* do in Perthshire?'

'Fish,' said Owen, curtly.

'What about Franklin's?' said Lindsay's father.

'Don't fret, Arthur,' Owen Franklin said. 'You won't starve. When it comes to ship design you know more than I ever did, and Donald is better at securing contracts than I ever was.' He pointed at one son and then the other. 'What's wrong with the pair of you? Don't tell me you're too timid to take over. Good God, you're twice the age I was when I struck out on my own.'

'Yes, but things were different in those days,' Donald said.

'Don't blather, son,' Owen Franklin told him. 'You're delighted to have your chance at last. And if you aren't, you should be. I'm stepping down, fading out of the picture. I'm going away into the Perthshire hills to threaten the salmon and that's an end of that part of it.'

'What's the other part, Pappy?' Aunt Lilias asked.

Reaching down by his chair Owen Franklin brought out five manila envelopes, each sealed with the firm's stamp, each with a name handwritten upon it. He held them in a little fan against his waistcoat while he looked around the table, his eyes travelling from face to face quite deliberately and without a trace of sentiment.

'This,' said Pappy Owen, and with a decisive little flick of the wrist began tossing envelopes down the length of the table to Donald, to Arthur, to Martin and to Forbes.

And finally, astonishingly, to Lindsay, who caught it in both hands.

CHAPTER TWO

An Eye to the Future

The house had been lit by gas for as long as Lindsay could recall. Cook and Maddy, the parlour-maid, had swan-necked jets to illuminate their rooms in the basement and Miss Runciman, the Franklins' housekeeper, had two of the same in her forbidding second-floor sitting-room. Only Nanny Cheadle eschewed the use of such new-fangled gadgetry and continued to go about the house with an oil lamp in her hand, trailing smoke behind her like a tugboat. Nanny's little idiosyncrasy drove Miss Runciman crazy, for she refused to accept that Nanny was a law unto herself and had earned the right to pretend that the nineteenth century was not drawing to a close and all was just as it had been before the Stephensons invented the *Rocket*.

The pungent odours of wick and paraffin had been all through the house when Eleanor Runciman had returned from evening service. She had hunted down her mortal enemy who, lamp still glowing, had taken refuge behind the locked door of the library and refused to come out. The spectacle of house-keeper and Nanny playing hide-and-seek amused Lindsay as a rule but neither she nor her father were in any frame of mind to put up with it that particular evening. Within minutes of entering the house Lindsay was placating Miss Runciman with a snifter of brandy in the downstairs parlour while Arthur beat a fist on the library door and ordered Nanny to give herself up.

'Five minutes, I can't leave you alone for five minutes,' Arthur shouted. 'Five minutes and you are at each other's throats. Behaving like children. Worse than children. At least children would be in bed by now. Nanny, Nanny Cheadle, come out of there this minute.'

'She wants to steal my lamp.'

'She doesn't want your blessed lamp. She just wants you to put it out.'

'Shan't.'

'Nanny, do as I say or I'll – I'll throw you out on the street.'

The library door opened.

'You wouldn't do that to me, Mr Arthur, would you?' Nanny Cheadle asked in a voice that managed to be both pathetic and shameless at one and the same time.

'No, I wouldn't,' Arthur said. 'I only want my library back, Nanny.'

'You don't want to steal my lamp?'

'For God's sake, what kind of a household . . . Take the lamp with you, just take the damned lamp and go to bed, Nanny, please.'

In the downstairs parlour Miss Runciman knocked back brandy, drew herself up inside her stiff black woollen dress and long-waisted corset and, with colour returning to her lips, said, 'I am perfectly all right, thank you, Lindsay. I should not have lost my temper.'

'No, you shouldn't, Miss Runciman,' Lindsay agreed.

'That woman so muddles my head I tend to forget myself.' She sniffed, elongated herself even more inside the corset. 'Did you have an enjoyable dinner?'

'Interesting,' Lindsay said. 'Interesting rather than enjoyable.'

'If I may ask, what was the nature of the surprise?'

'My Aunt Kay has arrived from Dublin,' Lindsay said, 'with her son.'

'A family reunion,' Miss Runciman said. 'How nice!'

It was on the tip of Lindsay's tongue to inform the housekeeper that her grandfather had announced his retirement and that he, the most gregarious man you could imagine, proposed to take himself off to a remote country house in the wilds of Perthshire. She could hardly believe it herself and, along with her cousins, suspected some hidden motive on Pappy's part. She said nothing about her own good fortune. Time enough for celebrations when everything had been signed, sealed and delivered and she better understood what was going on.

Lindsay didn't pretend to know what stocks were and how they differed from shares. Discussion in school of such erudite financial matters had bored her, though she had always been impressed by girls who knew who owned what and what dividends their fathers' companies paid out. Since leaving the Park School she had done what most other girls did with their time. Filled her days with piano lessons and lectures on art and literature. Went shopping in town with Cissie and Aunt Lilias. Played tennis, or skated upon the boating lake when it was frozen or upon the indoor roller-skating rink at the Causeway where there were potted palms, a melodic little orchestra and a tea-room that served hot chocolate and gingerbread.

Last summer she had gone on several excursions with her cousins, windswept trips downriver in a paddle-steamer to Rothesay or Millport. On one long sun-drenched day, they had cruised all the way around Arran and back again. And in August Uncle Donald had taken them all to London and on to Southampton for a special Naval Review at Spithead, a tiring but rewarding experience. Then there were launches, concerts, dances and rather grand dinners which, now that she had turned eighteen, Papa expected her to attend, sometimes with Cissie for company and sometimes not. What dramas and anxieties the future held in store did not concern her; she assumed that she would be taken care of until the time came to marry and settle down.

The cream-laid sheet of paper in the manila envelope that her grandfather had given her had changed all that, of course.

'Will your aunt be staying long in Glasgow?' Miss Runciman asked.

'I don't know,' Lindsay answered. 'Probably not. My cousin – his name is Forbes, by the way – has come to train as a manager. He will be lodging with Lilias and Donald.'

'A brand-new cousin?' Miss Runciman said, with a little tilt of the eyebrow. 'Is he handsome?'

'I really couldn't say,' Lindsay lied. Miss Runciman's interest in potential suitors for Lindsay had become all too apparent this last year or so. 'He's much, much younger than I am. Hardly more than a boy, in fact.'

'Ah,' said Miss Runciman. 'So he *is* handsome. Irishmen usually are. I was almost engaged to a gentleman from Cork once.'

'Really!' said Lindsay, dryly. She had too many things on her mind to be bothered with Miss Runciman's romantic anecdotes. 'I believe Nanny has gone upstairs now, Miss Runciman. I suspect my father would like tea brought up to the library, if that can be arranged. Some tea and toast, I think. For two.'

She had no notion what her father had made of the evening's events or how her grandfather's startling announcement had affected him. She had tried to introduce the subject on the way home in the cab but her father had been curiously withdrawn. She'd had sense enough not to press him. She had sat with the envelope in her hand, looking out at the city, wondering if the sheet of cream-laid paper and the arrival of the Irish cousin were somehow connected.

'For two?' Miss Runciman enquired.

'Yes. I've something to discuss with Papa and we may be some time about it. You may retire to bed whenever you wish.'

'Thank you, Lindsay,' the housekeeper said. 'I'll fetch your tea first.'

'And toast,' said Lindsay.

* * *

Outside the first-floor study there was little to indicate what Arthur Franklin did for a living. The house was comfortably appointed but had an uncluttered feel to it that her father had been careful to preserve. Lindsay suspected that the public rooms had changed little since her mother had arranged them and still reflected how the house had been when her parents had first taken occupancy twenty years ago.

Twenty years ago! She could not imagine it. In fact, she had been completely oblivious to the passage of time until she had arrived at her first bleeding and had altered mentally and emotionally. It was as if the tide of nature had affected not just her reproductive organs – Aunt Lilias had explained the mystery very scientifically – but her brain too, her ability to perceive all sorts of things that had been hidden from her before.

As a child she had believed that she loved Nanny Cheadle more than she loved Papa. Believed that she was Nanny Cheadle's child and that when she was old enough the truth would be revealed. Had even imagined that she might belong to Aunt Lilias and that the woman whose oval portrait hung above the fireplace in the big, seldom-used ground-floor drawing-room was not Margaret, her mother, but some ethereal substitute who had never really existed.

When the house had been quiet she would borrow the shell-backed mirror from Nanny Cheadle's dressing-table and bring it down to the empty drawing-room; the room in which a fire was lighted only on the coldest of winter days; the room with the little piano in it, the peaceful, faintly dusty room that seemed to have been preserved for no other purpose than to shelter the oval portrait over the fireplace. She would stand on toe-tip on the fender and angle the mirror so that she could see her face and the face in the portrait framed side by side. She had striven to recognise herself, to be able to say, 'Yes, this is who I am,' but could not, and had been both mystified and frustrated when Pappy or Uncle Donald in a soft, muddled moment had brushed her fair curls and told her that she looked so like her mama that she might be her double.

Lindsay had never been a 'kitchen jenny' like her smallest cousin, Pansy, who enjoyed spending time below stairs with the cook and the maids. Parlour, bedroom and library were the heart of the house as far as Lindsay was concerned and she left all domestic dealings to Miss Runciman.

When, as a child, she had toddled into the library, her father would patiently put away his pencils and squares and lift her on to the table, plonk her down on the sheet of crisp draft paper like ballast in the ship he was designing, and would listen patiently to her little tales of woe. Later she learned to respect his need for peace and quiet and would curl up in the battered old leather chesterfield and read quietly or watch him draw, his tongue between his teeth, his cuffs pushed back from his wrists.

He worked not at a desk or drawing-board but on the top of a huge pedestal sideboard in the window bay. The sideboard was flanked by a wall of books, elongated folios of diagrams, volumes of sheet music, bound sets of Scott and Smollett, Thackeray and Carlyle. Tucked modestly away on top of the open shelves were six or eight little postcard albums containing faded photographs of the weird and wonderful steam craft in whose construction her father had had a hand. On the mantel above the fireplace was a cased model of the *Charlotte Dundas*, complete with a miniature of Symington's engine. The model, the only one in the house, was not so much an ornament as an inspiration, for her father claimed that he had never designed anything that wasn't based on 'Old Willum's' perfect little boat which had been built over ninety years ago.

Once, when Lindsay had been convalescing from mumps, he had extracted the boat from its case and had brought it up to her bedroom. He had filled the internal boiler and fired it with shavings and had held it so that she could watch the tiny rods stir and click, the ratchet wheels spin, smoke wisp from the tall funnel and, at last, the paddle wheel begin to turn. Papa had smiled down at her, grinning above the boat, not showing how anxious he was to dispel her dullness and to bring back her liveliness.

Even now, a dozen years later, she could still remember the astonishing speed with which that tiny wheel had turned.

Leaving Miss Runciman to fetch the tea, Lindsay went upstairs and entered the library. She found her father seated not behind but upon the pedestal sideboard. The curtains had been drawn, the fire in the grate was low. He had pulled out one of the swivel jets to light the sideboard but there was no evidence of work on hand. He had unlaced one black shoe, just one. It dangled from his foot as if he had lost interest in taking off the other.

He sighed when Lindsay came in, and said, 'I suppose you want to know what's going on?'

'Of course I do,' Lindsay answered.

She seated herself on the chesterfield, quite upright, her small, wing-like shoulders pressed back as if she might fly at him at any moment.

'I've asked Miss Runciman to bring us tea,' she said.

'I'm not— yes, come to think of it, I could do with something.'

'Had you no inkling that Pappy intended to retire?'

'None. Absolutely none.'

'Has he never talked of it?'

'Oh, yes indeed,' her father said. 'He's been yapping about it for years. Whenever things got on top of him at the yard he'd threaten to pack it all in and retreat to a hut in the Highlands to practise his fly-fishing.'

'I didn't know he fished.'

'He doesn't,' her father said. 'Never cast a rod in his life. That's why none of us took him seriously.'

'He's not crying "wolf" now, by any chance?'

'Not this time.' Her father reached behind him and plucked his copy of the cream-laid sheet from the worktop. 'This may not look like much more than an office memorandum, Lindsay, but believe me it's serious stuff.'

'I rather thought it might be,' she said. 'I want you to explain it to me.'

'What is there to explain? Obviously Pappy wishes to ensure that Franklin's remains a family firm and that your generation has a stake in its future – nominally at least.'

'Nominally?'

'Well, you'll have no active part in running the business.' Her father sat back, braced on his hands. 'What your grandfather has done is draft a new deed of co-partnery which will form the basis of a legal document that will entitle you to receive a small percentage of our profits every year.'

'What will I have to do to justify this windfall?'

'Not a blessed thing,' her father said. 'You've no capital to contribute and I doubt if Pappy expects you to serve an apprenticeship.'

'I don't see why not,' Lindsay said.

'No. No. No, no, no.' Her father shook his head. 'Don't go embracing any fancy ideas, Lindsay. Don't imagine you'd be accepted into the College of Marine Engineers or the Maritime Institute just because you're a partner in Franklin's. That's not on.'

It hadn't occurred to Lindsay that it might be, as her father put it, 'on'. With the exception of drawing-office tracers and a few clerks and stenographers, the shipbuilding industry had no place for women.

Her father continued, 'I hope you appreciate just how even-handed your grandfather has been in allotting you a share in the partnership. Of course, you will have to accept some liability.'

'Liability? What does that mean?'

'If ever we happen to go bust,' her father said, just as Miss Runciman brought in the tea tray, 'you'll go down the drain with the rest of us.'

'Are we in danger of going bust?'

'Certainly not,' her father said and, hopping from his perch, made for the rack of hot buttered toast as if he hadn't eaten a thing all day.

In spite of many lessons and umpteen hours of practice, Lindsay was no more than proficient on a keyboard. She had no innate musical talent and – something her father could not understand – very little 'ear'. At best her performances were stiff, at worst clumsy. She envied her cousins, Mercy in particular, for their ability to sit down at a piano and busk a tune or sight-read any sheet of music that was placed before them. The closest Papa and she came to musical rapport was when she accompanied him at parlour soirées or picked out one of the Brunswick Park Choral Society's new arrangements while he got to grips with its harmony and tried to hide his dismay at her lack of musical flair.

There was more rapport between them that Sunday night than there had ever been in the piano alcove in the parlour. Leaning on their elbows, bottoms stuck out, they pored over the deed of co-partnery that set out the reconstitution of the firm:

Owen Franklin	6/64ths
Donald Franklin (son)	21/64ths
Arthur Franklin (son)	21/64ths
Martin Franklin (grandson)	7/64ths
Owen Forbes McCulloch (grandson)	7/64ths
Anna Lindsay Franklin (granddaughter)	2/64ths

Even to Lindsay it was obvious that Pappy wanted his sons to have sole authority and to transfer responsibility to their shoulders without upsetting the ship-owners and naval authorities who supplied the contracts. Pappy would not retire penniless, of course. He retained a stake in the firm and had personal equity in two or three ship-owning companies and shares in several of the cargo vessels that Franklin's had built for the Niger Flotilla. Even so, Papa told her, it was remarkably unselfish of the old devil to bow out before age or infirmity undermined his judgement.

'The current value of our assets is around two hundred and forty thousand pounds,' her father said. 'By no means large compared to some firms but not bad for a family-owned concern. The limitations of the site at Aydon Road have worked to our advantage, you see. We've never had space to tender for warships or transatlantic liners, so instead we build stern-wheelers and shallow-draught side-wheelers, craft so economical that you can operate them on fresh air and occasional handfuls of grass.'

'Like the ones for the Niger?' said Lindsay.

'Clever design, that. Simple to operate and maintain. We sent a small crew of experts over to Burutu to establish a repair shop and ensure that we stayed in the good graces of the Royal Niger Company. Don't think the chaps enjoyed it much, though.'

'Martin tells me that steam launches bring high profits.'

'Absolutely,' her father answered. 'Profit on delivery of a launch runs at about seventeen per cent compared with three or four per cent on a cargo ship.'

'And now we're moving into torpedo-boats?'

'You have been talking to Martin, haven't you?'

'Listening, mostly,' Lindsay said. 'Am I a partner, Papa? I mean, am I really and truly a partner in Franklin's?'

'You are, there's no denying it.'

'Martin will not be pleased,' Lindsay said.

'Nonsense, he won't mind a bit.'

'Owen Forbes might be less understanding.'

'Who? Oh, yes, your Irish cousin. Can't say I'm wild about the idea of taking on an outsider.' Her father leaned against the edge of the sideboard. 'I don't suppose I should look upon him as an outsider, though McCulloch will never have the authority that Martin has.'

'Will Martin inherit the major portion of his father's holding when Donald retires?'

'Assuming we're all spared, yes.'

'When you retire, if ever you do . . .'

He let out a bark of laughter. 'Dear God! Retirement. Still, still, I suppose we *do* have to think about these things.'

'I'm sorry,' Lindsay said. 'I didn't mean to sound morbid or mercenary.'

'No, dearest, you're quite right. I mean, I might pop off at any time. Stranger things have happened.'

'Papa, please don't say that.'

'Well, I might. People do.'

'You won't die, not for a long time yet.'

He drew in breath, held it, let it out again. 'To answer the question you haven't quite managed to ask, Lindsay: if Franklin's is still a family concern when I slip this mortal coil then, yes, you will inherit my holding.'

'I see,' said Lindsay. 'Well, if my destiny is going to be bound up with Franklin's, the sooner I perk up and take an interest the better.'

'A long eye to the future, do you mean?'

'Precisely,' Lindsay said. 'When's the next partners' meeting?'

'Monday week.'

'In the boardroom at Aydon Road?'

'Yes.'

'Am I permitted to attend?'

'Absolutely. You're a partner now and no one can stop you.'

'In that case, may I go with you?'

'Of course,' Papa answered and then, for no apparent reason, leaned over and kissed her on the brow.

Sleep did not come immediately. It had been a long day, not dreary and by no means uneventful but somehow not so exhausting as other more frivolous Sundays that she'd spent at Harper's Hill. Her premonition had had substance after all. Perhaps Martin had given her a hint. In the past few months he had become uncharacteristically sober, spending more time with his father and grandfather as if he were being drawn into maturity by responsibilities that neither she nor his sisters could be expected to understand.

Lindsay lay on her back in bed, the lace edge of the sheet pulled up to her nose, and stared at the plaster cornices above her.

The bedroom was in the 'old' part of the house, whatever that meant, since the whole building wasn't much more than thirty years old. The webby look of the high plasterwork intrigued her. She liked to imagine that the craftsmen had lost interest halfway through the contract, had toddled off to dinner one midday and had simply failed to return. The rosebuds and vine leaves did not seem quite complete, as if they were still forming themselves into unpredictable shapes that would take a geological age to settle.

She had never been frightened of being alone in this room. There were always reflections, a faint sifting radiance that the curtains didn't exclude, pattern and texture altering according to weather, the seasons and her changing moods. Tonight her mood was strange: anticipation tinged with regret that her grandfather would no longer be a consolidating presence in Harper's Hill and that Forbes would never know what life had been like in Glasgow in the 'good old days'. That any memories he and she might share would begin with an April evening grey with the threat of rain.

Owen Forbes McCulloch: new cousin, new partner.

She pursed her lips against the lace.

'Owen Forbes McCulloch,' she whispered, then, with a wistful sigh, turned on her side to sleep.

CHAPTER THREE

The Ladies' Man

For Lindsay history had never been much more than a matter of memorising the dates of famous battles and equally boring events such as the Repeal of the Corn Laws whose significance was lost on all but a few beastly swots and whose relevance to the average Glaswegian, male or female, was barely one point above zero. Her geography too was a little on the shaky side. If pressed, she might have managed to locate Peking or Korea in the colourful atlas that her father kept in the library. But Glasgow was Glasgow! Home was home! What did famine in Poona or riots in Milan matter when the Carl Rosa Opera Company were 'doing' *Carmen* in St Andrew's Halls or Daly's were displaying the latest spring styles in white and French regattas? Until she attended her first meeting of Franklin's board it had not even occurred to her that what happened in Cuba or on the fringes of the Ottoman Empire could affect the price of Aunt Lilias's new tea-gown, let alone the cost of bread.

The partners' meeting was scheduled for nine thirty and would be followed by the regular weekly meeting of departmental managers.

Lindsay and her father rode to Aydon Road in a hired hackney. Arthur Franklin preferred to use cabs rather than maintain a rig of his own, for Aydon Road was situated no more than a mile from Brunswick Crescent and in fair weather he liked to walk there and back again.

Lindsay was dressed in a pale brown outfit of Amazon cloth that Nanny said put years on her, which was, of course, the intention. She had even managed to unearth a hat that kept her unruly bubbles of blonde hair firmly in place. Nevertheless she was nervous and felt less like a woman than a dressed-up child. In spite of her uncertainty, she was not inclined to be intimidated. When her father suggested that she might care to leave the boardroom before the managers' meeting she jumped in with, 'Why should I?'

'I'm not saying you have to, exactly.'

'But you would prefer it if I did?'

'Well – candidly – yes, I would.'

'I won't say a word.'

'You'll be bored, you know.'

'Are you afraid that my presence will offend the managers' sensibilities?'

'Of course not,' her father said gruffly. 'Stay if you wish.'

'Tell you what, if Forbes stays I will too. New boys together. How's that?'

'McCulloch won't be at the meeting.'

'Why not?'

'He's started work at Beardmore's.'

'No favours?' Lindsay hid her disappointment.

'Absolutely not.'

The flat cobbles of the thoroughfare changed to the round cobbles of Old Farm Road. Lindsay could see the wall that marked the boundary of the shipyard, with a light crane and a couple of sheer-legs peeping over it. Even before the hack drew to a halt in front of the office block she could hear the thump of a punch and, rather eerily, two or three men crying out to each other in the aggressive drawl that was the *lingua franca* of workmen everywhere. When she stepped from the cab – her father helped her alight – she noticed a fresh pile of horse manure close to the kerb and surmised that Uncle Donald's four-wheeler was already tucked away in the yard's stables.

She wondered why she felt so out of place. Perhaps because she was no longer a little girl but had become an interloper in a world hostile to females, no matter how much of the company they owned. She could almost imagine the apprentices' snorts of derision when they learned that a girl had turned up in the boardroom: '*Two sixty-fourths, two sixty-fourths, for God's sake, and she thinks she owns the world.*' She did not feel as if she owned the world. She felt as if she owned nothing and had left her true self back home in the nursery.

Her father ushered her into the office building. Stout wooden pillars, a glass-front cubby, two stout wooden doors, a broad uncarpeted staircase leading upward: it was very quiet. Then Sergeant Corbett, the commissionaire, flung his newspaper aside, leaped out of his cubby and snapped a smart salute.

'G'mornin', Mr Franklin.'

'Good morning, good morning. Has my brother arrived yet?'

'Aye, sir, him an' Master – Mister Martin.'

'And my father?'

'Been upstairs for a good hour, sir, along with Mr Harrington.'

Mr Harrington, a moist little whelk of a man, was the senior partner in the law firm that handled all the Franklins' business, personal and professional.

Sergeant Corbett was scarlet-cheeked and cheery. He wore a dark green uniform, a broad leather belt and sported a huge pair of mutton-chop whiskers. He had been doorman for as long as Lindsay could remember. She had no notion what regiment had afforded him his rank or what battles he had fought in. Inkerman, perhaps, or Balaclava? Surely he wasn't old enough to be a veteran of the Crimea. Tel-el-Kebir, Egypt, or the campaigns in the Sudan were more like the thing.

'P'rhaps it's not my place, Miss Franklin,' the commissioner said, 'but I'd like to welcome you to our office. Nice to have a lady on board.'

'Thank you, Sergeant,' she said, then added, 'I'll do my best.'

Her father whisked her upstairs.

The boardroom windows provided a panorama of sheds and berths and a ribbon of the Clyde up which cargo traffic nosed and down which the products of the shipyards were tugged away to the open sea. The narrow strand of water did not look impressive. Sometimes it was brown, sometimes green; only on the flood with the wind against, crisp and silvery and smacking, did it bear a faint resemblance to a mighty waterway. On that April forenoon it lay calm and shrunken. Cows and sheep peppered the patches of grass between docks and railway tracks, and cheek by jowl with the Linthouse quays were trees, birch, lime and flowering cherry and the oaks of the old estates.

The Clyde ran eighteen miles from Broomielaw to Port Glasgow. It had a range of thirteen feet on ordinary spring tides and, since the rocks at Elderslie had been blasted away, a channel that allowed twenty feet of draught at low water. Lindsay recalled the figures effortlessly: they had been dinned into her like prayers. She might be ignorant of industrial processes but like every Glaswegian she lived with the smell of the river in her nostrils and its pride in her heart.

'Well, well,' Martin said, 'if it isn't my dear wee cousin.'

He wore tweeds, fine in texture but loud in pattern. He detached himself from Pappy and Mr Harrington and came around the oblong table to greet her. He had been a year on management staff. Lindsay was glad of a familiar hand on her arm.

'Ah, Lindsay.' Pappy did not offer his cheek for a kiss. 'I believe you know Mr Harrington.'

'She does, indeed,' said Mr Harrington. 'My, my, lassie, but you're growing like a weed.'

She knew him well enough to say, 'Like a weed, Mr Harrington?'

'A flower then, is that better?'

'Much better,' Lindsay said. 'I didn't notice you in the cathedral for the Easter Cantata. Didn't you attend?'

'Throat.' Mr Harrington tapped his collar stud. 'Quinsy throat.'

He was not quite so old as her grandfather. He was very small with a hunch to his shoulders that suggested not so much deformity as defensiveness. His skin was white and moist, always moist, which was why Martin had coined the nickname 'the whelk' for him. By contrast Martin was tall, broad-shouldered and open-featured. He continued to hold Lindsay's hand as if he felt she might be intimidated by men whom she had known most of her life.

He winked. 'Don't be frightened.'

'Why should I be frightened?'

'I'll take you down to the yard afterwards, show you the ropes. We've a full order book at the moment and an interesting collection of—'

'Martin,' her grandfather said, 'don't pester the girl.'

'I'm not pestering her. I just thought that if she's going to be a partner she should know *something* about what goes on here.'

At that juncture Donald ushered Aunt Kay into the room. She, it appeared, had been appointed to act for her son. After a few almost perfunctory introductions, Owen Franklin said, 'I believe all the relative parties are present now, Harrington, so I reckon we might as well push on.'

The lines of demarcation that governed who did what among shipwrights did not apply to managers. On to their shoulders fell responsibility not only for their own departments but for many other departments as well. Each of the umpteen processes that led from first rough sketches to a vessel's trials was fraught with the possibility of error and every plate, rivet and pipe had to be checked and rechecked at every stage.

Tom Calder coped with this pressure by keeping himself to himself. Managers like George Crush or Peter Holt never knew what Calder was thinking, what moved him to vote for this procedure against that or to dig in his heels over a problem whose solution seemed obvious to everyone else. The fact that Calder was right more often than not did not endear him to his colleagues. He was regarded as a stubborn devil who seemed not so much transparent as completely opaque, a quality that bouncy, bumptious George Crush and pragmatic Peter Holt found incomprehensible.

Even the men who had accompanied Tom Calder to the Niger did not know what made him tick. He had thrived in the stifling heat of the mangrove swamps and, unlike the rest of the crew, had remained abundantly healthy throughout their term on the fever-ridden river. He had grown brown and lean and lively while the rest of Franklin's team had been washed out by sickness. He had even volunteered to accompany the *Mungo Park*, largest of the stern-wheelers that had been assembled amid the sandflies and mosquitoes at Burutu, to test her engines against the fierce currents below Jebba, four hundred miles upstream. What impression the Niger had made upon Tom Calder remained a mystery. He had delivered his reports within days of returning to Aydon Road and had been back in the drawing office in less than a week, as if the African trip had never taken place at all.

On Monday morning George Crush ran Calder to earth in the drawing office. Wasting no time on pleasantries, he said, 'What's this I hear about a lassie taking over the management?'

'I've no idea what you're blathering about, George.'

'Come off it, man. The place is stiff with rumours.'

On Tom's board was a complete 'as fitted' drawing of Torpedo-Boat No. 56, an Admiralty-commissioned vessel 125 feet in length, with a 12-foot beam and a triple expansion engine that, on paper at least, would give a top speed of 26.4 knots. Tom admired the craft's sleek, purposeful lines and hoped that he would be invited to accompany her on her trials.

'Are you not going to tell me?' Crush insisted.

'Nothing to tell.'

'It's the old man's granddaughter, Mr Arthur's lass. Now you can't pretend you don't know her, since she's another music fiend. Is she the blonde who turns up at launches?'

'I expect so,' Tom said.

George knew perfectly well who Anna Lindsay Franklin was. He had met her several times and had gossiped about her in the manager's office, predicting that once she grew up she would make a perfect mate for young Martin, since neither of them seemed over-endowed with brains.

'They're up in the boardroom right now,' George went on, 'with Mr Harrington. You know what that means.'

'What does it mean?'

'It means the rumours are true. The old man's retiring and we're going to have a lassie telling us what to do.'

'If Mr Owen hands the reins to anyone it'll be Donald and Arthur.'

'So you have heard something?'

On Monday morning the draughtsmen were slow getting into their stride. The long room was filled with the scrape of stools, the stealthy rustle of paper being unfurled and the clump of the polished flat-irons that kept the ends of the rolls from scuttling shut. Visions of sleek, high-powered torpedo-boats cleaving the waters of the Gareloch evaporated. Tom couldn't be bothered with George's questions. They were based on the fact that Arthur Franklin and he were both members of the Brunswick Park Choral Society, and Crush's assumption that singing in a choir entitled him to share the Franklins' family secrets which, of course, was far from the truth.

'Come on, Tommy,' George Crush wheedled, 'what have you heard? Is Yarrow finally moving north and buying us out?'

'I don't know where you pick up these daft notions,' Tom said.

'Well, there's no smoke without fire. It seems to me – Peter agrees – that we're in for either a sell-out or a shift in management.'

Tom could hardly believe that men so skilled in the art of building ships would fall prey to every panicky rumour that floated up from the boiler shop. Every so often the tale would go about that Alfred Yarrow or Thornycroft of Chiswick was bidding for property on the Clyde. Heads would hang in the managers' office and the apprentices would go around looking as if they expected the axe to fall at any moment; then the threat would disappear and another unfounded rumour would replace it.

'George, George,' Tom said. 'You can't seriously believe that old man Franklin would put a female in charge of us?'

'Aye, well, you never know what rich folk will do when it suits them.'

'A girl? In charge of shipbuilding?'

'I suppose you're right,' Crush admitted reluctantly. 'What's she doing here, though? I mean, you can't deny she's been brought here for a reason.'

Tom glanced at the moon-faced clock above the drawing-office door.

'Tell you what, George.'

'What?'

'Why don't we walk over to the boardroom and find out?'

Lindsay had not expected fanfares to announce her entry into the partnership. She had also not anticipated that the proceedings would be so perfunctory and, to say the least of it, so very, very dry. Mr Harrington droned on about the new agreement for a good fifteen minutes before handing out typed copies of the document. Lindsay applied herself to reading but her attention soon slid away. Instead she found herself eyeing Aunt Kay who was scanning the agreement as if she understood every word of it. Perhaps, Lindsay thought, her Irish auntie was more of a businessman than anyone gave her credit for. After all, her husband operated a profitable brewery in Dublin and it was safe to assume that neither Kay nor her son had been entirely shut out.

'Mistress McCulloch, are there any points you'd like clarified?'

'No, it's all as clear as day, thank you.'

'Good.' Mr Harrington seemed about to put the same question to Lindsay, then thought better of it. 'Shall we move on?'

'Please do,' said Pappy.

Lindsay listened to Mr Harrington with only half an ear. She observed her grandfather who, most uncharacteristically, lolled in the tall chair at the top of the table as if he could no longer be bothered with the proceedings that he had inaugurated.

'Have you any questions?' Mr Harrington said.

'When will the articles of partnership come into force?' Martin asked.

'On the first day of May.'

'When will you announce the board changes, Pappy?'

The old man stirred. 'I'll inform the managers this morning and announce it to the men tomorrow. Rumours have already been flying so it's probably best to put a stop to them before the ship-owners begin inventing silly stories about us going to the wall. I want no fuss, you understand. I want the handover to be as smooth as possible. As far as the workforce is concerned nothing will change. Why should it?'

'Because you won't be here to look out for them,' Martin said.

'Daft beggar!' Pappy said, though he was pleased, Lindsay saw, by her cousin's remark.

Five minutes later the managers filed into the boardroom.

Lindsay made no move to leave. Her father did not press her to do so. Aunt Kay also remained seated. Only Mr Harrington, who apparently had urgent matters to attend to elsewhere, took his leave and departed. Lindsay looked around the table. She recognised Mr Holt, Mr Crush, and Mr Tom Calder, the tall stony-faced draughtsman who sang with her father in the Brunswick choir. She smiled at him. Rather to her surprise, he smiled back.

Owen Franklin got to his feet. He plucked at his lip with finger and thumb then spread his coat tails and put his hands behind him to hide the trembling. 'Gentleman,' he said, 'before we buckle down to the business of the day, I've an important announcement to make.'

Behind her, Lindsay heard someone hiss, 'Didn't I tell you, Tommy?'

And Mr Calder answer, *sotto voce*, 'So you did, George. So you did.'

'Were they surprised?' Miss Runciman asked.

'I think they had an inkling that something was in the wind.'

'Were they shocked?'

'No,' Lindsay said. 'They took it rather calmly, in fact. I expect they realise that things will go on much as usual with Papa and Donald in charge.'

'Your father . . .' Miss Runciman began, then stopped herself.

Chin held over her soup plate, Nanny Cheadle completed the sentence: '. . . is a wonderful man.'

'That's *not* what I was going to say,' Miss Runciman snapped. 'I do *wish* you would stop putting words in my mouth, Nanny.'

'Somebody's got to,' Nanny Cheadle said. 'Did they cheer?'

Lindsay was mildly confused. 'Pardon?'

'The men, did they cheer?'

'Hardly. They won't be given the news until tomorrow.'

'They'll cheer,' Nanny Cheadle predicted. 'They always cheer. If you were to stand up and announce that the seas had dried up, they'd still cheer. That's men for you. Cheer first, complain later.'

'I don't think they'll complain,' said Miss Runciman. 'With Arthur – with Lindsay's papa in charge they'll have no cause for complaint, I'm sure.'

'I'm sure,' said Nanny Cheadle. 'Where is his lordship anyway?'

'Donald and he have taken Aunt Kay to supper at the Barbary,' Lindsay answered.

'There's a sacrifice for you,' Nanny said.

'Now why do you say that?' Miss Runciman enquired. 'I think it's very nice, the three of them celebrating together.'

'Squabbling together more like,' said Nanny.

It was after seven o'clock. The dining-room windows caught the evening sunlight but the little park was already in shadow. Lindsay had returned home from the informal luncheon that had followed the managers' meeting at half past two o'clock and had mooched about the house for the rest of the afternoon. She was tempted to trot over to Harper's Hill to report to Cissie or take tea with Aunt Lilias but somehow she did not feel entirely welcome in her grandfather's house these days. The appearance of the Irish cousin had upset the equilibrium. Papa had been right about one thing, though: the managers' meeting *had* been boring. She had understood little of the jargon and the unfurling of plans and diagrams and the rapidity with which the men could make complicated arithmetical calculations had both impressed and dismayed her.

Nanny Cheadle finished her soup, licked her finger, dabbed a pea from the plate, put it between her teeth and nibbled like a squirrel.

Maddy cleared away the plates and brought in a dish of new potatoes, another of buttered cabbage and, finally, a tray of hot mutton chops.

Miss Runciman thanked the maid, and served.

The housekeeper looked different tonight. Her dowdy dress had been exchanged for a blue muslin blouse and she had arranged her thick brown hair in a style that softened her strong, almost masculine features. Lindsay watched Nanny stab a mutton chop and hack away the rim of golden-brown fat. Nanny Cheadle had arrived in Brunswick Crescent on the day that Aunt Kay had left, Miss Runciman a couple of years later. Neither had known Kay and probably had no knowledge of the quarrel that had left such a residue of bitterness so that even now, eighteen years on, it was all Papa could do to be civil to his sister.

'What makes you think they'll be squabbling, Nanny?' Lindsay asked.

The old woman looked up. For a moment she seemed more cunning than vague. 'Never you mind, Linnet, never you mind. He'll arrive home in a temper, though, mark my words.'

'You never did meet my aunt, did you?'

'Once, just that once, out there in the hall,' Nanny said. 'Had you in her arms, she did, all wrapped up in your shawl. Very pretty you were too.'

'My aunt – Kay, I mean – she told me I was ugly.'

'Nah, nah, dearest. *She* was the ugly one, that much about her I do remember,' Nanny went on. 'Luggage in the hall, hat on her head, white as a piece of chalk and shaking like a fig tree.'

'Where was my father?' Lindsay said.

'At the foot of the stairs. Whiter than she was, white as a ghost.'

'Why have you never told me before?' Lindsay asked.

'Never thought to mention it,' Nanny said. 'Anyhow, you never asked.'

'Did they say anything to each other?'

Nanny Cheadle closed her eyes and murmured to herself, as if to summon up the spirits of the dead. 'Nah,' she said at length 'not a word crossed between them that I can recall. She just gave me the baby, stuck out her arms and handed you over as soon as I stepped in through the front door. Then she walked past me, down the steps to the carriage. The carriage-man come up and lifted her luggage. And that was her gone for good.'

'Hasn't your father told you about this?' Miss Runciman asked.

'He won't speak of it.'

'Perhaps it's too painful for him.'

'What a good baby you were,' Nanny Cheadle put in. 'Never cross, never ugly.' She lifted her fork. 'Is there no mint sauce?'

'It's a chop, Nanny. There's gravy if you wish it. See, here's gravy.'

'Gravy,' the old woman said. 'I don't want gravy. I want sauce.'

At that moment the doorbell rang in the hall.

Miss Runciman rose to answer it.

She returned a minute or so later, looking puzzled and slightly annoyed.

'It's a young man,' she said. 'He claims that he's your Irish cousin.'

'Forbes,' said Lindsay, making to rise. 'Where . . .'

'I put him in the drawing-room,' Miss Runciman replied.

'I'll go to—'

'No, you will not,' said Miss Runciman sternly. 'You will finish your dinner before you do anything. Unannounced guests do not have priority over a well-cooked meal.'

'But what does he want?'

'To see you, apparently,' Miss Runciman said.

'He — he asked for *me*?' said Lindsay. 'He called to see *me*?'

Nurse and housekeeper exchanged a knowing glance.

Miss Runciman sat down at the table with a smooth, rather smug tucking in of skirts. She lifted her knife, and almost smiled. 'Yes, my dear, he has called to see you,' she said, then added, 'uninvited – which is reason enough for letting him cool his heels for a quarter of an hour or so.'

'Well,' Lindsay said, 'this *is* an unexpected pleasure. I apologise for keeping you waiting but we usually dine at seven and never receive before eight. You wouldn't know that, of course.'

She was flustered. Given more time she would have galloped upstairs and changed out of the pale brown outfit into something more becoming. She had kept Forbes waiting as long as she dared, however. Thank heaven Maddy had had the sense to light the fire and turn up the gas.

Forbes did not seem at all put out by being made to wait. Lindsay got the impression that he had been dozing and that if she'd dallied for another two or three minutes she might have found him asleep on the long, leather sofa. He wore a tweed jacket over unmatched trousers, a knitted vest. In the collar of his shirt was a scarf, not quite the coarse muffler that ordinary workmen wore but getting on that way. With his jet black hair and long lashes, though, Forbes could be forgiven any lapse in social etiquette. He was, Lindsay had to remind herself, not much more than a boy.

'I take it that you've had something to eat?' she said.

'Yes, Aunt Lilias saw to it.'

'Good. Please, please make yourself comfortable.'

She watched him settle, arm along the back of the sofa, his legs crossed. He looked directly at her, nowhere else. In the iron grate kindling crackled and fresh flames licked through a pyramid of coals.

Lindsay had never entertained a young man on her own before, not counting her cousins, of course, but Martin, Johnny and Ross knew how to make themselves at home without her attentions. It was different with her Irish cousin, though. He was far too confident for someone of seventeen. She was halfway afraid of him; not a deep fear, not dread, just a little quailing fear that he might suddenly pounce upon her and begin kissing her and that she would not have the gumption to push him away.

'Aren't you going to sit yourself down?' he asked.

'I – I – yes, of course I am.'

'Well, sit here then. Sit by me.'

'I've asked Miss Runciman to fetch coffee. Would you prefer tea?'

He patted the leather. 'I'd prefer you to stop fussin' and sit down.'

There were eight chairs in the drawing-room, armchairs, mahogany uprights, even a hard walnut stool that no one ever sat on. Forbes patted the leather again as if she, not he, were the guest. Meekly Lindsay seated herself on the sofa.

'There now,' he said. 'Is that not better? Is that not cosy?'

From the corner of her eye Lindsay studied his arm as if it were a snake that might suddenly entwine her.

'Are you afraid of me?' Forbes asked.

'Don't be ridiculous. Why should I be afraid of you?'

'I thought you might have heard.'

'Heard? Heard what?'

'I got sent down.'

Lindsay turned to face him. 'Sent down?'

'From my school, from Dunkerry.'

'Oh, you mean *expelled*.'

'Is that what they call it in Scotland?' Forbes said. 'Well, whatever name you care to be giving it, I got sent down.'

With relief Lindsay realised that he was only a callow boy after all and that being Irish had nothing to do with it. She felt brighter immediately.

She opened her eyes wide. 'Really?' she said. 'Why on earth did you get sent down?'

'Guess.'

'Smoking tobacco?'

'Nope. We all smoked like funnels in our school.'

'Drink then?' said Lindsay. 'The drink, I expect.'

53

'Not the drink either.' He tapped his fingers on the back of the sofa and smirked. 'I had the reputation of being a bit of a ladies' man.'

'A ladies' man! Really!' How she kept a straight face Lindsay had no idea. 'Aren't you a little young to be a ladies' man?'

'I'm not saying I am and I'm not saying I'm not,' Forbes told her proudly, 'but when it got out Pa reckoned I should come to Scotland straight away and not be waiting until I was eighteen.'

'I see,' Lindsay said. 'Very wise of him, I'm sure.'

'Mam wrote to Grandfather and he said, "Come." That's why I'm here. Coming to Glasgow was always on the cards. It's what Mam had planned for me since the day I was born. I was earmarked, you see.'

'Earmarked?'

'To follow in Pappy's footsteps.'

'I see,' said Lindsay, fluttering her eyelashes. 'Gosh!'

'You're not makin' fun of me, are you?'

'Not I,' said Lindsay. 'Have you told Cissie what you've just told me?'

'She was fascinated.'

'I'll bet she was,' said Lindsay. 'And Martin?'

'He said we were all born shipbuilders in our family but I should be minding my *Ps* and *Qs* if I really wanted to get ahead.'

'That seems like sound advice.'

'I knew you'd be saying that,' Forbes told her. 'My mam said you'd be sympathetic.'

'Did your mother suggest that you call here tonight?'

'She's out having supper with Donald and your pa.'

'I know,' Lindsay said. 'That wasn't the question.'

'Mam ha'nny got a clue I'm here. Not that she'd mind much if she did.' He leaned towards her. Lindsay no longer felt compelled to draw away. 'I thought I'd drop round, see where you live, and have a wee bit of a crack.'

'A wee bit of a crack,' said Lindsay, 'about what?'

He had the decency to pause before he said, 'Were you at the partners' meeting this morning?'

'I was.'

'Did Pappy say anything about me?'

'Your name was mentioned. Pappy welcomed you into the firm and I believe Mr Harrington, the lawyer, referred to you once or twice.'

'In what connection would that be?'

'Concerning the division of shares.'

Another pause: 'Did he say when I'd get my money?'

'What money?'

'My share of the annual profits.'

'I was under the impression that your mother was representing your interests. She was certainly at the meeting.'

'I ha'nny – I haven't spoken to Mam yet,' Forbes said. 'Since you and I are both in the same boat, I thought you might be the best person to ask.'

'Ah! Yes. Well, neither of us is of an age to draw profits. We'll have to wait until we're twenty-one before we receive our dues.'

'Jesus!' Forbes let the word slip with a vicious little hiss. Lindsay found the blasphemy shocking. He wriggled, uncrossed his legs, sat forward and clasped her arm. 'Twenty-one, twenty-one? That's almost four years away.'

'Meanwhile,' Lindsay said, 'our profits will be placed in a fund.'

'Who looks after the fund?'

'Mr Harrington.'

'Who's he?'

'The family's solicitor.'

Forbes tightened his grip. 'Are you happy with that arrangement?'

'Apparently it's required by law where juveniles are concerned.'

'Juveniles! God, is that how they think of us?' Forbes glanced at the door then put an arm about her. 'At least we're both in it together.'

'Yes,' Lindsay said. 'I would be obliged if you would take your arm . . .'

'What? Yes. Sorry.'

He swung his arm away and casually continued the conversation.

Lindsay wondered where Miss Runciman had got to with the coffee. She considered the possibility that the housekeeper was deliberately allowing her time alone with her handsome Irish cousin. She was tempted to leap to her feet, stalk out into the hall and declare her lack of enthusiasm for spending any time alone with Owen Forbes McCulloch. But the truth was that she didn't lack enthusiasm, didn't lack interest in this odd young man who could be so naive one minute, so sly and worldly the next.

'Have you got money?' Forbes said. 'Income of your own, I mean?'

'Papa gives me a small allowance.'

'How much?'

'For heaven's sake, Forbes!'

The rebuff was obviously expected and he rattled on without a blush. 'Four years is a long time to wait.'

'Doesn't your father give you an allowance?'

'Not him. Mean bastard!'

'Oh, come along. I don't believe he doesn't give you something.'

'If it wasn't for Mam I don't know what I'd do.'

'Don't you receive a wage from Beardmore's?'

'I'm an *apprentice*, a bloody apprentice, no better than a bloody *slave*.'

A discreet knock upon the drawing-room door: feeling decidedly foolish, Lindsay said, 'Enter.' Miss Runciman brought in a tray weighted with Georgian silver and the monogrammed English coffee service. She placed the tray on the sofa table and dropped a curtsey.

'Shall I serve, Miss Lindsay, or will the young gentleman help himself?'

'The young gentleman will help himself.'

'Will that be all, Miss Lindsay?'

'Yes, Miss Runciman. That will be all.'

The housekeeper's matt brown eyes were fiercely appraising. She sized up the Irish cousin and lingered long enough to receive a beaming smile and a soft, almost feminine flutter of Forbes's dark lashes. 'Thank you,' he said, his irritation replaced by something that Lindsay could only define as charm. It was a selfish, narcissistic performance, but she, like Miss Runciman, so wanted to believe that it was sincere that she, like Miss Runciman, could do nothing but respond to it. When the housekeeper finally left the room, Lindsay got to her feet and fussed with cups and coffee pot while her cousin hoisted himself from the sofa, wandered to the window and stared out over Brunswick Park.

'It's certainly a grand place to live,' he said.

Lindsay said, 'Nicer than Dublin? Surely not.'

'Well, Dublin's my home town and will always be close to my heart.' He returned to the sofa and accepted a coffee cup and saucer. 'But it's here on the Clyde that I'll make my mark.'

He stood close to Lindsay, balancing the miniature cup and saucer on his palm. His presence made her feel curiously mature, as if she had already inherited her father's house or become a wife in her own right.

'Is it a big house you have here?' Forbes asked.

'Big enough for two of us.'

'It'll not be as roomy as Pappy's place?'

'No,' said Lindsay. 'Few houses in Glasgow are.'

'I'd be as well digging in there then.'

'Pardon?'

'I thought I might be better off here.'

'You . . .'

'Nearer to you,' he said. 'Wouldn't you like that?'

Lindsay had been flirted with before, usually by men four or five years older than she was. In fact, she had almost been proposed to just before Christmas when Gordon Swann, Ethan Swann's youngest, had got carried away by the lights and the music at the Federated Ironmasters' annual ball in Finnieston Hall and had been on the point of popping the question. Lindsay had done nothing to encourage him, though she had let him kiss her out in the cold stone corridor under the bas-relief memorial to those who had died in the *Minerva* tragedy. That brief, breathless one-Christmas-night fling with Gordon Swann had not been serious, however. Somehow this was – desperately serious, even if Forbes lacked gravity and was far too young for her. Hot, calculating eyes and brash, impolitic hints of adult experience did not make him a man.

'I think you had better go,' Lindsay told him.

'I've offended you, haven't I?'

'You have,' said Lindsay.

'You're easily offended then.'

'Perhaps Dublin girls have thicker skins than I do.'

'They know a compliment when they hear one.' He drank coffee, put the cup back on the saucer and handed both to Lindsay. 'Anyway, I'm here to stay, Linnet, and Harper's Hill isn't so very far away.'

'Why do you call me "Linnet"?'

'That's what my mam calls you.'

'My name is Lindsay, plain Lindsay.'

'I'll remember that next time,' Forbes said. 'Do you really want me to go? I thought we were rubbing along pretty well.'

'No, I want you to go.'

'Walk me to the door then.'

'Why should I?'

'Because I'm your cousin and you are a lady.'

'Where's your overcoat?'

'Got none.'

'Your hat?'

'Got none. Lindsay, walk me to the door.'

Without knowing quite why she did so, she obeyed him.

Standing on the top step she watched him stroll off along the crescent, disappointed that he did not look back. In years to come, though, during and after her marriage, that was how she would remember Forbes, walking off into the gathering dusk — and deliberately not looking back.

CHAPTER FOUR

Sunday in the Park

Brunswick Park Choral Society had none of the pretensions of the big city choral unions. If there was such a thing as a written constitution no one knew where it was to be found, which is not to say that the society's members did not take singing seriously. On the contrary: they were just as dedicated to musical excellence as any of the great orchestral choirs, and what they lacked in timbre they more than made up for in gusto.

Mr Perrino, the choir's conductor, claimed his musical inheritance from an Italian knife-grinder who had docked at Greenock in the mistaken impression that he had reached the golden shores of the Hudson and who, being short on wit as well as cash, had decided to settle in Glasgow instead of re-embarking for New York. What had trickled down through three generations was an exploitable Italian surname, a perfect ear for pitch and a good set of vocal chords, attributes that had earned 'Perry' Perrino a decent living throughout the years and which – *Deo gratias* – he had passed on to his daughters, one of whom, Matilda, was presently the Brunswick's accompanist.

The choir met for practice throughout the winter months in the assembly hall of St Silas's School. It gave regular public performances in aid of the Tramways Servants' Sick & Benefit Society and other local charities in the Boilermakers' Institute in Partick, which was the venue for the final concert of the season.

Saturday was warm and sunny and drifted into one of those lovely clear evenings that now and then bless Clydeside. Because of the fine weather, though, the Boilermakers' was less than half full when, at half past seven o'clock, Mr Perrino shepherded the choir on to the platform to desultory applause. Matilda Perrino, slender and elegant in a black evening gown, took her place at the piano, Mr Perry Perrino his place at the podium. He had a trim grey beard and wavy hair and wore a loose pale grey jacket that, in contrast to the formal dress of the singers, lent him a faintly Bohemian air.

'Perry's developing a tummy,' Mercy Franklin murmured. 'That ratty old grey jacket won't hide it much longer.'

'How right you are,' Lindsay agreed. 'Soon he'll have to wear a bell tent.'

Mercy chuckled but when her little sister, Pansy, demanded what the joke was tapped the younger girl with her programme. 'Don't be nosy. Sit up. Pay attention. Look, there's Dada.'

'Where?'

'With the baritones, back row, fourth from the left.'

'I can't see him.'

'Behind the tall chap. See the tall chap?'

'Mr Calder,' Lindsay said.

'Oh, is that his name?' Cissie joined in the conversation for the first time. 'How do you know him? Does he come to the house?'

'No,' Lindsay said. 'I've met him at management meetings.'

'*You* go to those?' said Mercy.

'Of course,' Lindsay said. 'Didn't Martin tell you?'

'What on earth for?'

'To see for myself what goes on at the shipyard.'

'Rubbish!'

'All right,' Lindsay said. 'To annoy Papa. Is that better?'

'Much better,' said Mercy, and chuckled again.

Having brought the choir under control, Mr Perrino turned to the audience and delivered a brief speech of welcome, all flashing teeth and smiles.

'Do you know,' said Mercy from the side of her mouth, 'I do believe the poor soul is trying to appear cuddly.'

'Well, he's not succeeding,' said Pansy.

Aunt Lilias's daughters had been press-ganged into turning out for the last concert of the season and were none too pleased about it. The boys, Forbes included, had gone instead to the Theatre Royal to see the Wilson Barrett Company's production of *Hamlet* which, to the Franklin girls, was definitely the lesser of two evils. Even Pappy, seated next to Lilias, showed little enthusiasm when Mr Perrino with a little *tap-tap* of his baton swept the choir into Robert Lester's setting of 'Our Native Hills'.

Fifty minutes later the first half of the programme had run its course and the choir filed from the platform into the 'long room' where refreshments were served. Choir and audience mingled at the trestle tables. Uncle Donald waved but did not approach. Papa, engaged in carrying glasses of fruit squash to a brace of sopranos, did not wave at all. It was left to Mr Calder to approach the Franklin girls and enquire if they were enjoying themselves.

Lindsay replied politely that she was, and introduced Mr Calder to Cissie, Mercy and Pansy, who were not particularly interested in or impressed by the man. Tom returned to the safety of the choir and, seizing her chance, Cissie drew Lindsay off to one side.

'What do you make of Forbes McCulloch?' she said.

Lindsay was instantly on her guard. 'Why do you ask?'

'Tell me what you think of him.'

'Are you stuck on him?'

'No, but I think he's stuck on me.'

'Really?' Lindsay said. 'What gives you that impression?'

'The way he behaves.'

'Affectionately?'

'He's – he's – forward. Very forward.'

'In what way?' said Lindsay, frowning.

Cissie glanced round; her sisters were chatting to school friends and Aunt Lilias and Pappy had been trapped by Mrs Goldsmith who was angling to be invited into what she regarded as the Franklins' inner circle.

'If you don't want to tell me . . .' Lindsay said.

'I don't know how to put it.'

'It can't be that bad.'

'He shows himself to me.'

'What do you mean by "shows himself"?'

Freckles glowed across the bridge of Cissie's nose. Her blue eyes, normally bright and mischievous, were cloudy with concern. 'He comes home every evening like a navvy,' she said. 'He rides across town from Parkhead on the omnibus, you see. You can smell horse on him, and other smells too, soot or grease or something. He sidles in by the kitchen entrance and goes straight up to his room by the rear stairs still wearing his filthy boots.'

'How do you know?'

'I watch him.'

'*You* watch *him?*'

'I'm not spying on him, if that's what you're implying,' Cissie said, hastily. 'Fact of the matter is, it's impossible to avoid him. He's there, constantly there. Showing himself to me.'

'Precisely how does he show himself?' Lindsay asked.

'He comes out of the bathroom wearing nothing but a towel.'

'Perhaps that's what they do in Dublin.'

'No, he loiters in the bathroom until he hears me in the corridor before he comes out with just a towel, a tiny little hand towel about his . . .'

'Loins,' Lindsay suggested.

'Yes, loins.'

'Why don't you ignore him?'

'*I can't.*'

'Are you sure you want to?'

'Lindsay Franklin! How dare—'

'I'm sorry. Go on, please.'

'He swaggers towards me, looking at me, looking at me and *smiling*. I mean, our boys never parade about in that state. They'd be far too embarrassed. Besides, they have their dressing-gowns, and Mama insists—'

'Have you told your mama?'

'I haven't told anyone yet.'

Lindsay laid a sympathetic hand on her cousin's sleeve. 'We can't talk about this here. We'll have to meet in private.'

'When?'

'Tomorrow afternoon, after church. We'll meet at the iron bridge in Kelvingrove a half-hour after lunch,' Lindsay said.

'Good idea.' Cissie sniffed. 'You do believe me, Lindsay, don't you?'

'Of course I do, silly,' Lindsay said.

Eleanor Runciman believed that the world was full of women plotting to lure Mr Arthur to the altar. She lived in dread that one night he would not return home. For this reason she made a point of finding out which swan-throated soprano or full-bosomed contralto was running first in the field of Mr Arthur's affections, but as season succeeded season and the eager little divas became younger and more attractive Eleanor's anxiety increased.

She had no reason to suppose that the man she loved was anything other than honourable. Men were such weak creatures and so easily led, though, that she was afraid that Mr Arthur might eventually succumb to one of the grasping little harpies, a younger, slimmer, still fertile version of the woman that she had been when she'd stepped into his house sixteen years ago.

The sight of the man she loved rubbing shoulders with some sweet-voiced young thing so filled her with gloom that she no longer attended choral society concerts. Recently her fear of losing not just her place in the household but her place in Mr Arthur's heart had become so great that she could hardly bear to be civil to any of the women who turned up at Brunswick Crescent soirées. In the words of Osgood Turner's famous song, 'The years were passing, passing, passing, and the light in her heart grew dim.' The trouble was that the light in Eleanor Runciman's heart was *not* growing dim. Indeed, the older she got the more fiercely it seemed to burn.

When, just after eleven, Arthur opened the front door he found Miss Runciman waiting in the hall. He paused, a guilty silhouette, then whispered, 'Eleanor, what are you doing up at this hour?'

'Waiting to lock up, sir.'

'I can do that, you know.'

'I've left the whisky cabinet open and some cheese and oatcakes on a tray in the parlour in case you're hungry.'

He removed his overcoat. She took it from him. The fragrance of the night clung lightly to the cloth; the fragrance of the night or the perfume of one of the flowery young women with whom Arthur had shared a hansom. Eleanor gave the overcoat a violent shake, hung it on a hook on the hallstand and locked the outside door and glass-panelled inner door. Arthur watched.

He called her Eleanor only when they were alone. Now and then she had been tempted to try him with Arthur but she could not relinquish her ingrained feelings of deference. 'Do you wish me to pour your whisky, sir?'

'No, but do come and join me for a nightcap.'

'Thank you. I would like that.'

The parlour was lit by firelight and a single gas jet, the piano alcove filled with soft summery shadows. Eleanor wished that Arthur would play for her, would let her turn the music sheet and place a hand on his shoulder as Lindsay did, or Matilda Perrino, who was as slender as a willow and talented.

Mr Arthur didn't have to ask what she would have to drink: a thimbleful of brandy and *scoot* of soda water. He handed her the glass and invited her to be seated. He cut himself a sliver of cheddar and, nibbling it, lowered himself on to the upright chair at the edge of the alcove, half in and half out of shadow.

'Did the concert go well?' Eleanor enquired.

'It seemed to. What did Linnet have to say about it?'

'She appears to have enjoyed it. She did not say much.'

'She's changing,' Arthur said. 'Growing up.'

'She *is* grown up. She will be married and gone before we know it,' Eleanor said. 'Did you go back to Harper's Hill afterwards?'

'No, a gang of us went on to Pettigrew's.'

'For supper?'

'Hmmm. To celebrate the end of the season.'

'Another year gone,' said Eleanor Runciman. 'How it flies.'

Arthur dusted crumbs from his fingers, drank from his glass.

'Talking of change,' Arthur said. 'My father will be leaving Harper's Hill in a day or two. He takes possession of this Perthshire place on the first of June.'

'He will be missed.'

'Lindsay will be next to leave, I expect,' Arthur said. 'I'll feel very cut off when that day comes. Perhaps I should marry again. What do you think?'

Eleanor kept her voice level. 'Do you have someone in mind?'

He shrugged. 'No one in particular.'

'Miss Perrino, perhaps?'

'Matilda? Far too young for me.'

'What age is she?'

'Twenty-two or -three, I reckon.'

'Nevertheless, you have much in common.'

'Matilda already has a young man.'

'Does she?' said Eleanor, less evenly than before.

'In the other choir, the So-Fa. A Highlander, I believe, a tenor. She keeps rather quiet about him. Apparently her father doesn't approve. No doubt he'll be won over in due course.'

'If not Miss Perrino, Miss Douglas perhaps?'

'Rosemary? No, no. Rosemary's a kind friend but not . . .'

He got up suddenly and to Eleanor's surprise, laughed. 'What's all this about, Eleanor Runciman? Are you trying to marry me off?'

'May I remind you, sir, that you raised the subject.'

'Yes, I suppose I did. I don't know what I'm blathering about half the time. I've no intention of getting married again. It's all this blessed shifting about that's put me at sixes and sevens. Pappy pretending he's a country gentleman. Irish nephews descending upon us. Lindsay — well, Lindsay already planning what she'll do when I'm dead.'

'I beg your pardon?'

Amused by his own pessimism, Arthur said, 'It's true; well, half true. My dear daughter is beginning to show signs of ambition. She sits in on our management meetings and, when she remembers, makes notes. I wonder what she makes note *of*, for heaven's sake.'

'Do you wish me to have a word with her, Mr Arthur?'

'If you would, Eleanor. Try to find out what's going on in her head.'

'Could it be the young man, perhaps?'

'Young man? What young man?'

'The Irish cousin.'

'Forbes? Good God! I hope not.'

'He seems very personable.'

'Not to me he doesn't,' Arthur said. 'He's sly and self-serving, like his mother. Has he been here again?'

'No.'

'Is she seeing much of him elsewhere, I wonder?'

'I expect she encounters him at Harper's Hill. She could hardly avoid it.'

'Well, I'm glad he isn't lodging with us,' Arthur said. 'I wouldn't be happy having that particular nephew as a resident in my house.'

'If I might ask . . .' Eleanor hesitated. 'What do you have against your sister and her son?'

Arthur tugged his earlobe. 'I don't know.'

'Oh!'

'I've never liked Kay; Kay has never liked me. When we were children she was resentful of the fact that I got more attention than she did. That, at least, is Donald's theory. Doesn't really hold water, does it?'

'I do not think it does, no.'

'Kay and Helen were so damned outspoken. They gave Pappy and Mama a very hard time of it. Finally they gathered a little money from somewhere and struck out on their own.'

'Set up house together, you mean?' said Eleanor. 'I believe I did hear something of the sort.'

'They wanted to be independent, to have a life of their own. Wanted to behave like men, I suppose, but without responsibility.'

'Why did your father allow it?'

'Oh, they could wheedle the birds off the trees, that pair. Besides, Helen was practically an invalid and Pappy refused her nothing.'

'Much good it did her, poor thing,' said Eleanor.

Arthur was silent for a moment, then said, 'You know, I've never known if Helen realised she was dying when she set up with Kay in Shalimar Street. If Kay knew it too, or if . . .' He was silent again then, in a little rush, said, 'She had a lover. Helen, I mean. She had a lover that none of us knew about. They rented the apartment in Shalimar Street so that Helen could be with him.'

'Would he not marry her?'

'He was, I believe, already married.'

'Ah!' Eleanor said softly.

'Do *you* think that is a romantic thing to do? Do you approve?'

'I certainly do not,' Eleanor Runciman lied.

'Oh, dear,' Arthur said. 'I'm not so sure.'

'Really?'

'Well, she was never strong, our Helen. I vividly remember winter nights with the doctor coming and going, the stink of medicinal vapour and Nanny, our old nanny, running to fetch hot fomentations and glass cups from the stove.'

'Does Lindsay know about her aunts?'

'Certainly not, no.'

'Do you not think she should be told?'

'Why?' Arthur said. 'It isn't the sort of thing that a decent young woman should have to hear about her family.'

'That her aunt was loved?'

'That her aunt had a lover.'

'If I may ask,' said Eleanor again, 'did Kay also . . .'

'I don't know,' said Arthur. 'Perhaps she was already – ah – consorting with Daniel McCulloch. I wouldn't put it past her. She certainly let *us* down.'

'Us?'

'Lindsay and me. Left us in the lurch. How could she abandon her brother and her motherless niece with hardly a moment's notice? She was off to Dublin with her brewer within forty-eight hours of making the announcement. Married without any of her family present, not even Pappy. He was hurt, so hurt. I don't know how he found it in his heart to forgive her.'

'How old,' said Eleanor, 'is the boy?'

'No, it wasn't a pregnancy.' Arthur said. 'Kay was married for over a year before the first child was born. In my opinion it was Daniel McCulloch who forced her to choose between her family and marriage.'

'And she chose marriage?'

'That's how it seems to me.'

'Looking back?'

'Even at the time.'

'Perhaps she loved him,' Eleanor suggested.

'Love!' Arthur said. 'I doubt if Kay knows the meaning of the word. It was all very distressing. If it hadn't been for Nanny Cheadle – and you too – I don't know how I'd have coped.'

'Donald and Lilias . . .'

'She was *my* daughter, Eleanor. Lindsay was all I had.'

'Yes, of course. I'm sorry.'

For a moment Eleanor felt her sympathy waver. She had shared his life but not the making of him. She had no knowledge of the brief, loving marriage that had been brought to a close by premature death. She could forgive his bitterness but not the object of it. The boy, the nephew, could hardly be blamed for events that had happened before he was born. She got to her feet.

'Don't go,' Arthur said, 'unless, that is, you want to.'

If she had been in Kay's position and Arthur had asked her to run off with him she would have put everything away, every duty, every responsibility, every consideration. She would have shouted, '*Yes, yes, yes,*' and have been on the boat with him before he could change his mind. She sat down again.

'Now do you see why I'm less than enthusiastic about having Forbes McCulloch join the firm as a trainee manager?' he said. 'What's more I would prefer it if he did not come calling on Lindsay.'

'I'm not sure he can be stopped, not without appearing to be rude.'

'How many times has he been here?'

'Once, just once,' Eleanor said. 'His father, McCulloch, what's he like?'

'I have no idea,' Arthur answered. 'Never clapped eyes on the fellow. Apparently the boy's quite cock of the walk in Donald's house. I don't suppose I can stop Lindsay meeting with him there but I'd prefer him not to call on her here when I'm not at home.'

'Are you forbidding him the house, sir?'

Arthur considered. 'Yes, I do believe I am.'

'You're frightened of losing her, aren't you?'

'When the right chap comes along I'll let her go willingly; but Forbes McCulloch is not the right chap.'

'I would not say that to Lindsay,' Eleanor advised.

'Why not?'

'Forbidden fruit, Mr Arthur. Forbidden fruit.'

First there was a frown, then a wry smile. 'You're absolutely right. Negative effect, what? Tell me, Eleanor, what do *you* suggest I do about young McCulloch?'

'Nothing at all,' said Eleanor.

'Let nature take its course, you mean?'

'Precisely,' Eleanor Runciman said and shortly thereafter took herself off to bed.

It was a warm day with a touch of humidity, not oppressive. Hawthorn foamed with blossom, rhododendrons were in full bloom and on the river, under the willows, the first hatch of ducklings bobbed comically behind their mama. In the band-stand the band of the Royal Naval Reserve was thumping out orchestral selections just military enough to offend those Sab-batarians who had resisted the introduction of Sunday afternoon concerts. Most Clydesiders could not have cared less about preserving the Lord's day; they just enjoyed a good tune. Even those unwilling or unable to fork out sixpence for a seat in the enclosure were content to lean on the railings or loll on the riverbank and take the programme as it came, for cornet, bass, trombone and the wheedling notes of the piccolo floated freely into all the corners of the Kelvingrove.

The beat of the drum, or at least its vibrations, penetrated Owen Franklin's mansion on Harper's Hill where, at Lilias's insistence, Owen had finally addressed the problem of packing. The dressing-room on the second floor was strewn with tea chests, hampers and hat boxes. Mercy and Pansy had offered to assist but Pappy's temper was on short fuse and Lilias had ordered all her children out into the park with firm instruc-tions not to return home before half past five o'clock. Before Donald Franklin's troops could muster, however, Cissie slipped off on her own to rendezvous with Lindsay by the iron bridge.

'He's coming,' said Cissie breathlessly. 'They're all coming, in fact.'

'What's happening?' said Lindsay. 'What's all the fuss about?'

'Pappy's finally decided to prepare for departure,' Cissie explained. 'I've never seen so much luggage. I don't know where he's going to put it, for the house at Strathmore is already furnished.'

They strolled under the chestnut trees, clearly superior young ladies and thoroughly absorbed in themselves. 'Oh, yes,' Lindsay said, as if the topic had just entered her head. 'I believe you were going to tell me about Forbes.'

'Forbes!' Cissie made a unladylike gesture. 'Him! I can do without him, I may tell you. I'm heartily sorry that he ever came to Scotland.'

'Why? What's he done now?'

'Not only does he show himself off, he touches me,' said Cissie, primly. 'He *keeps* touching me.'

'Where?'

'In the hall, in the upstairs corridor, wherever he can.'

'No, I mean – where?' said Lindsay, agog.

Cissie glanced across the river as if afraid that her voice would be amplified by the trees and her confession made public.

'He's touched my – my breast.'

'*What!*'

'Stole up behind me, put his arms around me and placed his hands on my breast. He's always taking liberties, Lindsay, frightful liberties. When we were playing charades last evening – why didn't you come round, by the way? – when we were playing charades, he and I were sent out of the drawing-room, he pulled me into the cloakroom under the stairs and—'

'What?' said Lindsay again.

'Kissed me.'

'Why didn't you slap him?'

'I – I tried to.'

'What did he do?'

'He caught my hand and laughed. Then do you know what he said? He said that he liked a girl with a bit of fire in her, in her . . .'

'What?'

'Belly. That's what he said, Lindsay. Honestly! He told me that he liked a girl with a bit of fire in her belly.'

'How awful for you!'

'I asked him what sort of a person he thought I was.'

'What did he say to that?'

'He said he thought I was passionate.'

'Did he indeed?'

'I *swear* that's what he said. I'm not making it up.'

There was, Lindsay realised, more excitement than revulsion in her cousin's response. What worried Cissie, apparently, was that she could not predict just how unscrupulous their Irish cousin might turn out to be.

'Has he told you that he was sent down from school?' Lindsay said.

'Yes, he told me,' said Cissie.

'Did he tell you why?'

'Something to do with girls.'

'He prides himself on being a ladies' man,' said Lindsay. 'At first I thought he was boasting but now I'm beginning to believe him.'

'Oh, believe me, believe him,' Cissie said. 'He has absolutely no sense of propriety. And he's so ridiculously young.'

A tiny green worm of envy wriggled within Lindsay's breast. Its abrupt appearance had less to do with Forbes McCulloch's fumblings than his compliments. Plump, befreckled Cissie, passionate and desirable? Cissie had never struck *her* as passionate and desirable.

'If you really want to put a stop to his capers,' Lindsay heard herself say, 'surely a word in Martin's ear will do the trick.'

'Martin and the boys like him. Besides, I don't want to cause a fuss.'

'A fuss? He's *molesting* you, Cissie.'

'I think that's putting it rather too strongly.'

'If you don't put an end to it he'll take it as a sign that you're willing.'

'Willing?'

'To go further.'

'I hope you're not suggesting I that encourage him.'

'Of course not,' said Lindsay. 'None the less, a word to Martin . . .'

'Martin wouldn't understand.'

'Oh, I think he would,' said Lindsay. 'When he kisses you, Forbes I mean, does he——?'

'Yes,' Cissie interrupted, cheeks glowing. 'Yes, he does.'

'He must be stopped,' said Lindsay.

Cissie sighed. 'I know. I know.'

'He isn't in love with you, Cissie. He's just using you.'

'I'm not sure that is the case.'

'Cissie!'

'Well, yes, I suppose you're right. I just keep thinking: What if he really is in love with me? What if he's too inexperienced to . . .'

'Inexperienced?'

'You know what I mean – too young to express his feelings.'

'Look, would you like me to tackle him?' Such a solution had obviously not occurred to Cissie; it had only just occurred to Lindsay. 'Perhaps he'd take heed of me.'

'Why would he take heed of you?'

'Because I'm a fellow partner on Franklin's board.'

'That's plain silly,' said Cissie.

'No, it isn't,' Lindsay said. 'Forbes is very ambitious. I'd point out what he's risking by behaving so badly. Point out what he stands to lose if he persists in taking advantage of you.'

'Has he tried any of this nonsense with you?' said Cissie.

'No.'

'Perhaps you're too young for him.'

'I'm only six months younger than you are,' Lindsay said. 'It isn't me I'm concerned about. What if he sets his sights on Mercy or – heaven help us – Pansy? Think of the effect being molested would have on them.'

'Devastating,' Cissie agreed.

'Do you see,' Lindsay said, 'why we have to put a stop to it?'

'Perhaps we *should* tell Martin.'

'Let me talk to Forbes first.'

'Why you?'

'I told you, dearest. I think he respects me.'

'I'm older.'

'Ah, but I'm the partner.'

Tom Calder received four hundred and twenty pounds in annual salary. Being a man of abstemious habits with only one dependent relative – Sylvie – he managed to rub along quite well on that sum, for, unlike George Crush, he hadn't pushed himself into debt by taking a mortgage on a suburban villa. He lived in a residential boarding-house on Queensview where he rented not just a bedroom but also a snug little parlour. He had his career, his singing, his daughter and, by way of a weakness, a partiality for sugary foods that made the cry of the ice-cream vendor at the park's western gate seem like a siren song.

Tom purchased a cornet with two scoops of ice-cream decorated with raspberry syrup. He curled his tongue over the surface and uttered a little *hmmm* of pure pleasure. For a moment, satisfaction softened the bleakness of his gaze and, licking diligently, he wandered through the gate and along the pathway that led to the fountain.

Quite unhurried, quite unconcerned, he did not much care if he encountered Florence or Albert or if he did not. He had called upon them last week to settle the bills and had been received by Sylvie with an unctuousness that he found harder to swallow than her sulks. He had noticed that Sylvie had begun to show discernible signs of femaleness, an indication that Florence would not be able to dress her up like a china doll for very much longer. He was just spiteful enough to wonder how his sister-in-law and her husband would cope with a capricious adolescent and how long it would take them to realise that they had raised a wilful little monster. He was still thinking of Sylvie when he spotted the Franklin girls on the opposite bank of the river.

They were no great distance from him, fifty or sixty yards at most. Their summer frocks and hats made splurges of colour in the blue and green shadows of the trees and Tom contemplated them for a moment or two before recognition dawned. His first impulse was to ditch the ice-cream and call out to them. Instead, hastily munching, he matched his pace to theirs until their ways converged at the iron footbridge.

'Miss Franklin,' he said. 'Miss Lindsay.' He did not offer his sticky hand but took off his straw boater and held it politely by his trouser-leg.

'Why, Mr Calder,' Lindsay said, 'I hardly recognised you.'

'Oh! I'm sorry. I didn't mean to intrude.'

'It's not the intrusion,' Lindsay said. 'It's the hat.'

'Haven't you seen me in a hat before?'

'Often, but not a boater — or a striped jacket, for that matter.'

Cissie Franklin continued to glower at him as if he were a labourer who had forgotten his place.

'*Have* you been boating?' Lindsay said.

Tom felt like a small steam-powered engine that had been idle for too long. The pistons moved sluggishly: he could think of no witty reply. He told the truth. 'I've been eating ice-cream.'

'And that,' said Lindsay, 'is your ice-cream suit, I take it.'

He looked down at his perfectly ordinary blazer and cream-coloured flannel trousers. He had bought them in Dawson & McNicholl's, the merchant tailors, to wear on his trip to Africa but even before he'd arrived at Burutu he had realised how daft the notion had been and had left them folded in brown paper in the bottom of his trunk.

'What's wrong with it?' he said.

'Not a thing,' said Lindsay. 'It's very fetching.'

Tom was not so lacking in humour as all that. 'Now you're going to ask me where I fetched it from?'

Lindsay laughed. She looked remarkably pretty, a good deal less earnest than she did at management meetings. He was tempted to raise some serious matter of business to put her in her place but on a May day in the 'Groveries nothing, absolutely nothing, was more serious than a pretty girl in a floral hat.

Tom let out an undetectable sigh.

Lindsay said, 'Are you meeting someone?'

'No one in particular.'

'Why don't you walk with us then?'

'Lind-*say!* Cissie Franklin protested in a stage whisper. 'I don't wish to . . .'

He caught the glance that Lindsay gave her cousin but could not interpret it. Some female code or understanding veiled its meaning. He knew nothing about women really, just enough to be sure that the girls weren't flirting.

'Your company would be very welcome, Mr Calder,' Lindsay said.

'At least as far as the fountain,' Cissie added.

Then he thought he understood. Some chap, some masher had been making a nuisance of himself and the Franklin girls required male protection for a time. 'It would be my pleasure,' he said. 'As far as the fountain.'

They made their way on to the Radnor, the broad tree-lined avenue that divided Kelvingrove into two halves. Tom found Miss Cissie Franklin one side of him and Miss Lindsay Franklin on the other. Each slid an arm into his and step-in-step, like a team of dancers, they wheeled left and sallied through the foot traffic, heading Tom knew not where.

And didn't much care.

*   *   *

'Good Lord!' Martin said. 'We leave you to your own devices for five blessed minutes and you come back with some poor chap in tow.' He grinned, offered his hand. 'Tom, how are you?'

'I'm very well, thank you.'

'Beautiful day, is it not?'

'Beautiful.'

'We've been tossed out,' Martin said. 'My grandfather's in the throes of packing and Mama wants us out of the way. And you, what are you doing with yourself, apart from rescuing damsels in distress?'

'Hardly in distress,' Tom said. 'In fact, I think they rescued me.'

'Oh, from what?' Martin said. 'Some woman's nefarious attentions?'

'No,' Tom said.

'No such luck, what?' Martin extended an arm and gathered his flock to him. 'Ross and Johnny I believe you know. And surely you remember my sisters, Pansy and Mercy?'

'Indeed I do,' said Tom.

'From the choir,' said Pansy. 'You're a tenor, are you not?'

'I am.'

'Mr Calder also designs ships,' said Lindsay.

'I know *that*,' said Pansy. 'I'm not a baby.'

'You were in Africa, were you not?' Mercy said. 'You went to the Niger to put our boats together.'

Tom noted the pronoun, 'our' boats. Although she probably couldn't tell a spar from a splinter, young Mercy Franklin had more claim to ownership of the Niger stern-wheelers than he did. He felt no resentment. Unlike George Crush he wasn't tarred with the Socialist brush. Besides, Mercy was a pretty wee thing and he was becoming rather susceptible to pretty wee things. Cissie, he realised, had claimed his arm again.

'Did you like Africa?' Pansy asked.

'Not much, to be truthful.'

'Did you meet any cannibals?'

79

'Pansy, don't talk rot,' Ross said.

'Oh, yes,' Tom answered. 'I dined with them several times.'

There was silence. Tom wondered if he had overstepped the mark of decency, then Martin laughed and the girls followed suit.

Cissie nudged him in the ribs. 'Oh, Tom, you are a card,' she said, and darted a glance at the dark-eyed, dark-haired young man who loitered at the back of the group. 'Forbes, I don't believe you've met Tom yet, have you?'

'Tom's our chief designer, a wizard with compasses and scale,' Martin said. 'I don't know what we'd do without him.'

Cissie clung to him fondly. 'Nor do I.'

Tom detected sullen hostility in Forbes McCulloch's eyes. Snobbery or shyness? he wondered. Although he was a dozen years older than the oldest person in the group, the role that the girls had invented for him made Tom feel quite sprightly.

'Unless I'm mistaken,' he said, 'you're the new partner. We'll be seeing a lot more of you when you've finished your year at Beardmore's. It's a pleasure to make your acquaintance, Mr McCulloch.'

'Likewise, I'm sure,' Forbes answered sourly.

'I didn't know you had a lover,' Forbes said.

'He isn't my lover,' said Cissie.

'A fiancé then.'

'He isn't that either.'

'Is he bucking to be your sweetheart?'

'No, he's just a friend,' said Cissie.

'He's far too old to be your friend,' Forbes groused. 'Is he married?'

'No.'

Lindsay's inspired notion to pretend that Mr Calder was her sweetheart had worked a treat so far. Cissie had the Irish cousin right where she wanted him. She felt very gay as she strolled along behind Lindsay and the man who was supposed to be her sweetheart. Martin and Johnny were not far behind, though Mercy, Pansy and Ross had wandered off to the river to look at the ducklings. They would meet up shortly at the Refreshment Rooms where, Sunday or not, pots of tea and little iced buns were dispensed and there were green iron tables and green iron chairs upon the grass under the trees.

'How long have you known him?' Forbes asked.

Cissie felt her advantage slip slightly. She increased her pace to close the gap between her and the man in the striped blazer. From the rear he looked a little like one of those dandies that were the source of music-hall jokes; not a handsome chap, he had – *je ne sais quoi*, she thought – presence, character, something like that. 'Years,' she answered. 'Absolute years.'

'He thinks you're just a kiddie.'

'He does not.'

'You can tell by the way he treats you.'

'How does he treat me, Mr Know-All?'

'Like a kiddie,' Forbes said. 'Not the way I'd be treating you if you'd give me half a chance. Anyhow, he's a only draughtsman.'

'He's our chief designer and a department manager,' Cissie said. 'There's nothing wrong in keeping company with a manager.'

'He's more taken with Lindsay than he is with you.'

'He is not.'

'Sure and he is. Just look at them together.'

'Stuff and nonsense!' Cissie said haughtily, though she had a very uncomfortable feeling that Forbes might be right.

Lindsay said, 'I take it you know what's going on?'

'I have a vague idea, yes,' Tom answered.

'I hope you don't mind being dragged into it.'

'Not in the slightest.'

'He's *such* a painful young man, so pushing and conceited.'

'Is that why you like him?' Tom said.

'I do *not* like him,' Lindsay said. 'It's Cissie he fancies.'

'Fancying girls at his age — *tut, tut*,' Tom said.

'I'll bet you weren't so forward when you were seventeen.'

'No, but I'm not a Franklin,' Tom said.

She glanced at him quickly. 'Is that what you think of us?'

'The Franklins have always done well by me,' Tom said, 'as well as a person in my position can expect.'

'Your position?'

'Department manager.'

'You're our principal designer.'

'I'm really just an engineer at heart.'

Lindsay laughed. 'My father says that engineers don't have hearts.'

Tom laughed too. 'He's not far wrong.'

'That was during the strike, of course. Did you down tools with the rest?'

'I'm not a member of the Amalgamation.'

'You were on our side, you mean?'

'I'm on nobody's side but my own,' Tom said.

Conversation lagged: Lindsay wondered if she had offended him. The fact that they sat side by side on the board of management was immaterial. He would always be the worker, she the drone. Then she noticed that he was staring at a woman and child in the crowd, a girl, small and doll-like in a frilly dress and a tiny bonnet that barely concealed her ringlets. The girl clung to the woman's hand as if the bustle of the park scared her but when she caught sight of Tom she scuffed her high-button boots into the gravel and acted more coy than shy.

'Who is that?' Lindsay enquired before she could help herself.

'No one.'

'If you wish to speak with them, please do.'

'No.' Tom hesitated. 'I do not wish to speak with them,' and walked on, stiff now and resolute, leaving the woman and child behind.

'Tom Calder,' Lindsay said.

'What about Tom Calder?' her father said.

'Does he have a family?'

'I believe there's a daughter,' Arthur said, 'farmed out somewhere.'

'Farmed out?'

'Looked after by a relative, that sort of thing.'

'No wife?'

'She died some years ago.' Her father looked up from his dinner plate. 'Why the sudden interest in Tom Calder?'

'We met him in the park this afternoon.'

Miss Runciman said, 'Was the daughter with him?'

'No. He walked with Cissie and me for a while. He even took tea with us.'

'Tea at the Hill?' said Miss Runciman.

'In the park.'

'They serve tea in the park now, do they?' Nanny Cheadle said. 'What's the world coming too? It'll be dancing next.'

'What age is Mr Calder's daughter?' Lindsay asked, after a pause.

'About twelve or thirteen,' Papa answered. 'Calder had some time off at the birth, I seem to remember, then again when his wife passed away.'

'Before he went to Africa?'

'Long before.'

'Is this the same Mr Calder who sings in the choir?' Miss Runciman said.

'Yes,' Lindsay answered.

'Ah,' said Miss Runciman. 'I recall him. Tall gentleman, rather grim.'

'He isn't at all grim when you get to know him,' Lindsay said.

'Well,' Miss Runciman said, 'in my experience gentlemen with tragic pasts frequently develop hidden depths to compensate. How old is he, I wonder?'

'Ancient,' Lindsay said. 'Absolutely ancient.' And, before the housekeeper could press her further, swiftly let the matter drop.

CHAPTER FIVE

A Kiss and a Promise

For as many summers as Lindsay could remember, the Franklins had holidayed at the Bruce Hotel in Rothesay on the Isle of Bute. Rothesay was not regarded as a particularly fashionable resort but it had the advantage of being easily reached by boat from Glasgow and offered a multitude of diversions, from sea-water bathing to golf and tennis, and jolly concert parties in the Winter Garden. This summer, however, the pattern had changed. It wasn't off to the seaside but into the country that the Franklins trekked when the shipyard closed in mid-July. They steamed out of Queen Street in a first-class railway carriage and disembarked a couple of hours later at Perth railway station. There they were led by a team of porters to a horse-drawn charabanc that transported them across the Tay into the hills and forests of *terra incognita* where, for reasons that still remained obscure, Owen Franklin had chosen to hide himself away.

It was a two-hour drive but the weather was fair and the younger members of the family, Lindsay included, joined enthusiastically in the choruses that Martin insisted they sing 'to let the old man know we're coming'. Metalled roads gave way to tracks, small towns became hamlets, hamlets mere isolated cottages and then, at last, the horses clopped into the tiny community of Kelkemmit and on a hill among the pines across a dark loch the house of Strathmore hove into view, not giddy or grand but, to Lindsay at least, a bit of a disappointment.

'Is that it?' Cissie sang out. 'Martin, are you sure?'

'Ask Mama if you don't believe me.'

The driver, a youngish chap with hair like burned heather, called back, 'Aye, yon's the big house. We will be there in ten minutes.'

'What is it?' Pansy asked. 'I mean, what was it? I thought it was a castle. It doesn't look like a castle to me.'

'Nah, nah, it was never a castle, miss,' the driver informed her. 'It was Miss Pringle's home for many a year. Before that it was the old colonel's house and before that even, the priests' house.'

'Priests?' said Johnny. 'Good Lord!'

'It was a long time ago,' said the driver. 'There is no trace o' the fathers left now, sir, never fear.'

'Just the odd priestly ghost stalking the corridors perhaps?'

'Johnny, don't *say* that,' Pansy begged.

'*Whooo-ooo! Whooo-ooo-hooo!*' Johnny called out in a wavering voice and winced when all three of his sisters simultaneously punched his arm.

He waited for them on the strip of gravel that fronted the house. He had been waiting for half the day. Below him four or five sheep grazed the ragged shelves of grass that dipped down to the loch. All around were strips of pine forest and steep, smooth-shouldered hills. In the seven weeks that he had been in residence Owen had come to realise that he did not like Strathmore or the empty impartiality of the hills that surrounded it.

Fortunately Giles, a city-born servant, had quite taken to country living. He had quickly established contact with trades-men and farmers; had hired a cook and two girls to attend to cleaning and laundry; had bought a pony and trap at Perth sales and arranged for the animal to be stabled with Mr Tasker whose farm lay a quarter of a mile away, deeper into the hills. It was Giles who took out the rod of an evening, went down to the loch and came back, grinning, with a basket of trout to serve for supper or breakfast. Owen, however, could not shake off his melancholy. He even refused to climb to the summit of the ridge behind the house to admire a view that Giles assured was 'magnificent, sir, just magnificent'. He, Owen Franklin, had seen all the views he ever wanted to see and would have exchanged every mountain and shining loch in Perthshire for just one crowded brown acre of Clydeside.

He heard them singing long before the charabanc came in sight. He had ample time to assume a cheery air and pretend that he had done the right thing by retiring to the country. He even managed a smile when the conveyance finally lurched out of the trees and the horses, sensing journey's end, put a bit of effort into a trot. 'Lilias!' he shouted. 'Donald! Is that you hiding there, Pansy? By gum! I'll swear you've grown taller since I saw you last,' and rocked back and forth with affected delight, arms spread to welcome the children to his humble abode in the hills.

Cissie removed her bonnet and rubbed the elastic red mark on her plump chin. She placed the bonnet on a marble-topped washstand and seated herself on one of the two iron bedsteads that were tucked under the slope of the roof. She bounced up and down experimentally, and said, 'Solid granite.'

'A hard mattress is good for the spine, so they say,' said Lindsay.

'Not *my* spine,' said Cissie. 'Look at this place. I wouldn't expect a scullery maid to sleep here.'

'It's the country,' said Lindsay. 'We're supposed to rough it.'

'Where are the boys?'

'On the floor below, I think.'

'It's all very well for them. They're used to mucking in.'

Lindsay removed her bonnet and travelling cape. She seated

herself on the bed directly beneath the grimy skylight. She unlaced her boots.

'What's Pappy *doing* here?' Cissie went on. 'I mean, if he's tired of living with us in Harper's Hill he could sail to New York, or cruise the Mediterranean, or rent a villa in the south of France. Why Perthshire?'

'Perhaps he's in search of a quiet life.'

'He's not turning into a hermit, is he?'

'Ask him.'

'You ask him,' Cissie said. 'Oh no, don't bother. He obviously thinks this place is paradise. Did you see the grin on his face?'

'He was just pleased to see us, that's all,' Lindsay said.

Cissie tugged two long pins from her hair and shook her head.

'What are we going to do here for two whole weeks?'

'Enjoy ourselves, I suppose,' said Lindsay.

'How? There isn't even a tennis court.'

'Croquet?' Lindsay suggested.

'On that lawn, with those — those creatures?'

'Sheep,' said Lindsay. 'Chin up, Cissie. The boys will think of something exciting for us to do. Climb a mountain, perhaps. I've never climbed a mountain before, have you?'

Cissie did not deign to answer.

'Do you know what?' she said, at length. 'I'm almost beginning to wish that Forbes had travelled with us.'

'Oh, Cissie! I thought you hated him.'

'I do, but at least he'd cheer the place up.'

'No,' Lindsay said. 'Forbes isn't the cheering type.'

'When is he due to arrive?'

'Monday afternoon some time, I believe.'

'Is he travelling up with your father?'

'Somehow I doubt it,' Lindsay said.

The skylight darkened as clouds scudded across the blue and the attic bedroom turned even more gloomy. The cousins glanced upward.

'Rain?' Cissie said.

'Inevitably,' said Lindsay.

It had never been the Franklins' habit to travel with servants. There had been no need for servants when holidays were taken at the Bruce Hotel. Besides, Lilias was the daughter of a school-mastering couple, respectable but not well to do, and she was too thrifty to hand over to hirelings tasks that she was quite capable of doing for herself. She loved her husband not just for what he had given her materially, though, but also for the sort of man he was, frank, generous and devoted, lacking the sharp little edge of acerbity that had showed itself now and then in his father and brother and especially in his sisters, Helen and Kay.

Lilias had shed few tears when Helen Franklin had passed away and Kay had run off with Daniel McCulloch. She had no particular fondness for Kay and was not disposed to like Kay's son. She had accepted Forbes into her home only to please her father-in-law, because, in principle if not practice, Harper's Hill was not her house at all. Forbes was a good-looking boy, that she would concede, but the flaws in his character soon became too obvious to ignore. Unlike Donald, she was not prepared to forgive Forbes his transgressions merely because of his youth. She did not trust him an inch.

She tried to warn Cissie not to become too fond of her Irish cousin but Cissie was prickly and would not listen. Even Lindsay, normally so sensible, was unwilling to discuss the newcomer and Lilias was forced to accept that nothing she could say or do would slacken the hold that the young Dubliner had over her children. She regretted that Forbes would join them on Monday, that even on holiday she would have to suffer his egregious smiles and sly, slithering glances and catch the whispered innuendoes that her daughters, and Lindsay, seemed to find so fascinating.

It was, alas, a very wet weekend. Rain swept in on Friday

evening and brought with it a certain grey lethargy. By half past nine o'clock everyone had trailed off to bed.

Saturday was no better. Only the boys ventured out to explore the countryside and even they, wet through, were back within the hour. The march to church on Sunday was an ordeal; a long meandering sermon only added to the general disgruntlement.

No piano was to be found in Strathmore, an omission that Owen promised to rectify before the family's Christmas visit – 'Christmas visit? What's this about a Christmas visit?' – and the weekend deteriorated into bickering over endless games of draughts and cribbage and vain attempts by Martin to rouse interest in a round of charades. The atmosphere did not encourage fellowship let alone frivolity. The house reeked of dampness and a creeping decay that not even log fires in the parlours and coal fires in the bedrooms could dissipate. Small wonder that badinage between the boys took a macabre turn, turning to ghosts and corpses and the invention of a cod 'history' for the house that became so grisly that Pansy and Mercy were frightened and Donald had to put a stop to it.

By nine, armed with stone hot-water bottles, candles, books, bed-socks and, in Martin's case, a flask of whisky, the Franklins, male and female, trooped off upstairs with all the enthusiasm of prisoners ascending the gallows.

In the attic Cissie and Lindsay undressed by candlelight.

They brushed their clothes, folded their stockings, rolled up their ribbons and modestly slipped into their nightgowns. The day-maids from Kelkemmit had refused to attend on the Sabbath and Ross and Johnny between them had failed to ignite a fire in the gnarled iron grate, though in trying they had created more smoke than a kipper factory.

Cissie coughed and hugged the stoneware bottle to her breast.

'You're not going to read, are you?'

'I'm going to try,' said Lindsay.

'In this light you'll ruin your eyesight. What are you reading, anyway?'

'Oh, just a trashy romance.'

'About luh-urve?' said Cissie. 'What's it called?'

'*The Sorrows of Satan.*'

'I've read that,' said Cissie. 'I didn't think it was trashy. I thought it was rather spiritual and uplifting.'

Seated by the washstand on the room's only chair, Lindsay brushed her hair. The candle flame formed little pearls of light around the mirror's blown border, the only signs of warmth in the room.

'Lindsay,' Cissie said, 'do you think I'm clever?'

'Of course you are. At school, you were—'

'School doesn't count,' Cissie said. '*You're* clever. Everyone knows you're clever. I mean, that's why Pappy made you a partner.'

'No,' Lindsay said. 'He was just being fair.'

Cissie put the stoneware bottle on the quilt, then, not quite as seductively as Salome, raised her arms above her head. 'Do you think I have a good figure?'

'Better than mine,' said Lindsay.

'Fatter than yours, that's what you mean, isn't it?'

'Fuller,' said Lindsay, who knew better than to tell an outright lie.

Sighing, Cissie slumped on to the bed. 'I'm a frump, a fat frump,' she said. 'Heaven knows what I'll be like in five years' time. Too fat and horrible to contemplate.'

'Nonsense!'

Lindsay recommenced her grooming, counting strokes beneath her breath. Cissie and she had been as close as sisters and had shared many secrets. But there was a new note in Cissie's questions that made Lindsay uncomfortable. She waited, rather tensely, for the next question.

'Do you think that's all Forbes sees in me?' Cissie said. 'My figure, I mean. Do men really only care about how we look?'

Lindsay said, 'Has Forbes tried to kiss you again?'

'Not since that day in the park. He's wary of Mr Calder, I think.'

'Does that not answer your question?'

'Of course it doesn't,' said Cissie. 'I mean, it's not that I want him to . . .' Perplexed, she stripped back the covers and swung herself into bed. 'I don't know what I want, Lindsay. It's this place, this boring house. I was all right until we arrived in this hovel.'

'Perhaps Strathmore *is* haunted.'

'What do you mean?' said Cissie, more bewildered than alarmed.

Lindsay left the dressing-table and set the candle-holder on the shelf above the beds. Nanny Cheadle would love it here: a house without gas, a house as old and creaky as Nanny herself, a house filled with phantoms of unfulfilled desires. She eased herself into bed.

Cissie, not at all sleepy, said, 'Haunted? Tell me what you mean.'

'Haunted by star-crossed lovers doomed to linger here for all eternity.'

'Really?' Cissie lay back, arms above her head.

Lindsay reached for her book but did not open it.

Cissie said, 'I wonder what it's like to be a star-crossed lover.'

'Not much fun, I imagine,' Lindsay said.

'Better than being married to a man you don't love, though.'

'Or,' said Lindsay, 'to a man who doesn't love you.'

'Have you ever been in love, Lindsay?'

'If I had, I'd have told you about it.'

'Oh, yes.' Cissie chuckled. 'What about Gordon Swann then?'

'Don't be ridiculous.'

'What about our Martin?'

'I love Martin dearly,' Lindsay said, 'but not in that way.'

'What about Forbes?' Cissie persisted. 'Do you think you could love him — in that way?'

Lindsay pushed her feet down into the corners of the bed. The sheets were smooth and slippery and now that the bottle had warmed them felt faintly, not unpleasantly damp.

'Well?' Cissie said.

'If we're talking about husbands,' Lindsay said, 'I think I'd prefer Mr Calder to our cousin from Dublin.'

'Do you know something,' Cissie said, 'I think I would too.'

A week before the holiday Mr Sampson, the foreman, moved him out of castings and along to the engine shop. Forbes wasn't sorry to quit the foundry. When he enquired if his grandfather was behind the move, though, he was met with a blank stare and gathered the impression that he was being moved along not for the benefit of his education but because he had failed to make the grade.

He was used to being rejected. His father, Daniel, had had it in for him from the day he was born. His father wasn't a drunkard, a gambler, or a bully. He was fair with the farmers from whom he bought his grains and generous to his employees. He was known as a good, round, solid sort of family man, loved by his children — all except Forbes — and respected in the community. He had no obvious flaws to which Forbes could point and say, 'See, that's him, the real Daniel McCulloch, the ogre, the tyrant who reared and rejected me.'

Only his mother loved him, but his mother was weak. She seemed to expect more of him that he was ever able to deliver, but whenever he failed to live up to her expectations she was always willing to forgive him. When he grew he'd plucked up courage to ask her why his father hated him. Mam had denied that this was the case, had kept on denying it no matter how hard or how often he pressed her. So, by the age of eleven, he had begun to live up to the reputation his father had wished upon him. Had developed into a wild young rip, thoughtless, harum-scarum, always on the lookout for mischief — secure in the knowledge that his pa would punish and his mam forgive.

Thus was the order of Owen Forbes McCulloch's universe established.

He said nothing to his uncles about what had happened at Beardmore's. He knew when to keep his gob shut. Sooner or later they were bound to find out. Then, just like his pa, they would reprimand him for laziness or lack of interest or for scrapping with those apprentices who couldn't tolerate his accent and had ganged up on him at the dinner-hour, three and four and five of them to give him his licks, until finally he'd floored one of them with the back of a coking shovel, which had ended that daily dose of unpleasantness once and for all.

On the following Monday morning he was moved along.

He was surprised to discover that the engine shop was as cold and noisy as the forge had been. The foreman, Mr Gall, seemed to know who he was and why he had been sent there. Mr Gall took him straight to a small, oily upright machine and in a matter of ten minutes showed him how to face nuts. It was simple work, a fool could do it, but the monotony was crippling. That first week seemed like an eternity. His hands performed efficiently but his brain remained disjointed. He daydreamed of Cissie's freckles and full soft breasts, Mercy's rosebud lips and round hips, of Lindsay, with her fine blonde hair and a smile that suggested that if he played his cards right she might let him share her bed.

Amid the clink and clatter of metal he reinvented his past, excursions of the imagination in which he satisfied his desire with girls he'd hardly known, girls who had rebuffed him. He dreamed about holding a woman, touching a woman, having a woman hug him and tell him that he was so handsome and charming that she couldn't resist him. But as the week wore on all the girls became one girl, Lindsay, and his desire eased into a vague, wistful longing to be with her again.

When he strolled up the platform on holiday Monday toting

his scuffed leather valise the first person he saw was his Uncle Arthur nipping nimbly into a first-class compartment and slamming the door.

Forbes walked on, unperturbed. There would be time enough to chat to dear old Uncle Arthur after they reached Perth and were obliged to share a jaunting car for the second leg of the journey. In any case he was searching for a girl, some bonnie wee servant lass, say, whom he could sit next to and engage in conversation, or if she chose to be standoffish whom he could ogle for the duration of the ride. If he couldn't find a suitable specimen to talk to or admire – which, alas, he couldn't – then he would stare out of the window at the passing scene and anticipate the warm welcome that Lindsay would give him when eventually he reached Strathmore. Dreaming of Lindsay, Forbes rolled into Perth station and got out of the train.

'Ah, Forbes!' his uncle said. 'Were you on board? I kept an eye peeled at Glasgow but I must have missed you. Better day, is it not?'

'It is, sir, thanks be to heaven.'

The railway company had laid on a wagonette with a pair of horses between the shafts and a young driver on the high seat. The sky above Perth station was bright, the torrential rain that had raised the rivers and brought burns dashing down from the hills had eased away. Forbes sniffed the clean country air gladly and, without resentment, climbed up beside his uncle. They sat facing each other, knee to knee, as the wagonette rocked over the cobbles and the station dropped out of sight behind stout little houses that ringed the town.

Arthur cleared his throat. 'Ah, how are things at Beard-more's?'

'Just grand.'

'Have you seen Goliath in action yet?'

In spite of a general lack of interest Forbes had been impressed by the gigantic hydraulic hammer that had become a legend in the district of Parkhead, not least because of the damage its vibrations caused to surrounding properties. He had been even more impressed to learn that Goliath, though still in use, was in the process of being replaced by a new cogging mill with an engine that could do as much on a Saturday morning as Goliath could do in a month.

'Sure, and it was very spectacular, Uncle,' Forbes said.

'It's a white elephant now, however.'

'I did hear something to that effect,' said Forbes.

He decided not to force the issues that lay between his uncle and him. He wished to impress the man, not rile him. It had been easy to fool Aunt Lilias, hardly less so Uncle Donald. He was already aware, however, that no matter how far he advanced in shipbuilding he would always have Martin ahead of him, Ross and Johnny panting along behind, and had come to believe that his best hope for the future lay in Brunswick Crescent, not on Harper's Hill.

'I take you've seen the travelling crane?' his uncle said.

'Yes.'

'Have you been up in the operator's box yet?'

'No,' Forbes said. 'To tell you the truth, sir, I've been moved to the engine shop.'

'Have you indeed?'

'I asked for a transfer.'

'Did you indeed?'

Obviously his uncle had heard nothing of what had happened at Beardmore's and had no more than a passing interest in his welfare. Forbes felt no anger, no resentment, just a soft, slow infusion of confidence born out of the sure and certain knowledge that one day he would make Arthur Franklin sit up and take notice of him, that one day in the not too dim and distant future he would be far too important to ignore.

'I thought it would be better for me to get on with it rather than just hanging about,' he said.

'Get on with what, may I ask?'

'Learning about engines,' Forbes said.

'Now that you know all about casting and forging, you mean?'

'We don't make steel at Franklin's.'

'No, but we do have to know what sort of steel to order.'

'I'm aiming to be a manager, Uncle Arthur, not a coker.'

'You're not a manager just yet, Forbes,' his uncle reminded him. 'You have to learn to walk before you can run.'

'How long before you take me into Franklin's?'

'At least a year.'

'Am I being kept in Beardmore's as a punishment?' Forbes asked.

'A punishment? Of course not,' Arthur said, not harshly. 'You've been put out to Beardmore's to learn what it's like to be an apprentice.'

'Why can't I do that at Franklin's?'

'Because,' Arthur said, 'when you're brought into Franklin's you won't be an apprentice, you will not be serving your time at a trade.'

'What will I be doing?'

'Learning to manage.'

'And how long will that take?' Forbes asked.

'Probably for ever,' Arthur Franklin said.

On that lovely summer's evening on the hill above Strathmore, Lindsay fell finally and irrevocably in love with her cousin Forbes.

In a sense she had begun to devise excuses for doing so from the first moment they met. She had also begun to detach herself from Cissie who would no longer serve as her confidante and ally. The silly business of 'touching', the even sillier notion that Forbes was deliberately exhibiting himself were surely figments of Cissie's imagination. In the initial phase of disloyalty it even occurred to Lindsay that Cissie had made the story up because she *wanted* Forbes to kiss her and touch her breast. The temporary introduction of poor Mr Calder into the equation had been nothing but a bit of a lark. It did not dawn on Lindsay that her childish prank might have unforeseen consequences. Tom Calder was far from Lindsay's thoughts, however, that fine, clear summer's evening when the family strolled through the heather to the top of the ridge: three generations of Franklins – Pansy, Johnny and Ross scampering ahead, Martin, Mercy and Cissie next, Donald arm-in-arm with his father, then Arthur with Lilias, and at the rear, straggling, Lindsay and her cousin Forbes.

'For ever,' she said. 'No, I don't think Papa meant it literally. He was probably just warning you that managers have to keep up with the times.'

'I thought that's what he meant,' Forbes said. 'But it did give me a bit of a turn to realise what I've committed myself to.'

Lindsay was impressed by his seriousness. Stuck indoors for three days with Martin, Johnny and Ross she had almost forgotten that not all young men were so tirelessly hearty. She had been glad to see Papa, relieved to see Forbes. Cissie had hurled herself into Forbes's arms and greeted him as if he were a warrior returning from a campaign and not just a late arrival from the city. He had hugged her, bussed her cheek and then, Lindsay noted with satisfaction, had eased himself gently from her clutches. He had kissed Lindsay too, not on the cheek but on the side of the lips and as if once was not enough, had kissed her again, while Johnny and Ross chanted in unison, 'Oi, oi, oi! That's enough of that then,' as if they were rehearsing a musical hall turn.

Forbes had gone upstairs to wash and change. He had returned in time for afternoon tea, shirt open at the collar, flannel trousers fastened with a plaited leather belt that added a touch of the gypsy to his appearance. He was more robust than the image of him that Lindsay had cherished. She wondered if in a year or eighteen months the sinuousness would be gone, if he would have broad shoulders and a broad bottom like Martin, or if he would remain slender and sleek and heart-stoppingly handsome.

Even Aunt Lilias could hardly take her eyes off him when he stood, teacup in hand, in the bay window that looked out upon the loch.

'Air,' Martin had shouted. 'We must have air. We must all go out – you too, Pappy – and make our obeisance to the sun. Lord knows, we haven't seen it once since we arrived. Come along, drink up and let's take to the road.'

'For heaven's sake, Martin, calm yourself.'

'Can't help it. Been cooped up too long.'

'Where will we go?'

'Up to the ridge. We'll claim the summit in the Franklins' name. What do you say, Pappy?'

'If that's what you all want to do,' Owen answered, 'I'm game for it.'

A half-hour later the family moved out through the ever-greens on to the long, easy slope that led to the moors.

At the rear of the party Forbes and Lindsay conversed as if secretly, silently and separately they had both grown up at last.

'I was under the impression that you came to Scotland to make a commitment,' Lindsay said. 'I mean, nobody forced you, did they?'

'Nup. I'm a willing volunteer.'

'Then you've no right to complain.'

'I'm not complaining,' Forbes said. 'But I didn't come to Scotland just to learn about shipbuilding.'

'What did you come for?' Lindsay said.

'To be with my family.'

'Your family lives in Dublin.'

'Brothers and sisters, far too many of the wee beggars,' Forbes said. 'No, Linnet, I mean my real family, the kin I sprang from.'

'You're beginning to sound like Martin at his most pre-tentious.'

'God help me!' Forbes said, grinning.

'Do you really feel more Scottish than Irish?'

'Yes, I really and truly do.' He walked close by her, penned by the heather and bracken that defined the peat-cutters' track. 'I came here to find my family,' he said, 'and got more than I bargained for.'

'What do you mean?' said Lindsay.

'I mean,' Forbes said, 'I found you.'

'Oh, yes, you found all of us.'

'I mean,' he said, 'you.'

Martin and Johnny had dragged Pansy to the summit, a flattened ridge of rock and bare ground. Martin stretched his arms above his head and for a moment looked as if he were struggling to catch the sun and bring it down to earth like a gigantic ball for his sisters to play with. He looked grand and manly and not at all foolish – but he was Martin, just Martin, and Lindsay found that she suddenly understood just how affection differed from love.

'Do you not mean Cissie?' Lindsay heard herself say.

'Sure and I do not mean Cissie.'

'She's very taken with you, you know.'

Forbes took her arm. Her boy cousins had never seen any harm in hugging and hand-holding. Her father, like all fathers, was less demonstrative but even he would cuddle her when she was feeling low. Being touched by Forbes was different, though. If they had been alone on the hillside she might have sought his hand and pressed it against her skirts, answering sign with sign.

'Stop it, Lindsay.'

'Stop what?'

'I'm not attracted to Cissie.'

'Don't you like her?'

'I like her well enough but it's you I . . .'

Up ahead Aunt Lilias and Arthur had paused to admire the view of the glen. She leaned on him, resting against his shoulder as if he and not Donald were her husband. She looked back down the track and waved.

Lindsay, heart racing, waved back.

'Tell me,' she said. 'Tell me, Forbes.'

'It's you I'm going to marry.'

'Marry?' She was taken aback.

'Aye, marry,' Forbes said. 'What did you think I was going to say?'

'I – I don't know. That you – you liked me.'

'I'm not too young for you,' Forbes told her. 'It might seem like I am right now but in four or five years . . .'

'In four or five years,' Lindsay said, 'you will probably meet some other girl you like more than you like me.'

'No,' Forbes said. 'You know it, and I know it.'

'What do I know?'

'That we're made for each other,' he told her, 'and that one day you're going to be my wife.'

'I know nothing of the sort,' Lindsay protested.

If he had been older, if he had been less handsome she would not have protested. But she did not know how to respond to this moody boy, this dangerous young chameleon who had stepped into her life, who was her kin and yet a stranger, who was utterly unlike anyone that she had ever met before. She knew only that when he looked at her with that solemn, somnolent gaze she felt her heart beat like mad within her breast and all his flaws and Irish foibles mattered not one jot.

She believed him, trusted him, longed for him.

'You do, Linnet,' he said. 'Sure and you do.'

And Lindsay, already moving forward, whispered, 'Yes.'

From that moment the holiday sped past; the days seemed all too short, the nights far too long. Lindsay would lie awake under the skylight listening to Cissie's snores and recall all the things that Forbes and she had done that day, all the compliments he had lavished upon her, the loving look in his eye when he happened to catch her staring at him.

She could not help but stare at him. When they were not actually together she was possessed by an irrational fear that she had lost him, that the quaint old house or the great weeping moor had somehow swallowed him up. Or – a scene she played over and over again – that he had drowned himself in the loch for love of her and that Papa, Martin or Aunt Lilias was on the point of bringing her the tragic news: then, of course, Forbes would pop up again, her relief would be tremendous and it would be all she could do not to rush to him, take him in her arms and defy the family's opprobrium.

It was impossible to disguise the fact that they were starry-eyed about each other and had, in fact, fallen heels over head in love.

And the family, generally speaking, was not amused.

'Forbes, shall we go for a walk?' Lindsay would say.

'If you wish, Linnet.'

'I'll come with you,' Pansy would pipe up.

'Me too,' Mercy would say.

If the younger girls were not around then a signal would pass between Aunt Lilias and one of the boys and, before Lindsay could protest, she would be flanked by Johnny and Martin, by Ross and Johnny or some combination of cousins whose purpose was to ensure that Forbes and she were given no opportunity to slip off into the deep woods or even be alone together in plain sight upon the lawn.

The boys were rather entertained by this sudden outbreak of 'luh-urve' and inclined to be tolerant. Cissie, however, was fit to be tied. The same incidents that gave Lindsay joy drove Cissie into a fizzing sulk. Even at night, just before bed, she could not bring herself to be civil. Lindsay, equally stubborn, was not about to apologise for having won a famous victory; she regarded her relationship with Forbes not as the outcome of a contest but as something inescapable, something written in the book of Destiny.

Papa too was less than magnanimous. He was short with Lindsay, rude to Forbes. By the second week of the holiday the atmosphere in Pappy's country retreat was so volatile that everyone, in his or her own way, was having a grand time, for there was nothing the Franklins enjoyed more than conspiring against each other, an activity that beat sea-bathing hands down. Whispers rose from every corner, from behind every bush and tree. Martin, Johnny and Ross spent happy hours strolling by the loch, puffing cigars and nipping whisky while they analysed the pros and cons of marriage and romance. Only the youngest, Pansy, failed to see what all the fuss was about and had to be told, tactfully, that the flame of love was dangerous and that young people who did not know how to control their emotions might wind up ruining their lives.

'What does she see in him?'

'I'd have thought that was obvious. I mean, there's no denying he's a handsome young man.'

'I had the impression that he was making sheep's eyes at Cissie.'

'He was, but apparently he was rebuffed.'

'Ah, so it's Lindsay on the rebound, is it?'

'Of course it is. It won't last.'

'A holiday romance, you mean?'

'I'd stake my life on it.'

'Nothing to worry about then?'

'Oh, there's always something to worry about when a young man and a young woman imagine they're in love. But it'll soon blow itself out.'

Lindsay was wounded by their lack of faith in her judgement, saddened by the fact that nobody seemed willing to stand up for love.

The picnic, the ascent of Ben Cranachan, the march to church, the hike to Mr Tasker's farm, boating on the loch, a fishing lesson from Giles, bathing in the river – Forbes was constantly at her side: Forbes at the oar of the borrowed rowing boat; Forbes helping her cast a trout rod; Forbes taking her hand for the final pull up the big, broad-shouldered mountain; Forbes, muscular and hairylegged in striped bathing drawers, watching her step from the pool below the little waterfall, shivering in her flounced bathing dress; Forbes laying the Turkish towel about her shoulders, laying the towel gently about her while Cissie, still in the water, shrieked for attention.

'Forbes?'

'Yes, Aunt Lilias?'

'Help your cousin Cissie find her footing, if you please.'

'Sure and I will, Aunt Lilias.'

'Lindsay?'

'Yes, Papa.'

'Go into the tent and dry yourself before you catch your death.'

'But . . .'

'Now.'

Within the box-like bathing tent the grass was springy, the canvas walls musty, the light dim, the air warm. Lindsay could hear Martin shouting, Cissie shrieking, Johnny's laughter, very light and gay and genuine, floating like a feather in the emptiness outside. She struggled out of her bathing dress and, without guilt or shame, stood naked. She wished that he would come to her, snap aside the canvas flap and, without a word of warning or a by-your-leave, clasp her to him, his flesh against her flesh, his lips on hers.

'Lindsay, are you decent?' Mercy hissed.

'No. No, I'm not.'

'Do be quick. Pansy wants in. Her teeth are chattering.'

'All right,' Lindsay answered softly. 'All right. All right. All right,' and quickly covered herself with the towel.

Restlessness brought Lindsay downstairs early on Friday morning. Tomorrow they would all return home, the holiday over, and every second that remained was too precious to waste in sleep. It wasn't as if Forbes was returning to Ireland, thank heaven. Now that they had discovered each other they could be together as often as they wished. And if Papa would not allow Forbes to call on her at Brunswick Crescent they would meet at Harper's Hill.

Thursday had been a hot, cloudless day with an afterglow that seemed as if it would never fade. The family had eaten supper *al fresco* on the paved terrace at the rear of the house. They would have lingered out in the warm evening air if clouds of insects had not driven them indoors soon after the sun went down. They had spread themselves about the big drawing-room with the French doors wide open and had looked out at the shapes of the hills silhouetted against the sky. Then, quite unprompted, Lindsay's father had begun to sing. Lindsay had never heard him sing unaccompanied before, in the style known as *alla cappella*. He sang 'O'er the Seas Eternal', a song that she hadn't even known he knew. He sang quite naturally and spontaneously, as if the lovely evening had roused in him subtle emotions that could not be conveyed by words alone.

When he finished the song there had been no applause, only murmurs of appreciation and a few sentimental tears. Embarrassed, Papa had leaped to his feet again and had struck up with 'Many a Spree I have Seen and Heard and Many a Bumper Drunk', which, after Donald joined in, had led to a great knockabout chorus, with Aunt Lilias trilling away and everyone, even Pappy, stamping their feet. There had been other songs and choruses, solos and duets. Ross had performed his party-piece, full of rude noises, Pansy had lisped out 'Buttercups and Daisies', then Pappy had had Giles open several bottles of sparkling wine and the next thing they knew it was nearing midnight, the sky had turned dark and, in the very best of spirits, they had all gone off to bed.

Lindsay came downstairs in the hazy light of early morning with the words of the love song still running in her head. She had slipped on a summer dress but wore no stockings or shoes. The wine had left her with an unusual thirst; she longed for coffee but neither Giles nor the cook were up yet and she was reluctant to clatter about in the kitchen. It would be two hours or more before the maids arrived from the village to clear the glasses and empty bottles from the drawing-room and make the place spick and span. The French doors had been left open and the room smelled of mist. Lindsay could feel moisture against her skin, not clammy but cool, so cool that when she opened her mouth she could taste it on the tip of her tongue.

She went outside. Her grandfather was seated on the rustic bench at the edge of the terrace. Forbes was standing behind him. They were drinking from enamelled picnic cups and Forbes was smoking a cigarette.

Lindsay wondered if they were talking about her but then she realised that they were not talking at all. She observed from a distance as if she were a stranger and had no bond with either man, old or young.

Forbes straightened and turned round.

'Linnet?' he said. 'I thought it might be you.'

She came to him, barefoot, lifted herself on tiptoe and kissed him on the mouth. She leaned against him, sharing his breath and pleasant taste of coffee for a moment, then she leaned over the back of the bench and kissed her grandfather on the high part of the brow. Pappy turned and looked up at her. Forbes put an arm about her waist and offered the coffee cup. She took it and drank, and Forbes drank and, leaning against the bench, they shared the cup, as close as lovers in the tranquil morning.

'I suppose you think I'm too old to see how it is with the pair of you?' Owen said. 'Well, since you are both here, intruding into my quiet time, I'll tell you why I'm sitting here waiting for you all to go home to Glasgow.'

'Do you really want us to go, Pappy?' Lindsay asked.

'God, no!' Owen answered. 'I'd be happy for you to stay and keep me company for the rest of the summer, if not for the rest of my life.'

'Why are you here at all?' Lindsay said. 'It doesn't seem right for you.'

'I made a promise once . . .'

'To Grandmother?' Lindsay said.

The old man nodded. 'Kath was born and raised in Kelk-emmit. The family still think she came from Perth. Her father was a farm labourer and the family lived in the cottage by the church.'

'Are any of them still here?'

'No, they've been gone for umpteen years. There's a sister in Inverness, I believe, and another in Ayrshire but they didn't approve of me and after Kath and I married they refused to have anything more to do with us.'

'Perhaps they were jealous,' Forbes said, 'because she had made a better life for herself by marrying you.'

Owen put the picnic cup on the paving at his feet. 'Well, it doesn't matter now, since they're more or less all dead.'

'Except you,' said Lindsay. 'And this isn't where you belong.'

'I know,' he said. 'I know.'

'What did you promise her?' Forbes asked.

'I promised her we would live in the big house one day.' He pointed down the glen past the corner of the pine wood. 'I recall it as if it were yesterday; your grandmother looking across the loch, hurt and tearful because her family had spurned us. I promised then that one day we'd live in Strathmore.'

'You can't bring back the past, Grandpappy,' Forbes said.

'I know, son. I know it.' He shrugged. 'I have to try, though. Wouldn't you do the same?' He looked at Forbes, not at Lindsay. 'Wouldn't you want to honour a promise to someone you'd loved?'

'If I loved her enough, of course,' Forbes said. 'On the other hand, if she loved me she wouldn't expect me to keep a meaningless promise.'

'Then you don't understand,' Owen said.

'No, I don't think I do,' Forbes admitted.

'I do,' Lindsay heard herself say. 'I understand.'

Owen got up. 'I'm not as daft as you seem to think I am,

Forbes,' he said. 'At least I'm out of harm's way up here, by which I mean the boys have breathing space to get on with running the firm.' He came around the bench and spreading his arms gathered Forbes and Lindsay to him. 'Now, promise me you won't give away my secret. Arthur and Donald think I'm doddering anyway, so let them go on thinking it. I just need a bit more time to pause and reflect.'

'And then you'll come home?' said Lindsay.

'I might,' Owen said, 'or I might go on somewhere else.' He released them. 'Right now, though, I'm off to rouse Giles and tell him I want my breakfast. It's going to be another scorcher, by the look of it, and we don't want to waste it, do we? Besides, I've the feeling you two might like to have a bit of time alone, without your cousins hovering over you.'

Forbes said, 'Don't you object?'

Owen said, 'If you mean do I think it's wrong for the two of you to fall in love and want to marry, of course I don't.'

'The others don't think I'm serious,' Forbes said.

'Aye, son, but you are, aren't you?' Owen asked.

'Deadly serious,' Forbes answered.

Owen laughed and, without another word, went off into the house and left them alone on the terrace where for the best part of half an hour Forbes and Lindsay kissed and made promises that in the long run neither of them would be willing to keep.

PART TWO

1901

CHAPTER SIX

The Coral Strand

On the twenty-second day of January the old Queen died and her son Edward ascended the throne. In keeping with all shops, manufactories and businesses throughout the land, the shipyards closed for half a day.

For the Franklins a year that began in mourning soon brightened up. In January the owners of the houses in Brunswick Crescent had electrical wiring installed and even Nanny Cheadle could no longer find an excuse for stumbling about with oil lamps and candles. In January, too, telephone wires connected Brunswick Park and Harper's Hill and it was suddenly possible for Arthur and Donald to communicate without leaving home.

In the same month Donald replaced his carriage and horses with a two-cylinder, four-seater, petrol-fuelled Humber motor-car with three-speed transmission and the very latest in drum brakes, an essential component when portions of the family were on board and the damned contraption went hurtling down the steep cobbled streets that flanked Harper's Hill. Donald was a cautious motorist and Arthur wouldn't step into a motor-car at all. But Ross and Johnny were perfect daredevils, forever roaring off to test the vehicle's limit of adhesion on bumpy country roads, sometimes with Cissie and Mercy or Forbes and Lindsay hanging on to their hats in the rear seat.

Electrical light, telephones and motor-cars were just some of the devices whose appearance shook dust from the heels of many a young man and woman and fostered the illusion that theirs was the first generation in history to be entirely liberated. Speed and excitement were in the air. Older and wiser folk, Arthur, Donald and Lilias among them, could do little to check their offspring's enthusiasm and remind them that dignity and decorum, not to mention morality, were virtues not vices and that what had been thought proper under Victoria might still provide a benchmark for the twentieth century.

In the promulgation of such an ethic there was, of course, a fatal flaw, a paradox not entirely lost on all the smart young things who careered about in motor-cars and chatted on the black lobster-claw telephones that graced the hallways of every-one who was anyone: the paradox lay in the fact that while survivors of the nineteenth century preached traditional brands of humanity and enlightenment the seeds of Communism, Socialism, Anarchism and Nihilism had not only been sown but were sprouting like hog-weed, and there was blood all over the map.

God may still be in His heaven but all was not right with the world. Lindsay Franklin, for one, was well aware of it. News-papers were filled with reports from the Transvaal of the war in South Africa, not white man against black but white against white, Briton against Boer. Almost every evening now the Franklins discussed the latest developments in tactics and armaments. Armaments. The guns. 'Long Tom', mobile artillery, German-made Mausers that cut the Irish Guards to pieces at Bridle Drift. The siege at Ladysmith: Buller dragging sixty howitzers and ten long-range naval guns through the mud of the Tugela River to meet disaster on the heights of Spion Kop. Even the replacement of Buller with Lord Roberts, fiery little hero of Kabul, did not radically alter the course of the war. The French were mighty pleased at British defeats, the Russians no less so, and the Germans, naturally, were absolutely delighted at the success of their munitions.

The jingo press went haywire with every British defeat and celebrated every British victory with unquestioning enthusiasm. 'Kroojers' and pro-Boers were set upon and beaten up and when Lloyd George spoke in Glasgow the police had to put every spare man on the streets to quell the violence of the mob. Thus Lindsay learned the painful lesson that conscience has no part to play when business interests are at stake, that cause and effect are all the same on a balance sheet. In the months that brought her to her majority she learned more than a well-bred young lady should about the commercial forces that propelled her family's fortunes and was forced to acknowledge that every penny added to her trust fund had its origins in suffering, somewhere out of sight.

Franklin's order books were full. Admiralty contracts for torpedo-boats and torpedo-boat destroyers had been handed out to three or four British yards — including Franklin's — and the slips at Aydon Road were crammed with craft in various stages of completion.

Lindsay's father spent long hours cudgelling his powers of invention to improve the stress-bearing potential of everything from a new engine's connecting rods to the shape of a hull. There were launches and lunches galore, speed trials on the Gareloch, prolonged debates about the thermal efficiency of boilers and the loss of feed water per hour, aspects of shipbuilding whose importance Lindsay gradually came to understand. She attended weekly board meetings but said nothing, ever, in front of the managers. She did not dare put questions or let her voice be heard. Later, Martin or Tom Calder would explain things to her and Tom often escorted her into the yard to show her how the various processes of production dovetailed together. As she grew older, she could not help but marvel at man's ingenuity, a quality that many women tended to take for granted or, in their ignorance, mocked.

Hanging on to Tom Calder's arm, she would gaze at the cradled hulls and wonder at the beauty and menace of their lines;

the sleek speed-efficient shapes of torpedo-boats or the tapered, high-buttocked bulk of torpedo-boat destroyers – the infamous TBDs – one hundred and sixty feet of planed steel, the maximum length that Franklin's could accommodate. And when the dog-shores were knocked out and the *Mallard* or the *Boxer* or the *Havelock*, newly named, growled down into the waters of the Clyde it was the men she thought of, the men who had built them and the men who would sail them.

Seated at luncheon with managers and owners or smartly uniformed naval officers she would watch the champagne glasses being filled and laden silver dishes being ferried in and would glance out of the long window and think of the men out there in the rain, gnawing on dry bread rolls and brewing tea in cans. And she would wonder if they were proud and satisfied or if, as Forbes claimed, they thought of nothing but their pay-pokes and how much drink their shillings would buy come Friday night.

'How do *you* know what the men are thinking?' Lindsay asked.

Forbes had been pulled out of Beardmore's at the back end of 1899 and brought into Franklin's to learn the ropes. He studied engineering and ship design at the Maritime Institute one day and three evenings a week, a schedule that he didn't seem to find gruelling. Hard work had changed him and the brashness that had been so apparent when he had first appeared on Harper's Hill had gone, though he could still be infuriatingly opinionated at times.

'I've worked with them,' Forbes answered. 'I know what they're like.'

'Ah, but you're not really one of them; you've no right to condemn them.'

'I'm not condemning them,' he said. 'I'm just glad I don't have to trail home every night to a house full of wailing babies and a nagging wife.'

'Wailing babies and a nagging wife aren't the exclusive property of the working class, you know.'

'True,' Forbes said, 'but at least when we get married we won't have to set up in one stinking room.'

'Franklin's workers don't live in slums,' Lindsay said. 'Our shipwrights are reasonably well paid.'

'Really?' Forbes said. 'Have you ever been inside one of the tenements in Damaris Street or along the Portland Row?'

'I must admit I haven't,' Lindsay said.

'Then you've no right to talk.'

'I've every right to my opinion, Forbes.' She was aware that he had lured her on to thin ice. 'What about you? Have you ever been inside a tenement?'

'I've seen what they're like.'

'When?'

'None of your business.' He kissed her lightly on the brow. 'Just take my word for it, Linnet, poverty isn't something you should pontificate about unless you've experienced it for yourself.'

'And you have, I suppose?'

'No.' After an almost undetectable pause, he added, 'Never have and, thank God, never will,' which was something else that Lindsay would hold against him when the brand-new twentieth century picked up a head of steam.

It was the first time that he had taken her to Kirby's at the corner of Portland Row and St George's Road. The neighbourhood was bordering respectable but the big, brash tavern and the private club above it were not. Sylvie was not entirely surprised that Dada Hartnell knew where the doors were situated.

She had passed Kirby's now and then on the horse-tram coming home from Coral Strand meetings in town with Mama. She had peeked at the gaudy frontage and, with a shiver, at the dark green windows on the first floor, windows that hid the sort of goings-on that young ladies were not supposed to know about, though some of the girls at school did, of course; her classmates exchanged information – much of it inaccurate – on all manner of worldly things.

If they had only known where she, Sylvie Calder, had been and what she had seen perhaps they wouldn't have been so stuck-up. She did not confide in them, though. She did not correct their silly notions about what went on in public houses. She wasn't one of them. Had never made a friend at school, not even Amelia Rogers whose maid was a regular at Wednesday night Bible Study and whose brother, a divinity student, had once addressed the Coral Strand on the subject of 'Charity'. In eight years Sylvie had never been invited to tea at anyone's house, not even Amelia Rogers', though Mama Hartnell had had a lot to do with that because Mama did not encourage her to form friendships with girls who were unacquainted with God.

She, Sylvie, was acquainted with God. She knew God intimately. She knew the God who had created Eve out of dirt, the God who had expelled Adam, the God who had brought plagues down upon Egypt and who, a bit like Herod, had slain the children of the Egyptians in their beds; the God who had spoken to Moses, who, through His Son, had raised Lazarus from the dead; the God who looked a little, just a little, like Dada Albert, with his woolly moustache and watch-chain and the broad lap that she sat upon whenever she wanted petting or, less often now, whenever he felt the need to pet her.

When she imagined Satan, though, the serpent, the tempter, the defiant angel thrown out of heaven, it was Papa Calder who came to mind. She couldn't see herself sitting on his lap, kissing his thin lips, going out with him with the wickerwork collection basket and sheaves of leaflets that recounted the horrid life that poor benighted heathens had to endure in India or Africa or on the far-off Coral Strand; couldn't imagine Papa Calder bestowing charity on anyone, although he did pay for her schooling and her dresses which, so Mama told her, was just his way of striving to save his soul from damnation.

As far as Sylvie was concerned her father was damned

anyway. She hadn't missed him when he'd stopped popping up in the 'Groveries on Sunday afternoons. Had felt nothing but relief when he'd stopped visiting her at home every other week. She belonged to God, to Dada Hartnell, and her desire to make her other Papa notice her had been a weakness, particularly as he continued to pay for her schooling and her dresses and anything else Mama asked for on her behalf whether she was nice to him or whether she was not.

Generally speaking she liked being nice to people. The nicer she was the more generous they seemed to be. When Dada Hartnell introduced her to his acquaintances he would refer to her as 'my little lady', which was, she supposed, true and accurate. At one time he used to stand her on the bar counter and persuade her to recite a short poem about the Coral Strand and then the men would put money into her basket, heaps of money. Dada Hartnell had stopped doing that now. She was growing up, he said, and it was undignified to treat her as if she were a music-hall turn and that it would be better for them – that is, for the Coral Strand Foreign Mission Fund – if she just acted naturally, which was something Sylvie had no difficulty in doing, for she was a great deal less naïve than she appeared to be.

Albert had told Florence that they were going to tap the public houses on a stretch of Dumbarton Road between Patrick Cross and the bridges, a favoured beat for the seekers of charity who rattled tambourines or sold heather, flags or cheap paper florets. But, according to Dada Hartnell, there was no money to be made at that game. Instead he conducted Sylvie to the smoky dens of the docklands that lascars frequented, physical embodiments of the self-same heathens for whom the basket was being passed round and who, Sylvie thought, seemed grim and miserable so far removed from the Coral Strand. But they paid up. They were remarkably generous for poor people. They did not have to understand the message that Dada preached, they just had to look at her to know that God, in the shape of a blue-eyed little angel, cared about them.

Some so-called Christians were more difficult to deal with and on several occasions, when poetry and compassion had failed to take a trick, Dada Hartnell had had to pick her and the basket up and make a run for it.

To keep her from worrying, Dada did not always tell Mama where they were going or where they had been. He asked Sylvie to keep her mouth shut too and she was happy to oblige. She could keep a secret when it suited her. She already had a great deal of experience in keeping secrets. None of her classmates knew precisely where she lived or that Dada Hartnell wasn't her real father and did not work in an office in the city. She knew it was wrong to tell lies but there were occasions when not telling the whole truth could be an act of kindness and she believed that one thing balanced out another in the eyes of the Lord.

Sylvie was happy as she skipped down the road in the pretty frilled dress and shaped bodice that Dada Hartnell had insisted Mama buy for her, her bonnet bobbing as she tried to keep up with him; although he had short, stout legs Dada Hartnell's stride was much longer than hers. He wore a sober black wool-worsted suit, a soft-collared shirt and a tie with a trace of red in the pattern. His square-crowned hat was perched raffishly on his head. Except for the shallow wicker basket and the tarnished tin badge that identified him as a collector for the Coral Strand Foreign Mission Fund, he seemed no different from any of the other gentlemen who were heading, singly and in pairs, for the polished glass doors of Kirby's Tavern or, more circumspectly, for the unglazed door in the lane that led to the gentlemen's club upstairs.

Dada Hartnell pushed open the tavern door. It was Friday night. The bar was packed. He guided Sylvie before him into the throng. She couldn't see much except the backs and buttocks of the men in front of her. She looked round, tilting her head. Dada Hartnell gave her a reassuring wink. Parting the chaps before her as Moses had parted the Red Sea, he steered her towards the mahogany bar at the far end of the room.

There were mirrors everywhere, mirrors etched with adver-
tisements for beers and spirits, mirrors engraved with ladies in
floral shifts, mirrors even on the ceiling. When Sylvie looked up
she could see herself floating in the midst of all the men. She was
not in the least intimidated at being the only female person in the
room, except for the barmaids who were so large-busted and
brassy that they seemed to belong to another species altogether.
She inhaled the reek of sweat, spirits and tobacco smoke as if it
were incense and offered up a little prayer of gratitude that she
was here at last, inside the very tabernacle of wickedness where
somehow she felt so much at home.

'I say, Hartnell, what's this you've dragged in?'

'Ah, Moscrop, I don't believe you've met my daughter Sylvie.'

'I'll say I haven't. Daughter, is she? Not a bit like you, thank
God!' Mr Moscrop, all veined cheeks and bristling whiskers,
leered over his pint glass. 'Does she drink? Let me buy her a little
something, what? Little snifter of something to get her going,
what?'

'Enough of that, old man,' Dada Hartnell said. 'It's the
Lord's business that brings me here tonight. Sylvie's helping me
with my collections.'

'Damned tasty little mascot too, if I may say so.'

'You may not,' Dada told the man, rather curtly.

'So you're not takin' her hup-stairs to shake for you?'

'No, I'm not,' Dada Hartnell said. 'How about it, Daniel,
how about starting my little lady off with a bob or two for her
basket?'

'I know what I'd like to do to her basket,' put in a younger
man who had come up behind Mr Moscrop. 'I'd give it more
than a bob or two.'

'Do then,' said Dada. 'It's all in a good cause.'

'For the poor heathens on the Coral Strand,' Sylvie said.

'It speaks. Lo! it utters.'

'Charley, that's enough,' said another young man, one of
several who had gathered round her. She liked the sound of this

one's voice; liked being the focus of attention. She glanced from one to the other, smiling at each. Mr Moscrop, who had been pushed to the rear, was bobbing up and down, glass in hand, struggling to keep her in view.

'Ain't there enough heathens for you in Glasgow, Albert?'

'Far too bloody many of them,' Dada retorted. 'Far too many penniless engineers for a start.'

Sylvie wasn't offended by the swear word. She had known for some time that two men were contained within Dada Hartnell's skin: one who appeared at home, the other in places like Kirby's.

She slipped the basket from under his arm and offered it out, not too boldly. She gave the dark-haired, handsome young man a timid smile. She had already deduced that he was a student from the Maritime Institute on Sutter Street, that big sooty-black building where the lights burned all afternoon and blackboards and drawing-boards peeped above the window ledges. Perhaps he was hoping to become an engineer or a draughtsman, like her real father. She did not hold that against him. Dada Hartnell had told her that not all students were poor, that some were quite well-to-do and others, though not many, came from very wealthy families.

'What can I buy you?' the dark-haired young man said.

He addressed her directly, not through Dada. She did not answer him directly, though. She glanced up at Dada, waiting to be told what to do. He gave a light shrug, one of many secret signals that they had developed over the years. She smiled at the young man and said that she would be glad to partake of a glass of soda water.

'Soda water it is, then.' Half-a-crown appeared in his fingers like a conjuring trick and he instructed one of the others, Charley, to hop off to the bar and do the honours.

Sylvie said, 'It's all very well for us to be drinking soda water, sir, and I do appreciate your generosity, but what about the poor souls who languish in the heat of the Coral Strand, who is to buy them soda water?'

'Have you ever been to the Coral Strand?' the young man said.

Somehow he had gained prime position, had isolated her from the others – if isolation was the right word in such a crowded place. She noticed that the barmaids had spotted Dada and were none too pleased to see him. A burly man in a canvas apron and broad-striped shirt had appeared under the mirrors. She kept one eye on the man in the apron and the other on Dada while she spoke with the student who was paying for her soda water. She was relieved to see the man in the canvas apron shake his head and go off down a back staircase.

'What about me?' Dada was saying. 'Don't I get offered a dram?'

'You can buy your own, Bert. God knows you're rollin' in moolah after your win last week.'

'Shush,' Dada said. 'Shush.'

'Oh, I see. It's a domestic secret, is it?'

Sylvie did not quite know what was going on. But she had enough sense to pipe up and to try to rescue Dada from any embarrassment that her presence might cause. It had not occurred to her that he had tapped Kirby's before. They had visited several places where Dada was known and she had to remind herself that Mama and he had been collecting for the Coral Strand Mission Fund long before she appeared on the scene.

The young man sipped from the pint glass in his hand.

He said, 'You didn't answer my question, sweetheart.'

'I have not been to the Coral Strand, not yet.'

'Not yet?'

'I may enter mission work when I am old enough.'

'What age are you?'

'Fif—'

'Seventeen,' said Dada.

'Almost seventeen,' said Sylvie.

The young man ignored the guffaws of the jostling chaps at

his shoulder. He looked down at her from no great height – he was only a little bit taller than she was – and she felt her throat tighten, the soft band of flesh below her stomach become tight too, as if he had pulled an invisible string that drew all the parts of her together, narrowing and elongating them in the process.

She gave a little gasp.

'Sure when I was seventeen,' he said, 'I didn't even know where the Coral Strand was. Now here's a chance for me to learn something.'

'Pa'din?' Sylvie heard herself say.

'He's teasing you, dearest,' Dada said.

'No, I'm seeking information, really I am,' the young man said, so gently that Sylvie believed him even if Dada did not. 'Where *is* the Coral Strand and what do the folk there do all day long?'

'They do not believe in Christ our Lord.'

'Ah, so that's it!'

'They must be told that Jesus is their Saviour.'

'So that He can feed them with loaves and fishes?'

'Are you a Socialist?' Sylvie said.

'What makes you think I'm a Socialist?'

'All Socialists are Godless.'

'Well, I'm no Socialist. I'm only asking you to tell me where this place is. I'll make you a deal, sweetheart. Give me the latitude and longitude of the Coral Strand and I'll put a guinea straight into your basket.'

'For God's sake, Forbes, stop teasing her. She's only a wee kiddie.'

'I'm not teasing her,' the young man said. 'I'm deadly serious.'

Sylvie felt giddy with responsibility or something so akin to responsibility that she could not separate it from the other emotions that fizzed within her. She felt as if her bodice laces had had been tugged so tight that she could breathe only from the top of her lungs.

She said, 'A guinea?'

'Yes.'

'Do you promise?'

'Yes.'

'I cannot give you the navigational lines,' Sylvie said, 'but I can tell you that the Coral Strand is generally taken to refer to the white sand beaches of the remote islands of the Pacific, which include the New Hebrides, New Guinea and the Solomons. Exports trading is fair in some quarters but there is much disease because of the horrid climate and heavy rainfall. And there are pagan tribes all over the place, tribes who kill and eat each other and know nothing of Christ's salvation. The population of the Solomon Islands is forty-seven thousand souls, eighty of whom are white, twenty of whom are Christians financed by the Foreign Mission Fund. In New Guinea, that part for which Britain is answerable, there are—'

'Enough,' the young man said, laughing. 'Enough, enough, enough.'

'Do I get my guinea?'

'G'an, Irish, give the lass her moolah.'

'Put it in her basket, McCulloch, there's a good boy.'

'Ay-hay, but ain't she a clever little thing,' said Mr Moscrop. 'Near as clever as she is pretty, what!' Leaning, he dropped a florin into the basket. 'What else does she know, I wonder?'

'Does she know what the natives of Dublin do, Forbes? Ask her that.'

'They,' said Sylvie, 'are Papes and beyond redemption.'

'Oh-hoh! Oh-hoh!'

'They aren't all Papes in Dublin,' Forbes said.

'Are you?'

'No.'

'What are you then?' said Sylvie.

'I'm an engineer.'

'That isn't a religion,' Sylvie said.

'Wrong on that score, sweetheart. Wrong on that score.'

'Heathens we are, but we don't eat people,' Charley said.

'Unless we're very hungry,' said Forbes McCulloch.

'I hope you are not hungry now,' said Sylvie and, rather to her chagrin, heard everyone within earshot, even Dada, burst out laughing. 'I want my guinea. I've earned my guinea. You promised.'

'Promise you the moon if you're not careful,' Charley said.

'And get it for you, too,' said Forbes.

'I just want my guinea.'

'And you shall have it, my love,' the dark-haired young man said. 'I promise you shall have it. Bertie, why don't we all go upstairs?'

Lindsay's birthday celebrations had been strangely subdued. Reaching one's majority did not have the same significance for a young woman as it did for a chap; eighteen had meant something but twenty-one was just another milestone on the road to marriage.

Forbes had taken her to dinner at the Barbary. Papa had organised a lavish party at Brunswick Crescent. All the relatives had been present, together with some of her father's friends from the choir, four or five former school chums – from whom she now felt totally detached – and, at her request, Mr Tom Calder. Grandpappy had been there too. He had abandoned the notion of wintering in Strathmore and spent more than half the year at home with Donald and Lilias, returning to the dismal old house in Perthshire mainly in summer months when, like a Highland laird, he would entertain bits and pieces of the family and certain favoured friends who had a taste for fishing.

Aunt Kay had journeyed over from Dublin. She came alone to Glasgow once every year, usually in the February, and stayed no more than a week. She came, so she claimed, to keep an eye on Forbes and make sure he was behaving himself. Of Forbes's father, Daniel McCulloch, the Franklins saw and heard nothing. The brewer evinced no apparent interest in his son and

Forbes showed no inclination to return to Dublin, not even for a visit.

To Lindsay, even in their most confidential moments, he did not speak of his father or the sisters and brothers he had left behind. He was waiting, he told her, just waiting until he was old enough to marry and set up house with her. That was all he wanted out of life, a good steady job, a home of his own and Lindsay to share it with him; after that was accomplished the whole damned lot of them could go hang themselves.

For the best part of thirty months Forbes had behaved like a perfect gentleman, a suitor rather than a lover. He would kiss her, hold her in his arms, tell her he loved her and longed to be her husband. But he did not attempt to caress her intimately or hold her so close that she could feel his heart beat.

On those few occasions when Lindsay had got carried away he had disentangled himself and, with a bit of huffing and puffing, had apologised and explained that he respected her far too much to risk letting her jump the gun. He had it all drafted and documented, you see: a model future together, designed to scale. It was, he said, just a question of being patient, of waiting for the day when he would turn twenty-one, come in for his share of Franklin's profits, complete his courses at the Maritime Institute, and graduate to being a deputy manager. Then they would marry, settle down, have children. Then he would be able to call her his own, his very own. Then nobody would be able to point the finger and accuse him of being an opportunist.

Lindsay both admired and detested his conservatism. She did not know what had changed him from a brash and bragging boy into a man so stolid and constrained that at times he seemed almost dull. When it occurred to her that perhaps love had robbed him of his spark she cast the thought far to one side. He had lost something, something that she could not put her finger on. It wasn't his looks: he was more handsome than ever. He had not grown taller nor had he filled out and become coarse, like Martin and Johnny. He was just as slim and sinewy as he had ever been; heart-achingly handsome but, without conceit, somehow synthetic, like an artefact that one can do nothing with, except admire. She was still in love with him, still desired him – but in little fits and starts, in a spluttering, uncertain way that often left her headachy and depressed.

Forbes was busy, of course, occupied with making his way in the world, in proving himself worthy. Aunt Lilias – Papa too – had to admit that they had misjudged his determination. Once he was out of Beardmore's and into Franklin's he applied himself with a vengeance. He worked long hours in the drawing office, talked a great deal with George Crush about relations between labour and management, absorbed all that Tom Calder deigned to impart about design, everything that Peter Holt could tell him about engines. Dinner-time conversations at Harper's Hill were dominated by technical matters too important to encourage much gaiety.

Martin had become engaged to Aurora Swann, elder sister of the romantically inclined Gordon. They planned to marry in September. Mercy had been married for over a year, swept to the altar by a grandson of the McDades of Greenock who specialised in fitting out cargo boats and had branches all down the east coast. Mercy and Campbell McDade lived in a trim sandstone villa on the seafront at Langbank and were anticipating 'a happy event' in December. Pansy, no longer a schoolgirl, remained at home, dancing and skating and playing tennis, doing all the things that Lindsay had once done, before Owen Forbes McCulloch came along.

Cissie had become the Franklins' problem child. She was rebellious and recalcitrant, loud and silent by turns, moody and desperately unhappy as one squalid, short-lived courtship followed another. In the autumn of 1900 she had even entertained the notion of becoming the wife of Professor Duval, an ageing widower who held the Chair of Forensic Medicine at Glasgow University and whose obsession with music was so much in excess of Cissie's own that their brief, un-torrid affair had swiftly foundered and the old boy's engagement ring had been returned along with the ninety-six letters of love and musical analysis with which he had bombarded her.

There were times when Lilias feared that her daughter was turning into a hysteric. She would have taken her for examination by a medical specialist if Cissie had been willing. Cissie was not willing. Cissie saw nothing odd in her behaviour. Cissie would not discuss her behaviour or the course her life was taking, not with her mother, father, sisters or brothers; certainly not with Lindsay with whom she could hardly bring herself to exchange a civil word. She spoke to no one, confided in no one, kept her misery bottled up. She grew fatter. Her complexion suffered. Her dressing-table was littered with creams, astringent lotions, cosmetic preparations and enough pills to sink a small corvette.

Only Forbes knew what was wrong with his plump cousin, what would cure her but he, with uncharacteristic tact, chose to say nothing. Now and then, though, just for devilment, he would let her catch sight of him in the corridor on his way to the bath and, with a little wriggle of his backside, would let the towel flirt and once, albeit unintentionally, fall away completely so that she had at least one fleeting glimpse of his private parts to remind her just what she was missing.

'Do you know what this is, sweetheart?'

'Yes.'

'Do you know what you do with it?'

'Put the dice in it and roll them out on to the table.'

'Co-rrect,' Forbes said. 'Do you want to try?'

'Hold on,' Dada Hartnell said. 'She's too young for this.'

'Nonsense,' Forbes said. 'You're not too young, Sylvie, are you? It's just a game. You've played games before, haven't you?'

'If you think . . .' Dada said.

'I don't think anything,' Forbes answered. 'The mischief's all in your own head, Bertie. *Honi soit qui mal y pense*, and all that.'

'That means "Shame to him who thinks evil," Dada.'

'I know what it means,' Dada Hartnell snapped.

He had brought her here. Now he did not want her to be here. She had never considered him fickle before. She was not surprised that he did not want her to be here, though. It was all too much to take in. She felt greedy with the sheer pleasure of being in this grand room with its ornate gas chandeliers, big green billiards tables and an ornamental bar with brass rails and a brassware hood. The gaslight was low but the bar beamed brightly, illuminating the tiled mural behind it: 'Agriculture and Horticulture'. It resembled several paintings she had seen in art galleries except that neither of the ladies was wearing clothes and even the boy who accompanied them was as naked as the day he was born. She stared at the boy's tiny diddle and tried not to giggle.

Dada was saying, 'Look here, Forbes, if you think for one moment I'm going to roll for that guinea you owe us then you've another think coming.'

'I'm not going to roll against you, Bertie, not with the run of luck you've been having lately,' the young man said. 'Heaven forfend!'

'What, are you going to roll against her?'

'Irish, for God's sake, man, she is only a kiddie,' Charley said, without any weight of conviction.

Charley was the only one of the students who had accompanied them through a door at the back of the public house and up a narrow wooden staircase to the upper room. There had been a locked door at the top of the stairs but Forbes had a key to open it. Sylvie had followed him eagerly into the low-beamed, gleaming room. Dada had followed her.

There were fewer men present than she'd imagined there might be, given the number she had noticed darting into the entrance in the lane. Six or eight of them were playing billiards. Three by the bar. Eight seated round a long table in a quiet corner, enjoying a game of cards. She did not know where the

others had got to, unless they had slipped through the curtain left
of the bar, past the couch where four or five young ladies took
their ease.

'Sure and I'm going to roll against her,' Forbes said. 'Come
along, Bertie. I'm not going to swipe her on the odds. We'll make
it high pair on three with three in the cup. First triple takes all.
That way you don't need to be a veteran to scoop the pool. What
say?'

'Are we going to gamble?' Sylvie said.

'We're thinking about it,' Forbes told her.

'No,' Dada Hartnell said. 'I know what's going on here.'

'Nothing's going on that'll harm her. What do you take me
for? I've got sisters her age at home. Look, it's just a bit of fun,
Bertie. She'll never be out of your sight.'

The ladies on the couch were watching. They seemed a long
way off. Thick carpets and drapes muffled their voices but she
sensed that they were talking about her. She heard one of them
yell out but the greeting was distorted by a guttural accent.
Forbes glanced up and smiled, waved. Then the girl on the couch
did something that Sylvie had never seen done before, something
you could not possibly do if your dress was tightly laced. Dada
Hartnell seemed quite shocked but her new friend Forbes just
laughed.

Sylvie pressed herself against the edge of the table. It was
curved top and bottom like a baby's bath, longer than it was
broad and surprisingly deep. The cloth lining was the same
colour as mown grass. She looked down into it and automatically
stretched a hand to the worn horn cup that snuggled in one
corner. Two sets of dice, four dice in each set. One set was made
of ivory, the numerals spotted in black. The other was ebony
with white numbers. She gathered in the black.

'See,' she heard Forbes say. 'She already knows what's what,
Bertie. Must be instinctive — or inheritance, maybe. Something in
the blood.'

Sylvie put three of the four black dice into the cup, covered it with her palm and shook it vigorously. She *clumped* the cup down on the cloth, lifted the cup away and inspected the result. Five, three, one: very odd. She put the dice back into the cup and glanced over her shoulder.

She said, 'Let me do it, Dada.'

Dada Hartnell sighed, frowned, shrugged.

She said, 'We're playing for your guinea, aren't we?'

'That's it,' Forbes said. 'Double or quits.'

Sylvie said, 'I haven't seen the colour of your money yet.'

'What? Don't you trust me?'

'Implicitly,' Sylvie said.

'Do you know what you're doing, youngster?' Charley said.

'I shake the dice three times. I'm looking for pairs. If my highest pair is higher than his after three shakes then I win; if not, I lose. If somebody throws three matching numbers then they win immediately. Is that how it's done?'

'You've got it, honey,' Charley said.

'Presumably,' Sylvie said, 'if neither of us turns out a matching pair on three shakes of the dice we continue until someone does?'

'That's it,' said Forbes. 'They call it Sudden Death.'

She brought the rim of the cup to her lips. Closing her eyes, she kissed it and offered up a little prayer; not for herself, of course, but for the sake of the poor, benighted heathens who lived out of God's sight on the Coral Strand.

She smiled at him. 'Ladies first?'

'By all means,' said Forbes, graciously.

Sylvie drew back her arm.

'*How* much?' Florence Hartnell said.

'Forty-four shillings,' her husband told her.

'*Forty-four shillings!*'

'Not bad for a night's work, eh?'

'Not bad? It's — it's astounding.' She leaned against him,

bosom brushing his shoulder. 'Banknotes too, I see. One generous donor, Albert?'

'No, I exchanged some of the small stuff at the Merkland wine vaults. I didn't want to be caught jingling along Dumbarton Road after dark.'

Florence darted a glance behind her. Sylvie was seated in her old wooden high chair from which Dada had removed the arms, innocently kicking her legs and nibbling a crustless fish-paste sandwich. There was no point in quizzing her foster daughter: Sylvie would support Dada's story, come what may. She turned again and peered down at the cash on the tabletop. Three ten shilling banknotes, four half-crowns and a somewhat tarnished florin. There would be much 'counting out' to do tonight. She watched Albert smooth the notes with the flat of his hand, stack the half-crowns and place the florin on top.

He was grinning like the cat that ate the goldfish.

'Albert, what have you been up to?'

'Nothing, Mama.' Sylvie answered for him in her twittering little-girl voice. 'It was just that sort of night. God was good to us, wasn't He, Dada?'

'He certainly was, dear. He certainly was.'

'First we went into Mr Forsyth's, then to the Corona and then the King's Tavern. Everyone seemed possessed by a spirit of generosity wherever we went. I don't know why that should be, Mama. Perhaps it's the spring.'

'Did you give her drink, Albert?'

'Of course not.'

'And you? Have you been at the Allsopp's?'

'I had one glass, a half glass.'

'Albert! You promised.'

'Damn it all, Florence . . .'

'The Vigilance Society weren't there, Mama,' Sylvie said, without a trace of irony, 'and it was a very warm night. I had some soda water.'

'Did you put her up on the table?'

'I told you, I don't do that any more.'

'Very well.' Florence leaned against him. 'I believe you, though thousands wouldn't. Go on, Albert, count it out.'

Still grinning, Dada plucked up a ten shilling note and tossed it into the wicker basket. 'One for the Foreign Mission,' he said. He lifted another banknote, folded it and slotted it neatly into the biscuit barrel that Florence placed to hand. 'And one for us. One for the Foreign Mission . . .'

'And,' said Florence and Sylvie in perfect harmony, 'one for us.'

CHAPTER SEVEN

Postcard from Portsmouth

Combating nausea had never been a problem for Tom Calder. Even on a torpedo-boat bobbing like a cork miles from shore a couple of deep breaths would dispel any tendency to queasiness. The same could not be said for Martin. Of the six-man team that Franklin's sent to the Solent to test a brace of coal-fired boilers for the Navy Commission, Martin suffered most.

Personally Tom was not convinced that the navy really knew what it was doing by commissioning coal boilers at all. The Dutch and the Americans had recently obtained good results from the use of liquid fuel and Franklin's had designs on the drawing board for oil-fired steam-raising apparatus. Martin and Tom had argued the toss with Jason Melrose, R.N., but after the boilers had been installed and the *Banshee* put out for sea trials Martin rapidly lost interest in arguing the toss about anything.

The programme included trials at one thousand horse-power, trials at full power, and a coal endurance test. With Martin retching into a bucket below, it was left to Tom, aided by MacDougal, Franklin's foreman fitter, to record the calorimetric observations for the management. Engineer Lieutenant Jason Melrose was the main representative of the navy's Water-Tube Boiler Committee. Tom had respect for Melrose who had served his time with Thornycroft's but not for the petty officers and warrant-rank ship's engineers who seemed to think that wearing a uniform or navy-issue overalls endowed them with authority over everything that moved upon the face of the deep.

Tom was also put out by the fact that the navy insisted on the boilers being installed in the *Banshee*, a miserable old scow launched back in 1889 with a set of locomotive boilers that had never functioned properly. The new boilers were modifications of a Babcock prototype and by reducing the diameter of the tubes and redesigning the steam-collecting drum Mr Arthur, Peter Holt and he had adapted them for use in torpedo gunboats. Tom was familiar with every seam and joint in the boiler tubes and took pride in his work. He was as anxious as the naval commissioners to assess the trial data and had worked conscientiously through the twelve-hour stint at sea, measuring and recording everything from the carbon value of coal to the temperature of chimney gases.

He did not like being away from home, however. He had no taste for gossiping in the officers' club or the so-called 'ward-room' on the Parade and, on balance, preferred the Niger to southern England. Martin and he were billeted in a small hotel in Gosport across the harbour, MacDougal and the rest of the Franklin's team in a boarding-house nearby. The fitters had been sent home as soon as the job of installation had been completed and MacDougal, a stereotypical Glaswegian, spent his evenings touring the local pubs in search of a drinkable whisky and the chance of a brawl – all of which left Martin and Tom rather high and dry.

It was after eight o'clock before they sat down at a table in the hotel dining-room. Martin was still whey-faced and shaky after his ordeal but seemed determined to go out again tomorrow for the horse-power trial. Service was slow and grudging and in the long interval between the Windsor soup and the boiled mutton, conversation turned from technical matters to wistful speculation on what might be happening in that distant city on the banks of the Clyde.

Thursday night choir practice would be warming up in St

Silas's school, Perry Perrino working himself into a lather, the as-yet-unmarried Matilda pounding on the piano, sundry voices swooping and diving like swallows as each part of the 'The Cameronian's Dream' was rehearsed, adjusted and reassembled. Tom hoped that he wouldn't have fallen too far out of tune by the time he got home, for he was eager to appear in the Glasgow Choirs' concert in St Andrew's Halls, an event that would bring the season to an early conclusion.

Martin was dreaming not of his beloved homeland, apparently, but of the lovely Aurora Swann. He picked a piece of gristle from his teeth, put it on the side of his plate, and said, 'You've been married, Tom, haven't you?'

'I have.'

'What's it like?'

'Marriage in general?'

'The physical side of it. Is it – difficult?'

'No, not difficult; a bit awkward at first. Patience is essential, patience on your part, and the utmost consideration for the lady's modesty.'

'Hmmm. I'm not very good at being patient,' Martin confessed. 'I just hope Rora knows what she's doing.'

'I doubt if she will,' Tom said, with a little shake of the head. 'It isn't considered necessary – or proper – for a young woman to be informed about such things. I mean, you haven't . . .'

'Good God, no!'

Tom chewed mutton, drank water from a glass. 'It's somehow just taken for granted that the bridegroom will have all the necessary experience.'

'But I haven't. I mean, I've never . . .'

'Nor had I,' said Tom.

'But, I mean, it *was* all right, wasn't it?'

Colour had returned to Martin's cheeks. In spite of all the bombast, all the music-hall double-entendres that marked the chatter of young men these days the majority were just as ignorant of the basic facts of life as he, Tom Calder, had been.

Some, a few, would learn what to do from tarts or prostitutes but that had never been his style and, unless he missed his guess, it wasn't Martin Franklin's either.

'Yes,' Tom said, tactfully. 'It took us a little time to adjust to the intimacy of sharing — well, a bed. But believe me, Martin, nature will take care of things, provided you don't feel too strong an obligation to prove yourself.'

'I'm not sure I understand.'

Tom had no wish to discuss his marriage which, in the long run, had been a good deal less than ideal. He had gone to the altar filled with more apprehension than anticipation. Had fretted about his ability to support a wife, to pay household bills, far too many worries to let 'that one' dominate. Even so, he had been nervous when Dorothy and he had found themselves alone after the wedding supper and rather shocked to discover that she was more eager for conjugal relations than he was. The fumbling phase had not lasted long. Dorothy had been a sensual creature. Once she had found the key, her flighty nature had drawn her in directions that he would have preferred not to follow and had eventually lured her into adultery.

Martin would have no such concerns. By all accounts Aurora Swann was a well-brought-up young woman and there would be no worries about money to blight their bliss.

Tom said, 'I take it Aurora loves you?'

'Oh, yes, I'm sure she does.'

'And you love her?'

'Most positively.'

'Then the physical aspect will take care of itself.' Tom too was becoming embarrassed, not so much by the topic as by the suspicion that he was beginning to pontificate. 'Has someone been saying things that worry you, Martin?'

Martin pushed away his plate.

He hesitated, then admitted, 'My cousin.'

'Lindsay?' said Tom. 'Surely not!'

'God, no,' said Martin. 'My cousin Forbes.'

Tom had not forgotten that odd afternoon in the park when Cissie Franklin had used him as a defence against the young Dubliner. He had not liked Forbes McCulloch then and he did not like him now. To give the lad credit, he was a keen worker, very quick and intelligent. Nevertheless, Tom had often over-heard Forbes and George Crush discuss women in a callous and disparaging manner that he found offensive.

'What's Forbes been telling you, Martin?'

'How to — how to do it.'

'Is that all?'

'No.' Martin's face was aflame. 'He told me to take advantage of being away from home to — to . . .'

'Find a woman?'

'Yes.'

'Do you want to?'

'No.'

'Then pay him no heed.'

'Forbes says everyone does it.'

'Everyone does not do it,' Tom said emphatically.

'Forbes says that he's done it.'

The reason for Martin's anxiety was now clear. He had fallen foul of the influence of his Irish cousin. Martin was no sniggering schoolboy. He was about twenty-five years old, halfway to inheriting responsibility for running a shipyard that employed more than four hundred men, yet he was scared of losing face, of having to 'prove' himself by paying a street women to stimulate and satisfy not so much his lust as his curiosity.

'Do you want me to have a word with Lieutenant Melrose?' Tom said.

'What? What for?'

'He's bound to know where the brothels are in Portsmouth.'

'Oh, no. No, no,' said Martin. 'I just — I just wanted to . . .'

'It's the perfect opportunity,' Tom said, 'if you're that way inclined.'

'Have you ever — I mean, ever been to one of those places?'

Tom shook his head. 'Never.'

'Not even in Africa?'

'Africa?'

'I've heard that you can have native girls just for the asking.'

'Whoever spun you that idiotic tale doesn't know what they're talking about,' Tom said. 'Forbes, I expect, or was it George Crush?'

'Forbes, actually.'

'It's not my place to offer you advice, Martin, and you've no reason to heed what I say, but . . .'

'Go on, Tom. I'm listening.'

'Forbes is only trying to bring you down.'

'Bring me down? Why would he want to do that?'

'Perhaps he's jealous.'

'Why should he be jealous? I mean, he doesn't even *know* Aurora. He's only met her once, I think. He's engaged – well, practically engaged – to my cousin Lindsay.'

'Not of Aurora,' Tom said. 'Of you.'

'Me?'

There was an innocence in the well-to-do that Tom had noticed before, a vague kind of unworldliness that rendered them vulnerable to manipulation. The Franklins weren't sufficiently rich or well-bred to have lost touch with reality but Owen Franklin's influence was waning, watered down by the passage of years and the pace of the twentieth century. Others less moral, less honest and upright would in time corrupt not only the shipbuilding industry but all industry, through their malice and greed. In the cousins' relationships Tom could already detect a blurring of the line between deed and achievement, between responsibility and exploitation. And it galled him to think that Martin had been taken in by McCulloch's insinuations; galled him even more that Lindsay seemed destined to marry the Dubliner and that it was only a matter of time before McCulloch's generation gained the upper hand.

'Because you'll always be top man,' Tom said.

'Oh!' The idea was obviously new to Martin. 'Oh, you mean because I'm a major shareholder in the partnership?'

'Hmmm,' Tom said.

'I don't think Forbes is like that. He's — well, I consider him a friend.'

'I know,' Tom said. 'But sometimes, Martin, you have to treat your friends just as cautiously as you treat your enemies.'

'I don't think I have any enemies. Do I?'

'No,' Tom said. 'I don't suppose you have.'

Martin was silent for a moment or two, then said, 'Forbes is one of us, Tom. He wouldn't do anything to harm the family, would he? I mean, I might act the fool at times but Lindsay — well, Lindsay's going to marry the chap and, whatever you may think of me, you have to admit that Lindsay has her head properly screwed on.'

'How soon will they marry?'

'I don't know,' Martin said. 'Sooner rather than later, I think.'

'Is Mr Arthur reconciled to it?'

'He thinks Forbes is far too young even to contemplate marriage.'

'What do you think?'

'Well, I say good luck to them.' Martin paused again. 'It might be no bad thing for Forbes to move out of Harper's Hill, actually.'

'Why is that?' said Tom.

'He upsets my sister Cissie no end,' Martin said, then added, hastily, 'Not that it's Forbes's fault, mark you. I mean, if it were Forbes's fault my father would soon put a stop to it. No, it's Cissie. She's gone all queer. We think — my brothers and I — that she fancies Forbes for herself.'

'I see,' Tom said.

'Forbes, of course, has been in love with Lindsay from the moment he first set eyes on her.'

'Did he tell you so?'

'Not in as many words,' Martin said. 'But you'd have to be

blind not to see how much he adores her. That's why I can't imagine Forbes wishing any of us ill.'

Tom did not contradict him, did not point out that several of love's manifestations were ill-wrought things indeed.

He said, 'Do you want me to have a word with Melrose then?'

'About what?'

'Where to find the Portsmouth brothels.'

Martin, it seemed, had almost forgotten his marital anxieties.

He shook his head. 'I think not. I'm feeling better now, thanks to you. Probably just needed a bite to eat and a bit of sensible chat to set me right. I think, in fact, I'll toddle off to bed soon, pour myself a glass of whisky and write a nice long letter to Aurora.'

'You're sure?'

'Oh, absolutely.'

Tom put down his knife and fork and signalled to a bored young waiter in a stained apron to come and remove the plates.

'What's for pudding?' Martin asked.

'Spotted Dick,' the waiter answered.

And both of the Scottish gentlemen burst out laughing.

The display of postcards in the hotel lobby was limited to a faded view of Langstone Harbour, another of the old Bermuda Dock and a doctored print of Nelson's flagship *Victory* which, in reality, wasn't much more than a floating heap of firewood these days. None the less Tom picked the picture of the flagship, put tuppence in the box on the reception desk and, postcard in hand, climbed the stairs to his room on the second floor.

Still chuckling over the joke the waiter had unwittingly foisted on them, Martin had retired some ten minutes earlier. When Tom reached the brown-painted corridor, which reeked of gas and something that smelled suspiciously like bad fish, he found that a half glass of whisky had been placed on the carpet by the door of his room. He glanced along the corridor but Martin's door was closed. Smiling, Tom carried the glass into his own room and shut his door too.

Unlike the corridor, the bedroom boasted 'electrically installed fitments', which meant a small table lamp with a parchment shade and a naked ceiling light-bulb that did nothing but flicker no matter how impatiently Tom fiddled with the switch on the wall. The window curtain had been closed, though, the bed turned down, the ewer on the dressing-stand refilled with fresh water.

Tom left the whisky glass and postcard on the stand and went to the window. He lifted a corner of the curtain and looked out at a vista of tiled roofs and brick walls. He could not see the sea but he could hear it sifting and sucking on the uncultivated piece of coast around Gilkicker Point.

It would be rough tomorrow, certainly too rough for Martin. Perhaps it would be too rough for an accurate horse-power test and the trial would have to be postponed until the wind eased. He hoped not. He wanted it done with, wanted to put the tedious ninety-hour coal endurance trial behind him too, wanted to be on a train heading back to Glasgow as soon as possible. If the weather stayed gurly he would try to persuade Martin to return home early and let MacDougal and him finish up here. He would write to Mr Donald explaining why Martin had not been needed in Portsmouth, a plausible lie to spare the young man's blushes. He liked Martin Franklin. He liked all the Franklins come to think of it, and, peculiar though it seemed for a man in his lowly position, felt quite protective towards them.

Tom took off his jacket, loosened his collar and seated himself at the dressing-stand. He poured half the whisky into a tooth-glass, added water from the ewer then pulled the postcard towards him and uncapped his fountain pen.

He had promised Lindsay a letter but a postcard would have to do. He sipped whisky, pondered for a moment, then, in the amazingly neat hand that years of meticulous draughtsmanship had taught him, printed a few lines of casual chit-chat about the weather, the *Banshee* and the appalling food. He would stamp and post the card at the Post Office by the harbour and not risk depositing it in the box in the hotel foyer.

He finished off with 'Hope to see you soon', and signed it simply, 'Tom'.

He directed the pen-nib to the panel to print Lindsay's address and then, frowning a little, hesitated. He sat back, elbow braced on a pillow. Then he put down the pen. He sipped whisky once more and reflected on all that Martin had said about Forbes's relationship with Lindsay and Cissie Franklin.

So far Tom had managed to keep Lindsay separate from Donald's rambunctious sons and pretty, plump-cheeked daughters. He knew, of course, that Lindsay and Forbes were regarded as 'a couple' and that marriage between them was almost inevitable. But he seldom saw them together and had blinded himself to the fact that Lindsay was not so intelligent as he believed her to be, that she, like far too many girls of her generation, was willing to be ruled by the heart and not the head.

Seated there in the drab hotel room in Portsmouth, Tom felt a sudden sense of grievance, as if Lindsay too had betrayed him. It was, of course, nonsensical to suppose that she spared him even a passing thought outwith the boardroom and the shipyard. He was not, he reminded himself sternly, one of the Franklins' inner circle. Even the promise of a letter from Portsmouth had been casually made, casually accepted. He owed Lindsay nothing. In fact, the more he thought of it, the more foolish it seemed. She would be so caught up in her own affairs that his letter – his postcard – would be tossed aside or, if Forbes happened to be in her company, slyly mocked.

He reached for the card to tear it up, then, again, stopped.

He listened to the wind buffeting the window pane, the rattle of the glass behind the curtain. Tomorrow would indeed be rough. The *Banshee* would not put to sea. He felt suddenly cut off from the meagre companionship of half-formed wishes and vague desires that had sustained him for several years. He wondered fleetingly what his daughter would be doing tonight, what Mission Fund meeting she had attended or what church soirée she had graced with her presence. At one time, he had tried to compare Sylvie with Lindsay when, in reality, there had never been anything to compare. He should send a postcard to Sylvie, but he knew that she would just sneer at his simple communication and tear the card in two.

He reached for the postcard again, hesitated again. Then, for no very good reason save a vague feeling of empathy with the plump, freckle-faced young woman who had once clung so gaily to his arm, he lifted his pen and carefully addressed the panel not to Sylvie, not to Lindsay, but to Miss Cecilia Franklin at her home on Harper's Hill.

One of the functions of Mrs Dunn, the Franklins' housekeeper, was to collect the morning's mail directly from the postman and deliver it to the breakfast table. When Grandpappy was in residence, of course, Giles would take charge of any letters addressed to Mr Owen, whisk them off to the library where, as soon as breakfast was over, the old man would sift through them and separate business from personal correspondence.

Since Owen's 'retirement' the volume of personal correspondence had increased threefold. Many of his old acquaintances were partial to long weekends out of the city and, unlike Owen, had a fondness for Perthshire's rivers and hills. In fact, an invitation to a weekend or week-long house party at Strathmore had acquired a certain kudos in shipping circles and folk that Owen barely knew or could hardly remember were for ever calling upon him cap-in-hand in the hope of striking up a friendship. Whatever intention the old man had had about closing the door on society had, in the words of the minstrel song, gone floating down the Swanee. He was more in demand than ever and in the course of a year spent as much time being entertained in Glasgow as he did entertaining at Strathmore, so that he was glad to sneak off to the country on his own now and then just to restoke his boilers.

Pappy Owen was at home in Harper's Hill that calm March morning, lording it over the breakfast table as if nothing whatsoever had changed since the old century gave way to the new.

Melancholy moods and bouts of guilt seemed to have left him at last, or perhaps *he* had left *them* with the oil-cloth coats, deerstalkers and leggings in the rummage-room up north. While in Glasgow he was, or appeared to be, quite his old self again, except that he did not rush off to Aydon Road of a morning or express much interest in the state of business. Energy thus conserved manifested itself in a tendency to interfere in domestic matters and Lilias and he were constantly at loggerheads over who had the right to order whom to do what or, to put it another way, who ruled the roost in Harper's Hill. Mercy's betrothal had almost brought them to blows. It had been all Donald could do to prevent his dear wife walking out in exasperation and abandoning the lot of them. Eventually Forbes and Lindsay had taken the old chap out to dinner at the Barbary and had had a quiet word in his ear – something Donald and Arthur seemed incapable of doing – after which Grandpappy left such esoteric matters as the choice of material for Mercy's wedding dress and the selection of a guest-list to his daughter-in-law and her team.

He had been back from snowy Strathmore for the best part of a fortnight. He had spent this time haring from concert hall to art exhibition, from luncheons with the Association to dinners with the Federation, with hardly a minute to call his own. He seemed to thrive on it, though, and was totally oblivious to the fact that his grandchildren were no longer children and found his playfulness, particularly at breakfast, just a tiny bit wearing.

Mrs Dunn brought in the post.

She was a small, stooped elderly woman, very sour and solemn, a holy terror to Cook and the maids. She bobbed a

curtsey and, crabbing around the table in predetermined se-
quence, distributed letters to Donald, Lilias, Ross, Johnny,
Forbes and, skipping Pansy, last but not least to Cissie; one
rare, almost shocking picture postcard that, by its gaudiness,
seemed desperately to be trying to compensate for days and days
without a communication of any kind, with nothing to open,
nothing to read.

'Good God!' Johnny exclaimed. 'Our Cissie's got a postcard.'

'Someone loves her after all,' said Pansy.

'That's enough,' said Lilias.

'The *Victory*.' Pappy lifted himself a little in his chair and
peered through his half-moon spectacles. 'I thought it had sunk
years ago. Portsmouth. Must be from our Martin.'

'Oh, yes, of course,' said Pansy, disappointed. 'Martin.'

Although she had not touched the postcard yet – it lay by her
plate picture side up – Cissie said, 'It isn't from Martin.'

'How can you tell?' said Johnny. 'Psychic emanations, or
what?'

'You *could* read it,' Ross suggested. 'There's writing on the
other side.'

Cissie said, 'It can't be from Martin.'

Forbes was seated opposite her. He was leaning back in the
indolent half-sprawl that they had all had to learn to put up with
and that, much to Mama's annoyance, Johnny had decided to
emulate. Ross, Johnny and Forbes were dressed for the office, all
three clad in near-identical pinstripe suits, the accepted rig for
deputy managers who hadn't come up the hard way. On a
weekday morning they would have been gone long since but on
Saturday, out of deference to their exalted positions, they were
not obliged to appear at Aydon Road until nine o'clock and
would knock off shortly before one.

Cissie glanced up and caught her cousin's eye. He had a
smile on his face, a familiar little smile that tugged at the
corner of his cheek and created something appallingly like a
dimple. He was eating grilled kidneys and, without taking his

eyes from her, speared one with his fork and put it in his mouth. He said nothing, not a word, but that smile, that insinuating smile remained upon his face even while he chewed and swallowed.

Cissie loathed him, loathed and feared and loved him. She could not shake off the sensation of his hands upon her. She knew what his body looked like, was privy to that information. Information was all it was, a fierce, cunning sort of mischief that he and she shared but that she could share with no one else. For who would believe her? These days she was regarded as a nuisance, a hysterical trouble-maker, Forbes as sane and sensible. Only she seemed to have realised that he was two people, three people, a whole anthology of different and differing characters, one of whom – only one – she loved without regard for the hurt it brought her or the satisfaction it afforded him.

Forbes said, 'Perhaps it's from her lover.'

'Yes,' said Pansy, 'or a secret admirer.'

'Do not be ridiculous, Pansy,' Donald told her.

'Professor Duval?' Johnny suggested.

'Resurfaced in Portsmouth,' Ross added.

'Run off to sea to mend his broken heart,' said Pansy.

'Go on, Cissie, turn it over,' Forbes said.

'Put us out of our misery,' said Ross.

Forbes watched her unflinchingly, still chewing. He was confident that the postcard would be harmless, meaningless, a damp squib. That she would be made a fool of once more, driven back towards him, fluttering and squawking like a chicken in a coop. That he – all of them – would have the last laugh on poor, fat, frightful Cissie.

She lifted a corner of the postcard and, like a gambler who must keep his hand hidden, peeped at it. Everyone at table watched, some anxiously, some eagerly. She flattened the card again and rubbed it with her forefinger.

'It is,' she said. 'I knew it would be.'

'What?' said Johnny. 'From Duval?'

'No.' Cissie looked straight at Forbes. His jaw had stopped working and the smile was gone. 'It is actually from my lover.'

'Your lover!' Pansy exclaimed. 'You with a lover!'

'And who might that be?' Forbes asked.

'None of your damned business,' Cissie answered and, taking up the card and pressing it to her breast, quietly left the dining-room.

'Her lover?' Lilias said as soon as the door closed. 'Cissie doesn't have a lover? Does she? Pansy, does she?'

'How would I know? She never talks to me any more.'

Donald laughed, rather uneasily. 'Tom Calder's down in Portsmouth along with Martin testing the Babcock boilers for the navy, so bored, I imagine, that he's sending postcards to anyone whose address he can recall.'

'Tom Calder,' Forbes said, with a smug little nod. 'Of course.'

'Nothing wrong with Tom Calder,' Pappy Owen said.

'For Cissie, our Cissie?' said Johnny.

'At least Tom's one up on old Duval,' said Forbes.

'Really?' said Pansy. 'In what way?'

'He's still breathing, isn't he?' said Forbes.

And everybody laughed.

Cissie went straight upstairs to the third floor of the mansion, an ill-lit region of attics and storerooms where, some years ago now, an apartment had been fitted out to accommodate the nurses who had attended her grandmother in her last illness. She went into the water-closet that had never been plumbed properly and that still groaned and dribbled when pressure was low, a narrow, shadowy refuge with a single tinted glass window high on the wall.

She often came here to weep in private, to wash away her despair. She was not in a weepy mood this morning, though. She felt quite gay in fact, buoyed up less by the manager's postcard than by the capital she had managed to make out of it. She intended to read what Tom Calder had written – clichéd greetings, no doubt – then tear up the card and sluice the pieces away so that no one would ever know who had taken the trouble to drop her a line. It would probably come out sooner or later: Mr Calder would mention it to Papa, Papa would tell Mama and Mama would chide her for being so secretive over something so simple and ordinary.

She closed the door, bolted it and slid the heavy mahogany lid across the pedestal. After making sure that all the surfaces were clean and dry, she carefully seated herself.

She was far up in the house, high above the bedrooms, the library, the music-room, the dining-room, the sundry parlours. Outside pigeons crooned and scrabbled in the roof ridge. She felt not isolated but airy. Holding the postcard between her palms she studied the depiction of Lord Nelson's flagship from several angles. It didn't look at all like a famous piece of history, more like something that Coleridge's Ancient Mariner might have encountered in one of his nightmares. She turned the card over and read what Mr Calder had printed in an amazingly neat hand.

She ran into him quite frequently at choral events and concerts and, most recently, at the launch of an A-class torpe-do-boat destroyer that everyone, including Lindsay, seemed very excited about. He always made a point of speaking to her but, like the other men, seemed to have far more to say to her pretty cousin Lindsay. With the edges of the postcard pressing the flesh of her thumbs, Cissie recalled that daft Sunday in the park when Mr Calder, sporting a striped blazer and straw boater, had played his part so well. It seemed like an eternity since she had been that carefree, when her life had been uncomplicated and unstained by emotions over which she had no control.

She read the postcard again.

Simple greetings, ordinary news, not in the least clichéd.

The *Banshee*, she gathered, was the naval craft in which Franklin's boilers had been installed. The weather had not been kind. She wondered how Martin had coped with rough seas; Martin had a habit of turning green while crossing the Clyde on a ferry. She wished that Mr Calder had dropped a hint that he too remembered that day in the park when she had flirted with him and hung on to his arm.

On the ridge above the window pigeons crooned. She could see their plump shadows strutting behind the glass. For a moment she felt like crying – then suddenly she did not. She unbuttoned her dress, slipped the postcard inside and buttoned up again. It would be unjust to Tom Calder to tear it up. She would hide it somewhere in her bedroom, and when she was feeling blue, she would re-read it, a gloss to happier times.

Cissie, rising, unbolted the closet door.

'Where are we going tonight, Dada?' Sylvie asked as soon as they came out of the close mouth.

'Where would you like to go, sweetheart?'

'Kirby's.'

'Kirby's? My goodness, you are becoming adventurous. Is it that young man you're hoping to see? He's not going to let you win again, you know.'

'He didn't *let* me win. I beat him fair and square.'

'Of course you did, honey,' Albert Hartnell said. 'McCulloch's a clever devil but even he can't rig a dice cup.'

'I asked God to let me win.'

'Obviously He heard you,' Albert said, without irony.

'Take me to Kirby's then.'

'I can't.'

'You mean you won't.'

'No, honestly, sweetheart, it'd be more than my reputation's worth to sneak you into Kirby's again.'

'Why?'

'The boss wouldn't stand for it.'

'You mean Mama?'

'No,' Albert said. 'I mean Mr Bolitho, the owner.'

'Mr Bolitho? Is he the chap in the apron who came to look us over?'

'The same,' said Albert.

They were walking towards the thoroughfare. Although the sky was clear, the gaslamp-lighters were out and about with their long poles, and midden men were popping in and out of closes, hunched under their baskets. Children paddled in the gutters or gathered about wide-open windows where their mothers leaned and chatted and distributed bits of bread and jam and other little titbits, none fancy. From the slums south of Portland Row came violent shriekings and shoutings, almost indistinguishable from the noise of the shunters that delivered ore to Maclintock's iron works, as if little men and little machines became one now that night had fallen on Clydeside.

To all of which, pretty, frilly Sylvie remained heedless. She clung to Albert's hand, skipping as if she were ten again and not a month short of sixteen.

'Now,' she said, 'if you were to take me to Kirby's and I were to talk to Mr Bolitho, tell him how important the work of the Coral—'

'No,' Albert said patiently. 'No, honey, no, no.'

She stopped abruptly, dragging the man to a halt.

'I want to,' Sylvie said.

'Mr Bolitho isn't interested in our Mission work.'

'I want to.'

'Look,' Albert said, 'it isn't just Mr Bolitho. It's the – er – the ladies. The ladies won't like you showing up too often.' He raised his eyebrows, spread one hand, trying to appeal to reason. 'I mean, honey, Dada's a member. I admit that I like the odd night out and Kirby's – what I'm trying to say is . . .'

'*I want to.*'

Her cheeks glowed. Her features were so knotted with temper that for an instant her grey eyes all but disappeared.

Her skin was so fine that it creased as easily as silk or chiffon or, as now, drew tight across the delicate bones of her skull so that she appeared not very young but very, very old.

'Sylvie, sweetheart, Dada can't take—'

She stamped her foot. 'You can. You can. You can.'

'*Ssshhh, ssshhh* now, honey. Please don't make a scene.'

'Take me to Kirby's.'

'No.'

'I'll tell Mama.'

'Tell Mama what?'

'Where we go, what we do.'

'Mama knows what we do.'

'Not everything.'

'No,' Albert admitted. 'Not everything. But I still can't take you to—'

'*I want to see him, I want to, I want to, I want to.*'

Her voice rang from the lean, neat tenements of Portland Row and echoed into the ramshackle courts behind the iron works like a pitiful cry for help. Albert crouched as low as his girth allowed. If he hadn't been wearing his suit, he might have knelt at her feet. He let the basket fall from under his arm, reached out both hands to her hands and, when she stamped and wriggled away, caught her about the waist.

'Sylvie, Sylvie, stop it. Stop it, please.'

As soon as he touched her she became calm, so pale and pretty and composed, so sweet and guileless that Albert felt like an ogre.

'Listen,' he said, 'the Irish lad won't be there. He only shows up on Fridays along with the other students. Take my word on it, sweetheart, he won't be at Kirby's tonight.'

'Take me, Dada, please.'

She pressed against his palms, tilting her hips. Albert capitulated.

'All right.' He got to his feet, picked up the basket, gave her his hand. 'But don't blame me if you're disappointed. He won't be there, you know.'

'He will,' said Sylvie. 'I just know he will.'

In the City Hall in Candleriggs, Dickens had once given readings from his works, Thackeray had delivered a lecture on 'The Four Georges' and, courtesy of a grateful public, David Livingstone had received a banker's draft for two thousand pounds. These fragments of Glasgow's history were embedded not only in the fabric of the building but also in Lindsay's imagination. Seated by her father's side, awaiting the appearance of the Edinburgh Choral Union's orchestra and choir, she tried to picture what Dickens would have looked like at his reading desk, dwarfed by the organ, and wondered how Livingstone had made himself heard in a crowd of three thousand adulatory admirers; on balance she would have preferred to be attending a reading by Dickens than a performance of Elgar's *Judas Maccabeus*, a work she always found depressing.

The hall was three-quarters full before 'the gang' from Harper's Hill made an appearance. Aunt Lilias led them along the aisle and, with fussy little gestures, ushered her remaining sons and daughters into the row. Donald and Grandpappy brought up the rear and Lindsay, to her surprise, soon found herself seated shoulder to shoulder with Cissie.

The organist, Mr Bradley, coaxed notes from the vast golden pipes and the orchestra tuned up in the amphitheatre. From far off behind the scenes floated the sound of a contralto voice – Madame Dumas, perhaps – running through scales. Lindsay's father, alert and excited, rubbed his hands together, leaned over and said to Cissie, 'So you couldn't resist turning out to hear one of Europe's finest choirs?'

'No, Uncle Arthur. It should be a wonderful evening.'

'Well, I'm certainly looking forward to it,' Arthur said, and sat back.

After a moment Lindsay whispered, 'What are you doing here, Cissie? I thought you hated Elgar.'

'Spare ticket,' Cissie said. 'Martin's. Couldn't let it go to waste. It's not every week one gets the opportunity to hear the ECU in Glasgow.'

'No, I don't suppose it is,' Lindsay answered.

She was relieved that Cissie wasn't sunk in introspective gloom. That she had deigned to exchange even a polite word seemed to augur a truce in their undeclared war. Lindsay, however, remained guarded.

'I do like your coat,' she said.

'Thank you. It's new. Daly's.'

'Tailored?'

'Of course.'

The organ uttered a declamatory warning, programmes throughout the hall rustled, the orchestra began to file on to the platform. Arthur rubbed his hands again and exchanged a thumbs-up signal with Donald. From the end of the row Pappy waved his programme, like a racing tout.

'He isn't here then?' Cissie whispered. 'He didn't come?'

'Who?'

'Forbes.'

'No,' said Lindsay. 'Didn't he tell you he wasn't coming?'

'He was vague about it. You of all people know what Forbes is like. Actually, we don't have much to say to each other these days. I mean, we don't see that much of him at home.' Cissie's question had a hint of point: 'I suppose you do know where he is this evening?'

'Oh, yes,' said Lindsay. 'A prior engagement.'

'Hah!' said Cissie.

'One of his college friends has been signed on by Cunard and has taken his classmates out to celebrate.'

'They'll have gone drinking, I expect.'

'Dinner, I believe, at Miss Cranston's.'

'I just hope I don't have to put Forbes to bed afterwards.'

'Come now,' Lindsay said. 'Forbes isn't a boozer.'

'That's true,' Cissie conceded, then added, 'Well, at least you know where he is and who he's with.'

'I'm not Forbes's keeper, you know,' Lindsay said.

'Which is probably just as well,' said Cissie as Mr Dambmann, leader of the orchestra, appeared from the wings, and the audience broke into applause.

'Greetings to you, Bertie,' Forbes McCulloch said affably. 'Sure and I didn't expect to see you here on a Saturday night.'

'Well, I . . .'

'Riding your luck, are you?'

'Well . . .'

'Where is she?'

'Downstairs.'

'In the public?'

'No, in the street.'

'In the street! That's takin' a bit of a risk, old man,' Forbes said. 'I mean, there's no saying what she might not get up to in the street.'

'Please, it's my daughter you're talking about.'

'All the more reason to bring her up.'

'How can I? Bolitho will have my guts if I do.'

'Not if she refrains from shaking her little basket, he won't.'

'She wants to see you,' Albert said.

'Thought that might be the case.'

'She insisted on coming. I told her you wouldn't be here, but . . .'

'But I am here, aren't I, old chap? Ready and waiting.'

'Look, Sylvie's my responsibility, a — an innocent child.'

'No, Bertie, whatever else she may be,' Forbes said, 'she isn't a child.'

'I don't want her to come to any harm.'

'Then bring her up.'

Albert shook his head.

'Can't,' he said. 'Daren't.'

'Who are you really afraid of? Me, or Billy Bolitho?'

It was on the tip of Albert's tongue to confess that he was more afraid of Sylvie than anyone else, but somehow that did not seem like the sort of thing you should be admitting to a stranger. Billy Bolitho's ladies were strong in number, for the upper room was crowded with gentlemen intent on pleasure. Albert had never been through the curtain at the rear of the room, had never been seriously tempted by the painted whores, even though some of them were hardly much older than Sylvie. He looked across the tables to the bar where Billy Bolitho, minus apron, was bossing the barmaids about and, at the same time, joshing the customers. Even when he laughed Mr Bolitho managed to look hostile. He was manager, and co-owner along with Mr Joseph Kirby whom nobody could recall having seen about the place in many a long year.

Forbes said, 'I'll go down and fetch her, shall I?'

'No,' Albert said. 'Please don't.'

'God, what a timid chap you are, old son,' Forbes told him. 'Aren't you going to have a flutter since you're here?'

'Not with Sylvie waiting in the—'

'She could be my guest. I'm not afraid of Billy Bolitho, even if you are.'

'She just wants to see you.'

Forbes grinned, showing what Albert interpreted as a dimple. It didn't do to study the Irishman too closely; with his long, dark lashes and charming smile it would be all too easy to fall under his spell, even if you were a man. He wore a fawn-coloured sporting coat and a high-necked pullover, no collar, no cravat. He had the appearance of a wealthy farmer or landowner, older, much older, than his years. Albert knew who Forbes McCulloch really was, though, and what his connections were and that there was more brass than copper behind him.

'Well then,' Forbes said, 'why don't you have a shake of the dice if that's your fancy, and I'll go down and keep your little pet lamb company for a quarter or half an hour?'

'Did you come here just to see her?'

'Don't flatter yourself – or her, Bertie. I came here because I'm off the leash for once and fancied a bit of a drink and a bit of a spin.'

Albert glanced wistfully around the mirrored room. He loved Kirby's, had loved it from the moment he had been in a position to fork out the stiffish annual fee and elevate himself from the public bar to the company of the gentlemen upstairs. No riffraff here: it was, in its way, more respectable than the Western Club – or so Albert liked to believe. Some came to drink, some to gamble, others to seek consolation with the ladies, so free and uninhibited in their behaviour that only a prude could object to them.

All God's children, Albert thought, each and every one of them.

He heard the toothy rattle of the dice-cup, the snicker of billiard balls on the long green tables, breathed in the rich effluvia of perfume and cologne, cigar smoke and whisky and the blond beer that the barmaids drew so expertly into tall fluted-glass steins, frothy with head, beaded and beautifully chilled.

'Oh, sod it!' Albert said. 'Half an hour then. No, twenty minutes. But don't bring her up here, please. I need your word that you won't do that?'

'You have it, Bertie,' Forbes said.

'And don't . . .'

'Pardon me?'

'Don't, you know, do anything to scare her.'

'Heaven,' Forbes McCulloch said, 'forfend!'

He came down the steep staircase towards her. Three men had gone in and up just before him and, seeing his approach, had left the door open. She watched him from her stance in the lane, from under the hissing gas lamp on the wall. Two of the men had addressed her, had made suggestions that she was too mature to find offensive and, if truth be known, had actually found rather flattering. She had told them she was waiting for her father and could not go with them because her father would be very annoyed if she did.

'Aye, and who's your pa then?' they had asked her.

'Mr Bolitho,' she had answered.

They had gone scurrying away like frightened rabbits and had opened the door with a key and then she had seen him, Irish, coming down the stairs.

He had his hands in his pockets and he was dancing. Dancing down the steep wooden stairs with all the agility of the brown-skinned man, an acrobat, that the London branch of the Coral Strand had sent to Glasgow to put on a show last summer, to drum up contributions for the fund. He looked dark too, dark and acrobatic. He looked quick and rhythmic and poised. His hat was tipped back from his forehead. His lips were pursed as if he were whistling a tune that only he could hear, a tune to which his feet kept time.

She felt the breath go out of her at the sight of him.

God had answered her prayer. What she was doing could not be wrong if God had answered her prayer.

He was here, he was coming for her.

Her dandy, her destiny.

'Hello, sweetheart.' He stepped across the lane, tugging his hands from his pockets: Sylvie felt as if he were reaching for her, reaching out to claim her. 'Dada's got business to attend to. He sent me down to look after you.'

'Yes.'

He offered his arm, not his hand.

She took it naturally, fell easily into step with him, not skipping.

'Where are you taking me?' she asked, at length.

'You'll see,' Forbes answered, grinning, and led her briskly round the corner into St George's Road.

It had been the devil of a week, the devil of a journey home.

Tom had persuaded Martin to leave Portsmouth before the horse-power trial which had taken place in seas that Melrose deemed 'moderate' but that seemed a little more steep than that to Tom. Fortunately the wind had flattened before the *Banshee* had steamed out into the Channel for her coal-endurance test and the run to Bilbao and back – a distance of over a thousand nautical miles, a fair haul for an old torpedo-boat in the spring season – had been completed almost without incident. He had nursed the boilers as best he could and had had MacDougal stand guard over the navy stokers who were inclined to be lazy and erratic. And there had been a spot of bother during the brief coaling dock at Bilbao when one of the stokers had somehow lost a tooth and MacDougal had somehow acquired a shiner – neither mishap being related to the other, of course.

On returning to Portsmouth, it had taken him half a day to check his figures against those on Jason Melrose's records and sign for the accuracy of the reports, then MacDougal and he had hot-footed it to London just in time to catch a Friday-night sleeper to Glasgow. He had arrived, bleary and stiff, in Central Station in the grey light of morning, had bid the foreman farewell and, indulging himself for once, had hired a hackney to take him out to Queensview which he reached just as breakfast was being cleared away.

Mrs Grogan, the landlady, had been kind enough to find him a spare plate of porridge and a couple of fried eggs, however, and he had eaten alone in the dining-room, relieved to be back where he belonged.

His mail, such as it was, had been put in his room and, as soon as he had washed, shaved and changed his clothing, he carried the letters into the parlour, seated himself in the dusty moquette armchair in the window alcove, lit a cigarette and opened the first of the three envelopes.

It was, as he'd expected, the monthly bill from his sister-in-law, Florence. He cast his eye down the list of items: camisole, stockings, a moirette silk petticoat — whatever that was — at twelve shillings and ninepence, Nainsook knickers at five shillings and sixpence. Tom didn't doubt the accuracy of Florence's accounting — purchase receipts were enclosed — but he did sometimes wonder where the great heap of clothing that Sylvie had acquired at his expense was stored, for the Hartnells' apartment was small and spartan. He checked Florence's addition, found it correct, sighed and put the bill to one side to deal with shortly.

He opened the second envelope: a personal memo from Perry Perrino scripted in bright green ink informing him that there would be a massed choirs practice in St Andrew's Halls at two o'clock on Sunday afternoon and that he, Perry, hoped that he, Tom, would be able to attend.

Pleased that he had not been left out, Tom put that letter aside, too.

He opened the third envelope and gave a little grunt of surprise: a printed invitation to a musical evening with Mr Owen Franklin at Harper's Hill. Across the bottom of the card Owen Franklin had scribbled: 'Do hope you can come, Tom,' as if he were already one of the inner circle and deserved the old boy's personal attention.

He lifted his cigarette from the ashtray and inhaled deeply.

This Sunday, 'The Cameronian's Dream'.

Next Saturday, an 'At Home' at Harper's Hill.

By gum! Tom thought. Things *are* looking up in the world.

CHAPTER EIGHT

Floating Capital

'What,' Lindsay said, 'do you want to do this afternoon? Go out for a walk?'

'In this dreary weather?' Forbes said. 'No, I'm perfectly happy to sit tight and wait for Runciman to fetch us afternoon tea.'

'Miss Runciman.'

'Miss Runciman then.'

Forbes stretched an arm along the back of the sofa and toyed with a lock of Lindsay's hair. She felt no particular excitement. She knew by experience that nothing would come of his flirting. She would have preferred to be out of doors, even if only for a short promenade along Brunswick Crescent. Forbes was right, though; the weather was not conducive to exercise.

A mild, misty drizzle enveloped Clydeside. Drab evergreens and trees not yet in bud dripped moisture, the big windows of the drawing-room were opaque with condensation. Church that morning had smelled distinctly damp, not wintry but bluff and loamy. The weather had failed to quash Papa's enthusiasm for the massed choir rehearsal, however. He had hurried off straight from kirk to catch a bite of lunch at Harper's Hill before Donald and he walked the short distance to St Andrew's Halls together.

Forbes had appeared at the front door about half past two o'clock. Miss Runciman had shown him into the drawing-room.

Lindsay had been been upstairs in the library engrossed in the latest issue of *The Shipbuilder* when Miss Runciman, wearing her everlasting smile, had announced Forbes's arrival. Showing no sign of annoyance at the interruption, Lindsay went downstairs at once, prepared to behave as if she were overjoyed. The sight of Forbes in his Sunday best had given her a lift, for however tedious she found his conversations of late his charm more than made up for it.

By half past three, though, she was bored again. She was loath to admit even to herself that she took less and less pleasure in Forbes's company these days. She still loved him, of course she did, but she could hardly recall the magnetism that had once attracted her to him.

He toyed with her hair, then, letting his hand slide from her shoulder, appeared to lose interest. He rolled out of the sofa, put his hands in his trouser pockets and meandered to the window.

Then he said, 'Are you in a position to get married yet?'

He jingled coins in his pockets and did not seem in the least interested in her reply.

'What do you mean, Forbes, "in a position"? Of course I'm in a position to get married. I'm single and over twenty-one.'

'I mean,' he said, 'financially.'

'Ah!'

He returned to the sofa and leaned his forearms on the back of it, giving her his full attention. 'How much did your trust turn up?'

'I'm not sure you have a right to ask me that,' Lindsday said.

'Oh, come on, my love,' Forbes said. 'If I'm going to take you on then I'm entitled to know how much you're worth.'

'What did you say?'

'Sorry.' He smiled sheepishly. 'That didn't sound right, did it?'

'Just for a moment you sounded like a real Irish horse-coper.' Lindsay let her pique show. 'Take me on indeed! What a callous way of putting it.'

He slid an arm about her, cupped her shoulder, nuzzled her neck. His cheek was shaven smooth and she could smell cologne. She wondered when he had taken to wearing cologne.

'I mean,' Forbes said, 'if we plan to set a date this year then we have to be practical about it. I want you, Linnet. Can't you tell how much I need you? I really can't wait much longer.' He kissed her neck, letting his lips linger. 'That's all I meant.'

She felt guilty. The touch of his lips was so tender and loving that she could not help but forgive him. She covered his hand with hers. It was so still and clammy in the drawing-room that the rustle of her skirts sounded like a crackle of thunder. Where was Miss Runciman? Probably in the kitchen personally preparing the neat little sardine sandwiches that Forbes professed to adore. What would Miss Runciman say, Lindsay wondered, if she came into the drawing-room and found them sprawled on the carpet in a passionate embrace?

'It's too early to consider announcing our engagement,' Lindsay said. 'I'm no less keen than you to be married but my father does have a point.'

'What point is that, sweetheart?'

'You're not twenty-one yet.'

'What's that got to do with it?'

'You're not − not established.'

He came swiftly around the sofa, seated himself by her side and took her face between his hands. 'Look at me, Linnet. Do I seem like a boy to you?'

She shook her head. His hands tightened, fingertips finding and resting on the pulses behind her ears. He said, 'Do you think a man has to be twenty-one to make a woman happy?'

'Forbes . . .'

'Linnet, I don't want to lose you.'

'Lose me?'

'To someone else.'

'There is no one else.'

He took a deep breath, released it. 'No,' he said. 'No, of

course there isn't.' He slid his hands from her face and sat back. 'Anyhow, I thought we were going to be practical.'

'And talk about money, you mean?'

'If you like,' Forbes said.

'Are you asking me how much I'm worth?'

'Oh, I see. That's what's got you riled, is it? No, Lindsay, that's not what I'm asking, not at all.'

'What then?'

'I want to know how much *we'll* be worth when the time comes.'

'Haven't you asked Martin?'

'He claims he doesn't know.'

'Donald then, or Pappy?' Lindsay said. 'You're fully entitled to see the figures — or your mother is. I'm not sure how trust law works when juveniles are involved.'

'Juveniles! Jesus, I hate that expression. I'll be twenty-one next year. I'll have finished my diploma course and most of my managerial training. I'll be established. You've seen the figures. You know what I'll be earning. Will it be enough, Linnet, just tell me that? Can we make do?'

'Don't be ridiculous, Forbes. Of course we can make do. Good Lord, you're carrying on as if we were being condemned to nail-biting poverty.'

'I don't want to have to depend on anyone.'

'I applaud that sentiment,' Lindsay said. 'But it doesn't alter the fact that my father doesn't want us to marry until you're older.'

'How old? Twenty-five, thirty-five? Forty, fifty? Until my cock withers and drops off?'

'*Forbes!*'

'Well, it's the truth, Linnet. Your daddy doesn't want you to get married at all, especially not to me. He likes having his little girl at home. It makes him feel ageless. And then along comes this hairy Dubliner—'

'Nonsense! Absolute nonsense!'

'Are you blushing?'

'No.'

'You are, damn it, you're blushing.' He touched her again, brushing her hair with his palm. This time she shivered. 'Is it that naughty word I used? I notice you know what it means?'

'Forbes, please. Don't.'

'No,' he said. 'You're right as usual. I mustn't taunt myself. We've got to be sensible, practical — *nice*. Nothing else for it.'

'Twelve hundred pounds,' Lindsay said.

He whistled.

'Twelve hundred and eighteen pounds and eleven shillings.'

He whistled again.

'Including accrued interest.'

'At what rate?' Forbes asked.

'I've no idea,' Lindsay answered.

'Say, eleven hundred base over three years. Say, three hundred and sixty per annum. Halve it for one per cent. Multiply by seven. Good God!'

'It's a great deal of money.'

'I'll say it is.' He whistled once more, not silently. 'If you add in the interest, I'll be picking up not far short of five thousand quid on my birthday.'

'Had you no idea that Franklin's were doing so well?'

'None. Not really. Not in hard cash.' He permitted himself a grin. 'Small wonder that Rora Swann considers our Martin a rare old catch.'

'I don't think the money matters. I think she loves him.'

'Of course she does,' Forbes said. 'Same as I love you.'

'Are you sure?'

'Well, I can't just be after your money, my love, can I?' He eased himself back in the sofa and put his hands behind his head. 'Do you know what the arithmetic means, Lindsay?' He did not allow her to answer. 'It means we don't have to kowtow to anyone. We can do as we damned well please, whenever we please.'

'Forbes, I really don't think we should get carried—'

With startling agility he leaped forward and snared her about the waist. He was alert and animated, no longer distant. No longer boring. He kissed her mouth firmly, kissed it again.

'Let's do it, Linnet,' he said.

'Do – do what?'

'Between you and me, Lindsay, just between ourselves, let's agree a date.'

'For what?'

'Our wedding, of course,' said Forbes.

Tom could not make up his mind if the Hartnells deliberately set out to make him feel small or if it was merely negligence that caused them to offer him a low wooden chair. He didn't think that Florence was the devious type but he was less sure about her husband. Something about Albert rubbed Tom up the wrong way and it would not have surprised him to learn that the chap had sawn the legs off the chair just to increase his awkwardness.

The tenement apartment was furnished with odd bits and pieces of furniture and not much of it at that. It was, however, clean; far too clean, not just spotless but scrubbed within an inch of its life, every plate, spoon and fork, every square inch of worn linoleum buffed by one of the damp bristle brushes that were propped like artillery shells on the draining board over the sink. Even the pan of tripe and onions that bubbled on the stove smelled more antiseptic than appetising.

Tom tucked his heels under the spar of the chair and, bent almost double, tried not to click his chin on his knees. Florence and Albert were seated at the kitchen table. There was nothing on the table, not so much as a crumb.

'You've brought payment, I assume?' said Florence.

'I have,' Tom answered.

He fumbled to free an elbow, dipped into his overcoat pocket and produced a signed cheque. He craned forward, chest to thighs, reached up and offered the cheque to the couple. Albert glanced at Florence. Florence nodded. Albert took the cheque and passed it to Florence. Florence studied it with care.

'I think you'll find it in order,' Tom said.

'Hmm, you took your time with it,' Florence said.

'I've been away on business. Working.'

Tom gave the word 'working' a little extra emphasis. He had a suspicion that work was anathema to Albert Hartnell who, when interrogated, admitted only to being a 'contractual storeman', whatever that entailed, and would not be drawn into naming his current employers. If, fourteen years ago, Tom had known the Hartnells better he would not have handed his daughter into their care: it was too late to reclaim Sylvie now, though.

Albert said, 'Africa again?'

'Portsmouth.'

'At the naval dockyard?' Albert said.

'Yes,' Tom said, to save further explanation.

'Rule Britannia!' Albert said. 'Britain rules the waves, what!'

'Albert,' Florence warned in a dreadfully deep voice. 'Enough out of you.'

Tom squirmed. His joints were locking up. He eased back, tried to stretch, felt the knob of the chair-back dig into the base of his spine like a poking finger.

'Where's Sylvie?' he said.

'Out,' said Albert.

'Resting,' said Florence.

Tripped on a small lie, the Hartnells frowned at each other.

'Which is it to be?' Tom said. 'Out or resting?'

'Ah, is she in then, dear?' Albert said, widening his eyes. 'Has she returned from being, from being – out?'

'She's lying down in the room,' said Florence.

'Of course, of course she is,' Albert said. 'Having a nice wee nap, I expect. I wouldn't want to disturb her, would you, Tom?'

'What's wrong with her?' Tom asked. His indifference to Sylvie's welfare was only skin deep, it seemed. He could not entirely erase the guilt and responsibility that were the very essences of fatherhood. 'Is she ill?'

'Ill? Oh, no – hah-hah – course she ain't ill,' said Albert.

'She's – unwell, shall we say,' Florence told him.

'I'd like to see her,' said Tom.

'She is asleep,' said Florence.

'Has she been missing her schooling?'

'Not a single day,' said Florence. 'She isn't that unwell.'

'I see,' said Tom uncomfortably. 'I trust she hasn't been overdoing it.'

'What do you mean?' said Albert. 'Overdoing what?'

'Church work, Mission work, school,' Tom said. 'Burning the candle, sort of thing.' He was tempted to add 'like her mother before her', but he did not consider the remark appropriate. Besides, Florence had been just as shocked as he had been when her sister's moral collapse came to light.

'She's very dedicated to the Coral Strand,' said Florence.

'No stopping her,' said Albert.

'I would like to see her,' said Tom again.

'She's asleep. I'm certain she's asleep.'

'I won't waken her,' Tom promised.

'You might,' said Albert.

Tom tried to rise with dignity but the little chair seemed to be glued to his bottom and rose with him, sticking out like some piece of medieval mummery. He struck at it with his elbow, failed to dislodge it and, fearing for his balance, sat down again.

'I'll wait,' he said.

'Wait?'

'Until she wakens. Or until you waken her for supper.'

'Not enough in the pot for four,' said Florence.

'I'm not scrounging,' said Tom. 'I just want to see that Sylvie's all right.'

'Why shouldn't she be – all right?' Albert enquired.

'I don't know,' Tom said. 'I haven't seen her in months, you know.'

'She hasn't changed,' Florence said.

'We thought you'd forgotten about her,' said Albert.

'Is that what Sylvie thinks too?' said Tom.

'Oh, no,' said Florence calmly. 'She's a real pet lamb, our Sylvie. She goes her own way and gets on with her own life.'

'In the service of others,' said Albert.

'Yes,' Florence said. 'In the service of others.'

'She finishes her schooling soon, doesn't she?' Tom said.

'In July, yes,' said Florence.

'What will she do then? College, perhaps?'

'She's a girl,' said Albert.

'Some girls do go to college these days,' said Tom. 'If it's a matter of cash, I don't mind paying for her to learn how to utilise a typewriting machine, or some other skill for that matter.'

'Park School girls do not become stenographers,' said Florence.

'Don't they?' said Tom.

'In any case,' said Albert, 'she wants to be a missionary.'

'A medical missionary?' said Tom, surprised.

'She ain't clever enough for medicine, alas,' said Albert. 'Knows her own limitations, does our wee sweetheart. No, she has her heart set on working on the home front for the Coral Strand. She'll do the training course, like I did.'

'You didn't,' Florence reminded him. 'I did.'

'Same thing, dearest,' said Albert. 'However, working for the Coral Strand is what our Sylvie has set her heart on.'

'You won't stand in her way, will you, Tom?' said Florence.

'No, probably not,' Tom said. 'I'd like to find out more about it, though.'

'More about what?' said Albert.

'This organisation: the Coral Strand. What precisely is it? What does it do with its funds? Where are its offices and what training will Sylvie receive?'

Florence glanced at her husband who raised a weak eyebrow.

Florence said, 'We can answer all your questions, Tom.'

'Quite right and proper, quite natural for you to ask,' said Albert magnanimously. 'Got the papers handy, dearest?'

'Not just to hand.' Florence paused. 'Next time you come, Tom, I'll have them all laid out for your inspection. Meanwhile, to save you hanging on, I'll slip through to the room and see if she's awake yet.' Florence smiled. 'If she's not you can have a little peep at her, Tom. Would that not be nice?'

'Yes,' Tom said. 'That would be very nice. Thank you.'

'No thanks necessary,' Albert said, and like a true gentleman rose to open the door for his wife.

She lay with her head on a silk pillow, one small fist curled against her cheek. Her hair was spread about her head and babyish perspiration dewed her upper lip. She wore nothing but a shift. Tom could see the outline of her breasts against the cambric, the nipples curiously elongated. She looked, he thought, slightly flushed but not unhealthy. He was embarrassed to be hovering over her while she slept, unaware that she was being observed, but the fact was that he preferred her asleep to wide awake.

The net curtain over the window was too flimsy to filter out the evening light and he could make out Sylvie's clothes folded over a high chair, drawers, stockings, an embroidered garter of which the staff of the Park School would certainly not approve. On the mantel above the fireplace two plaster-cast bookends held a dozen books in line; two little black boys knelt in prayer, foreheads pressed to Latin primers and English grammars as if to acquire knowledge by osmosis. There were no other ornaments in the narrow bedroom, not even functional objects like a mirror or a candlestick and the only furnishings were a dressing-table and a head-high tallboy.

Sylvie sighed, opening one hand and closing it again.

'Aw, she's dreaming,' Albert whispered. 'Sweet dreams, dearest.'

'Have you seen enough, Tom?' Florence murmured from the doorway. 'It's just flushing, quite natural in a girl of her age.'

'Yes.' Tom eased himself out of the alcove. He had seen enough, more than enough. It was the first time that he had observed his daughter's slumbers since her infancy, and somehow he wished he hadn't.

'I'll tell her you called, shall I?' said Florence.

'Please do,' said Tom, and left.

Arthur Franklin had nothing against marriage between cousins. The upper brackets of the shipping industry were full of such unions, encouraged to protect the closed nature of family firms and keep predators firmly beyond the pale. Arthur was willing to concede that Forbes McCulloch would probably wind up as his son-in-law but until that day came he was determined that Forbes would not be given the run of the house.

He entered the hall cautiously, handed hat and overcoat to Eleanor Runciman and peeked at the door that led to the drawing-room.

'Is he still here?'

'No, sir. He's gone.'

'He *was* here, though?'

'Yes, most of the afternoon and much of the evening.'

'I guessed as much,' Arthur said. 'When neither Lindsay nor he showed up at Harper's Hill for dinner I thought they'd be here.'

'I provided him with dinner.'

'Did you indeed?'

'I assumed that you had gone back with your brother,' Eleanor said, 'and that there would be meat to spare here.'

Arthur hesitated, then, still buoyant with the pleasures of the afternoon, headed for the parlour.

'Eleanor, gin or brandy?'

'Brandy, if you please.'

A late evening *tête-à-tête* had become part of the pattern in Brunswick Crescent. Arthur liked to have someone to talk to at the end of the day. Now that Lindsay was growing away from him he depended increasingly upon the housekeeper to provide him with company and, when required, advice. He did not, of course, take advantage of their intimacy and Eleanor was far too respectful to impose upon their close relationship.

'Did you dine with them?' Arthur said.

'Of course.'

'Any plans discussed?'

'What sort of plans?'

'Matrimonial plans.'

'Not in front of me,' Eleanor said.

'Pappy declares they'll marry before the year's out.'

'Do you have no say in the matter?'

'It seems not,' Arthur said. 'It seems I'm just expected to conform.'

'You could surprise them.'

'Could I? How?'

'Give them your blessing.'

Arthur was seated in an armchair, she on the sofa.

He said, 'You rather like the Irish cousin, don't you?'

'I see no harm in him.'

Arthur smiled. 'Because he's a handsome young devil, eh? Does he remind you of that chap from Cork?'

'Chap from . . . Oh!' Eleanor almost blushed. 'How did you hear about the chap from Cork?'

'You've told the tale to Lindsay so often it would be a miracle if I hadn't heard it. I'm not deaf, you know,' Arthur said. 'Fiancé, was he?'

'No, not — not quite, sir.'

'Not good enough for you, eh?'

'Rather the other way around, I fear.'

'How long ago was this near-run thing?'

'Years and years ago. Too many to count.'

'Why do women have such a soft spot for Irishmen?' Arthur sat back and unloosed his collar and cuff links. Eleanor held his whisky glass while he did so. 'I mean, is it the gift of the gab or the brooding looks or the elfin charm? Damned if I can see the attraction.'

'I think' – Eleanor gave him back the glass, fitting it carefully into his outstretched hand – 'I honestly think it's the charm.'

'Skin deep.'

'That's as may be,' Eleanor said. 'Better skin deep than not at all.'

'Don't the Scots have charm?'

'Some do, some don't.'

'Aren't I charming enough?'

'At times, sir, yes – fairly.'

Arthur shook his head ruefully. 'Damned with faint praise.'

'It isn't charm that makes a marriage.'

'Really? What is it then?'

'Mutual respect.'

'Try telling that to two young people who fancy themselves in love.'

'I would not dare,' said Eleanor.

She had gauged his mood at last. He wasn't really fretting about Forbes McCulloch. The great lift of voices that had filled St Andrew's Halls that afternoon had lifted his spirits. For a time, she thought, he had soared above pettiness while Donald and he, and two or three hundred other singing souls, had shared in musical communion. She wished sometimes that she had a voice that could soar and that she might share that exquisite pleasure with him.

She said, 'Is there no one for you, sir?'

'No one? What do you mean, Eleanor?'

'I mean . . .'

Arthur laughed, a little uncomfortably. 'Ah, so you're still dwelling on the fellow from Cork, are you? Lost opportunities, and all that?'

'I was thinking of your welfare, your happiness.'

'I'm happy enough with things as they stand.'

'And after Lindsay goes?'

'She won't be far away. McCulloch has his work . . .'

'She need not go at all,' said Eleanor.

'Hmmm?'

'They could live here with us. With you, I mean.'

'So,' Arthur said, still not riled. 'So that's what's on my darling daughter's mind, is it? Did she ask you to sound me out?'

'I think it's only a vague suggestion.'

'Lindsay's idea, or McCulloch's?'

'It is a very large house for a single gentleman to occupy,' Eleanor said.

'I might consider moving.'

'Do you wish to move?'

'No,' Arthur said. 'But I think I'd prefer moving to sharing.'

'It would be a simple thing to arrange,' Eleanor said. 'The couple could have the entire upper floor and use the drawing-room for their parlour.'

'Where would you go?'

'I could take the little bedroom on the second floor, next to Nanny.'

'Cramped, very cramped,' said Arthur.

Eleanor paused. 'Nanny may not be with us for much longer.'

Arthur sighed. 'That's true.'

'It is, of course, only a vague suggestion.'

She watched him swirl whisky in his glass. He put the glass on the carpet at his feet, crossed one knee over the other and tugged at his earlobe.

'*Did* Lindsay put you up to this?' he asked.

'I don't think she's frightfully keen to leave you.'

'Leave me?' Arthur said.

'She worries about your future.'

'Good God! I'm not in my dotage yet, you know.'

'She thinks you might be lonely.'

Arthur picked up the glass again. 'Did she actually say that?'

'Not in so many words, no.'

'Ah, but you know her too well to be fooled, Eleanor.'

'I've known her most of her life,' Eleanor said.

She was hedging his questions skilfully so far and felt rather pleased with her deviousness. The 'suggestion' hadn't come from Lindsay but from young Mr McCulloch who had enlisted her help when Lindsay was out of the room.

'I'm not surprised that McCulloch wants to plunge helter-skelter into matrimony,' Arthur said. 'I expect he'll want to take on a house of his own too.'

'I think,' Eleanor said, 'that the young man may be more sensible than you give him credit for, sir.'

'Well, he certainly isn't short of a shilling or two,' Arthur said. 'At least he won't be when he reaches his majority.'

'Floating capital,' Eleanor said, 'looking for a berth?'

'Perhaps I should offer to sell McCulloch this place and look out for something smaller and more suitable to my needs.'

This was precisely what Forbes McCulloch had warned her against.

'I would not be able to accompany you, sir,' Eleanor said.

'What? Why ever not?'

'I am unmarried.'

'You're unmarried now and nobody gives a fig.'

'There is, or was, a child in the house.'

'And that's all that respectability requires, is it?'

'Do you remember the sensation when Mr Fingleton employed a young housekeeper? What talk there was about that?'

'Malicious gossip,' Arthur said. 'Nobody could ever prove that he was sleeping – that the young woman was anything other than she appeared to be. Besides, Ronald Fingleton was a notorious old rake and she was such a pretty young thing. No, no, no. There's no comparison.'

'Even so . . .' said Eleanor, and let it hang.

Arthur sighed again and finished his whisky.

He was settled in now and would keep her talking for a good hour or more. She had laid out the hand, had planted the notion that he might lose her as well as his daughter and, with luck and a little manipulation in the course of conversation, she might discover just how much he valued her.

'If this does come to pass,' Arthur said, 'he'll have to pay his way.'

'From what you've told me, sir, that would not be a problem.'

'No, I don't suppose it would,' Arthur conceded. 'It wouldn't take much to convert this barn into two separate establishments. What's up there? Five apartments?'

'Yes, five.'

'I'm not giving up my study.'

'Lindsay would not expect you to.'

'You *have* discussed this with her, haven't you, Eleanor?'

'In a general way, sir, yes.'

'Well, if McCulloch does move into my house after marriage there's one thing I would insist upon.'

'No dogs?' said Eleanor.

'No mother-in-law,' said Arthur.

Lindsay had never known what it was like to be other than prosperous. She accepted her position in society with the equanimity that is the birthright of all middle-class children. Money, like time, had had no real significance for her.

'Live here?' she said. 'Papa would never stand for it.'

'For a time, a year or two, while Forbes — your husband — establishes himself,' Miss Runciman said. 'Did I not hear you discuss some such thing with him yesterday afternoon?'

'Did you? No, I think you're mistaken,' Lindsay said hesitantly.

'Ah, in that case . . .'

'Well, perhaps we did,' said Lindsay, frowning.

She had been half asleep yesterday, particularly in the hour before dinner. She was under the impression that Forbes had been going on about the state of the war, particularly de Wet's invasion of Cape Colony, details of which had just appeared in *The Times*. She had her own views about the war in South Africa but she did not have the temerity to argue her case with Forbes. Something less distant might have been said in the course of the evening, however. She tried to recapture the ebb and flow of the conversations that had marked out the dreary Sunday: some talk of money, much talk of marriage, a brief interlude of kissing – then what? She could not for the life of her recall.

'I rather received the impression that you and Forbes were in agreement,' Eleanor Runciman said.

'About what?'

'Marrying and coming to live here.'

'Oh, did he say that? I mean, did I agree?'

'I seem to remember,' Eleanor went on, casually rather than cautiously, 'that when Forbes said it might be an acceptable means of persuading your father that you aren't too young to marry . . .'

'Yes?'

'You agreed with him.'

'In that case,' said Lindsay, 'I suppose I must have. Now, if you'll excuse me, I really must dash. I'm meeting Aunt Lilias in town at noon.'

'Shopping?'

'Lunching. Uncle Donald's off somewhere working on a tender and my aunt's feeling a little bit out in the cold.'

'Poor soul,' Miss Runciman said tactfully, and tactfully said no more.

'Are you rich?' Sylvie asked.

'What makes you think that?'

'Because you bring me here.'

Forbes looked round. It hadn't occurred to him that the

lounge of the Imperial Hotel in North Street was a particular haunt of the wealthy.

'I bring you here because it's convenient,' Forbes said.

He was drinking tea in an effort to create the impression that Sylvie was his sister. But there was no deceiving the sly-eyed waiters who lurked behind the varnished pillars and palm fronds of the so-called orchestral lounge which, if Sylvie had but known it, had only slightly more class than the average Dublin knocking-shop. Three elderly ladies scraping away on stringed instruments to a piano accompaniment did not cloak the fact that the Imperial's rooms could be rented if not by the hour at least by the half day and that very few of the couples supping on oysters and champagne in the dining-room were married, at least not to each other.

'I don't tell Dada that we come here,' Sylvie said.

'What do you tell Dada?'

'That you take me to Miss Cranston's.'

She wasn't as daft as she seemed, Forbes realised. Her naïveté must be superficial. He, a Dubliner, had learned long ago how to differentiate between innocence and experience. If he *had* been her brother he *would* have taken her to Miss Cranston's Tea-rooms which was so respectable that one almost expected the table legs still to have rufflettes around them. At least she, Sylvie, had got that right. He was beginning to wonder what sort of an education she had received from wily old Albert, her dada.

Forbes wondered many things about Sylvie Hartnell, not least what she would look like with her clothes off and if that fine, flawless skin would be soft to the touch and if her honeysuckle sweetness would translate into compliance, even complicity, once the barrier between them had been broken.

He felt a soft chug of desire in his belly, a stirring below. He was tempted to try to take her there and then, to persuade her to go upstairs with him. He had just enough cash in his pocketbook to spring for the bridal suite. But, no, it was too soon, too premature. Albert would go haywire if he did not return her within the hour, delivered safe, sound and intact to the door in the lane around the corner from Kirby's. Besides, he could not be sure that she would be willing, if she would understand what it meant to be willing and what he would do to her if she was. He needed to be patient, to exercise cunning, to play the long game just as he had done with Lindsay, albeit to quite another end.

'What does Dada say to that?' Forbes asked, huskily.

'He says *that's* all right then.'

It was their third outing together. So far they had done nothing but sip tea, nibble little gammon sandwiches and sniff at each other like puppy dogs.

Forbes sensed that this was no ordinary wooing, no ordinary, uncomplicated seduction, for Sylvie was Albert Hartnell's daughter. Whether he liked it or not, Albert was part of the equation, and Forbes could not discount the possibility that he was being set up.

'Do you tell your dada everything?' he asked.

'Not everything. Only what he needs to know,' said Sylvie.

'What do you say about me?' Forbes asked and then revised the question. 'I mean, what does your dada have to say about me?'

'He says you're rich.'

Forbes blew out one cheek. 'Does he now?'

'I think you are. I think you are and you're not telling me.'

'Why would I not be telling you?'

'In case I ask you for money.'

Forbes paused, swallowed tea-tasting saliva from the back of his throat, then asked, 'Money for what?'

'The Mission, the Coral Strand.'

'Oh, yes, of course.'

'What did you think I meant? For myself? For me?' She laughed, a glassy little sound, far from being a giggle. 'I would never ask for money for myself, not from a gentleman, however nice he seemed to be.'

'Am I nice?'

'Very nice. The nicest man I've ever met.'

'Aye, but you haven't met that many men, have you?'

'A few,' she stated, matter-of-factly. 'Quite a few.'

'In what context?' said Forbes.

'In the context of collecting for the Fund.'

'How long has Albert had you out on the road?'

'Since I was tiny, as small as I can remember.'

'Don't you mind?' said Forbes.

'Why should I mind? It is good work, and God—'

'Yes, there is God to think of, I suppose,' said Forbes.

'*Are* you a Roman Catholic?'

'I told you before, Sylvie: no, I'm not.'

'Good.'

'Why? Don't you like Papes?'

'Oh, I don't object to them,' Sylvie said. 'But I could never marry one.'

'Marry . . . ah, yes, marry,' said Forbes, briefly caught off guard.

'Or a Jew or an Indian gentleman.'

'Hindoo.'

'Hmm. Hindoo.'

'Not even if he was nice,' Forbes said, 'and rich?'

'You're not a Hindoo,' Sylvie said, not seriously.

'Are you sure?' Forbes said. 'I might be, you know.'

'Hindoos wear turbans.'

'Sikhs wear turbans, I think. I don't know what Hindoos wear.'

'Perhaps they wear nothing at all,' said Sylvie thoughtfully.

He felt the chug of desire once more, stronger than before.

He said, 'Anyway, I'm not one of those, any of those.'

'Then I could marry you,' Sylvie said, 'if I wanted to.'

'Is that what you want, Sylvie, to be somebody's wife?'

'Or a missionary,' she said. 'I think I am going to be a missionary.'

'In a foreign field?'

'No, here at home.'

'Is that what Dada and Mama want you to do?'

'It's what I want to do. I only do what I want to do.'

'And what is that exactly?' said Forbes.

'I haven't *quite* made up my mind. I'm still waiting to find out.'

He took coins from his trouser pocket and placed them on top of the bill that a waiter had laid on his tea plate. The waiter seemed surprised that they were leaving so soon. Obviously the fraternal pretence had failed. Forbes eased from behind the brass-topped table.

The aged female quartet hidden behind the palm fronds were playing a version of the Scarlatti *Caprice*, one of Pappy's favourites: Forbes did not want to be reminded of his grand-father just at that moment.

'I'd better get you back,' he said.

She rose too, light as a soap bubble, and took his hand.

'Put me back, you mean,' she said. 'Put me back where I belong.'

Looking down at her Forbes felt thoroughly wicked and at the same time completely disarmed.

'We had better go,' he said.

And Sylvie, in a whisper, answered, 'Yes.'

CHAPTER NINE

A Musical Evening

Tom had long since trained himself not to be impressed by the trappings of wealth. Even so, as he approached the Franklins' mansion at half past seven o'clock on that soft March evening, he experienced a twinge of awe at the sheer scale of the building. He had always respected the Franklins' professional abilities rather than the sham quality that Robert Burns had called 'the guinea stamp'. It wasn't a Burns' song that he had brought along with him as his party-piece, however, but Andrew McConnachie's setting of Joseph Grant's 'The Blackbird's Song is Sweet'. Tom was no soloist but he knew enough about musical evenings to realise that as a member of the Brunswick Choral Society he would be expected to take part in the programme.

As he climbed the steps to the front door, a hackney cab clattered over the brow of the hill from the direction of Woodlands Road, and at the same moment a small, very spluttery horse-less carriage negotiated the broad corner from Park Gate. He checked. He was tempted to wait for the occupants of the vehicles to enter before him so that he might slip meekly in behind them. How daft! he thought. I probably know the Franklins as well as anyone. Taking a firm grip on the handle of his old canvas music case, he rang the bell.

The door opened instantly. 'Tom! How good of you to come.' Much to Tom's surprise, Owen Franklin ushered him across the threshold as if he were a long-lost son. 'By God, I can't tell you how pleased I am to see a friendly face. Nothing in there but choristers – not that I've anything against choristers – but you know how clannish they are when they all get together. And as if that wasn't bad enough, most of them are girls.'

Owen Franklin's protracted greeting puzzled Tom. It seemed just too effusive, too hearty to be entirely sincere: 'Brought your music, I see. Good, good. Lizzie will take your coat. Do you want to hang on to the case? Put it up by the piano, that way it won't get lost. Hah, somebody at it already by the sound of it.'

From behind the partly open door of the drawing-room came the strains of a piano being played very, very well: one of Edvard Grieg's early Norwegian pieces, Tom thought, though a bumble of conversation almost drowned out the melody. He heard a girl's laughter. Four or five servants were assembling tables in the hallway and from the mouth of the stairs floated delicious smells of cooking. Someone was smoking a cigar. Owen Franklin's home seemed warm and welcoming and Tom puts his doubts behind him.

The doorbell rang. 'Ah, that'll be the Lucases. I thought I saw his motoring car weaving down the street. Know Jack Lucas, do you? You should, Tom. Pumps.'

'Oh,' Tom said. 'Yes.'

'Go in, lad. Help yourself to drink. Go on, don't be shy. You'll find plenty of folk you know. We'll make up a programme shortly.' He angled Tom towards the drawing-room door and just before a booming voice called out, 'Owen, you old rogue, back home from your bloomin' cave, are you?' he caught Tom's eye and with a peculiarly gentle smile, said, 'Cissie will take care of you.'

'Thank . . .' Tom began but Owen, arms extended, had swung away.

'Jack, damn me!' the old man roared at the latest arrivals. 'Did I send you an invite? Must have been a mistake.'

Tom glimpsed the younger of the Lucas brothers wrapped in

a huge brown, flapping motoring coat, goggles stuck up on his brow. Behind him, almost blotted out, was his windblown young wife, Olivia. He had seen the couple at concerts and had done business with Lucas senior whose company made pumping equipment. Perhaps, Tom thought, this was a gathering with a bit of purpose. He hoped so; he would certainly be more comfortable talking business than singing 'The Blackbird's Song'.

Then, from within the drawing-room, leading him on, came the sounds of the Norwegian peasant dance, and the laughter of girls.

Holding his music case against his chest, Tom went in.

'Isn't that him?' Pansy said.

'Isn't that who?' said Cissie.

'Your swain, your postcard lover?'

'Don't be ridiculous,' said Cissie, blushing.

She had been blushing since a quarter past six o'clock, for Mama's maid, Nancy Coutts, had been sent upstairs to help her into her corsets and when it came to tight lacing Nancy Coutts had less conscience than Torquemada. By strength of arm and sheer determination she had managed to reduce Cissie's waist to fit the boned high-necked Russian blouse that Cissie had bought for the occasion. The effect, even Cissie had to admit, was dramatic. Whatever there had been to spare about her middle had been pushed up to fill the blouse's pouched front which was some compensation, Cissie supposed, for not being able to breathe.

'Oh, don't be so coy,' said Pansy. 'I know Tom Calder. He isn't a stranger. He seems to have been about for ages.'

'I don't know what gave you the impression that—'

'Martin told me.'

'Told you?' Cissie said.

'What happened in Portsmouth,' said Pansy.

Cissie hesitated. Tom Calder had just entered the drawing-room and was loitering, lost, by the door. There were twenty or thirty guests already present. Mercy and her husband were fighting one of their duels at the piano in the window bay, she aloof and composed at the keyboard, he itching to take a turn. They never played duets together, so Mercy said, for while they were very much in love there were certain stresses that no marriage could hope to survive and an accurate rendering of four-handed harmony was one of them.

Cissie said, 'What did happen in Portsmouth?'

'I know, and you don't,' said Pansy, who knew nothing very much about anything. 'Anyway – look, you're too late. You've missed the boat.'

'Oh, shut up,' said Cissie and, abandoning her sister, headed past the punch-bowl and sherry glasses at a fair old rate of knots.

'Mr Calder – Tom?' said Lindsay.

'Miss Franklin,' the manager said.

'I did not expect to see you here.'

'Didn't your father mention that I had been invited?'

'No. I'm not sure he knew. In any case, I'm pleased to see you.'

'I'm pleased to be here,' Tom Calder said.

'Would you like to me introduce you?'

'I think your cousin may wish to do me that honour.'

'Cousin? Forbes, do you mean?'

'No. Ah . . . Cissie, as a matter of fact.'

'Cissie,' Lindsay said, then, voice lifting with something that may have been amusement, repeated, 'Cissie?'

'Your grandfather indicated . . .'

'Cissie,' said Lindsay again. 'Well, well, well,' just as the cousin in question barged indignantly out of the crowd.

'Tom!' Cissie exclaimed. She was red-faced and breathless. 'Tom! How *wonderful* to see you. How *marvellous* of you to come.' She snared his arm.

'Entirely my pleasure,' Tom murmured. If he was discomfited

by the girl's enthusiasm, he managed to hide it. 'Lindsay was just going to—'

'Lindsay, Lindsay, Lindsay, that's all I ever hear.' Tiny beads of perspiration clung to Cissie's brow and her cheeks glowed with indignation. 'Isn't one enough for you, Lindsay Franklin? Do you have to have them all?' And with that she snatched Tom away and drew him after her towards the piano in the window bay.

She stopped short of the couple who were squabbling at the keyboard and, pressing herself against him, looked up into his long, lugubrious face.

'Thank you for writing to me,' she whispered, 'for the postcard.'

Tom had not forgotten the postcard. He was, in fact, beginning to regret having yielded to a casual impulse to drop a line to Cissie. He had, he supposed, felt vaguely sorry for her while distance separated them. But when he looked down into her eyes, he felt that sense of pity well up again, less vague this time. This was no act, no coy or flighty performance: Cissie Franklin was desperate for attention. He glanced up, saw Lindsay watching them from across the room, brows raised questioningly. Behind Lindsay, Forbes McCulloch was watching too, a scornful smile on his sleek, handsome face.

Tom set down the music case, leaned it against his calf.

He bowed, reached for Cissie's hand and lifted it to his lips.

The hand, ungloved, felt lead heavy, fingers cold. He pressed his lips to her knuckles. He felt a quiver go through her and saw tears in her eyes. And somewhere between his breast-bone and stomach, he experienced a weird little click, like a ratchet slipping his sympathy into another gear.

Cissie turned away. 'I'm sorry. I'm so sorry. I don't know what . . .'

'I do,' Tom said.

He put a hand on her shoulder and, like the lover he had once pretended to be, fished out his pocket handkerchief to wipe away her tears.

'Did you know he was coming?' Lilias said. 'Did you bring him here?'

'Certainly I knew he was coming. I invited him,' Owen replied. 'It's my party after all, this is my house and I can invite—'

'It isn't your house.' Lilias regretted her outburst even as she charged on with it. 'It's *our* house, and I should have been consulted.'

'Why?' Owen said, smiling over his daughter-in-law's shoulder at Olivia Lucas and Miss Broughton, younger daughter of the Anglo-French shipping agent, Auguste Broughton, who were carrying laden plates from the buffet table into the dining-room. 'Why should I have to ask your permission—'

'You know how sensitive she is,' Lilias interrupted.

'Cissie? Cissie isn't sensitive. She's lonely.'

'Nonsense! She has just as many things to do to occupy her time as the rest of us. I mean to say, Pansy isn't—'

'Pansy isn't in love.'

'Oh, love, is it?' Lilias said: it was her turn to bestow a brilliant, brittle smile on passing guests, to pretend that nothing was wrong. 'I suppose you think that all you have to do is trail some man, any man, across my daughter's path and she will automatically fall in love with him?'

'Nothing wrong with Tom Calder, dear.'

'I did not say there was.' Lilias sipped from a cup of strong fruit punch to cool her temper. 'I just do not want you interfering in my daughter's . . .' She hesitated. 'Has Calder expressed an interest in Cissie? Has he had a little private word in your ear?'

'How could he? I haven't seen him in months.'

'There are such things as telephones.'

Owen shook his head ruefully. 'For heaven's sake, Lilias! Do you think Tom Calder would have the temerity to telephone me to express an interest in my granddaughter? Preposterous. He's an employee – and a gentleman. He'd never stoop to that sort of thing and I wouldn't let him. What do you take me for?'

'I'm not at all sure what I take you for these days.'

'Not a fool, though.'

'No,' Lilias conceded. 'An interfering old devil, but not a fool.'

'The girl isn't happy.'

'Oh, I'm well aware of that. But is having a middle-aged widower trail after her going to make her any happier?' Lilias said. 'Doesn't Calder have a daughter about Pansy's age tucked away somewhere?'

'I believe he has,' said Owen. 'But that doesn't make him Methuselah.'

'First you bring Forbes here for Lindsay . . .'

'Rubbish!' said Owen, not forcefully. 'I found him a place with the firm because Kay requested it. It seemed a fair request to me considering he's my grandson, just as much as Martin or—'

'Stop twisting my argument.'

'Argument? I'm not arguing with you, Lilias. You're the one who's doing the arguing. Look, I'm wanting my supper and I do have to talk to my guests, so why don't we just let this matter rest. Let the lass enjoy herself for once.'

'I warn you, if that man trifles with Cissie's—'

'Dear God!' Owen exclaimed and with an exasperated shrug turned his attention from Lilias to the dishes arrayed on the buffet table.

'Will this do for you?' Cissie asked.

'Perfectly,' Tom answered.

'Not too uncomfortable?'

'No, it's fine. Really.'

They were seated on the staircase just below the first landing.

Cissie steadied her plate on her lap, leaned against him and whispered, 'We can look down on everyone from here, can't we?'

'That we can,' said Tom.

'The dining-room will be so crowded.'

'I prefer it here,' Tom said.

'Do you?'

'It's not every evening I get to eat my supper sitting on a grand staircase with a beautiful young woman for company.'

'Are you teasing me, Tom Calder?'

She held her fork in one hand, twirling it a little. Her face was turned towards him and now that her tears had dried her eyes seemed luminous and trusting. She had been brought up in a house full of siblings and was probably used to being teased. None the less, Tom was unsure whether she expected it of him or whether her need was so great that she had lost her sense of humour. He decided not to risk it.

'I've never been more serious in my life.'

'Where do you live?' said Cissie.

'In a residential boarding-house, the Queensview.'

'Where is that?'

'Off the Crow Road, in Partick.'

'Is it comfortable?'

'Comfortable enough for me.'

'Good company there?' Cissie said.

'It's quiet,' Tom answered, 'very quiet in fact.'

'I get so tired of crowds, don't you?'

'Sometimes.'

'But you don't mind your own company?'

'I get tired of that too occasionally.'

'Were you tired of your own company when you wrote to me?'

Tom looked down at his plate. The servant had been over-generous; he doubted if he could do justice to four slices of cold roast beef, two portions of salmon mayonnaise and a lump of potato salad.

'Mildly homesick more than anything,' he said.

'And were you thinking of me?'

'Martin and I — we'd been talking about . . .'

'About me?' said Cissie, frowning slightly.

'About home in general, about the things we missed.' Tom was stretched; it wasn't a question of being tactful, he had to be cunning as well, and deceit did not come easily. 'I thought of home quite a lot when I was in Africa. If I'd known you better I'd have written to you then, Cissie. Would you have answered?'

'I'm not much of a letter-writer,' Cissie said, then added quickly, 'Yes, I'd have answered. It's better, though, to be together, to talk like this, don't you think? If you go away again, I'll write. Now that we know each other, we'll have lots more to write about.' She peered at him, frowning. 'Are you going away again?'

'I hope not,' Tom said.

'It wouldn't be Africa, would it?'

'I doubt it,' Tom said.

'I suppose,' Cissie said, trying to make light of it, 'I could come with you, with the team, I mean. High time I saw more of the world.'

'There are better places to visit than the Niger,' Tom said.

'Do you have a child?'

'Yes, a daughter.'

'What's her name?'

'Sylvie.'

'She's not as old as I am, is she?'

'I wouldn't think so,' Tom said. 'She's fifteen.'

Cissie nodded. She steadied her plate, broke off a fragment of salmon mayonnaise with her fork and ate it absently. She seemed to be thinking of other things — more questions, perhaps. In profile she was not unlike Lindsay. Tom considered volunteering more information about Sylvie but he was apprehensive lest Cissie and his daughter had met at some point, at school say.

'I'm twenty-two,' Cissie said. 'I'm older than Lindsay, you see. He really was far too young to take an interest in me.'

Owen Franklin's guests were well into the spirit of the evening.

Noisy and cheerful, they transported cups of punch, glasses of wine and plates of food from drawing-room to dining-room.

A programme of sorts had been arranged. Already Mercy had played a complex Chopin *étude*, her head held high and haughty while her husband turned the pages for her. Mr Arthur had opened the batting for the Brunswick choir with 'White Wings They Never Grow Weary'. Amanda Bailey, the Brunswick's prettiest soprano, had made the light fittings ring and Mr James Holcomb, heir to the Pressed Steel empire, had embarrassed everyone by croaking out 'Turn the Mangle, Joe', just before supper was called.

Tom looked down at the heads below.

Owen's guests were those and such as those: choristers, shipping people, pretty young women whom Tom had noticed at concerts in the City Hall or in boxes at the Royal when the D'Oyly Carte were in town. He wondered why he had been invited. He tried to pretend that he did not know the answer but it was all too obvious that the old boy had asked him along to court Cissie.

Tom said, 'Heaven knows, it's not my place to criticise a member of your family but . . .' He shrugged.

'I thought Forbes was right for me.'

'I'm not sure he's right for Lindsay either,' Tom ventured.

'Lindsay can take care of herself.'

Perhaps she was right. Perhaps Lindsay would be able to make something of the Dubliner. Tom tried to blot from his mind the disparaging manner in which George Crush and Forbes McCulloch talked of women.

'Do you like Lindsay?' Cissie said.

The question was too direct to be avoided.

Tom said, 'Yes.'

'Is she not too young for you?'

The question was skewed towards an unfavourable answer. He thought for a moment before he replied: 'I've always regarded Lindsay as a very intelligent young lady,' he said, 'but she – how can I put this? – she doesn't seem quite mature enough to be a good wife just yet.'

'So *you* wouldn't marry her?'

He shook his head, lying first by gesture then by word.

How could he tell Cissie that he would marry Lindsay Franklin like a shot if she had not been so far above him. Age had nothing to do with it. He was just the right age, the proper age to take a wife again. He'd had most of the rough edges knocked off over the years, and was materially settled. If he fancied a wife then in an ideal world Lindsay would have been his first choice.

He managed to laugh. 'No.'

'Are you sure?'

'Yes, I'm sure.' Still smiling, he said, 'Miss Franklin, for a well-brought-up young lady you ask far too many questions.'

'Do I?' she said, pleased. 'Let me ask you one more then?'

'What now?'

'Are you on the programme tonight?'

'Yes.'

'Doing what?'

'I've brought along the sheets for "The Blackbird's Song".'

'Don't sing that,' Cissie said.

'Why not?'

'Do you know "The Kerry Dancing"?'

'Yes, but I'm not convinced I can do it justice,' Tom said.

'I have the music. I'll accompany you. I'll lead you through it. Any key that suits your range.'

'I'm not rehearsed,' Tom said. 'Couldn't you manage . . .'

She leaned against him again and crooned, ' "Oh, the days of the Kerry dancing. Oh, the ring of the piper's tune. Oh, for one of those hours of gladness . . ." Isn't it a beautiful melody?'

'It is,' Tom agreed.

He wondered why she had chosen that particular song, why she insisted upon it. She seemed far too young to be dreaming of days that were gone.

'Please, Tom, sing it for me.'

And Tom, gently capitulating, said, 'If you insist.'

'Sickening, isn't it?' Forbes said.

'What is?' said Lindsay.

'How she's throwing herself at him.'

'I don't think she's throwing herself at him at all.'

'He walks in off the street . . .'

'Absolute rot!' said Lindsay. 'Pappy invited him.'

'And we know why, don't we?' said Forbes.

'I expect you have some theory about it,' said Lindsay who, without definite reason, felt testy and defensive. 'And I expect you're going to expound it whether I like it or not.'

'What's got into you all of a sudden?'

'You,' Lindsay said.

'Not yet.' He grinned. 'Soon, I hope, but not yet.'

'For God's sake, Forbes!'

'Tut-tut! Such language. No, she's desperate. She'll take anything. Even old Long Tom there. She won't find what she's looking for in his trousers.'

'You really are foul sometimes.'

'It's true, though,' Forbes said. 'Doesn't she realise she's making a damned fool of herself, whipping him upstairs, hogging him all to herself.'

'Tom doesn't seem to object.'

'Sure and he doesn't object. It's the way in, isn't it?'

'The way in?' Lindsay said. 'If you mean —'

Forbes laughed. 'Such a nasty thought didn't even cross my mind. It's her money he'll be after, not her endearing young charms.'

'Cissie doesn't have any money.'

'There will be a settlement, though. Bound to be a settlement. If Calder hasn't the brain to work it out for himself then Martin will have told him.'

'Not everyone's as calculating as you are, Forbes.'

'Do you think I'm calculating, dearest?'

'Candidly, yes.'

'Well, it's just as well one of us is, otherwise we'd both die virgins.'

She was conscious of his hand upon her waist, his forearm against the swell of her dress. His touch was discreet, not impolite. She was almost betrothed to him and no one would think him forward for holding on to her.

'It always comes down to that with you, doesn't it?' Lindsay said. 'To – to what happens in the bedroom.'

She had imagined that she would want him less as she liked him less, but the illogical desires she had suffered in the first months of courtship had not diminished. Forbes had taught her to think of marriage as something detached from the setting up of a home, from the bearing and raising of children. He had found weaknesses within her that she had not even suspected, moist little hungers that shame and innocence had kept hidden.

'Sure and it does,' Forbes said. 'If Cissie wants him and Calder wants her money then who am I to complain? Not jealous are you?'

No, Lindsay thought, not jealous, just regretful that Cissie and she had somehow exchanged tracks.

'Oh, look,' Forbes said, 'she's going to play for him. How sweet!'

Tom wore a suit of navy-blue worsted with a high collar. He had put on a string tie. A watch-chain draped his waistcoat and his hair, greying slightly over the ears, was swept back with a lick of brilliantine. He looked, Lindsay thought, perfectly in place and competent in this company. He glanced down at Cissie who had taken her sister's place on the piano bench. Smiling up, she gave him a key. There was something so dignified about them as a couple that Lindsay realised how sad her father must feel at the passing of the age of innocent communion and companionship.

'God!' Forbes hissed. 'It's the bloody "Kerry Dance".'

'What's wrong?' Lindsay whispered. 'Does it bring back memories?'

'Does it hell!' said Forbes.

And Tom, one hand on Cissie's shoulder, began his song.

It was close to midnight before the evening's entertainment concluded. The last song was a stirring male-voice rendition of 'Hearts of Oak' which, though English in origin, seemed highly appropriate to a room full of shipbuilders and sent everyone off content.

On tables in the hallway, urns, jugs and teapots had appeared, together with trays of orange sponge cakes to provide Owen's guests with 'a chittering bite' to sustain them on their journeys, short or long. They stood about the hall in topcoats, cloaks and long-fitting pelisses drinking tea or hot chocolate, chatting, reluctant to bring such a jolly evening to an end.

Coat over his arm and music case by his side, Tom sipped tea. He had seldom sung so loudly or so heartily and his larynx was just a little raw; a minor discomfort, he reckoned, a small price to pay for the pleasure he had received and – he was not so modest as all that – the manner in which he had been accepted into the company.

'Tom!' Owen Franklin slapped him on the back, almost causing him to spill his tea. 'Tom! What can I say? How can I thank you for coming this evening? Your contribution was amazing, quite amazing.'

Tom could not recall the old man ever having been so fulsome during his years in management. But Owen Franklin in retirement, Owen Franklin at home, Tom had come to realise, was quite a different fish from the fellow who had ruled the workforce at Aydon Road.

'Well, thank you, sir, but I wouldn't call it amazing.'

'Ah! You don't know the half of it, lad,' said Owen. 'That song you sang, "The Kerry Dancing", beautiful, just beautiful. Why did you pick that one, may I ask? Been a favourite of mine since first I heard it – what? – fifteen or twenty years ago in the old halls in Mint Street. My dear wife and I both loved it. Devereux – yes, that was his name, Robert Devereux – he sang it. He wasn't Irish either. Canadian, I think, a fine, light tenor, very smooth. Before your time, of course. Before your time.' The hand remained on Tom's shoulder. 'You'll come again, Tom, will you not, now you've found the way?'

'I'd be del—'

'Ah-hah, here she is,' Owen declared, stretching out an arm. 'Our little Cissie, the belle of the ball.' He brought his grand-daughter into the circle of his arms and, while Tom juggled teacup and saucer, incorporated Tom too, all three awkwardly linked. 'What do you think of our Cissie then, Tom?'

'She's . . .'

'She's a grand lass, isn't she?' Owen said. 'A grand lass in every way.'

Tom felt a tickle of amusement in his chest. It occurred to him that if Owen Franklin had been *this* obvious in merchandising the products of the shipyard the firm would have gone into liquidation years ago.

'Pap-paaay,' Cissie protested.

'It's true, though. Isn't it, Tom?'

Tom answered obediently, 'Indeed, it is.'

'I see you have your shawl on, dearest,' Owen said. 'It seems that you are going to have an escort as far as the pavement's edge, Tom. I've sent Giles to the rank so there will be cabs along presently. Cissie, don't catch cold.'

'No, Pappy, I won't.'

Tom put down the cup and saucer, slipped into his overcoat and picked up his music case. Cissie took his arm. The loose silk-tasselled shawl draped about her shoulders lent her, Tom thought, a Romany touch that suited her high colour. He shook hands with Owen Franklin, shook hands with Mr Donald and with Martin who was at that moment just about to escort his fiancée, Aurora Swann, down the steps to a waiting carriage.

'Are you travelling in my direction, Mr Calder?' the young woman asked. 'I am going out to Kessington.'

She was very tall and handsome, smothered in furs, as if winter had not yet given way to spring in Glasgow's suburbs.

'Thank you,' he said, 'but I do believe I'll walk home. It's not far.'

'I hope we will meet again,' Aurora said.

'I'm sure you will,' said Martin, just as Cissie drew Tom away.

As soon as they were alone, Cissie relaxed. She did not, however, release her hold on his arm. Several hackney cabs came clopping up from the stand at Woodlands Road, one after the other like a parade. The Franklins' neighbours were probably used to occasional late-night disturbances and in five or ten minutes it would be over, the Hill grave and quiet again. Tom glanced round but saw no sign of Lindsay or of Forbes McCulloch who, in a manner not quite studied, had managed to avoid him all evening long.

Obeying his own little ritual of propriety, he was reluctant to let Cissie walk him further than the corner of Harper's Hill or to pass out of sight of the mansion's wide-open door.

She said, 'I want to see what's happening in the Kelvingrove.'

'What there is left of it,' Tom said.

'Have you seen it?'

'How can I not have seen it?' Tom said. 'Building's been going on for months. There are those who think that Dumbarton Road is beginning to look rather too much like Cairo or Bombay.'

Cissie had gained sufficient confidence to disagree. 'Nonsense,' she said. 'It's an international exhibition, after all, and I for one like all those minarets and domes. Pansy and I have been sneaking out for weeks now to watch them being erected. It's very exciting, don't you think, to have such a thing right on your own doorstep? Come along, let me show you.'

It was a harmless concession to let her lead him across the curve of Park Circus to look down on the almost-completed site of the Great Exhibition whose ornate halls and international pavilions would, so it was said, put Crystal Palace in the shade. Tom was not sure he agreed with the optimistic view, or the principle behind it. He was as proud of his city as the next man but with war still raging in South Africa he regarded the exhibition not as a jewel in the crown of the municipality but rather as a means of stiffening the sinews of empire.

'There,' Cissie said, nudging him towards the railings. 'Don't tell me you're not impressed.'

In spite of himself, he was; the glint of moonlight on the vast area of parkland and the buildings rising spectrally out of leafless trees reminded him of the last great exhibition on this site, thirteen years ago.

As if reading his mind, Cissie said, 'I remember the last one, do you?'

'Yes,' Tom said.

'I remember the orchestral hall . . .'

'Which had terrible acoustics and a whining echo.'

Enthusiasm undampened, Cissie went on, 'And the sweet manufactory rolling out comfits and peppermint rock. And,' a breath, 'the gondolas on the river and the little steamer that my pappy built. We sailed up and down the Kelvin on that steamer under fairy lights and lanterns in the trees – oh, I don't know how many times.'

Tom remembered the steamer only too well, a tiny craft, hardly more than a launch with a miniature coal-fired engine, and how he had worked on its design with Mr Owen and what he had learned in the process. The steamer had been Franklin's contribution to the municipal commonweal, but this year the firm had not been invited to contribute.

Tom remembered other things about the 1888 exhibition too, things that he would not reveal to Cissie: a week before it had opened his wife had admitted her adultery, one of them, and a week before it had closed she had died.

He had taken Sylvie, aged two, to the Groveries several times, just his tiny, doll-like, vacant-eyed daughter and he queuing for a ride on the switchback and, like Cissie, riding down river on Franklin's steamer amid the gondolas and electric launches. He still remembered how uninterested Sylvie had been, how nothing had seemed to excite her attention, nothing except the captive balloon advertising Waterbury's Watches that floated high overhead, swaying and waltzing on the end of its cable. How Sylvie had loved that balloon. Roused from her infant trance, she had pointed at the sky and cried out to possess it, to have him bring it down and place it in her hand like an orb. He also remembered how three days after Dorothy's death he had allowed Albert Hartnell to wheedle him into the Bodega Bar in the main building and how, for the first and last time in his life, he had got raging drunk; how all the bitterness, all the venom in his soul had spewed out and it had taken Hartnell and three of Franklin's employees all their strength to drag him outside into the rain.

Shawl around her shoulders, Cissie leaned her forearms on the painted railing and looked down into the park. She was smiling, her memories not his memories, her past not his past, not blighted. He had a sudden urge to put his arm about her, not to give but to receive comfort.

She said, 'The Duke and Duchess of Fife are performing the opening ceremony on the second of May. Will you take me, Tom? I mean, will you take me to the concerts and exhibitions, to sail on the river? Will you take me to see all the sights?'

'Aren't your family . . .'

'I don't want to go with my family. I want to go with you.'

'I'll take you, Cissie.'

'As often as you can?'

'Yes, as often as I can,' he promised.

Then, putting propriety aside, he kissed her.

Something told him that they would cherish that moment just as poor Joseph Grant had cherished the memory of a blackbird's song in the winter of his dying and Owen Franklin, widowed now and old, still remembered the ring of the piper's tune.

'Goodnight, Miss Franklin,' Tom said.

'Goodnight, Mr Calder,' Cissie answered, and before he could see the tears in her eyes again, turned and ran pell-mell for home.

CHAPTER TEN

The Great Exhibition

If they had been acquainted, which naturally they were not, shy Princess Louise, wife of the Duke of Fife and King Edward's eldest daughter, might have taken time off from her royal duties to offer young Sylvie Calder a quiet word of advice. She, the Princess, had seen it all before, every act of deception and betrayal you could possibly imagine, for, although she was a woman of impeccable moral character, she knew only too well what went on in the Court of St James and the hurt that acts of adultery could cause to all parties involved. In the spring of 1901, Sylvie Calder was in no frame of mind to listen to advice from anyone, however, not even a daughter of the new King of England, and any lesson that the Princess might generously have passed along to the young commoner would almost certainly have been ignored.

As it was, Sylvie, like a hundred and forty thousand others, got no nearer to the beautiful Princess Louise than the crowd that flanked the avenue to the Industrial Hall. She saw nothing of the golden key with which the Princess opened the exhibition's gates, very little of the lady herself, nothing, in fact, except the feather in her hat and, Sylvie later claimed, a long-fingered, white-gloved hand waving in her direction; an omission that Sylvie speedily rectified by the invention of a little white lie: 'She looked at *me*, I tell you. She looked straight at *me* and smiled.'

'I'm sure and she did.' Forbes already regarded Sylvie's war with reality as one of her most endearing traits. 'She probably thought you were a princess too.'

'Do you think so? Do you really think so?' The excitement of a royal occasion had added a frenetic element to Sylvie's effervescence. 'Perhaps I should have gone to the opening of the new art gallery where she could have seen me better.'

'Well, it's too late now,' said Forbes. 'Maybe she'll come back with old Teddie when he visits later in the year.'

'Is *he* coming? Oh, is the King coming? I didn't know that.'

'Once he's out of half-mourning, or whatever it is that kept him away,' said Forbes, 'he's promised to come up and see us. I mean, if the Princess tells him what pretty girls there are in Glasgow he'll be on the train like a shot.'

'I would like to meet the King,' said Sylvie. 'Do you think the King would like to meet me?'

'I'm sure he would,' said Forbes sincerely. 'Oh, yes, I'm sure he would.'

She preened. He liked it when she preened. He knew precisely where he stood with Sylvie when she put on airs and graces. All he had to do to amuse her when she was off on one of her self-adoring little trips was flatter her.

Sylvie giggled. 'I know what the King would like to do to me.'

'Uh-huh! And what's that?' Forbes said.

'He would like me to sit on his big fat tummy and – and . . .'

'And?'

'Light his cigar.'

'Would you like to sit on his big fat tummy?'

'He's the King. He could order me to do it.'

'Ah, but would you like to?'

'I don't know.' She pouted, giving him the eye. 'It might be rather jolly.'

Forbes had become an expert in innuendo. He'd had plenty of practice at the yard, for George Crush had a dirty mind and had told Forbes tales of the royal family's goings-on that, if broadcast, would have had him arrested for treason. 'He's far too old for you,' Forbes said. 'The King, I mean.'

'Do you think age matters?' Sylvie said. 'I suppose it does to a man.'

'What about girls? Do you fancy a big fat old fellow lying on you?'

'What a thing to say!' said Sylvie.

'It's a genuine question, a serious line of enquiry.'

'I don't know if I fancy *anyone* lying on me. I'm not very big, you know.'

'Perhaps you'll get bigger.'

'I think I'm as big as I'm going to get.'

'I doubt it,' Forbes said. 'There's probably some stretching to be done yet. Girls often get bigger after they're married.'

'Babies swell them out.'

'Babies – or the making of babies.'

'I'm not sure I want to have babies.'

'Well, I'm not wildly keen on the idea myself.'

'I thought all men wanted sons to follow in their footsteps?'

'Not all men,' said Forbes. 'Trying to make babies might be more fun than having them, Sylvie. What do you think?'

'I don't know,' she said. 'Maybe,' and giggled.

They were drinking coffee in an alcove of the Imperial, tucked away from the visitors who streamed through the hotel's lounges. Glasgow had already filled up with foreigners, French and Italian, Dutch and English, and the string quartet among the palms had refreshed its repertoire with gentle, unmilitary pieces by Offenbach and Waldteufel as well as the inevitable 'Greensleeves'. Across West George Street, Kirby's had laid in extra supplies of lager beer, cognac and schnapps and, for those industrial and commercial gentlemen who had arrived in Glasgow without their loved ones, Mr Bolitho was offering short-term membership of the club upstairs at a very reasonable fee. Russians, though, were frowned upon; the members of the seventy-strong team imported to raise and man the exhibition's

'Russian Village' weren't interested in gambling, only in drinking everyone under the table and hauling off through the curtain anything that vaguely resembled a female, language, it seemed, being no barrier to international relations.

For this reason – the terrifying carnality of the Russians – Albert had more or less handed Sylvie over to his young friend Forbes, though Sylvie's perpetual wheedling and whining may have had something to do with it, plus the fact that Forbes was willing to pay for the privilege of her company, a guinea here, a fiver there, cash that Albert badly needed to support his current losing streak.

Forbes snipped at a wafer biscuit.

He said, 'Would you not like to try to make babies, Sylvie?'

'I do not know how it is done.'

'Liar!' Forbes said, grinning.

'I don't. I don't,' Sylvie protested, rising beautifully to the bait. 'It's not the same as it is with fishes and frogs, is it?'

'I don't know how it is with fishes and frogs,' Forbes told her. 'I've a better idea how it is with human beings.'

'Have you . . .' She was suddenly attentive, more adult. 'Have you – tried?'

'Now what do you think?'

'I don't . . . I think – you have, haven't you?'

Forbes popped the rest of the wafer into his mouth and wiped his lips with a napkin. Mimicking her seriousness, he leaned forward. 'It isn't making babies that's difficult, sweetheart, it's knowing how *not* to make babies that's important for people like you and me.'

'Like you and me?' She pounced on it at once. 'What do you mean?'

'People,' Forbes said, 'who are falling in love.'

Sylvie was surprised. She had not expected this manoeuvre, he realised, and congratulated himself on his impeccable sense of timing. She had laid herself open to seduction, at least on the verbal front, but he had introduced the word, the crucial, magical word 'love' into the conversation and had, it seemed, found the golden key. He softened his smile, warming and moulding it like wax.

'I'm sorry if I've offended you,' he said.

'Offended . . . Oh, my heavenly Lord, no.'

'I'm sorry if I've misjudged the situation then. I speak only as I feel, dearest; but that doesn't give me the right to put words into your mouth.'

'Forbes, I don't – I don't know what to say to you.'

He leaned across the brass-topped table, across coffee cups and china pot, spoons, jugs and sugar basin. He touched her lips with the tip of his forefinger as gently as if he were wiping away an infant's tears.

'Say nothing,' he whispered. 'Just let me look at you, remember you as you are now, so pretty that I feel as if my heart will stop.' He did not even have to compose the lines in his head; they seemed to flow from him as naturally as breath. 'I've known many – several – girls in my time, I admit, but, dearest Sylvie, I've never known any more attractive, more – dare I say it? – more desirable than you. You're such a good, trusting, innocent child that I flinch from expressing what I really feel for you.'

'What? What? What do you feel for me?'

'Love,' he said. 'Love like I've never felt for any other woman.'

'Not even your mama?'

He shook his head, irritated at her stupid interruption. He caught himself, said softly, 'It's a different kind of love, Sylvie, dearest. Real love, true love. I want to *be* with you.'

'You are with me.'

She was either a fool, he decided, or a subtle tease. He touched her mouth with his forefinger again, temporarily sealing in her inanities. 'With you, I mean. With you, my dearest darling sweetheart. *With* you.'

'On top of me?'

He sighed. 'Yes.'

'Like Mama and Dada do?'

'Yes.'

'But not to make babies?'

'No, not to make babies.'

'All right.'

'All right?'

'Hmm. Now all we have to agree on,' she said, 'is where and when.'

'Are you sure you know what we're — ah — agreeing *to*, dearest?'

'Of course,' little Sylvie Hartnell said. 'Don't you?'

Tom had shelled out two guineas for a pair of season tickets to the exhibition's Grand Concert Hall shortly before the season's programme was announced and a mad scramble for seats began. He suspected that by summer's end a feast of entertainment would be offered to lovers of bands and choirs and that the huge Venetian-style dome would ring to the sound of some very famous voices indeed. Meanwhile there were evening recitals on the electrically powered organ and a regular supply of parochial choirs seeking sufficient resonance to drown out squawking infants and the clump of feet from the exhibit gangways next door.

The Brunswick had already been engaged to perform on a Thursday night in late September and the Glasgow Massed Choir to repeat 'The Cameronian's Dream' on the first Saturday in October.

Autumn, however, seemed a long way off and Tom had purchased the season tickets for a purpose somewhat more devious than an urge to see what was going on under the gilded dome. It was, in effect, his first deliberate step in the courtship of Donald Franklin's daughter. He propped the tickets behind the clock on the shelf above the fireplace in his little parlour and admired them from time to time, rather smugly. Eventually he acquired a printed programme of events which, with a draughtsman's hand, he marked with tiny stars and circles and squares to separate possibilities from probabilities and the latter from racing certainties. The Sousa Ensemble was a racing certainty, a performance of the finest marching band in America, an event not to be missed.

Tom's letter of invitation to Miss Cissie Franklin took the liberty of emphasising that very point.

Cissie's reply to Mr Tom Calder made the point that if all she had heard of Sousa's band were true then she would probably be able to listen to it perfectly well just by opening the window of her bedroom but since it wasn't every day she received an invitation from a respected naval architect she would none the less be delighted to accept.

Mr Calder wrote back to Miss Franklin suggesting that they might partake of a light repast in the Royal Bungalow restaurant in the exhibition grounds before John Philip took the stage.

Miss Franklin wrote back to say: wonderful.

Consequently, at precisely six o'clock on a moist Friday evening, Mr Tom Calder, looking suitably American in a new hand-sewn seersucker suit, arrived in the hallway of the Franklins' mansion to be inspected by Lilias, teased by Pansy, warned to 'watch out' by Martin and, with Cissie hanging on his arm, was sent off into lightly falling rain under one of Mr Owen's gigantic Strathmore umbrellas.

Hot weather had left the air still and the smell of rain rose from dusty pavements and dusty trees. A rainbow haze stretched behind the minarets of the new Renaissance Art Gallery and above the disapproving presence of the university's Gothic tower were little slips and smears of azure that promised a return to fine, warm weather before the night was through. Cissie did not care about the weather. Cissie would have walked through fire, let alone flood, with Tom Calder. Although she hadn't seen him since they had parted at the railing above the Kelvingrove on the night of the musical evening, he had been constantly, comfortingly in her thoughts.

'Tom sends his regards,' Martin would now and then inform her on returning from Aydon Road; Tom had done nothing of the kind. 'He asked me to tell you that he misses you.'

'He did not.'

'He did, too,' Martin would assure her. 'Honest, cross my heart.'

'What else did he say?'

'That's all,' Martin would tell her. 'He's quite bashful, you know.'

'Tell him . . .'

'That you miss him too?'

'Just – just that I hope he's well.'

'He is well. He's thriving.'

'Tell him, Martin. Please.'

'I will, dear. I will.'

Tom held the umbrella over their heads and Cissie folded up the fancy little parasol that Pappy had purchased for her at the Japanese stall on the Main Avenue on the occasion of the family's initial tour of the 'Groveries earlier in the month. It had been hot that day, very hot. Pappy had bought all the ladies parasols and all the boys floppy cotton sun hats which, though they looked ridiculous, had kept them cool throughout the long afternoon. They had all been there, even her soon-to-be sister-in-law, Aurora, a great straggling trail of Franklins wending their way from exhibit to exhibit in blistering heat; all except Forbes who, to Cissie's relief, had gone into the Institute to work on a set of scale drawings for his diploma examination.

'Did you really miss me, Tom?' she asked.

'Who told you that I missed you?'

'Martin.'

'Ah, well, yes, it's true. I did.'

'Why did you not call upon me at the house?'

'It didn't seem – I mean, Cissie, my position is such . . .'

'Your position? Oh, Tom, don't be so stuffy.'

'Cissie, we can't just ignore the fact that I'm employed by your father,' Tom said. 'At least I can't.'

'Papa's not going to sack you just because you like me. For one thing, Pappy wouldn't let him.'

'No, it isn't just that,' Tom said.

'You mean you don't like me?'

'Of course I like you,' Tom said. 'I wouldn't be here with you now if I didn't like you.'

'Then,' said Cissie, hugging his arm, 'that's all that really matters.'

'I just feel that you don't know me very well.'

'Well, that's easily rectified,' said Cissie airily.

'Look,' Tom said, 'I don't want you to become too – too fond of me.'

'I see,' Cissie said. 'You're worried in case I paint you into a corner.'

'I wasn't thinking of you, of us,' Tom said. 'I was thinking of what your family will say if our friendship continues to flower.'

'What will my family say, O fount of all knowledge?'

'That I – that I'm . . .'

'After my money?' Cissie was undismayed by the line that the conversation had taken. 'Tom, Tom, my dear Mr Calder, don't you see that my family will be only too relieved to be rid of me? I'm the black sheep, the poor spinster daughter. They are terrified that they'll have me hanging around their necks for the rest of their lives.'

'Now, now, Cissie, surely you're exaggerating?'

'Yes,' she said. 'I am.'

He glanced down at her. In spite of the umbrella the rain had wetted her freckled cheeks. Her face looked glossy, not tearful but cheerful, and there was no mistaking the mischief in her eyes.

'Are you teasing me, young woman?' Tom asked.

'After a fashion, yes.'

'I'm not used to being teased.'

She pursed her lips and frowned slightly. 'Very well, sir: I will not tease. I will simply point out a fact that seems to have escaped your attention and that should allay any fears you have about my family's attitude towards you.'

'What fact is that?'

'Our meeting was engineered.'

'Ah!'

'We weren't flung together. We were brought together.'

'Ah-hah!'

'Ponder for a moment,' Cissie said, 'and you'll see that I'm right.'

'Yes,' Tom said. 'I believe you are.'

'Pappy thinks you're the man for me, and what my pappy says goes.'

'What do you think, Cissie?' Tom asked.

'I think,' Cissie answered, 'that my dear old pappy has the soundest judgement of any person I know.'

'Does that mean . . .'

'That you are the man for me? Of course it does,' said Cissie. 'There now, my dear Mr Calder, does that put your mind at rest?'

'No,' Tom said.

'No?'

'It means I've got to start taking you seriously.'

'Not too seriously, I hope.'

'No,' Tom said, 'not too seriously. Not just yet,' and, holding the brolly high, swept her through the gate of the 'Groveries into the ground of the Great Exhibition.

Thin grey cloud brought a prematurely early dusk. By nine o'clock the house on Brunswick Crescent was in shadow and, to Lindsay, seemed empty and sad.

Papa had somehow managed to obtain tickets for the Sousa concert and had taken Miss Runciman with him as a treat. Cook and Maddy had also gone to the exhibition but their tastes ran more to riding the water chute and the switchback. Lindsay had volunteered to stay at home to look after Nanny Cheadle who was too frail now to be left alone.

Nanny had been fed early. Lindsay had read to her until she had fallen asleep. She slept a great deal. Papa said that she would simply sleep her life away without pain or concern, for she knew that her time on earth was almost over and that she would soon have her reward in heaven. It was, Lindsay knew, no mawkish sentiment but a reflection of the crusty belief in God's mercy that sustained all die-hard Presbyterians. She didn't know what she believed in these days or what would sustain her when the end became the beginning, the beginning the end for, unlike Nanny Cheadle, she did not dwell secure in a knowledge of God.

She ate a cold supper in the dining-room, cleared the table and carried the dishes down to the kitchen. She looked in on Nanny once more, offered her tea, but the old woman was too drowsy to respond and, after lighting a wax night-light and placing it in a water-dish, Lindsay came downstairs again.

She was restless, loose-endish, agitated. She tried to study an article in *The Shipbuilder* but couldn't summon up concentration. She tried to lose herself in a novel but found that she had no interest in the fate of the fabricated characters. She closed the parlour door, tinkled listlessly on the piano, listened for Nanny, picked out another few bars of musical-hall melody, then, to her vast relief, heard the front doorbell ring. She went at once to open it.

'Forbes! What are you doing here?'

'I want a quiet word with you,' he said. 'You don't seem awfully pleased to see me. Aren't you going to let me in?'

'Of course.'

She stood back and allowed him to enter. She watched him take off his oilskin slicker and hang it and his cap upon the hallstand. His hair was damp and he had a slightly dishevelled look that suggested he had walked from Aydon Road or, though she could not imagine why, all the way from the Institute.

She said, 'Is it still raining?'

'No, it's stopped.' He glanced at the darkened staircase; Lindsay had not yet thought to put on the lights. 'Where is everyone?'

'They've gone to the exhibition.'

'What, all of them? Nanny too?'

'No, Nanny's too sick to go anywhere.'

He pointed at the ceiling. 'Is she upstairs?'

'Yes.'

'Breathing her last?'

'She's asleep, Forbes, that's all.'

He sauntered past Lindsay into the parlour.

'Can't last much longer, though, can she?' he said.

'Probably not.'

Lindsay reached for the electrical light switch but Forbes said, 'Leave it. Gloaming's more romantic, don't you think?'

'I'm not feeling terribly romantic to tell the truth,' Lindsay said. 'Do you want something to eat?'

'I thought you said the cook was out.'

'She is. I'll make you an omelette if you like. I'm not entirely useless.'

'I know you're not,' he said. 'So they're all out, are they? Well, well!'

Lindsay moved away. Circling the upright music-stand, avoiding the sofa, she perched on one of the hard chairs that flanked the fireplace.

The fire had been set but not lighted. The day had been stiflingly hot and the air in the parlour had a sour, bakehouse smell that the rain had not eliminated. The recesses of the room were in almost total darkness but the light in the window was strengthened by contrast and Forbes moved against it like a shadow-shape.

'I haven't seen you in days,' she said. 'Where have you been?'

'Busy,' he said. 'Very busy.'

'When are the diploma exams?'

'Too damned soon.'

'Are you not prepared?'

'As prepared as I'll ever be.'

She put her hands on her knees and rocked a little. She was embarrassed to be alone with him. She struggled to find something to say, anything to say: 'You won't fail, will you?'

'Of course I won't fail,' he said. 'And once I've got it, Linnet, I'm not going to hang around. I expect she'll be gone by then, your old Nanny, and those rooms upstairs will be vacant.'

'Forbes . . .'

'Talk to him. No, sod it, *don't* talk to him. *Tell* him. Tell him you want to marry me and can't wait any longer.'

'You're too young, Forbes. You're—'

'Christ!' he said.

She lost sight of him as he merged with the shapes in the room.

Then she felt his hands upon her. He caught her under the armpits, pulling taut the fabric of her tea-gown.

She gave a little cry as he lifted her, then yielded, sliding from the chair into his arms. He thrust his mouth down, licked her neck with a tongue that was as rough and as sleek as a cat's. He kissed her mouth. She felt the sudden thickness of his tongue, the fierce weird thickness of penetration. When he pulled away she pursued him, seeking that wet, writhing contact once more. She did not even enjoy it: she needed it. He swung her around him, both her feet off the floor. He kicked the piano bench. It toppled and fell. He pushed her against the piano. She felt the hard satinwood mouldings press on her buttocks and spine, crushing her summer garments. He pinned his forearm across her breasts and pushed his hand between her legs.

She groaned when the heel of his hand found her, cupping her so fiercely that even through three layers of clothing she felt as if he might tear that part from her. She tilted her hips. When he took his hand away and pressed his body against her skirts she wrapped her arms about his waist and pulled him closer, so smotheringly close that there seemed to be nothing between them. She was aware that his breathing had become shorter and sharper until it seemed to have within it an element almost of panic; then, as she sagged against him, spending, he released three or four sharp little cries, high-pitched and more feminine than her own. She clung to him, trembling, appalled at the alacrity with which it had come about, at its clumsiness.

It was not as she had imagined it would be. She felt weakened by her inability to refuse him his will. She tried to stand upright but her knees were like jelly and Forbes, gasping, held on to her, not tenderly or demandingly but simply for support.

After a moment or two he pushed himself away. Saying nothing, offering no apology, no explanation, no word of gratitude or affection, he turned his back on her and attended to himself.

'Forbes . . .'

He glanced over his shoulder, his face chalk white in the half darkness.

'You'd better do something about that mess,' he said.

Lindsay touched a hand to her dress.

'Yes,' she said, 'I'd better,' and hurried upstairs to change.

Her father looked up from his bacon and eggs. He had already demolished a full plate of porridge and several slices of hot buttered toast and, with the sun at his back, had a purring, contented air that Lindsay could only put down to the influence of John Philip Sousa bouncing through 'The Washington Post'.

She seated herself cautiously at the breakfast table. She had no pain, no actual discomfort, for nothing had been taken from her, but she felt leaden and listless and more than a little guilty at what had occurred last night.

'How was the concert?' she made herself enquire.

Miss Runciman, also purring a little, doled out porridge.

'A wonderful experience,' the woman said. 'Do you not agree?'

'I do. I do,' Arthur Franklin said. 'Quite stunning, in fact.'

'Scintillating, I believe, was the word you used last evening.'

'Was it? Yes, that's the word for it — scintillating.'

'Such precision,' said Miss Runciman, passing a plate to Lindsay. 'Such meticulous phrasing. I have never heard trombones like it.'

'And the timpani . . .'

'Certainly made my heart beat faster,' Miss Runciman said.

Arthur scooped up a forkful of crisply fried egg and put it into his mouth. He made a round eye, then said, 'How are *you*, Linnet? How was *your* evening? Did anyone call?'

'Call?'

'On the telephone?'

'No, no one called,' said Lindsay.

'You were in bed early, were you not?' said Miss Runciman.

'Well, Eleanor, we were rather late coming home,' Arthur put in. 'After eleven it must have been.'

'I heard you,' Lindsay said. 'I wasn't asleep.'

'Nanny no trouble?' said Arthur.

'None. She slept through — all evening, I mean.'

'She is not a well woman,' Miss Runciman said. 'I fear she—'

'Hush now,' Arthur said. 'Let's not hurry the poor soul away. She'll leave us in her own good time.'

'In God's good time,' said Miss Runciman.

'Quite!' said Arthur. 'Oh, by the way, Lindsay, guess who we saw in the concert hall last evening?'

'I can't.'

'Go on, have a pop at it.'

'Papa, I can't. Really.'

'Your cousin Cissie.'

'Oh?'

'In the company of Tom Calder, no less.'

'Together?' Lindsay said.

'Absolutely,' her father said. 'No question about it, is there, Eleanor?'

'None whatsoever,' Miss Runciman said. 'Behaving like love-birds they were. That, if you ask me, is a match in the making.'

'Nonsense!' Lindsay heard herself say. 'Tom isn't interested in Cissie.'

'Oh, yes, he is,' Arthur said. 'And if he isn't then he ought to be horse-whipped for leading the poor lass on.'

'Love-birds, what do you mean by "love-birds"?' Lindsay said, almost indignantly. 'Tom isn't the "love-bird" type.'

'How do you know?' said Eleanor Runciman.

'I – I just do.'

'Men change,' Miss Runciman said. 'Do they not, Mr Arthur?'

'Indeed, they do. "Take a Pair of Sparkling Eyes", and all that.'

'Cissie's eyes don't sparkle,' Lindsay said.

'Ah, but they do,' her father said. 'At least Tom Calder thinks they do.'

'What were they doing?' Lindsay said.

'Listening to the music,' her father said.

'And holding hands,' Miss Runciman added.

'In public?'

'Good Lord, Lindsay, what's got into you today?' said her father. 'Got out of the wrong side of the bed, did you?'

'She isn't for him,' Lindsay said. 'Cissie isn't right for Tom Calder.'

'That's not for you to say,' Miss Runciman reprimanded. 'After all there are those who might think that Forbes McCulloch isn't right for you.'

'Who?' Lindsay said. 'Come along, out with it – who?'

'Oh, please,' Arthur said. 'Don't squabble. It's a beautiful morning and we should all be glad to be alive and fit enough to enjoy it.'

'Do you think Forbes is wrong for me, Miss Runciman?'

'Not I,' Miss Runciman answered, emphatically.

'Papa?'

Arthur Franklin shrugged. 'Not for me to say, dearest, though I admit that Forbes isn't the sort of chap I'd have picked for you, given choice.'

'You don't have a choice.' Lindsay realised that she was behaving badly. She had ruined her father's breakfast and his bountiful mood, but guilt made her headstrong and she pushed on, angrily. 'Forbes is my choice. My choice, do you hear? What's more I do intend to marry him.'

'Well,' her father said placatingly, 'we'll see, we'll see.'

Lindsay threw down her napkin and got to her feet. 'We will not see. I will marry Forbes if I want to and there's nothing you can do to stop me.'

'That's true,' said Arthur, sighing.

'I'm tired of waiting. I intend to marry Forbes as soon as possible.'

'Where will you stay?' Miss Runciman said innocently.

'Here.'

'Perhaps Forbes – your young man,' Miss Runciman said, 'will not be so keen to share you and a house with us.'

'Yes, he will. It was his idea in the first place.'

'I might have known it,' Arthur said. 'I might have damned well known that he would find a way of getting his feet under my table.' He leaned an elbow on the tablecloth and crashed his cheek into his fist. 'There's no stopping them, is there. Like mother, like son.'

'What do you mean by that?' Lindsay demanded.

'He doesn't mean anything by it,' Miss Runciman said.

'Keep out of it, Eleanor, please,' Arthur Franklin said. 'This is a family affair now and doesn't concern you.'

'Pardon me, sir, but I think it does,' Miss Runciman said. 'I think you're going to need a cool head and an objective opinion in the very near future.'

'Do you?' said Arthur, suddenly more puzzled than annoyed. 'And what might that "objective opinion" be?'

'That you consider Lindsay's suggestion very, very carefully.'

'And then what do I do?'

'Accept it graciously,' Eleanor Runciman said.

Monday was incredibly hot. The torpedo-boat destroyer, the first of six ordered by Baron Yamamoto, Japan's Minister of Marine, was taking shape in the stocks. She was partly plated and her lines well defined but blistering temperatures inside the hull meant that work upon her had slowed to an unacceptable degree.

Mr Arthur had ordered butts brought down to the slip and had appointed several lads to relay canisters of fresh water up the ladders to help the platers and riveters survive, for the Clyde-siders – hard men, as tough as they come – were more used to coping with drenching rain and biting cold than a Mediterra-nean-style heat-wave. By midday several apprentices and one elderly ganger had collapsed with heat-prostration and the moulding loft had been transformed into a hospital where Hector Garrard, an ex-ship's doctor, applied cold packs, hot tea and Belladonna powders before deciding if the patient was fit to return to work or had better be sent home.

George Crush disapproved of Mr Arthur's mollycoddling approach. He regarded the heat-stroke victims as mere mal-ingerers and had spent the morning tramping up and down the planks, berating the foremen for condoning laziness. He would have invaded the loft too, to prod and poke at the prostrate forms on the stretchers there but he was afraid of Hector Garrard who had told him more than once that he would be fortunate to see fifty if he continued to let his temper play havoc with his blood pressure.

The drawing office wasn't much cooler than the yard in spite of wide-open windows and a couple of motor-driven fans that seemed to do nothing but stir the heat like broth in a pot. Pencils became slippery, pens recalcitrant. T-squares, compasses and scales accumulated sweat no matter how often they were wiped and two complex drawings of emergency steering equipment were so badly stained that they had to be scrapped. Nobody was comfortable, nobody happy; nobody, that is, except Tom Calder who seemed to thrive on shimmer and glare and who, on that particular Monday morning, would have crawled inside a Scotch boiler with a smile on his face.

Tom would have preferred to be sipping iced tea under a striped awning on the veranda of the Mackintosh Tea House, of course, or sampling a dish of lemon sorbet under the trees, or if push came to shove strolling the shady side of the piazza with his arm about Cissie Franklin's waist. Life was never quite perfect, however, and mere contemplation of such pleasures kept Tom from boiling up and boiling over like several of his managerial colleagues.

It was early afternoon before he abandoned his board and left the drawing office for a breath of air. He went downstairs into the lane that split the yard, turned right and headed for the snout of land at the corner of the slip around which, in nine weeks' time, the first of the Jap destroyers would slide smoothly into the river. He had rolled down his sleeves, put the stud back into his collar and tightened his tie. He did not, however, deem it necessary to wear his jacket, for, manager or not, he had no intention of melting just for the sake of dignity. He lit a cigarette and, between inhalations, hummed the opening bars of 'Under the Double Eagle' which, though not the most romantic of tunes, had connotations that Tom could not ignore.

He glanced up at the half-built torpedo-boat destroyer and waved cheerily to two half-naked platers who were hanging, gasping, over the stern.

They, rather startled, waved back.

Still singing to himself, still puffing on his cigarette, Tom moved towards the water's edge to catch a faint whiff of breeze and enjoy the luxury of a few minutes of privacy while he tried to fathom why he had been invited to spend a week of the July holiday at Mr Owen Franklin's country house in Perthshire. He had nothing to keep him in Glasgow but he knew that if he did accept and if Cissie were there too – which undoubtedly she would be – then he would be committing himself irrevocably, and that among the ranks of middle-class traditionalists she would become 'his Cissie' and he would be stamped as 'her man'. He was not dismayed at the prospect.

The river smelled of tidal mud and sewage, tarry, metallic and strong. He tossed away the cigarette, stretched his arms like a man holding up a barbell, and took in a contented breath. He had already decided that he would go to Strathmore and risk committing himself to Cissie. If Lindsay or Forbes McCulloch didn't like it – too damned bad.

'Calder. I say, Calder. Stop there, will you?'

George Crush came hopping down the ladder-way. He sported full managerial fig, brown wool three-piece suit, hard collar, even the tight brown bowler that left an angry red mark on his forehead on the rare occasions when he removed it. His moustache was glossy with perspiration, his complexion slightly more mottled than that of a cooked crab.

'What do you think you're doing, man?' George shouted.

In the clotted air of the afternoon his voice was as penetrating as a needle or a knife. Tom stopped, turned: 'Pardon?'

'Where do you think you're going – like that?'

'I'm out for a breather, George, that's all.'

'In that state?'

'What state?'

'Half naked.'

'Half what?'

'Where's your jacket? Where's your hat?'

'George, for heaven's sake, it's touching ninety degrees in the drawing office. God knows what it's like—'

'No excuses, no excuses.'

'Are you feeling all right, George?'

'This is how it starts,' the manager shouted. 'This is how it begins. First it's water for the men, then it's managers throwing off their clothes. Next thing you know we'll have 'Tallies selling ice-cream and bare-naked women waving palm fronds. I'm surprised at you, though, Tom. Fact, I'm disgusted.'

'George, are you sure you're all right?'

'I've seen it,' the manager went on. 'Oooow, I've seen it. I've seen governments overturned and blood flow in the streets for less.'

'What the devil are you going on about?' Tom asked.

The manic flicker of the eyes steadied. He stepped closer. Tom could feel heat radiating from him, smell the pungent odour of unhealthy sweat. He had often heard the little tyrant raving on before but never like this, never without a rationale. George snorted and poked a forefinger into Tom's breastbone.

'Hoy!' Tom stepped back.

George Crush followed him, pace for pace.

'Got your leg over, haven't you, Tom Calder? I've heard. I've been told. Aye, got your leg over, you cunning bastard. Butter won't melt in your mouth, aw naw, but it'll melt on her fanny, won't it? That's your plan, that's your strata— strata – stratagem. Get her on the bed and yourself on the board.'

'I don't know what you're talking about,' Tom said, though he had an inkling that it had something to do with Cissie and his equanimity had already been shaken by the manager's vehemence. 'Look, George, I think you should get out of the sun for a while. Come on, I'll take you up to the office and we'll ask Hector to take a look at you.'

'I'm not sick. You're the one who's sick, Calder.' For a split second his accusations seemed almost justified. 'Swanning about the 'Groveries arm-in-arm. Holding – Christ! – holding hands.'

'If you mean . . .'

'Could you not have taken her some place private?'

'George, whatever you may have heard, Miss Franklin and I are not—'

'Fat cow. Fat—'

'That's enough!'

'Forbes, my pal Forbes, keeps me a – abreast of the situation.'

'What situation?'

'It's the same old story, old as the hills. You'll step into the partnership and I never will.'

'I thought you said you wouldn't take a partnership in a gift. You told me it would be against your principles to desert the workers.'

'Just because I'm not in a position to stick her.'

'What did you say?'

'Because I can't stick it in her.' Crush manufactured a raspberry, a sound whose crassness shattered Tom's control completely. 'Because I can't give her the old pole. That's all they ever want from us, all they think we're good for, these people – the old pole, the old pig-sticker. Well, I wouldn't waste mine on that fat wee Franklin cow, not if you—'

It was hardly a fight, not even a scrap. The gallery that had gathered on the upper level of the hull were none the less impressed that a dour, long leek of a man like Mr Calder had enough savvy to throw a feint before bringing in the right hand; a neat clip, a short jab and finally an uppercut so perfectly timed that it caught Mr Crush right on the button and by God, wouldn't you know it, he went down like a half ton of bricks.

Surprised, impressed and delighted, the gallery cheered.

Tom was less surprised, less impressed and by no means delighted.

He caught George by the lapels as the manager swayed and, dipping his knees, dragged him forward and draped him over his shoulder.

George was no light weight and it took Tom a moment to settle the body with boots foremost and bowler to the rear and set off towards the moulding loft where that old sawbones, Hector Garrard, had set up shop. He felt nothing at first then, dimly, he heard cheering. They were cheering him from the rail. An odd little glow stole over him, a unfamiliar sensation that caused him to straighten his spine and, almost jauntily, step out in time to the Sousa march tune that still pumped away in his head. He hoisted George higher, grasped the broad buttocks with one arm, and raised the other hand not in triumph but in acknowledgement of a satisfaction shared.

Five minutes later he unloaded Crush on to a stretcher in the moulding loft and stood back to let Hector Garrard do his work.

The doctor knelt. 'What happened? Did he fall? Did he strike his head?'

'No,' Tom answered. 'We were just chatting when he suddenly became agitated and began shouting, then – then he fainted. I managed to catch him before he struck the ground.'

'That's all?'

'That's it,' Tom said. 'Is he dead?'

The doctor lifted a lifeless eyelid, felt for the carotid artery, examined poor George's tongue then, raising a bushy eyebrow, glanced up at Tom.

'Unfortunately,' he said, 'not.'

It was seven weeks before Manager Crush was considered fit to return to work. By that time summer had begun to fade, Baron Yamamoto's torpedo-boat destroyer was almost ready to be launched, the Great Exhibition had been declared a rousing success.

And Tom Calder and Cissie Franklin, after a brief courtship at Strathmore, had officially announced their engagement.

CHAPTER ELEVEN

The Launching Party

'Look,' Albert Hartnell said, 'you might say it's none of my business but it is, you know. I'm mean I'm her father, more or less, and if *I'm* not going to look out for her then who is?'

'Heck of a way you've looked out for her so far,' Forbes said.

'What's that supposed to mean?'

'Parading her in pubs and bars all over town.'

'She never minded it. She liked it.'

'Showing off her petticoats.'

'Oh, now! Come now!'

'Dancing on tables like a music-hall queen.'

'Did she tell you that?' Albert said.

'I know what you did to her, Bertie,' Forbes said. 'The only thing that surprises me is that she doesn't seem to hate you for it.'

'What I – what I did? And what's that, may I ask?'

'Corrupted her.'

Albert dipped his mouth to the beer tankard, drank, wiped his moustaches with his knuckle, then said, 'She didn't need much corrupting, boy, I can tell you. Took to showing off like a duck to water. Took to wrapping men around her finger too. Got that off her mother, I reckon.'

'Her mother?'

'Florence's sister.'

'I was under the impression that Florence's sister was a paragon of virtue.'

'Some paragon!' said Albert.

'Devout churchgoer, staunch Christian, that sort of thing?'

'All front, all face,' Albert said.

'You don't mean to say . . .'

'I do mean to say.'

'Good God!' Forbes said ruefully. 'Like mother, like daughter?'

'In a nutshell, my friend. In a nutshell.'

Albert finished the beer and glanced in the direction of the bar. The new football season had just kicked off and that, together with the attractions of the exhibition, had drained the club of customers. Dice and card tables were deserted and, apart from one listless young country girl, the sofas by the curtain too. Kirby's was peaceful, quiet and cool. Forbes could think of worse places to spend a Saturday afternoon but he wasn't yet prepared to forgive Albert for having telephoned him at Harper's Hill.

'Is that what you dragged me here to tell me?' Forbes said.

'I thought it was time we had a bit of a chat.'

'How did you get my telephone number?'

'Asked the exchange. Owen Franklin's house. Right?'

'How long have you known where I live?'

Albert tutted and shook his head. He was less cowed than Forbes would have liked him to be. He had something up his sleeve. Forbes had a notion what it might be and was not entirely unprepared to deal with it. He still smarted, though, at the recollection of Albert's voice coming at him through the earpiece of the instrument in the hallway of Pappy's house and the realisation that he could not keep the various pieces of his life separate much longer.

'Months,' Albert said. 'Months and months. Since the first.'

'The first what?'

'Since you first started making eyes at our Sylvie.' He glanced around at the bar again and made an ineffectual signal to the barmaid who seemed to have been struck deaf and blind.

'The first *what*, Bertie?'

Albert said, 'You may not have much of an opinion of me, Irish, but I'm not so careless as to let my daughter be wheeled away by a man I know nothing about, not even for an hour or two.'

Forbes drank a mouthful of black stout. 'Listen, Bertie, I haven't laid a glove on her.'

'I know. That's what she's complaining about.'

'*She's* complaining? Sylvie's complaining?'

'Loud and long.'

'Jesus!'

'She's besotted with you,' Albert stated. 'And I want to know what you're going to do about it.'

'Do about it?'

'Are your intentions honourable, or what?'

'If you mean am I going to marry her then the answer's no.'

'I didn't expect it to be otherwise,' Albert said, 'not when you're hooked up with a nice young lady, a nice *wealthy* young lady like Lindsay Franklin.'

'Who the hell told . . .'

Albert tapped the side of his nose with his forefinger. 'We knows, you know, Florence and me. Makes it our business to know these things.'

'Is that why you—'

'Trusted you?' Albert said. 'Of course it is. If you can't trust a chap who's practically engaged to one of the Franklins who can you trust? I mean, what would a nice, wealthy young lady like Miss Franklin say if she found out that you'd been squiring another girl to tea at the Imperial?'

'I'm not marrying Lindsay Franklin for her money,' Forbes blurted out. 'I don't need her money. Damn it, I have money enough of my—'

He bit off the boast, aghast at his own stupidity. He had

walked right into it. He blinked at Albert, waiting for the axe to fall, for the fatuous smile, the wink, the setting of terms. Panic possessed him, wave after wave in those few seconds when he realised that he had given himself away, then it receded, rushed away like water from a sluice and suddenly he felt very clear-headed.

'Bertie,' Forbes said, 'are we making a financial arrangement here?'

'You know,' said Albert, 'I do believe we are.'

The launching of any vessel, no matter how small, is fraught with the possibility of disaster. In the week preceding the arrival of the Japanese Naval Ambassador, Mr Tiroshumi Kimura, his wife, six of his children and several uniformed representatives of the Nipponese Empire, Donald Franklin became very anxious indeed. With two more TBDs under construction and three on the slate, Donald knew how important it was to impress the paymasters.

He also knew what sticklers the Japanese were for protocol and consulted by telephone two commercial shipping agents who gave him the low-down on the sort of ceremony that would appeal to foreigners and advised him to learn a few words of Japanese with which to greet his guests when they stepped off the overnight sleeper from London.

Lindsay had charge of arrangements for the formal luncheon. She plumped for fish, shellfish, pork and a variety of exotic trimmings, such as artichokes, quinces and green plums. She hired a chef and staff from the Barbary to serve lunch for fifty in the mould loft which, as it happened, was the only space big enough to accommodate such a large party.

Pappy Owen, wise fellow, had taken himself off to Strath-more. Without his steadying hand management meetings deteriorated into discussions about whether or not the christening bottle should contain wine, sake or holy water and whether or not the Reverend Brough would be prepared to bless a heathen craft. Mr Kimura solved this problem by indicating that the London party would include – his words – 'a parson' and that the Franklins need not worry about offending the gods of the river and the sea, which were just about the last things that Donald was worried about offending.

It was all Arthur could do to keep Donald from blowing a valve, particularly as the Japanese would be three days in Glasgow to tour the Great Exhibition and Donald didn't think that his ability to bow and scrape would stretch that far. It was all very well for Arthur, Donald declared: all Arthur had to worry about was greasing the standing way and sliding cradle and building the launching platform, tasks that could safely be delegated to the foremen, for, Japanese or not, a boat was a boat and the foremen had the procedure off pat.

According to Tom the acid test would come not with the launch but after the destroyer had been fitted out and armed. Baron Yamamoto had demanded a maximum speed of thirty knots and, Tom said, if Donald thought that the launch party would be difficult to please just wait until he encountered the squadron of Japanese officials who would turn out for the trials.

'Are you teasing my dear old papa, Tom?' Cissie asked.

'No, I'm perfectly serious.'

'Why is this boat so important?'

'Because the Japanese have money and are willing to spend it,' Tom said. 'There's a strong rumour going about that their government intends to invest two million in Britain's shipyards over the next five years.'

'Yen?' said Cissie.

'Pounds,' said Tom.

'I'll have to be nice to them then, I suppose?'

'That you will, dearest,' Tom told her. 'That you will.'

As it happened it was impossible not to be nice to the Japanese. Mr Kimura was a perfect gentleman and he, his wife and each of his six children spoke almost perfect English. He had been a naval attaché in Britain for the best part of ten years before his elevation to Naval Ambassador and had been resident in Dulwich for so long that all his children, even the littlest, behaved more like Westminster choristers than fierce sons of Nippon.

The sun managed to blink through moments before the Franklin brothers ushered the Japanese contingent up the short steep wooden steps to the canvas-draped platform where, hanging from scarlet cords, a bottle of Dom Ruinart champagne rubbed shoulders with a small porcelain flask containing some mysterious liquid that the 'parson' had brought along with him. All the Franklins were present, all save Mercy who was four months pregnant and had elected to stay at home. Below the platform workmen with mallets waited to knock away the dog-shores as soon as the ship had been blessed and Madam Kimura had done her bit with ribbons and draw-cords.

Across the bow of the *Hashitaka* hung an odd circular cloth cage of red and white stripes which, a moment after the bottles crumbled against the plate and the ship was released, ripped open to free eight white doves that fluttered away over the heads of the onlookers and circled around the destroyer as she went down the launching way; also a shower of flower petals that drifted like snowflakes over the heads and shoulders of the spectators, an unusual touch that Donald feared would rouse the shipwrights to raucous laughter. Not a bit of it: even the most hardened among them fell silent at the sight, as if they were just as superstitious as the foreigners and believed in a blessing of birds and flowers. The *Hashitaka* shuddered when her hull struck the water, then, with a dip and lift of her bows, she lunged bravely out into the river to be picked up by the tugs and steered away to Copeland's fitting-out basin a quarter of a mile away.

Cheering continued. Little Kimuras waved Union Jacks and Rising Suns, one in each hand in respectful equilibrium. Mr Kimura smiled and bowed to the uniforms present as if he, and he alone, had been responsible for seeing the new destroyer safely off to sea. Under cover of the canvas, Cissie sought for Tom

Calder's hand and gave it an affectionate squeeze while, just in front of his daughter, Donald let out his breath and leaning towards his brother murmured, 'Thank God that's over.'

'Hmm,' Arthur answered. 'One down and five to go.'

The party assembled in order of precedence and began to file towards the steps, Donald and Arthur bowing and deferring to their guests while in no formal order at all the Franklins and managers fell in behind.

The *Hashitaka* was still visible, still being manoeuvred into the deep channel by the skilful tugs. She looked well in the water, Lindsay thought, not large but spry and pugnacious even without her armaments. Lindsay paused to admire the Franklins' latest production and, at that moment, realised that she had lost Forbes. She glanced round, did not discover him at first, then, stepping back a pace or two, found him pressed against the corner of the platform rail. His hands were clasped on the woodwork, elbows raised up like chicken wings. He was staring down into the roped enclosure from which family and friends of the workforce were permitted to watch the proceedings. A hundred or so women and small children, done up in best bonnets and shawls, were still milling about, waving to husbands, fathers and sons now that the show was over and the great and the good had all but disappeared.

The girl, and the man too, were obvious. He, though not tall, had a bulky bearing enhanced by a high-crowned hat and fulsome moustache. Although the day was warm he wore a brown alpaca overcoat thrown open to show off an ornate waistcoat and heavy gold-plated watch-chain. He had the girl by the hand, hugged close to him. For an instant, Lindsay thought she was a child, then, looking more closely, realised that she was older than her daintiness suggested. She was extremely, almost excessively pretty in the pale pink, rosebud fashion that prevailed on Christmas cards and in gallery pictures of angels, delicate but so scrubbed that in her tight little plaid pelisse and matching tammy she appeared almost sinfully wholesome.

'Forbes?'

He spun round abruptly.

'Forbes, who are they?' Lindsay asked.

'Who?'

'The man and the girl?'

He did not look, did not glance downward. He gathered Lindsay with a hand on her upper arm and hastily steered her away from the rail; not quite hastily enough, however, to prevent Lindsay from noticing that the girl in the plaid pelisse raised one lace glove and with a gesture so tiny and coy that it seemed more infantile than childish, fluttered her fingers in Forbes's direction.

'I've no idea,' Forbes said.

'They seem to know you,' Lindsay said.

'I don't know what you're talking about.'

'The man and the pretty little girl, they seem to know who you are.'

'Well, damn it, I don't know them,' Forbes told her gruffly and, almost lifting her off her feet, steered her along the platform and down the steep wooden steps to the yard.

Miss Runciman brought her the news. She heard nothing of the muffled commotion on the staircase or in the hallway, whispered voices, the scuffle of her father's bedroom slippers as he hurried down to the telephone. By the time Miss Runciman wakened her, therefore, the inexorable ritual was already under way.

She heard someone breathing and, not alarmed, opened her eyes. The room was in half light, for hazy autumnal cloud had not yet burned off and the hour, Lindsay sensed, was early. Miss Runciman stood over her, big, mannish chin exaggerated by the angle. She was dressed not in brown but in black, the black pearl buttons that cinched the neck of her dress mirroring her solemn, shiny-black eyes. Lindsay knew at once what had happened.

'Is it Nanny?' she murmured.

'Yes, my dear,' Eleanor Runciman answered. 'I'm afraid she's gone.'

Lindsay was no longer drowsy but she had no inclination to slide out of bed, even to shift position. She lay on her back and thought – or tried to think – what it would be like not to have Nanny to look after her, though Nanny had not been Nanny for many months, many years. That she had survived so long had been a miracle, Papa said, not of willpower but of lassitude, as if at the end she had been too weary to let go. Now, last wispy breath released, she was gone, lying still and tranquil upstairs, a burden to no one.

'Who found her?' Lindsay said.

'I did, when I took her tea.'

'Has my father been to look at her?'

'Yes.' The housekeeper's voice lowered by half an octave, not sad but sonorous. 'He has sent for the doctor and the minister.'

'The minister?'

'Mr Mackenzie did ask to be informed.'

'What can the minister do for her now?' Lindsay asked.

'Nothing,' Miss Runciman said. 'He will say a prayer for our comfort.'

She put out a hand and would have stroked Lindsay's brow if Lindsay had permitted it. There was nothing possessive in the gesture, nothing harmful, but *she* wasn't Nanny and it was only Nanny's hand that Lindsay wanted, Nanny's hand to comfort her for Nanny's death. Anger welled up in her, a moist, crackling sort of anger at Eleanor Runciman's presumption. She thrust the housekeeper's arm away and bounced out of bed.

'I don't need his stupid prayers,' Lindsay declared. 'And I don't need you telling me how sorry you are. You hated her. Don't pretend.'

'Oh!'

Miss Runciman's lips remained fixed around the utterance. She turned and headed for the door while Lindsay, too selfish to recognise hurt, reached for her robe and slippers.

✻   ✻   ✻

'You must have been fond of the old bird,' Forbes said, 'to make such a song and dance about her popping off. I mean, she *was* old and it wasn't unexpected, and she didn't appear to suffer at the end.'

'I wish I'd been with her, though,' Lindsay said.

'You couldn't be with her all the time. She pegged out too long for her own good, if you ask me,' Forbes said. 'You're not feeling guilty, are you?'

'No, not guilty, no.'

'Nothing you could have done. She had a decent innings, really. You must admit that it was long past her time to go. I'm surprised at Runciman, though . . .'

'Miss Runciman.'

'. . . weeping like a fountain. Think she means it?'

'I think she does,' said Lindsay.

'Haven't noticed you blubbing much,' Forbes said. 'I suppose you were reconciled to it. Bit of a relief in a way, is it?'

'No, not a bit of relief, Forbes, no.'

'When will she be buried?'

'Tomorrow afternoon.'

'Where?'

'Brunswick Park New Cemetery, next to my mother.'

'Your mother?'

'My father purchased plots some years ago.'

'Sure and that's good management for you. Always looking ahead.' Forbes moved closer on the sofa. 'Will there be room down there for me?'

'I don't know,' Lindsay said. 'I haven't given it much thought.'

'Didn't she have any family that would take her?'

'Take her?'

'Dispose of – somewhere else she should be.'

'There's no one,' Lindsay said. 'No one I've ever heard of.'

'Is she worth anything?' Forbes said. 'If she's worth something then you can bet your bottom dollar relatives will come crawling out of the woodwork sooner or later.'

'There are no relatives. She had us, that seemed to be enough.'

'Where's the bo— where is she now? Upstairs?'

'Yes.'

'Have you been to see her?'

'Of course.'

'How did she look: peaceful?'

'If you want to go up . . .'

'No, no. I mean, Linnet, I hardly knew her.' He paused, then said, 'But I wouldn't mind taking a look at the rooms some time.'

'The rooms?'

'What we talked about, to see if they're suitable.'

'Suitable?' Lindsay said stupidly. 'Suitable for what?'

'For us, for moving in.'

'Oh God, Forbes!'

'It's not going to affect poor old Nanny now, is it? I mean, she's had her fling and we're still here with all of our lives ahead of us.' Forbes shifted against her, placed his hand upon her thigh and rubbed it up and down, gently, sensually. 'She wouldn't want to stand in your way. She'd be happy to see you living in her old rooms. See you happily married. Not having second thoughts, Linnet, are you?'

Lindsay hesitated. 'No.'

He moved his hand inward, not forcefully, tucking it into the folds of her mourning dress. 'The quicker we're spliced the better.'

'Forbes, don't,' Lindsay said.

'I'm only offering comfort.'

'No, you're not,' Lindsay said.

'What's wrong? Is it because of what's upstairs?' Forbes said. 'Well, you know the old saying: "In the midst of life we are in death"? Works the other way too, I reckon.'

'Forbes, please, don't,' Lindsay whispered.

✻   ✻   ✻

237

'Mama,' Sylvie said, quite out of the blue, 'have you ever been in love?'

'I am constantly possessed by love.'

'I don't mean God's love. I mean with a chap, a fellow.'

Florence stiffened but did not release her grip on Sylvie's hand nor break stride. Her heart, which had been light a moment before, turned leaden in her chest, however. She felt the mysterious muscles that attached her breasts to her ribs become as hard and inflexible as the whalebone that encased them. She tried to breathe naturally but the snort, the sniff that came up from below would not be checked.

'Hah!' she said; then again, 'Hah!'

'You must have been in love with Dada?' Sylvie said. 'If you hadn't been in love with him then he would not have married you.'

'Ha-ah!'

It was a fine clear night with a half moon hanging above the glow from the 'Groveries. Dumbarton Road and the delta of streets that spread out from the bottom of Byres Road were busy, for it was the witching hour when pubs released their clientele to mill and mingle with the honest, abstemious folk who had better things to do with their money than squander it on drink. Walking home from prayer meetings or, as now, from an uplifting lecture in the Baptist Hall in Purdon Street, Florence Hartnell was usually at her best.

'Did Dada court you for a long time?' Sylvie rattled on.

Florence gave no answer at first. She increased the length of her stride in direct ratio to the shallowness of her breathing. It wasn't the act of lying that bothered her so much as the quality of lie that would be necessary to appease her foster child.

'Why are you asking me these questions, Sylvie?' Florence tried not to allow the engine of admonition to overheat. 'Is a young man interested in you?'

'There might be.'

'Is it Mr Currie?'

'Mr Cu . . . Oh, Mr Currie?' Tinkling laughter, a palpation of silly Mama's hand. 'Mr Currie is not the sort of man who would be interested in someone like me. Mr Currie is only interested in getting back to his mission in . . .'

'Kituta,' said Florence, automatically.

'Kituta, yes, as soon as the war is over.'

'I thought,' said Florence, 'that he seemed interested in you.'

'I think,' said Sylvie, 'that Mr Currie might be more interested in little boys than little girls.'

'Who told you that?'

'Did you not see his lantern slides?'

'Yes, but those – that – that is just the nature of his mission.'

Florence was shocked that her daughter had voiced a doubt that had flitted across her mind too in the course of Mr Currie's illustrated lecture. She had cast the doubt from her, feigning an ignorance that was not true to her character.

'No, it isn't Mr Currie,' Sylvie said, laughing again.

'Who is it then?'

'It isn't anyone. I just wondered if you had ever been in love.'

Florence remembered some of the things Albert had done to her in the name of love and how reluctantly she – in the name of love – had surrendered to him before she had learned to turn the same robust and pleasurable acts against him so that he had no option but to take her as he found her and let her call the tune in that department of their relationship and, by slant and inference, in all others too. Bull by the horns now, Florence told herself, bull by the horns.

'Who is he, this young man of yours?'

The changed tone of Sylvie's laughter gave the game away: her little Sylvie had fallen in love. A strange, terrible pang clasped Florence in the unyielding region under her stays, a jab, a flutter, a breathless catch beneath the breastbone. She slowed her pace and let Sylvie's hand slip.

'There is no young man,' Sylvie said, dying to be pressed for the truth.

'Aye, miss, but there is,' Florence said. 'What's there about him that makes you so reluctant to tell me who he is? Is he of the Roman faith?'

'No, he isn't of the Roman faith.'

'Is he married?'

'No, he isn't married.'

'Hebrew?'

'Not a Jew either.'

'Who is he, Sylvie?'

'How do you know,' Sylvie said, 'that I haven't fallen for a black fellow?'

Florence's lungs collapsed as if she had received a body blow. She felt her heart thud and cramp. Gasping, she put her hand to her throat, and staggered.

'Wha' — what this you're telling me?'

Sylvie laughed and skipped. 'Oh, Mama,' she said. 'It's only my joke. There is no chap in my life. If there was he certainly would not be a black fellow.'

'Sylvie — Oh my dear Lord! Sylvie!'

She could feel muscles working against organs, a weird churning sensation that stretched from her brain to the pit of her stomach. She was relieved. And in her relief she doubted. And in her doubt she denied herself the pleasure of relief. Round and around and around and around.

'Mama, are you unwell?'

'I'm — I'm just a wee bit — a wee bit faint.'

'I gave you a fright. I'm sorry, Mama. I shouldn't give you frights.'

Florence righted herself. She made a pretence of arranging her frock, straightening her bonnet. She breathed from the middle of her chest to shake off dizziness, as if the dusty odours of Dumbarton Road might revive her like a whiff of sal volatile or a snifter of brandy.

'I-am-perfectly all right, Sylvie. Give-me-your hand.'

'Lean on me, Mama.'

'I do not have to lean on you,' Florence said. 'Walk properly, please.'

Men were slithering out of the public house ahead of them like rats from a butter barrel. Florence straightened her shoulders, let righteousness adjust the balance within her. She gripped Sylvie's hand firmly as they detoured from the pavement's edge out on to the cobbles of the back way that, via the alleyways where Sylvie and her dada had preyed, connected Dumbarton Road to Argyll Street and Portland Row.

The men watched, growled, lurched, traded obscenities as the scent of piety and sex, Florence and Sylvie, excited them, then they shouted, roared, whistled for attention. But Florence, feeling stronger by the minute, ignored the voices which, like evil deeds or bad memories, faded away behind her. She was herself again, quite herself, unshaken, unswerving and able to cope with any iniquity, in others if not in herself.

'Mama,' Sylvie said, once they were heading safely for Portland Row, 'Mama, please tell me, what is it like to be in love?'

And Florence, having no answer to give, stumbled and fell down dead.

CHAPTER TWELVE

A Lesson Ignored

Cissie volunteered to accompany him to Florence's funeral. Tom politely refused. He had already told her all the lies he intended to tell her about his marriage and his daughter. He felt rather mean about it, for he had supported Cissie at the funeral of the old woman, Miss Cheadle, whom he had hardly known at all. It was only a week to the day after Nanny's funeral when a note from Albert Hartnell informed him that Florence had died suddenly.

Tom had just returned to Queensview from choir practice when the courier turned up. He had read Albert's scribbled note in disbelief, had even asked the messenger, 'Are you sure?' before running out to find a hackney to take him to Portland Row to comfort his daughter and, if necessary, bring her back with him.

Florence's body, he discovered, had been transported to the Kelvinhaugh morgue where a police surgeon would perform an autopsy, standard procedure in cases of sudden death. Sylvie had been taken off to the police station and questioned before being escorted home to break the news to her foster father. By the time Tom reached Portland Row, therefore, Albert and Sylvie had had the best part of an hour to compose themselves and decide how they were going to face up to a future without Florence.

Albert was seated at the bare table in the kitchen, vest removed, shirt unbuttoned, fists clenched around a whisky glass.

Sylvie, too, seemed abnormally calm. She sat in the high chair munching a hot buttered tea-cake and dabbing her lips – not her eyes, Tom noted – with an embroidered handkerchief. She said not a word while Albert explained what had happened.

'Heart,' he concluded. 'Must have been her heart.'

'Had Florence complained of pains or breathlessness?' Tom asked.

'Not a peep out of her. If she was suffering,' Albert said, 'she never told us nothing about it. That was her way, of course. That was Florence for you. Now she's gone and left us.' He brought the whisky glass to his mouth, paused then said, 'Gone and left us to our own devices. Aye, Tom, I tell you, she'll be hard to replace.'

'Replace?'

'In my heart,' Albert said.

'How long will it be before the body is released?'

'Three or four days, so I'm told.'

Unlike her sister, Florence had always seemed robust. What age had she been? Only three or four years older than he was. He glanced at Sylvie. 'It must have been a terrible shock for you, dearest.'

'Hmm.' She nodded. 'Terrible.'

'Did you try to revive her?'

'She was dead,' Sylvie stated.

'What did you do?'

'Went back to find the men.'

'What men?'

'The men from the pub. They thought Mama was tipsy but when I told them we had been to a missionary lecture they changed their tune. One of them touched her and said she was a goner, then the policeman came and he took me to the station and gave me tea while Mama was removed.'

Her cool, precise manner appalled him. There was no numbness, no suggestion that she was not in complete control of herself.

'I think,' Sylvie said, 'that they had seen dead persons before.'

'She means the men,' Albert explained. 'The men from the pub.'

'She was happy, you know,' Sylvie said, matter-of-factly. 'We were chatting about Mr Currie when she fell down. She did not suffer.'

'Sylvie,' Tom said. 'Sylvie, you don't seem very . . .'

'Upset? Why should I be upset? Mama's with God now.'

'You see,' Albert said, 'Florence believed in redemption.'

'*He* doesn't believe,' Sylvie said, 'that's why he doesn't understand.'

She had alighted on his weakness, his lack of faith in a divine power, in a life hereafter. He was too practical a man by half. He needed proof, a pattern, a system that would explain everything that went on on the road to heaven and no book, no preacher been able to provide it.

Tom cleared his throat. 'What will you do now?'

'Do?' said Sylvie. 'I will say a prayer for Mama, of course, and—'

'I mean where will you go, where will you live?' Tom said. 'If you don't want to stay here you can come home with me. I'm sure we can find you a bed in the Queensview.'

Sylvie snorted. 'I'm not going with *you*.'

'She's going to stay here, aren't you, sweetheart?' Albert said. 'She's going to look after me and see that I'm all right.'

Tom was lost for words. Florence had once been his ally, had supported him across the bridge of doubt, had taken his daughter from him at a time when he thought that would solve everything. He needed her advice now, but she was no longer here to give it.

'We'll be all right, won't we, dearest?' Albert said.

'Yes, Dada. We will be fine.'

'In that case . . .' Tom got to his feet.

He had come with the intention of shouldering responsibility for the daughter he had once discarded but when it came down to it he really only wanted to shake off once and for all the emotional debts that had accumulated over the years. He had always felt more indebted to Florence than to Sylvie. He had never been able to engage with Dorothy's child, to forgive Sylvie for being Dorothy's legatee. He realised now that self-recrimination, the folly of fatherhood, had been his one besetting sin.

'Everyone will be at the funeral,' Sylvie said. 'All the folk from the church, officers from the Coral Strand. Mama, looking down, will be very proud of what she achieved with her time here with us.'

'Will there be room at the graveside for me?' Tom asked.

Sylvie said, 'Yes, Papa, we will make room for you.'

Tom stepped back, fumbling at the buttons of his overcoat. 'If there's anything I can do . . .' he said, lamely.

'Well, yes, there is, as a matter of fact,' said Albert.

'What's that?' said Tom.

'Funerals are expensive, Papa,' Sylvie said.

Twice in the space of ten seconds she had addressed him as 'Papa.' Under the circumstances it gave him no comfort. Sylvie wasn't asking for his love, only his money. Even so, he nodded.

'You may send the bills to me for payment.'

'All of them?'

'All of them,' Tom said, then turned on his heel and left.

Hundreds turned out for the service in the Mission Hall in Damaris Street. Relegated to the rear, Tom listened sceptically to the roll-call of his sister-in-law's virtues. Albert and Sylvie were in the front row, the girl in pure black velvet and, in spite of her tender age, half veiled. Mr Chappell, a Coral Strand representative from London, spoke eloquently about the Hartnells' contribution to the work of the foreign mission and, like a stage magician, produced a small wooden plaque which would be displayed on the wall in the Holborn offices to remind everyone of Florence's dedication.

It was all rather touching and so perfectly sincere that Tom's

eyes grew misty when the mission choir sang 'One Day the Lord
Will Walk on Every Coral Strand', and Sylvie, adhering to
Albert's arm, led the way up the aisle, out of the hall on to the
pavement where, amid a rabble of ragged urchins, a carriage and
plumed horses waited to carry Florence's coffin to the Auld Kirk
burial ground, near Merkland Quay; the same shabby graveyard
in which, a dozen years ago, Dorothy had been laid to rest and
which he, Tom, had hoped never to clap eyes on again. He
clambered into one of the horse-drawn charabancs that had been
laid on at his expense to carry the menfolk to the cemetery.

The last he saw of Sylvie was at the pavement's edge, a little
posy of forget-me-nots in one hand, a white handkerchief in the
other. She was flanked by women, some shawled, some hatted,
but as the procession rolled off down Damaris Street she looked
up in a manner just distracted enough to suggest that at last she
was missing the woman who had reared her and was moved to
search for her presence not in heaven but lingering here on earth.

'Where were you? I wanted you there. You promised you would
come.'

'I *did* come,' Forbes said. 'I *was* there.'

'Where?'

'In the close opposite.'

'The whole time?'

'The whole time.'

'What was I wearing?'

'Black, all black, and a hat with a half veil.'

'What was I carrying?'

'A bunch of flowers, small blue flowers.'

'What kind, what variety?'

'I don't know, do I?' Forbes said.

'You didn't go to the cemetery with the others?'

'No, I did not.'

'Why not?' Sylvie said.

'I didn't want to be seen.'

'I thought you might have offered me a kiss, or something.'

'I wanted to, honey, truly I did. But I didn't dare show myself.'

'Mama's not here now, Mama's gone, so it doesn't matter.'

'I'm afraid it matters more than ever,' Forbes said.

'Dada says you will look after me.'

'Does he?' Forbes said. 'Does he, indeed? Where is he, Sylvie? Has he gone out collecting on his own?'

'He doesn't want to go collecting any more.'

'I'll bet he doesn't,' Forbes said. 'He knows I'll take care of you.'

'Marry me?'

Forbes refrained from answering that question. 'Is he over at Kirby's?'

'I think he might be. He said you would take me home.'

'I will. Of course and I will. But not until you answer me one question.' He reached across the Imperial's brass-topped table and caught her hand. Through the suede gloves he could feel the delicate structure of her fingers. 'Why was Tom Calder at your mother's funeral?'

'Who?'

'Tom Calder, chief designer for Franklin Shipbuilders.'

'I really and truly don't—'

'Your name isn't Hartnell at all, is it?' Forbes said.

Another veil was attached to her hat tonight, not black but grey. She had escaped from full mourning already, from black to grey and dark green, shades that flattered her. He doubted if Lindsay had such an expensive range of clothing. Sylvie stared at him, eyes empty. If she had been a true artist, she would have squeezed out a tear or two to temper her eagerness. Perhaps she sensed that he and she were stamped from the same mould and painted the same colour, like little tin soldiers.

'I think you're Tom Calder's daughter.'

'What if I am?' Sylvie said.

'Why didn't you tell me? Did Bertie imagine there might be an advantage in keeping quiet?'

'I thought you might leave me if you knew who I was.'

'I'm not going to leave you,' Forbes said.

'Are you going to marry me?'

'It depends what you mean by "marry".'

'Become my husband. Make me your wife.'

'No, I'm not going to do that,' Forbes said.

'Because you don't love me?'

'Because I do love you,' Forbes said. 'I love you more than any other girl I've ever met and I'm going to go on loving you, come what may.'

It was enough, just enough, to give her pause.

She snuggled her hand into his and squinted at him from under the veil.

Then she said, 'You just want to take me to bed.'

'Yes, I do want to take you to bed.'

'I've never been with a man before.'

'I'm glad of that,' Forbes said.

'Have you been in bed with her?'

He did not have to ask who. Everything was moving in the right direction, though, and he felt his desire grow and expand: a strange sort of desire, not like his feelings for Lindsay, not calculating. The things he'd said to shock his cousins were coming home to roost at last, for in Sylvie Hartnell – Sylvie Calder – he recognised not just compliance but complicity.

'No,' he said.

'Don't you want to be in bed with her?'

'I want to be in bed with you.'

'She's the one you'll marry, though?' Sylvie said.

'Yes, she's the one I'll marry,' Forbes said. 'There you are, darling. I'm being straight with you. I'm not making false promises. The fact that you happen to be Tom Calder's daughter makes no real difference. If anything it just makes things more interesting.'

'Interesting?'

'Complicated,' Forbes said. 'I like things complicated, don't you?'

She was beginning to comprehend. She might have been fathered by Honest Tom but she had been raised by Bertie Hartnell. He had never met the woman whom Sylvie had called 'Mama' and could only guess how her influence had acted upon the wild inheritance that George Crush had told him about in lurid detail, how Tom Calder had had the horns put on him by his wife, Sylvie's mother, who had slept with half the men in Glasgow apparently before she had succumbed to a galloping consumption.

'Yes,' Sylvie answered, with just the trace of a lisp. 'Yes, I do.'

'Did your dada tell you why I'm going to marry Lindsay Franklin?'

'For the money?'

'Exactly.'

'I thought you had money of your own.'

'I do – but not enough.'

'Not enough to let her go and marry me instead?'

'Not nearly enough for that,' he said.

Forbes felt the lies thicken in his throat. The ease with which he lied to Lindsay failed him when he studied Sylvie's grey eyes, blonde ringlets and unblemished complexion. She did not have to seduce him. She did not even have to deceive him. She loved him. He knew that she loved him and that she would do anything he asked of her because of it. For an insane moment he was tempted to throw away his future, snatch Sylvie's hand and run off with her.

'No,' he said, sharply. 'No.'

'It is her money you want, isn't it, dearest? Not her?'

'I want you,' he said, not lying. 'Only you.'

'Then we will not speak of it again.'

'What?'

'Her.'

'Sylvie, I . . .'

'Dada says you may take me home.'

'To your house, do you mean?'

'Yes,' Sylvie said. 'To my house.'

'Will Bertie – will your dada be there?' Forbes asked.

And Sylvie answered, 'Not until we've done what it is we have to do.'

Lindsay was quiet all through dinner.

Arthur was concerned that Nanny's death had left a mark upon her, though her appetite did not seem affected and she ate with her usual gusto. Eleanor had been a brick. Cook too. Even Maddy had had sense enough not to go whistling and rattling about the house but to observe respect for the mourning atmosphere. He missed Nanny Cheadle but there was an element of relief in him too, for the house was undoubtedly more civilised now that the old woman had taken her leave.

It had been a strange end to summer, all fuss and bother, everything askew. He had not been able to enjoy the things that would normally have given him pleasure. He had lost enthusiasm for the choir's performances under the exhibition dome and had not, so he believed, sung as well as he was able to do. Even the Glasgow Choirs' rendering of 'The Cameronian's Dream' had lacked punch, though why the paleness of one male voice out of three hundred should make a difference Arthur was at a loss to explain.

The Japanese launching, the *Hashitaka's* imminent trials, Nanny's funeral, a procession of up-and-coming weddings, Lindsay's, perhaps, among them, and a programme of work that allowed no rest had resulted in moods of uncertainty that manifested themselves as anxiety about absolutely everything.

He went upstairs after dinner, not really to work but to ponder. He had been set a problem in the design of air supply to boiler-rooms and had no idea where to begin. He sat on the edge of the table with a pad on his lap and a pencil in his hand and waited for inspiration. He could not apply himself, though, could not bring his mind to bear on fan casings and deflectors, on cowls and foul weather shutters and was relieved when Lindsay entered the study.

'Am I disturbing you?'

He put the pad to one side. 'Not at all.'

He watched her warily, sensing her seriousness. Her mother had had the same sort of transparency, an inability to hide her feelings. It had been one of Margaret's more appealing qualities but in Lindsay directness was more challenging. She looked so pretty and mature in black, almost, he thought sadly, like a little widow herself.

'May I speak with you?' Lindsay said.

'Of course.'

'It's important.'

'I gathered that by your expression.'

'Forbes and I wish to marry.'

'That isn't exactly news,' Arthur said.

'To set a date,' Lindsay said.

'Before or after Martin's wedding?' Arthur said. 'Before or after Cissie and Tom Calder make their trip to the altar?'

'I'm serious, Papa.'

'I know you are.'

'We want to come and live here with you.'

'Forbes's idea?' Arthur asked.

'It's a sensible thing to do.'

'Practical, certainly,' Arthur said.

He had already considered the matter and knew that he would capitulate. If she had come in off the street with some beggar as a would-be husband his answer would have been exactly the same. He felt shrivelled inside, though, withered by the realisation that his safe, sad, comfortable existence was coming to an end, that he had fulfilled his dream, and Margaret's too, by successfully raising a child to adulthood.

She stood before him now with her hands on her hips like some little washerwoman. 'It need not be a large wedding, if that's what concerns you.'

'That isn't what concerns me,' Arthur said.

'Forbes doubts that his father will attend.'

'Kay will come, no doubt of that.'

'What do you have against your sister?'

'I honestly do not know.'

'Can't you forgive and forget, Papa?'

The question was too raw. He still could not answer it without heat. At all costs he must avoid a squabble that could escalate into bitterness. He had been through that already with the self-same sister, with Kay. There was no drama in their feud, only a vain need to prove that she was right, he wrong, without ever defining what had been at stake in the first place.

'It's the upper floor you want, isn't it?' he said.

'And the ground-floor drawing-room.'

'What will happen to Miss Runciman?'

'Nothing,' Lindsay said. 'She will remain where she is.'

'And look after us all?'

'Oh, I see,' said Lindsay. 'You want us to pay for another servant.'

Arthur hesitated. He was tempted to explain that the cost of change meant nothing to him. He had a queasy feeling, however, that Lindsay had already been tainted by the mercenary Irishman and he was determined not to let them off entirely scot-free.

He said, 'If Eleanor thinks another servant is necessary, yes.'

'That will be satisfactory.'

She spoke with a coldness that he had never detected in her before; a first glimpse of how she would be changed, perhaps? He felt the heart go out of him, felt it shrivel like the last orange in the dish.

'You aren't short of money,' Arthur said. 'Your income—'

'We will pay rental too, never fear.'

'Why do you want to stay here?'

'To look after you,' Lindsay said.

'I do not need looking after.'

'In time, perhaps you will.'

'Oh!' Arthur said. 'I was under the impression that this was to be a temporary arrangement.'

'Are you trying to prevent me from marrying Forbes?'

'Of course not, not if you're sure that he really is the man for you.'

'He is. He is.'

'Very well.' He managed not to sigh. 'Let me talk this over with Forbes. Then we'll inspect the rooms upstairs and see what alterations are required. When that's in hand you may, if you wish, set a date for the wedding.'

'How long will it all take?'

'Not long,' Arthur said.

He knew what his daughter's haste implied: that she was unsure of the untrustworthy longings that she could not inter- pret or excuse, desires that a well-brought-up young woman could satisfy only with a husband.

'When can the work be started?' Lindsay asked.

'As soon as you — you and Forbes — agree on what you want by way of alterations,' Arthur said and then, because he was still her father, added, 'Where is he, by the way? I thought he was coming round for dinner?'

'He told me he was,' Lindsay said. 'We agreed that we would talk to you together.'

'I see,' Arthur said. 'Perhaps he just didn't feel up to it.'

'What do you mean by that?'

'Nothing, dearest, nothing, nothing.'

'Forbes isn't afraid of you, you know.'

'I'm well aware of that,' Arthur said.

'He may turn up yet,' Lindsay said.

'If, however, he doesn't appear,' Arthur said, 'you may tell him that everything's settled.'

'Is everything settled?'

'Everything,' Arthur said, 'except a date.'

'Would January be too soon?'

'No,' Arthur said, gravely, 'January would be just about right.'

It was his first experience of forbidden things. No matter how long he lived Forbes knew there would never be another experience to match it: curiosity could not be satisfied twice. It seemed fitting that it would take place in the apartment in Portland Row where the presence of Sylvie's mama lingered like a whiff of carbolic. From the moment the outer door closed behind them and Forbes realised that Bertie had sanctioned what was about to happen, he felt complete and coherent, no longer patched together.

Sylvie lit the gas jet and removed her hat. She moved quickly. She tossed her hat on to the table and began to unbutton her coat. They had not exchanged a word since they had entered the close. There was nothing left to say, nothing left to negotiate. He did not know what she thought of him, what she wanted from him. He wondered just what he did mean to her, if he really was more than the avatar of her arousal, a means to an end.

The gas jet flared and smoked. The smell layering the soap-smell was as harsh as the roar of the jet itself. Sylvie struggled with her coat. Blonde ringlets framed her face, bobbed on her brow.

Forbes stepped forward, not to help but to trap her. He caught the coat sleeves and knotted them in his fist, pinning her arms behind her. He kissed her. He put his mouth down and let the kiss alight upon her lips. He felt her lips part just enough to allow him her tongue, moist, without taste. He placed his hand on her breast, encased in the grey dress and mysterious under-garments. Then, ashamed of his haste, he released her, let her slip out of the overcoat and toss it too on to the tabletop.

'Do you want me to take my clothes off?' Sylvie asked.

'Yes.'

'Do you want to go into my bedroom?'

'If you want to.'

'I will bring a light.'

He remembered the promise she had made to him months ago, how bold her words had seemed, how knowing. She did not seem knowing now, though. She spoke in a whisper, like a bewildered child. That there would be light in the bedroom, a gas jet, did not matter. Sylvie had her own means of compelling desire and of satisfying the wicked fantasies that had chased her out of childhood. By the light of a flaring taper and a stout candle in a brass holder she led him by the hand through the hallway into the bedroom.

She blew out the taper and set it and the candle-holder down upon the edge of the iron guard. Above the fireplace the hunchbacked shadows of bookends flickered on the wallpaper. In the wedge of candlelight Sylvie's throat, face and hair were underlit like that of a painted angel. He no longer burned with a fierce need to grasp and impress. Caught in the aura of her prettiness he was, for a moment, helpless.

'Do you want me undressed?' she said.

'Yes, I do.'

'Do you want to watch me?'

He nodded.

'Do you want to love me, Forbes?'

He nodded again, dumbly.

The dress was cumbersome. He did not offer to help. He could not have helped even if he had wished to do so; Sylvie was intent upon herself. Every hitch, every delay took him further out of himself too. He was fascinated by Sylvie's mouth, her hair, her slender bare arms, her wide grey guileless eyes. He had no thought of others now, of Lindsay, of Cissie, no recollection of the girls after whom he had lusted and upon whom, in his ignorance, he had tried to foist himself. In that moment Sylvie became unique and irreplaceable and he knew that he would never tire of her.

The unbound corset, the rustling silk petticoats with lacy frills, the awkward arrangement of suspenders, the expert manipulations of her small fingers: he watched her clothing slip away. She undressed unself-consciously, not preening, not posing, arms and shoulders, breast and thighs glimpsed in the shadows, in the candlelight. She seated herself on the side of the bed and removed her boots then peeled her stockings over her knees and calves, leaving nothing to cover her but the woven silk ceinture. She turned away from him, tilted a shoulder, twisted her body and brought the garment away in her hands like a carapace. She dropped it into the darkness by the bed and turned again.

Facing him now she put her arms out by her sides, pressed her fingers into the quilt, gave her head a gentle toss and smiled.

He inched towards her, a half pace to the side to remove his shadow from the smudgy shadows that cloaked her belly and her thighs. Her breasts were small-nippled, pale and contrite, her waist narrow. Her belly, rounding out from her hip-bones and dipping down into her lap, was silky soft and the hair, darkened, more unruly and profuse than he would have imagined.

He was still fully dressed. He wore no hat, no overcoat, but even so he felt coarse and ugly in his tweeds. He stepped closer and clumsily touched her knees.

'Lie back,' he said.

She lay back across the bed and though he hadn't dared ask it of her, opened her legs in a gesture that was both lewd and beautiful. She lifted her feet, placed them on the quilt and raised her hips.

'Do you like me?' she enquired.

'Yes. Yes, I do,' Forbes whispered.

'Show me,' she said.

He stood helplessly before her, staring down. He was unable to believe what was happening to him, unable to relate his gnarled fantasies to this small individual who had already given him more than he had demanded and who, he felt certain, would give even more before she was done with him.

'Show me, Forbes, show me,' she hissed.

He put his hands to his trouser buttons then, overcome, knelt before her. He kissed her knees, her thighs, her stomach and breasts while little Sylvie Hartnell, roused by his adoration, gasped and sighed and grappled to bring him into her, to make him part of herself.

CHAPTER THIRTEEN

The Winter Rains

The fixing of a wedding date, the purchase of an engagement ring, the family celebration, oddly sober and unmusical, that followed the official announcement, together with Forbes's obsession with 'getting the house just right' left Lindsay rather out in the cold. She saw little of Forbes in the autumn months and even when they were together they were seldom alone. Matrimonial rituals, it appeared, were not designed to bring a happy couple closer together but to drive them, at least temporarily, apart.

The house rang with the thud of mallets, the rasp of saws and a shrill and constant whistling without which, it seemed, carpenters and joiners could not properly function. Eleanor Runciman retreated to the basement kitchen. Even there she could not avoid the interminable racket and knew that weeks of disturbance lay ahead, for Forbes had told her that woodworkers would be followed by plumbers, plumbers by plasterers and plasterers by painters and decorators, all culled from Franklin's employment roster.

Donald had been less than delighted by this appropriation of part of the labour force. He had pointed out that Martin had paid out of his own pocket for work done on Rosemarket House, where Aurora and he would set up home, and had suggested that Forbes should do the same. An argument ensued between the brothers, and Arthur – who actually agreed with Donald but felt obliged to defend his soon-to-be son-in-law – was drawn into a quarrel that only Pappy's intervention prevented from becoming a feud. He, Pappy, footed the bill for labour and materials and, to be even-handed, offered to do the same for Tom and Cissie in their newly acquired apartment in Sandyford Avenue, an offer that Tom politely but firmly refused.

Domestic matters did not distract the Franklins from turning profit on their current contracts, in meeting delivery dates and conducting trials to the satisfaction of their several clients, including Mr Kimura, who turned out to be an even worse sailor than Martin and had to be ferried off the *Hashitaka* before she had covered a sea mile out into the Gareloch. There was another launching almost identical to the first except that the little Kimuras did not put in an appearance and the weather was at its worst, a day of blinding grey rain driven by a strong south-westerly. Lunch afterwards was a damp affair and that evening, for no obvious reason, Lindsay had a fit of panic about her wedding and wept into Eleanor Runciman's broad, boned bosom.

No panic for Martin and Aurora Swann. They were married in style in St James's Church in Aurora's home parish and everyone who was anyone in the shipping trades received an invitation to the service and to the reception in the Congleton Halls thereafter. The Swanns, it seemed, were intent on setting a benchmark for grandeur and expense that the Franklins would be hard pushed to top. Tom and Cissie were quite prepared to settle for a quiet wedding in St Anne's but Lilias wouldn't hear of it and immediately swung herself on to a new heading, trading dressmakers for caterers and nagging Donald almost nightly to allow her to expand the guest list and increase the budget.

The Calders' recently purchased apartment in Sandyford Avenue was swiftly taking shape. Electrical wiring was installed for lighting, the old lead gas pipes were replaced and Tom personally tackled the erection of shelves in kitchen, bathroom and the servants' pantry, and made a jolly good job of it too.

In Harper's Hill, with Martin and Mercy gone and Cissie soon to follow, the mansion had already begun to seem empty and Lilias had taken to dogging her three remaining children about the place as if to make sure that they too had not flown the coop or, like Cissie, were not about to be spirited away by some stranger and leave her to stare vacantly at Donald down the length of the dining-table night after night.

In contrast Arthur and his housekeeper would have been only too pleased to have an opportunity to stare vacantly at each other over the soup bowls. The house in Brunswick Crescent had been turned into a Bedlam and even after the workmen had left for the day there would be Forbes McCulloch to contend with, Forbes stalking about with renovation plans tucked under his arm, a pencil behind his ear, Forbes pointing to this, kicking at that, complaining loud and long about shoddy workmanship or that some minor detail had been overlooked in the fulfilment of his grand design.

'Have you been up there recently, Eleanor?'

'Yes, Mr Arthur, I have.'

'How many rooms do you make it?'

'Six, I believe.'

'Hmm, that's what I counted, too. Six, plus the downstairs drawing-room. Dear God, I didn't realise we had so much unused space in the house.'

'Knocking down head walls and inserting steel beams does appear to be having the desired effect. Did you not approve the plans, sir?'

'Plans, what plans? The little beggar keeps amending them every time I turn my back. I don't know what he thinks he's building; a damned transatlantic liner has less bunk space, for heaven's sake.'

'Have you had a word with him?' Eleanor asked.

'A word with him? How can I have a word with him when I

can't be sure what he's up to from one day to the next or, for that matter, even *find* him half the time when he's crawling about among the sawdust and shavings under what used to be my roof. I pale to think what it will be like when the painters arrive.'

'Please,' Eleanor said, 'don't.'

'Well,' Arthur sighed, 'it can only get worse before it gets better.'

'*Will* it get better, do you think?' Eleanor asked.

'You know,' her master answered, 'I'm beginning to have my doubts.'

Lindsay caught him as he strode down the hall with his overcoat slung over his shoulder and his hat in his hand. 'Forbes, where are you going?'

'I have work to do at home.'

At least he had the decency to pause and, hand upon the door handle, let her catch up with him. 'Work? What sort of work?' Lindsay said. 'Haven't you done enough for one day?'

'It's business,' Forbes said. 'The Admiralty tender.'

'What Admiralty tender?'

'We're on for a new type of torpedo-boat and Donald is very concerned that we get our figures right first time.'

'First I've heard of it.'

'Donald's playing it close to the chest.'

'So close it hasn't even come up in management meetings?'

'It will, it will, quite soon I expect.'

Lindsay moved closer but did not touch him. He did not take his hand from the door handle. 'I thought you were staying for supper?'

'I can't, honey. Truly.' He smiled indulgently. 'You see how it is?'

'No, I don't, Forbes. All I see is the back of you these days.'

'Not for much longer, I promise.'

'Why are you doing this?'

'Doing what, Linnet?'

'Ignoring me.'

'Oh, now, I'm not ignoring you. Everything I do is for the both of us.'

'Does that include borrowing money from me?'

'I thought I'd explained that,' Forbes said, not quite crossly. 'It's only until I get my hands on what I'm owed. Won't be long now, Linnet. By the way, you haven't told your father, have you?'

'Of course not. He'd be furious if he thought I was lending you money.'

'He's just too old-fashioned to understand how things are.'

'I'm not sure *I* understand how things are.'

'Sharing. What's yours is mine, and vice versa,' Forbes said. 'If you really don't trust me to pay you back . . .'

'It isn't that.'

'What is it?'

'I just – I don't know,' Lindsay said. 'I just never see you these days, to be alone with you, that's all.'

'You'll be alone with me soon enough, honey, all snug in our nice new suite of rooms, just you and me and no one else. I'm doing it for you, Lindsay. I mean, I don't care if I live in a garret. But that isn't what I want for you. I only want the best for you.' He released the door handle and adjusted the roll of papers under his arm. He remained encumbered with coat and hat, though, and his caress was awkward. 'Look, I'm sorry. Here, give me a kiss and a cuddle, will you, please?'

Obediently she put an arm about him and kissed him on the mouth. She could sense his urgency but his lips were warm and he let the kiss linger just long enough to appease her. She was the one who drew away.

'There now,' he said, 'wasn't that nice?'

'Yes,' Lindsay agreed, 'it was.'

'Now,' he tugged open the door, 'I really must toddle.'

'Forbes,' Lindsay said, 'why do we need six rooms?'

When he grinned she remembered why she had fallen in love with him.

'For the little 'uns,' he told her.

'Little 'uns?'

'Our children, silly,' Forbes said, then, cramming his hat on to his head, hurried down the steps into Brunswick Crescent and, in a moment, was gone.

St Mungo's Mansions were far from the river, almost on the city boundary, in fact. East of the tall, sharp-cornered building with its chip-carved frontage was a sprawl of less salubrious tenements occupied by workers from the locomotive repair shops. To the west, however, beyond the thin, metallic strip of the old sugar canal, lay a vista of rolling green hills and distant mountains that Forbes hoped would give the girl pleasure and bring a breezy touch of colour to her pale cheeks.

He had selected the property with care and forethought. The building was less than ten years old, well tended and solidly constructed. Its rear entrance was discreetly screened by trees so that he could come and go as he pleased without being too obvious about it. There were churches, mission halls and public houses within walking distance and at least three music-halls no more than a halfpenny tram ride away. The opening of the new electrical tram-line had clinched it: he could travel from the city centre in a matter of twenty minutes and, with one change of car, be home in Brunswick Park in half an hour. The rent was considerably less than he would have paid for a third-floor West End apartment and, best of all, the place came fully furnished, right down to bed linen.

He opened the door with a latchkey and ushered Sylvie inside.

The hallway was papered in heavy plum-coloured wallpaper. A potted plant in an enamel bowl occupied a blank corner. There was a huge coat rack with a mirror in the centre, a grandfather clock and other bits and pieces of bric-à-brac, none tawdry. The kitchen to the rear was bright and airy, parlour and dining-room even more so. There were three bedrooms with brass bedsteads, horsehair mattresses, clean sheets, quilts and spreads.

Forbes put his hand upon her waist and showed her round. He could sense her apprehension like a kind of vibration but reckoned that he had done well by her and that once she got used to it she would be happy here. He steered her into the parlour and let her test the armchairs and the sofa. She did not bounce upon them, did not squeak or squeal. Her sweet little face was puckered with concentration as if she were trying on a new dress or a new pair of shoes.

At length, Forbes said, 'Do you like it, sweetheart?'

'Has Dada seen it yet?'

'He came last night, I believe. Didn't he tell you?'

'I haven't seen him since yesterday morning. I was asleep before he arrived home last night. I think he had been drinking again. He misses Mama so much, you know.'

'A blow for him, yes, a terrible blow,' Forbes said. 'It'll do him no harm to get out of your old house into somewhere new, somewhere like this.'

'Will you stay with me?'

'What?' said Forbes. 'Now?'

'Stay here with me?'

'Sure and I will,' Forbes said. 'Whenever I can.'

'Will you be here when I come to stay?'

'When you move in, you mean?' Forbes said. 'I will do my very, very best to be here to welcome you. If I'm not, though, I'll come just as soon as I can.'

'Dada says you're going to look after us.'

Forbes waved his hand, shaping a circle in the air. 'Is this not looking after you, sweetheart?'

'Care for me.'

'Care for you? God, Sylvie, don't you know I love you?'

'And I love you.'

He experienced a tremor of annoyance at the wan, matter-of-fact manner in which she accepted what was being given her. Had Bertie not told her what this place was costing every month? Did she not realise that a girl in her position could hardly expect to do better, that there were thousands of young women who would have been overjoyed to be brought to live in a brand-new, well-furnished apartment, thousands of young women who would have been delighted to have him for a lover on any sort of terms? Irritation brought a surge of sexual longing in its wake.

All he had to do was look at her, not listen, just look at the colour of her eyes, the curve of her lips, her satin skin. How many other girls could claim that they were desired with such unreasonable intensity? On impulse he kissed her and inserted his tongue into her mouth. He fumbled at his trousers, released himself, let her see how urgently he needed her attentions. He was not obliged to pay homage to her refined sensibilities; unlike Cissie, unlike Lindsay, she carried no weight of prudence or, he had discovered, of modesty.

She would do anything he wished her to do.

Provided he loved her.

Holding her against him, rocking against her, he said, 'Now look, I have to know, dearest. Is this it? Is this the place for you? If it's not . . .'

'What? You'll find another?' Sylvie said. 'Ah-hah, ah-hah.' She wagged a finger in his face. 'You will never find another like me, though, will you?'

'That's true.'

'Will you, Forbes?'

'No, damn it. Never,' he told her. '*Do* you like it here?'

'Ye-eees.'

'Will you be happy?'

'Will *I* make *you* happy?'

'Sylvie, please answer me. Will you be happy here?'

'Perfectly so,' she said, then, still dressed in coat and bonnet and wearing her grey suede gloves, she knelt before him like a slave.

Albert opened the door. Bleary-eyed, haggard and unshaven, he was clad in a nightshirt, bedsocks and a greasy old overcoat in lieu of a dressing-gown. He looked, Tom thought, absolutely terrible. He managed a smile, though, and signalled Tom to follow him into the kitchen.

To Tom's dismay he found that the room had been stripped of every stick of furniture. God knows, it had been bleak enough in Florence's day but now, with even the linoleum peeled away, it was nothing but rough floorboards and bare walls. Albert ate soup not from a bowl at the table — there was no table — but directly from a blackened pot upon the side of the stove. A crust of bread and a bottle of milk stout made up the elements of his supper.

'Can't offer you much, old son,' Albert said. 'Share my stout with you if you like.'

'So it's true,' Tom said. 'She has gone.'

'Ah, yes. You got the letter. She said she would write to you before she departed but I wasn't certain she would do it. You know what she's like, a wee darlin' most of the time but with a mind of her own when it suits her.'

'I received the letter this morning,' Tom said. 'I came as soon as I could. I didn't expect her to be gone already.'

'Got the offer. Took the chance.'

'Abandoned you?'

'Oh, no, no. I urged her, I pressed her to go.'

'When did she leave?'

'Yesterday forenoon. I took her to the railway station myself.' Albert rested one foot on the guard rail of the stove and dipped a spoon into the broth pot. 'Shed a tear too, I may tell you, to see her going off like that, all on her own, clutching her little bag. Florence . . .' He swallowed, wiped his moustache with a knuckle. 'Florence — ah, well, you know how it is, Tom, you know how it is to lose a wife when you least expect it.'

Tom looked around for somewhere to sit and finally propped himself against the sink. He glanced round, frowning; even Florence's scrubbing brushes were gone.

'What happened to everything?' he said.

'Sold.'

'All of it?'

'Except for some of the clothes. I kept some of the clothes.'

'Are things that desperate, Albert?'

'Not desperate, no. I just wanted rid of the stuff. I wasn't going to give it away, was I? Florence would have turned in her grave, bless her, if I'd just given it away. Sold it down Paddy's market. Price' — he shrugged — 'reasonable.'

'What about Sylvie's wardrobe?'

'Sold it too. Furniture fetches.'

'I mean her dresses, her shoes,' Tom said.

'She took them with her.'

'All of them?'

'I got some to post off later.'

'Why didn't you tell me what was happening?' Tom said. 'If you needed money for her railway train fare or her lodging then I—'

'You've done enough,' Albert said. 'More than enough.' He paused. 'Besides, you'll be needing all your hard-earned once you've got a wife to support and a house to look after.'

He ate soup noisily, his back to Tom.

Tom said, 'I suppose Sylvie spotted the engagement announcement in the *Glasgow Herald*?'

'I expect that's it,' Albert said.

Tom said, 'Is that why she accepted the post with the Coral Strand?'

'Uh?'

'Was she offended because I intend to marry again?'

'She didn't say much about that,' Albert said. 'She misses her mama. She wants to do right by her mama. When the position in London was offered, she jumped at it. She always had it in mind to work for the Mission, you know. I was never all that for it, but her mama was. Her mama would have done anything for the Coral Strand. Now, God rest her, she has given up her daughter to God's cause.'

'So my engagement to Miss Franklin . . .'

'She isn't bitter, Sylvie. She'd have wished you well. She did, in fact. She did wish you well. Last thing she said to me before she left: "Tell Papa I wish him well." Last words to me at the railway station.'

'Who offered her the position?'

'Mr Chappell.'

'May I see the letter?' Tom said.

Albert pushed the soup pot aside. 'What letter?'

'From Mr Chappell.'

'I think Sylvie took it with her. Had an address on it, yes.'

'What address?'

'An address in London.'

'Albert, are you lying to me?'

'No, Tom, I ain't lying.' He wiped his moustache again and, with a little grunt of resignation, dug his hands into his overcoat pockets. 'She don't want you to have it.'

'I don't believe you.'

'It's true, I swear,' Albert said. 'I told her, I said, "Your papa's going to want to know all about what's happening to you, how it's working out for you in London." And she said, "No, he has done enough for me. He has his own life to lead now and a new wife to look out for. I will not have him burdened. I am going to do God's work and God will look after me." '

'Sylvie said that?'

'Her exact words. Didn't she hint as much in her letter?'

'No.'

'She ain't yours no longer, Tom. She ain't mine either. She's

269

gone off to do the work she was trained for, was born for, you might say.'

'Will she be sent to the foreign field?'

'I don't know, do I?' Albert said. 'After her training, perhaps.'

'Where is she staying in London?'

'In the Coral Strand's hostel in Holborn.'

'Does she pay to lodge there?'

'No, not while she's under training.'

Tom nodded. He was filled with guilt: guilt kept doubt at bay. He wanted desperately to see his daughter again, to talk with her, to be assured that it was not his marriage that had driven her away, had precipitated her into a career that seemed unsuited to such a delicate wee thing. He had been to Africa, if not the Islands, and he knew how bad the tropics could be, how dangerous, how unhealthy, and suspected that his daughter's illusions would soon be shattered and her heart broken by the work.

He was gripped by terrible emptiness, a fear that had no base or bottom but that seemed to go down and down inside him, like a pit shaft. He felt bleak, as bleak as Albert looked. He crossed his arms over his chest, closed his fists on his shoulders and drew in a shuddering breath.

Albert said, 'It's what she wants, Tom. It's what'll make her happy.'

'And you, how will you manage without her?'

'I'll make out somehow.'

'This Mr Chappell, didn't he offer you a position in London?'

'He did not,' Albert said. 'I expect I might go there, though, to London. Might find something to keep body and soul together. Work for the Mission on a voluntary basis just like I did here. Be near to Sylvie, case she needs me.'

'You're not — can't you stay here?'

Albert tugged his hands from the overcoat pockets. Thrust out by his massive belly, the nightshirt protruded before him. His shins, Tom noticed, were as hairy as his forearms.

'How can I?' Albert declared. 'How can I stay here when all there are is memories, everywhere, memories? I've lost them both, Tom, and there's nothing left for it but to start out somewhere new. Somewhere cheap.'

'Don't you have work, a job?'

'You know I don't.'

'Albert, are you broke?'

'I'm not asking for nothing. You don't owe me a penny, Tom Calder. You done well by our lass and for that Florence and me were eternally grateful. But it was my pleasure, my privilege I mean, to share what I had with Sylvie. Now it's over and all I have left – well, you know how it is? You done all right. You stuck with your career and you've earned your reward. Marry your young lady, I say, and be happy. I've had my high days, Tom, my days in the sun. Don't you fret about me. I'll be all right, right as bloomin' rain, old Albert.'

'If it's work, perhaps I can find you some . . .'

'No!' Albert jerked his head. 'No, that would never do. You've got your own life to lead and you don't want no rusty anchor holding you down.'

'When do you have to leave here?'

'Tomorrow.'

Tom nodded. He slipped a hand into his vest pocket. He had taken the notes from the reserve that he kept in a cash-box in a locked drawer in his room at the Queensview. He had thought that he would find Sylvie still here, had, in all honesty, expected to find her with her hand out. But she had taken her own direction, had selected her own destiny. Nothing he could do about it. No more could he give her. Perhaps in a week or two he might write to Mr Chappell at the Coral Strand's London headquarters and send a donation in Sylvie's name.

Meanwhile he brought the three ten pound banknotes from his pocket, hesitated, then, extending his hand, offered them to Albert.

'I can't leave you like this,' Tom said. 'Let me help.'

'No, Tom. No. I still got my pride.'

'Please take it. For my sake.'

'I – I can't.'

'For Sylvie's sake then.'

Albert started down at the floorboards.

Tom said, 'Sylvie wouldn't want to see you stranded.'

He sighed, a little roar. 'You're right, of course. Sylvie would want me to have it. She would be charitable. When I write to her I'll tell her what you've done, how kind you've been.'

'When will you write to her?'

'When I'm settled.'

'Will you also let me know where you are, Albert?'

'If that's your wish.'

'It is.'

He came forward, wrapped an arm about Tom and hugged him briefly. 'You're a good man, Tom Calder,' Albert muttered. 'A damned good man. God knows, you done the best you could. I wish you a marriage as happy as my own.'

They shook hands.

'Albert.'

'Uh?'

'When you're in touch, tell Sylvie I'm here if ever she needs me.'

'I will, Tom,' Albert Hartnell said. 'Rest assured, I will.'

He let himself in with the copy of McCulloch's latchkey that he'd had made in a cobbler's shop on the Maryhill Road late yesterday evening. He entered the hall and, groping, found the electrical light switch, then he called out, 'It's only me, dearest. It's only Dada. Where are you?'

'In here.'

He followed her voice into the largest of the three bedrooms and found her propped up in bed. She was clad in a fancy nightdress with puffy sleeves and did not bother to cover herself

272

when he entered. She had taken the ribbons from her hair and, with the rays of an electrical lamp around her, seemed to be burnished in light gold leaf. Through the fabric of the gown he could make out the protrusions of her breasts and he thought how lucky a man McCulloch was to have this treasure all to himself.

She was reading, not a novel but a textbook, a big blue cloth-bound tome with a Roman gentleman in a toga gilt-stamped on the front. Her eyes were not grey tonight but dark and slaty and she looked, Albert thought, weary and more in need of sleep than education.

He went to the bed and seated himself upon it.

She looked up from the book. 'Did Papa come?'

'He did.'

'Did he receive my letter?'

'Indeed, he did.'

'Did he swallow the story?'

'Yes, swallowed it in one gulp.'

'How much?' Sylvie said.

'Twenty quid. Under the circumstances I didn't feel it wise to push.'

She placed a forefinger in the book to mark her place and held out her hand. 'Give it here, please.'

'I thought I would put it into the bank first thing tomorrow.'

'Here.'

He laid the notes, still folded, across her palm and watched her fingers close on them. She obviously knew that he had diddled her and he waited for a reprimand, an argument. She seemed satisfied with the sum her papa had given her, though, the parting gift that would separate them once and for all.

'Did Forbes . . .' Albert began.

'Yes. He came. He brought me.'

Albert risked brushing a lock of hair from her brow.

'Goodnight, Dada,' Sylvie said pointedly.

'Goodnight, dear,' Albert said, and kissed her cheek.

He rose reluctantly and took himself to the door. It was a fine apartment but still strange and he was still lost in it. His bedroom, at one remove from Sylvie's, was small but comfortable. It had a single brass bedstead, a high-boy, a dressing-table and a washstand. It did not have Florence in it, though, and at this lonely hour of the night he missed his wife more than he cared to admit, not only for her company but for the fact that she, and she alone, had kept Sylvie from overwhelming him.

He paused in the doorway on the edge of the vast hall with its tick-tocking clock and fleshy pot plant, its gigantic hat-stand and oval mirror. He looked at his foster-daughter, Tom Calder's child, more beautiful now than pretty, her pert little chin raised, her slate grey eyes fixed grudgingly upon him.

'What is it, Albert?' Sylvie enquired. 'What do you want now?'

'Have you said your prayers yet?'

'Not yet.'

'When you do . . .'

'What?'

'Put in a word for me,' said Albert.

It seemed to Cissie that the Great Exhibition had gone on for ever, that when it closed not just the summer of 1901 but her youth would close with it, vanishing into memory like the bands and fireworks, the water-splash and gondolas, switched off like the sweeping beam of the Schuckert searchlight that flashed over every corner of the site and even penetrated the velvet draperies of the mansions on Park Circus and the corner of Harper's Hill.

Since August the 'Groveries had been illuminated after dusk but now the rains had arrived, the winter rains, and the lights had a bleary shimmer that indicated an imminent return to melancholy reality for the city and its citizens.

Closing-night looting was anticipated. The police would be out in force to check the stampede of souvenir hunters. Tom and

Cissie had decided that they would forgo the last-night concert and tuck themselves away from the festivities. To make up for it, however, Tom had invited her to dine in the Royal Bungalow four days before the gates were finally locked.

It was already cold and Cissie wore furs, lisle stockings and Russian boots to walk down from the Hill into the park. In the elegant cloakroom of the Bungalow she changed into the dress and shoes that she had carried with her in a waterproof bag and joined Tom at a table by the window. Rain poured from the restaurant's slanted eaves and the wind blew stridently across the river, making the boats dip on their mooring ropes and whipping the water about the weir. Wild weather was not without its excitement, however, and when they had finished eating and had drunk a bottle of wine between them, they went out for a last tour of the glistening piazzas and leafless walkways lit by swaying lanterns and the broad, ethereal beam of the Schuckert.

Cissie was snug enough inside her furs and Mica hood but Tom, carrying her shoe bag over his shoulder like a knapsack, was soon soaked. He was not dismayed by the discomfort, though, or too cold to enjoy their last parade before the Great Exhibition was diligently packed away. He kissed Cissie under the boughs of the chestnut trees and, because there were few folk around, kissed her again in the centre of the main piazza, his legs spread and braced like a mountaineer's against the swirling wind, his lips wet against her wet cheeks, both so wet and so exhilarated that they laughed and, with arms linked, set off for the gate that would lead them home.

As they strode along arm in arm, Tom said, 'My daughter has gone to London, by the way.'

'Has she?' said Cissie brightly.

'To train as a Mission worker.'

'Really! That will suit her very well.'

'Yes,' Tom said. 'I do believe it will.'

'Did you talk to her before she left?'

'Unfortunately, no.'

'She will write to you, will she not?'

'I expect so,' Tom said.

'But she will not be at our wedding?'

'No.'

'Tom?'

'Hmm?'

'Tom, I can't say I'm sorry, not actually sorry.'

'Why?' he said, then, hugging her arm, added, 'No, I know why.'

'Do you?' Cissie said.

'I think you just want me for yourself.'

She laughed and lifted her face and let him kiss her on the nose almost without breaking stride. 'What a conceited pig you are, Tom Calder.'

'It's the truth, though, isn't it?'

'Of course it is,' said Cissie. 'But I'm not telling you that.'

They walked on, Cissie and he, past the concert hall and the bandstand, the Russian village, their heads down, battling together into the rain.

He remembered how it had been in the not-so-old days when Sylvie too had loved him without question; then he thought of her as she had been that Sunday by the fountain before he had sent the postcard from Portsmouth, that afternoon when he had seen Sylvie for what she was, a stranger.

In five weeks' time he would be married to Cissie Franklin and as secure as a man could ever hope to be, any man who was loved as he was, that is. Cissie would never know that he had almost fallen in love with her cousin Lindsay, that he regretted the putting away of that love, the wistful evocation of what might have been and never would be now. He would not hurt her, could never, ever hurt her. He would pay for her love with loyalty and devotion, would dedicate himself to ensuring that she never found out how it had been with him once, long ago, or that he had chosen her only because she had chosen him.

'Tom?'

'What is it, dear?'

'Look.'

He turned and watched fireworks pouring upwards into the cloud, rockets bursting and a spray of sparks showering down upon the heights of Gilmorehill, showering down and winking out, extinguished prematurely by the rain.

'Why are they setting them off them tonight, Tom,' Cissie asked, 'when there's nobody here to see them? It seems such a waste.'

'It's a demonstration,' Tom said, 'a sort of rehearsal, I suppose.'

'For what?'

'The big show,' Tom answered and, suddenly cold, drew her close and hurried her away towards the exit gate.

PART THREE

1906

CHAPTER FOURTEEN

A Marriage of Sorts

The morning song of Harry Forbes McCulloch began earlier each day. Soon, so his grandfather claimed, one end would meet the other and there would be no sleep at all for any them. It was not that young Harry was a crosspatch. He did not shriek to be fed or wail for attention or whine when things did not go his way. He was, in fact, a cheerful wee chap, possessed of such a sunny disposition that it was impossible to believe that the havoc he caused in the Franklin household was not more the fault of those who cared for him than of the child himself.

What Harry was not was a sleeper. He had never been a sleeper. Even as an infant, still on the breast, he had lain gurgling in his cradle or in the huge, barge-like baby carriage that his grandfather had bought for him and had refused, not stubbornly but with winning little smiles, to close an eyelid while there was so much of interest going on around him. Now, aged three, he was not only vocal but mobile and the onset of the morning song would be accompanied by the rattle of the bars of his high-sided crib and the thump of feet as he jumped down to the rug in the nursery and, chanting happily, headed for the top of the stairs.

'Mammm-eee, Papp-eee, Grand-eee.' There was a definite lilt to it, a striving for cadence as if he were already practising to dispense with the spoken word altogether and converse only in song. 'Papppeeee, Grand-eee. Up, up.'

Bare toes on the lowest rung of the pine-wood gate that Franklin's carpenters had constructed and Arthur had erected, a gate so stout that it would not have been out of place in a cattle yard, a gate that young Harry had almost mastered and, given another inch of growth and another ounce of strength, would not keep him in his proper place much longer. Bare toes on the rung, fists on the bar, nose – a trifle moist – peeping over the top, he chanted a cheerful greeting to the new day.

Arthur groaned.

Forbes sat up.

Lindsay smiled into her pillow.

Cook eased out of bed with a rueful shake of the head. Maddy, still unmarried, tried to hang on to her dreams by not opening her eyes. And Miss Eleanor Runciman, who did not trust the nursemaid, Winn, even if she was Mr Forbes's sister, shot out of her room and on to the first-floor landing, muttering, 'The stairs, the stairs,' in a voice so deep and tragic that it would have put Sarah Bernhardt to shame.

The housekeeper's morbid obsession with what might happen on the stairs was not entirely unjustified. Harry was a devil for staircases. He spent many hours, even in chill winter, clambering up and down the funnel of the house, crooning to himself. What was more disturbing – even the imperturbable Winn admitted it – was that he had recently taken to hoisting his baby brother, Philip, from his cradle to introduce to the joys of runners and rods if not yet to vertical fall, though that, Eleanor feared, might be next on the list of Harry's adventures with gravity.

She ascended rapidly from the first to the second-floor landing and, holding her robe about her, peered up into the January gloom.

A light shone in the nursery. Harry, innocent as a snowball in his fleecy night shirt, had levered his arms on to the top of the gate and rested his chin on his elbows. He looked down at the housekeeper out of chocolate-drop eyes and, breaking off his chant for a moment, said very distinctly, 'Philip wants a egg.'

'Where is Aunt McCulloch? Where is Winn?'

'Philip's wet again. Why is he always so wet, Miss Runkelman?'

'Because,' said Eleanor, 'he is still a baby.'

'I'm not a baby.'

Now that she had him in view her concern diminished and with it her severity. It was cold in the upper reaches of the house. She hadn't paused to put on stockings. Harry, though, seemed quite oblivious to the low temperatures and the fact that dawn was still two hours away. She could make out his little bare toes protruding through the lower rungs, realised that he was supported entirely by his arms, and marvelled at his sturdiness.

Though she had no dominion over the upper floors now and did not even hold keys for that part of the house, she crept further up the staircase.

'I know you're not a baby, Harry,' she said. 'You are not wet, are you?'

'Nooo,' scornfully.

'Do you need wee-wee?'

'Done it. Pulled the chain.'

'Can you reach the chain, Harry?'

'Stand on the seat.'

'Of course,' Eleanor said.

She could hardly believe the rate at which children acquired self-sufficiency these days. Nanny Cheadle had done everything for Lindsay for fully five years before she had allowed the child to tackle things for herself. Now, it seemed, a little boy was expected to contribute to his own welfare and that of his baby brother almost before he could walk. How times change, she thought: how times do change.

'I think,' said Harry, 'Philip ack-tully does want a egg.'

'Is Philip hungry?'

'Yes.'

'Are you hungry too?'

'Yes.'

'What is Nanny Winn doing?'

'Washing Philip.'

'Do you want to come downstairs, Harry?'

'That would be very nice, thank you, Miss Runkelman.'

He squirmed and struggled to lift himself over the top of the gate. It was just as well that Arthur had designed such an ingenious lock otherwise the boy would probably have worked out the mechanism by now and would have been unstoppable. As it was, in three or four months the gate would not hold him; nothing would hold him.

Harry was such a handsome wee fellow, though, Eleanor could forgive him almost anything. He had his father's dark colouring, but the shape of his face suggested that he might soon grow to resemble his grandfather. Appearance mattered less than character, however, and Eleanor prayed that he might prove to be more Franklin than McCulloch in this respect.

In the four years since Forbes McCulloch had moved into the house in Brunswick Crescent, Eleanor's attitude had altered drastically. At first she had been taken in by his charm and, like everyone else in the household, had put herself out to do his bidding, a phase that hadn't lasted long. The arrival of first one McCulloch sister and then another – Winn following Blossom – had so weakened Eleanor's authority that she had even been tempted to resign her position. If it hadn't been for Arthur, who was in this matter more ally than master, then she would have sought other employment.

Gowry McCulloch, the brother, was next to arrive; the smiling, iniquitous brother who, though he did not reside in Brunswick Crescent, was never out of the house and could usually be found lounging in the kitchen chatting to Maddy, drinking tea or, worse, sprawled in the ground-floor drawing-room smoking cigarettes and working his way through his brother's stock of spirits.

Although he was officially employed by Franklin's to service, polish and drive the firm's new Lanchester and keep Donald's new model Humber in trim, Gowry McCulloch seemed to spend most of his time hanging about the garage in the lane behind the crescent tinkering with Forbes's bright yellow Vauxhall. He did not have a room in Brunswick Crescent, thank the Lord, but lodged somewhere in the direction of Partick where he returned to catch up on his sleep after a hard day doing, it seemed, very little.

Blossom, Winifred, Gowry: who would be next to arrive from that outpost of the McCulloch clan, Eleanor and Arthur wondered, and why, if Daniel McCulloch was so wealthy and well-connected in the fair city of Dublin did his daughters and son feel the need to export themselves to Scotland and take up positions that were, however you looked at it, menial? Servants they were but also siblings, a combination that, in Eleanor's experience, did not lend itself to domestic harmony.

In the four years since Lindsay's marriage to the Dubliner there had been no sign of Forbes's father, no gifts, no letters, no words of congratulation at the marriage or the birth of the children, no signals of approval at the success Forbes had made of his chosen career.

Kay's visits to Glasgow had become increasingly frequent and more than made up for lack of paternal interest. She would stay with Donald and Lilias for a few days, then, without so much as a by-your-leave, would appear on the doorstep at Brunswick Crescent. Gowry would lug her baggage up from the motor-car and she would sweep in to occupy the guest-room upstairs with hardly more than a nod to Eleanor or Arthur or even to Lindsay who was just as mystified by the doings of her Irish relations as everyone else: everyone, that is, except Forbes. Forbes remained in control of every situation and, riding high on the crest of a shipbuilding boom, seemed to have more income than he knew what to do with.

Eleanor took another step up the steep staircase.

Harry was straining to cock one leg over the topmost bar. His nightshirt was ruched up around his hips and she glimpsed his miniature parts, already perfectly formed and masculine. She was embarrassed on his behalf and, holding out a hand to catch him lest he should topple over the gate, called out sharply, 'Winn. Nurse Winn, are you there?'

'I'm here,' said a voice behind her. 'I'm going up in any case.'

Lindsay emerged soundlessly from the door of the bedroom on the second floor. Quietness was her way now, her habit. She moved quietly, spoke quietly, talked to the children in a quiet voice, not so much serious as subdued.

'Will you feed him in the nursery?' Eleanor said.

'Mam-ma, Philip wants a egg.'

'Yes, dearest. I heard you.'

In a cupboard to the rear of the nursery a little kitchen had been set up. Forbes had insisted that the nursery had its own separate facilities and had designed a system with a cistern and motorised pump that would lift water to the attic floor and allow the installation of a bath and a water closet.

'Will it not be too cold for him in the nursery?' Eleanor said.

'Don't fuss, please,' Lindsay told her quietly. 'I'll wrap him in the big shawl until the fire is raked and lighted.' She moved past the housekeeper, let herself through the gate on to the nursery floor and, taking her son by the hand, led him away into the room.

Shivering slightly, Eleanor watched the door close behind them before she turned to come downstairs again. From the bedroom on the landing below came the sound of a yawn, then a cry of, 'Bloss. Blossom, do you have my tea there?'

Out of the darkness loomed the bulky figure of Blossom McCulloch. Although it was barely six o'clock Forbes's sister was already dressed for the day in a loose cream-laid blouse and adjustable brown skirt that Mr Arthur said made her look like a lady golfer. Eleanor watched her enter the master bedroom, heard the murmur of Irish voices as sister and brother conversed, then the woman re-emerged and without so much as a glance in Eleanor's direction lumbered downstairs to the hallway.

In the wintry half-dark she felt quite lost for a second or two. Lost in her own house, indeed? How ridiculous! From the nursery came baby Philip's cry, a single peevish wail, silenced by the application of Lindsay's breast.

Ah, how times change, Eleanor thought again, how time does fly, and, pulling herself together, hurried down to the first floor, into her own domain.

Lindsay did not feel comfortable in the attic nursery but then, if she were honest, she did not feel comfortable anywhere in the house, save possibly in the piano parlour which was where she took herself and the children when Forbes was not at home and she could exert a little bit of authority over Winn and Blossom. There, with Miss Runciman for company, she would play with her sons, released from the feeling that her every move was being observed and would be reported back to Forbes.

Even with her baby pressed to her breast and the sensual rapport that feeding him brought her, she could not entirely shake off a feeling that Philip wasn't hers at all, that she had merely been allowed to borrow him for a little while as a concession to necessity.

She felt him tug, suck again, rest and sigh.

She gave him only three small feeds a day now. Winn had begun to wean him on sweet milk and saps, which was the way it was done in Ireland, so Winn said. Lindsay had no means of knowing if it were true, for everything Winn told her Blossom or Forbes would, without question, endorse. She could not deny that Philip seemed to be thriving, though he was as unlike his brother as it was possible to be, fair-haired and slight, and so passive that there had been times when Lindsay, in fits of panic, had wondered if he were quite right in the head.

Aunt Kay had assured her that Forbes had been just the same at that age, quiet and untroublesome, inclined to sleep the clock round. Lindsay was not consoled and after her mother-in-law had returned to Ireland she had asked Dr Hough to call and examine Philip, which the doctor duly did. He had assured her that the infant was perfectly normal, that maternal anxiety was a common postnatal condition, and had prescribed a mild sedative to soothe her nerves.

She had never had any worry with Harry. Her first-born had flopped out into the world after seven hours of labour and had been a joy to her from the start. Philip, though, had been a fortnight overdue, seemed reluctant to be born at all and had kept her in labour for twenty-nine hours. Since that ordeal she had not been herself, had felt cut off from what went on around her and disinclined to engage with anyone or anything.

Aunt Lilias had advised her to ask Forbes to take her away for a breath of sea air or to Strathmore for a week or two, with the children but *sans* servants. Forbes, however, had declared that he was too busy to go anywhere that summer and had refused point blank to let her travel to Strathmore with Cissie, Tom and their small son. Travelling, Forbes said, was bad for nursing mothers.

Forbes reminded her that she was ill, and she believed him. Forbes told her that she was exhausted, and she did not doubt it. Forbes informed her that the best thing she could do was to let Winn take care of the children and rest as much as possible; without question Lindsay did just that. He also told her that in her own best interests, and to speed her recovery, he would refrain from intercourse, for, he said, it wasn't proper for a woman in her debilitated condition to enjoy sexual relations. Finally, he forbade her to attend management meetings or take any active interest in the business of the yard. This she found easy to do, for during her pregnancies she had lost contact with Franklin's affairs and after Philip's birth had retreated into a quiet, sullen world of her own, a world dominated by her children and her husband.

'I'm thinking,' Winn said, 'that he has had enough.'

'He's only resting.'

'It's you that should be resting. I'll walk him to bring up the wind.'

Lindsay had been nursing her son for less than ten minutes. In that time Winn had raked out the fire, transferred ashes to a bucket for Maddy to collect and, with Harry kneeling at her side, had reconstructed the fire with kindling and small coals and brought flame to the fore by pumping the ornamental bellows. Harry would love to experiment with the bellows but was forbidden to go near the fire or touch any of the hearth utensils.

Winn had put up the iron fireguard, had filled a basin from the tap in the kitchen, had washed her hands and Harry's face, had dressed the boy in warm woollens and pantaloons; had lighted the gas stove, filled a pan and put two eggs to boil in it, then, almost casually, had set the nursery table for breakfast. She rubbed her palms on her pinafore and held out her arms.

'Give him here to me,' she said.

Lindsay looked down at the small face nestled against her breast. She was swollen still but not massively so and the tender ache than had troubled her at the beginning had all but vanished. Her nipple remained taut, though, with a single droplet of milk caught on the crown. Philip, eyes closed, was not satisfied, merely resting; instinct told her so. She gathered the shawl and drew the folds about her and the baby.

'He will need to be winded,' Winn said.

'I know he will need to be winded,' Lindsay said.

Philip was almost eight months now. Recently he had put on enough weight to be cumbersome and had strength in his grip when he chose to use it, which was not often. His passivity still worried her a little. Harry had been active even at that young age, hated being walked and winded and had kicked and struggled and, once or twice, had even cried. Harry, now, was seated at table, playing with the spoons and butter knives. In some recess of her mind Lindsay recalled that she had heard Miss Runciman invite the boy downstairs for breakfast but Harry had obviously forgotten about it.

The dining-room was the only communal room in the house, the one place where McCullochs and Franklins met face to face. Even here, though, it was her husband and not her father who set the rules. The evening meal had become something of an ordeal, with three or four McCullochs lined up against Arthur and Miss Runciman in an atmosphere so tense and icy that Lindsay could hardly bear it. Because she was afraid of favouring one side over another, even in trivial matters, she tended to say little and eat even less.

It was all so different in the apartment in Sandyford Avenue where Tom and Cissie and their little boy, Ewan, resided. Less well off than the McCullochs, the Calders had only one day-maid to attend them, yet somehow their life seemed much fuller and happier than her own.

Now, in the gloom of mid-winter after over four years of marriage, she could hardly bring to mind the memory of her passion for Forbes, their romantic meetings at Strathmore or those first few nights after their wedding when Forbes had taught her what it meant to be a wife and had all but exhausted her with strenuous love-making. She still caught her breath at the sight of him as he stood, unaware, by the window in his hand-tailored suit or in the privacy of the bedroom, where he stripped off his clothes and padded towards the bed. Summer and winter he slept naked, shoulder and arm visible in the half light, dark hair like a stain upon the pillow. Then she would long for his attentions, to be loved as a wife should be loved, but would do nothing, make no move, for, all evidence to the contrary, she believed that she was still ailing.

Winn said, 'Give me the baby. I will do the rest.'

Lindsay felt trapped between what she wished to do and what she had been trained to do. Before dawn on a cold mid-winter morning the only comfort she could find came from the child in her arms, the passive form of her son resting against her under the big woollen shawl.

'I want to stay here,' Lindsay said.

'You must go downstairs. Forbes will be wanting you downstairs.'

'No, I want to stay here.'

'The nursery is no place for you,' Winn told her 'in your condition.'

The nursery *was* the place for her, the one and only place where she felt whole. She closed her eyes and, rocking a little, hugged Philip to her.

'Are you for smothering him?' Winn said.

'Mammm-eee?'

'What is it, Harry?' Winn said.

'He's frightened,' Lindsay said.

'He has nothing to be frightened of,' Winn said. 'Unless it's you that's frightening him, you not doing what you're told.'

Lindsay opened her eyes. She glanced down. Philip had gone to sleep. She could feel the rhythm of his breathing slight against her heart, the warm sussuration of his breath against her skin. She needed nobody, least of all her husband's sister, to tell her that her child was asleep.

'Mammm-eee?'

'Philip is perfectly all right, dearest,' Lindsay said.

'Doesn't Phil-lup want a egg?' Harry asked, a little incredulously.

'Later, perhaps later,' Lindsay said.

Winn stood directly before her.

The nursery seemed filled by the girl's indignation, though there was no visible sign of it in her posture or expression. She was only nineteen years old, but resentful enough to be ninety. She had jet black hair and eyes like Forbes but the shape of her face was longer, less regular, the flesh around her mouth and nose oddly pouched like that of a burrowing mammal. Plainness had not undermined her self-assurance. She gave the impression that she considered herself to be the salt of the earth and everyone else pitiably inferior.

'There now, are you not going to give him to me?' Winn said

softly. 'He will be better with me to take care of him, you being as you are.'

Lindsay knew the tone of voice only too well: the lilting, cajoling brogue that disguised demand as request. She recognised the wilfulness behind it, the charm and easiness that were not charming and easy at all. She had been listening to that voice for years but she could still be taken in by it and, for the sake of peace, concede and yield up everything.

As if from a distance, a long way back, Lindsay heard herself say, 'And how am I, Winn? Tell me, how I am.'

A smile, just a shade too stiff to be winsome: 'You are not yourself this morning at all.'

'How am I then?' Lindsay said again. 'Tell me, Winn, how am I?'

Philip sighed against her breast. A butter knife, balanced until then on the table's edge, clattered to the floor. Winn paid it no heed. Lindsay, looking up, waited, but no answer was forth-coming from the girl, no intelligence.

'Well?' Lindsay said.

'I'll get Forbes.'

'For what?' Lindsay said. 'To answer a simple question?'

The voice within her which had started out from some vague hollow source became clear in her mouth. She was startlingly conscious of her disappointments, her inadequacies. She felt no kinship with Winn, her sister-in-law. Intimidation and com-pliance were the bases of their relationship and at that moment she saw why Winn had to appeal to her brother, *her* husband, concerning such a petty matter. Forbes would not arbitrate or negotiate. He would back his sister without question, would support Winifred just as he supported Blossom. The sisters were his barriers, buffers to keep her at a distance. In that early morning hour in the nursery at the top of the house, Lindsay suddenly realised how she had been duped.

'Harry,' Lindsay said, 'did Miss Runciman say that you could take your breakfast downstairs?'

'Miss Runkelman, she said . . .' The little boy appeared puzzled then, with a laugh, he scampered around the table, around the nursemaid and hid behind the nursing chair. 'She said . . . yeee-sss.'

'Would you like to go downstairs, Harry?' Lindsay asked.

'He is not to go downstairs until the men are gone,' Winn said.

'You can tell me, Harry? Would you like to go downstairs and have breakfast with Papa and Grandee?'

He put his head around the side of the chair. 'I'll eat Phil-lup's egg.'

'You may have an egg of your own.' Lindsay cradled the baby carefully in the crook of her arm and got to her feet. She buttoned her robe then offered her hand to Harry who took it eagerly.

'I must talk to Forbes about this,' Winn said. 'You must not be going anywhere until I've talked to Forbes.'

'About what, Winifred? About me?'

'Forbes doesn't like to have the children downstairs in the morning,' Winn protested. 'You know the rules.'

'Oh, yes,' Lindsay said, clearly, 'I know the rules, but they are Forbes's rules, not mine.'

'You'll upset him,' Winn told her tersely.

'Not before time,' said Lindsay.

Then, with the baby in her arms and her first-born by the hand, she went to the head of the staircase, showed Harry how to unlock the gate, and led her tiny army boldly downstairs to the dining-room.

'I don't know what came over you this morning,' Forbes said. 'Winn's exceedingly upset by the whole incident.'

'Bringing our children into the dining-room to join us for breakfast is hardly my idea of an incident, Forbes,' Lindsay said. 'Why is Winn upset?'

'She feels it was her fault.' He paused. 'They weren't even decently dressed. Besides, the dining-room's no place for a baby.'

'My father doesn't seem to agree with you; nor does Miss Runciman.'

'Miss Runciman? Yes, we'll have to have a talk about your Miss Runciman. It seems that she's been interfering again.'

'Disobeying the rules, do you mean?'

'Lindsay, a household must be properly governed. Since your illness . . .'

'What illness?'

'Come along, you know how ill you've been.'

'Tell me, Forbes, how ill have I been?'

'You've not been yourself. Everyone says so.'

'Everyone? Who, for instance?'

'Lilias, Donald, Martin, even Tom . . .'

'Tom?'

'. . . have all remarked how exhausted you seem. They're concerned for you, dearest. We're all concerned for you.'

'Because I won't do just what you want me to?' said Lindsay.

She was seated at the inlaid dressing-table — one of several antique pieces that Forbes had picked up at auction — brushing her hair; brushing her hair as she had not brushed it in years, brushing with long, smooth, rhythmic strokes that she counted under her breath as if she were a girl again and still had a motive for making herself pretty. She wore a peach silk peignoir and a flannelette nightgown in pink and blue that had been left untouched in the bottom drawer of her wardrobe since her honeymoon. She had unearthed it that afternoon, not because it was alluring, but because it was warm.

'Forbes, all I did,' she went on, 'was bring the children downstairs. It's not a hostile act, for heaven's sake. I mean, they're not lepers.'

'Unfair!' he said. 'That's unfair!'

The mirror on the dressing-table was not authentic. The original triple mirror had been damaged. Forbes had had it replaced by an identical copy. Lindsay had no more than a hazy recollection of the conversation about the mirror; she had been three or four days out of labour with Philip when Forbes had pranced into her bedroom to tell her of his purchase.

He said, 'I love my children as much as any man alive.'

'Provided you don't have to see them too often?'

'Linnet, what *has* got into you?'

She glanced at his reflection in the side mirror. He had been out for the best part of the evening, dining with a couple of shipping agents and, she suspected, with Gowry. It did not seem to strike her husband as anomalous that he insisted on propriety at home yet patently flouted the rules of society by trailing his uncouth brother about with him.

He had removed his evening jacket and starched shirt front. He sat upon the bed, suspenders dangling, shirt open to the waist. He looked, Lindsay thought, as if he had been playing scrimmage, not eating out with gentlemen. Unaware of her scrutiny, he rested his forearms on his knees and stared down at the Japanese carpet, a gift from Mr Kimura to commemorate Admiral Togo's destruction of the Russian fleet at Port Arthur and the small — the very small — part that Franklin's had played in the victory. Why the carpet had wound up on the floor of their bedroom and not in store at Harper's Hill Lindsay couldn't imagine.

Forbes said, 'Have you been hearing things?'

'What sort of things?'

He glanced up. 'I don't know. Things?'

'I've no idea what you're talking about, Forbes.'

'Oh!' he said. 'Well, that's all right then.'

She put down the brush and turned on the chair. 'What things?'

Once more he paused, frowning. 'About the Admiralty contract.'

'That isn't what you meant.'

'It's the work, the work is very demanding right now.'

It was the first time in months that he had spoken of his work. Her father and he would discuss aspects of business now and then or engage, often heatedly, in arguments over technical detail, all far above her head. What few crumbs of information she had picked up concerning Franklin's projects had come to her through Tom. She saw little of Martin and Rora who seemed to move in different circles from the rest of the family and had not even attended the traditional New Year's Day celebration at Harper's Hill. Ross and Johnny were practically strangers. Only Aunt Lilias visited her regularly, and Aunt Lilias had no interest in anything these days except babies and weddings and gossip.

Lindsay said, 'I thought the order books were full?'

'They are – or will be,' Forbes said.

'Well then, what is it that concerns you?'

'I can't tell you.'

'Can't tell me? I'm a partner, Forbes, in case you've forgotten.'

'It's a state secret,' he said. 'Sorry.'

'Suit yourself,' Lindsay said.

He got up and flexed his arms in the chicken-wing manner that she had always considered both ugly and comical. He stepped out of his trousers and folded them across his arm. Lindsay went back to brushing her hair.

He said, 'What you need is a lady's-maid.'

'Oh, I see. You've another sister waiting with bags packed on the quay at Rosslare, have you?'

'You shouldn't have to brush your own hair.'

She laughed: yesterday she would not have laughed. Yesterday she would have been incapable of raising a smile. She wondered what had changed. Something small, obviously, some small shift in balance. She did not know what had come over her or why on that cold January morning she had recognised ridicule for what it was and had allowed disappointment to alter in character, to become resentment. She laughed again and swung round, catching him unaware. He had lowered his striped drawers and, with his back to her, seemed to be admiring his parts or, perhaps, examining them critically. She could see his rather flat buttocks, very white, tapering down into hairy thighs. He looked, she thought, remarkably skinny, something that she hadn't noticed during her 'illness'.

'What have you been doing to yourself, Forbes?'

He shot round. 'What?'

'I do believe you're losing weight.'

'Me? I'm fine. Nothing wrong with me. It's you yourself. Look at you. Skin and bone, just skin and bone.'

She glanced at herself in the side mirror. Her breasts were heavy but even through the nightgown she could discern the prominent 'salt-cellars' that framed her collar bones and, no doubt about it, her arms *were* thin. She was willing to concede that perhaps she had lost the watery fat that had coated her body in the wake of her pregnancy but she did not take his criticism to heart, did not take it, or him, very seriously.

'What if I am?' she said.

'Sure and I'm not losing weight, am I?' he said, lifting his shirt.

'You don't have to look at me. You don't even have to touch me.'

'I'm just the same as I always was,' he said.

'I don't think I need a lady's-maid, thank you, Forbes.'

'It's muscle. I'm just lean by nature.'

'Yes,' she said. 'Yes, you are.'

He plucked at the winter drawers, drew them away from his thighs, peered down. 'You may be right, though. Perhaps I am. Jesus!'

'It'll be worry about the contract that's doing it.'

'What contract?'

'The secret contract for the Admiralty.'

The frown changed to a scowl, dark and severe. He stripped off his shirt, under-vest and drawers and threw them over a chair.

He crabbed to the bed and got into it, punching at the bolster and then the pillow. He lay down, arms folded across his chest, nose pointing at the ceiling.

'I don't want to talk about it, Lindsay.'

She put the silver-backed brush into its case and the case into the right-hand drawer of the dressing-table. She shook her hair, making it swing prettily. She was drawn, yes, but not ugly, not old. Good Lord, she wasn't even in the prime of her life, yet the man in the bed did not want her, her husband was no longer aroused by her. At least she had managed to cut through his indifference. For a moment or two they had even come close to bickering. Bickering, she supposed, was better than nothing.

She switched off the overhead light, shed the peignoir and felt her way through the darkness of the big bedroom, a darkness that had never seemed so complete and intense before marriage. She encountered the bed-end, the seam of the quilt and, groping, tugged back the blankets and sheets and slid in beside her husband.

Forbes stirred, moved away, made room for her. She could sense his truculence, his apprehension. He was still on his back, arms folded across his chest. She wriggled down beside him, deliberately letting her nightgown tighten and drag against her flanks. The inclination of the mattress threw her weight gently against him. He flinched and shifted another inch or two on to the upward slope. Even on this, the coldest night of the winter, he slept unclothed. He generated a little layer of heat but when she touched his shoulder she found that his flesh was icy cold as if the engine of his body had some original part to it that defied the laws of thermodynamics.

She laid an arm over his stomach. He breathed in stiff, short, bellows-like breaths. She hoisted herself a little higher until her cheek shared his pillow and her mouth was close to his ear.

'Forbes,' she whispered urgently. 'Forbes.'

'What is it now?' he said.

'Tell me about the Admiralty contract.'

'For God's sake, Lindsay,' he growled, 'go to bloody sleep.'

'Thank you, dearest,' she said. 'I will,' and with a chuckle that made his blood run cold, turned on her hip and rolled away.

CHAPTER FIFTEEN

Weapons of War

Soon after nine o'clock, she dressed Harry and, leading him by the hand, left the house. She walked to the rank at the corner of Sheddon Street where two motorised taxi-cabs stood aloof from a line of hansoms. She chose one of the old-fashioned 'clip-clops' and lifted her son into it. He perched on the slippery seat, humming to himself as he gazed at the tall tenements, the tram-cars, all the bustle of the January morning streets. He looked, Lindsay thought proudly, quite a little gentleman in his new navy blue topcoat and pantaloons and a cap with velvet earflaps.

There had been quite a rumpus with Winn before they had left. Lindsay had almost lost her temper with the nursemaid who had protested that it was far too cold for a small boy to be taken out of doors, no matter how well wrapped up he was.

'He will not be out of doors for long,' Lindsay had said.

'Where are you going, then?' Winn had asked.

'I don't think that is any of your business.'

'What if Forbes telephones and wants to know where you are?'

'Tell him we have gone shopping.'

'You will be tiring Harry out, you know.'

'I don't think so, Winn.'

'What about the poor baby?'

'Poor baby?'

'He will be hungry.'

'I will be back long before Philip needs fed again,' Lindsay said. 'But if I am much after twelve o'clock you may give him a bottle.'

Still protesting, Winn had trailed her down to the hallway and had demanded, 'Where are you going? Where are you taking him?' as if she, Lindsay, were planning an abduction.

Stubbornly, Lindsay had refused to answer.

It was not until the hansom trundled into Aydon Road that Harry turned to her and said, 'Are we going to see Papa?'

'Yes, Harry, we are going to visit our shipyard.'

'To see Papa?'

'Perhaps.'

'And Grandee's boats?'

'Oh, yes, and Grandee's boats.'

'Hurrah!' the little boy yelled, throwing out his arms. 'Hurrah!' as if he had been awaiting this moment from the day of his birth.

'Why, if it isn't Miss Frank— I mean, Mrs McCulloch,' Sergeant Corbett said. 'It's a pleasure to see you again. And who might this be, ma'am?' He stooped, hands on knees, and inspected Harry critically. 'Is this the first-born?'

'It is, Sergeant. His name is Harry.'

'Welcome to Franklin's, young man,' Sergeant Corbett said. 'I hope we'll be seeing a lot of you in future.'

Harry stared up at the broad leather belt and mutton-chop whiskers and enquired, 'Are you a soldier?'

'I used to be a soldier, aye.'

'When I'm big I'm going to be a soldier,' Harry said.

'A fine soldier you'll make, I'm sure,' said Sergeant Corbett, then to Lindsay, 'There's no management meeting today, ma'am.'

'I know, Sergeant.'

'I think Mr McCulloch is out this mornin'.'

'And my father?'

'He's upstairs. Will I ring for him to come down?'

'I'll go up. We'll both go up, if we may.'

'Is this the laddie's first visit?'

'It is.'

'Then he'll be wanting to see the boats.'

'Boats,' Harry said. 'I want to see the boats.'

'First,' Lindsay said, 'we'll go and find Grandee.'

'Is Grandee on a boat?'

'I don't think so.' Lindsay took her son by the hand and directed him towards the main staircase. 'Perhaps, if he has time, Uncle Thomas might take you down to see the boats.'

'Is Uncle Thomas on a boat then?'

'Mr Calder,' the sergeant said, 'is in the mould loft with a party.'

'What sort of party?' Lindsay asked.

'A party from the Admiralty,' Sergeant Corbett said.

The long wooden-walled corridor on the second floor of the block was situated directly above the boardroom and the offices that opened from it were occupied entirely by Franklins and their kin. At one time there had been space for all departments on the upper floors but over the years Owen's sons and grandsons had claimed priority, all except Tom Calder who was quite content with his cubicle at the end of the drawing-office. Forbes, however, had complained bitterly about having to share space with Johnny and Ross and had insisted on being given an office of his own next door to Martin's.

The clack of typewriting machines flooded up from the clerks' room, the brutal thud of a power punch, the shriek of a saw and the clang of riveters belting on hammers sifted in even through windows sealed against the frost that held Clydeside in its grip. Lindsay heard men whistling and, like mammoths trumpeting, the hoots of bum-boats and tugs and the ineffable churning of propellers from the miasmic waters that stretched into the frozen haze.

Harry too heard these sounds, his first experience of the rhythms of a song that would sit close to his heart: no Kerry Dance, no piper's tune, no sentimental ditty recalling days that were dead and gone or that had never been, but an overture to the future. Eyes wide and ears pricked, Harry accompanied it, making up his own little song as he went along.

Arthur was delighted to see them. Surprised too. Somehow it had not occurred to him that his grandson was of an age to be brought to the yard. He swept the boy into his arms, carried him to the window and stood him on the narrow ledge over the steam pipes.

'Boats!' Harry said. 'Boats, Grandee! I see the boats.'

Her father's room was cluttered. He shared the old Founder's Office with Donald now. Racks of plans in brown-cloth folders and tall teak filing cabinets backed the desk. Donald was out on the road with Martin. Ross and Johnny too were out of the office, and of Forbes there was no sign behind the pebble-glass door that bore his name.

Lindsay watched her son and father fondly. Her father's hands were on Harry's waist, Harry's palms pressed against the window, his cap askew. As they surveyed the slips and rails and jibs that lay before them in the dead, dunning January cold, the bond between the generations had never seemed stronger.

'Wha's 'at, Grandee?'

'That's a destroyer, son, for chasing torpedo-boats.'

'Big-gun boats?'

'Yes, guns, but we haven't put the guns on yet. Do you see the men on their knees? They are fitting the deck, the place where the sailors will stand.'

'Wha's 'at?'

'Oh, that,' Arthur Franklin said. 'That's a boiler, for boiling the water to make the steam.'

'For the tea?'

'No, it's too big for tea. Steam, to drive the engines.'

'Wha's 'at?'

'A crane. If we wait a wee bit we'll see it turning.'

'Wha's it doing?'

'Lifting steel plates up to the second deck.'

'Where the sailors stand.'

'Absolutely.'

'Wha's that noise, Grandee?'

'The saw in the wood-frame shop. A circular saw, for cutting wood.'

'For the fire?'

'Not quite, son,' said Arthur. 'Would you like to go down and watch the saw cutting timber?'

'*Yes.*'

'Would you like to see the boats?'

'YES.'

Lindsay said, 'If you're too busy, Papa, perhaps Tom could spare a few minutes.'

'To give my grandson his first tour of Franklin's? No, no,' Arthur said. 'I'm not handing that privilege over to Tom Calder, no matter how busy I am.'

'Where is Forbes, by the way?'

'Gone off to Beardmore's, I believe, to discuss special castings.'

'In the motor-car, with Gowry?'

'Naturally,' said Arthur.

Mr Albert Hartnell and his daughter had been resident in St Mungo's Mansions for so long that the motor-car and the gentleman caller who got out of it had become an accepted part of the scene. It would have been naïve of Albert to pretend that his neighbours did not know what racket he was in or what the young man was up to when he vanished into the close at the rear of the building. Besides, Mr Hartnell was by no means the only person in the Mansions who had secrets worth keeping. Albert knew more about other folks' business than they did about his which was, he reckoned, as good a safeguard as any against inquisitiveness and disapproval.

Even Mrs O'Connor who lived across the landing with her cat Snowball and her crotchety maid Evelyn had a secret not so far removed from the secret that Sylvie lived with. Mrs O'Connor's revenue, Albert had discovered, came from interest in shares left her by three grateful gentlemen who had wives and children and posthumous reputations to protect even although they were personally long past caring. In fact, if the self-appointed widow had been ten or a dozen years younger, on the sunny side of sixty, say, Albert would not have been averse to marrying her to secure himself a comfortable old age.

He was such a worrier, was Albert. He worried when things were going badly and he worried when, as now, things were going well. He worried about the past and he worried about the future. He worried most of all that Sylvie would do something to offend Forbes McCulloch and bring the entire rocky edifice tumbling down about his ears. He was always very careful to bow to Forbes's wishes and exit the apartment speedily whenever the young Lothario put in an appearance.

As for Sylvie, he was never less than sugar-sweet to Sylvie who, as she'd grown older, had become sharper in some respects, more fey in others. What really stirred Albert's anxiety was her belief that it was only a matter of time before Forbes McCulloch would desert his wife and children and come to live with her on a permanent basis. Gently, tenderly, he had tried to explain 'reality' to Sylvie, to make her appreciate that what she had was all she was ever going to get and that she was fortunate that Forbes chose to share even a small a part of his life with her. Sylvie would have none of it, simply closed her ears to anything that ran counter to the fantasy that she was more than just a mistress who might at any time become a liability.

At least Albert had Gowry for company; honest, amiable,

garrulous, down-to-earth Gowry, who was all that Irishmen were reputed to be and who, in the dreary hours of late evening or in the morning, stood him a pint or two while Forbes was upstairs with Sylvie taking, or delivering, lessons in love. Many a peaceful hour Albert spent with the chauffeur in the Old Barge Inn before Gowry hooked out his pocket watch and murmured, 'Time, Albert, time to be rousting out his majesty and be on our way,' for Gowry, it seemed, was not so much his brother's conscience as his clock.

It was from Gowry that Albert learned what may or may not have been the truth about the McCulloch family; not a family united or, as he'd been led to believe, a family swimming in beer money like the Guinnesses or the Goodisons. They did not even live in Dublin but in a sprawling cottage attached to a tiny brewery in the sea-coast village of Malahide, about nine miles north of the famous city. Here McCulloch's Black Irish Stout was produced in limited quantities and the annual turnover was just enough to keep things ticking over. Apparently Donald Franklin had been the only one from this side of the water ever to visit the place, and Donald had somehow been persuaded to accept the lie that old Daniel McCulloch was a magnate in the industry and not an indolent old reprobate whose only interest in life was buying, breaking and backing horses and dabbling in Home Rule politics.

Such half-truths and exaggerations Albert swallowed whole. Gowry was so full of brogue and blarney, so utterly *un*-insistent about anything that everything he said seemed plausible. If he had informed you that the moon was blue or the Pope an Orangeman then you would have been more than inclined to believe him and would certainly not have been boorish enough to question the source of his information.

'But, Forbes' – Albert sought reassurance – 'I mean, your brother has done well for himself. He's financially secure, is he not?'

'Done well and will be doing better,' Gowry had answered.

'Wait until he has the lot of us over here, then you'll be seeing the sparks fly.'

'All of you?' said Albert.

'He'll be leaving him with nothing before he's done.'

'Leaving who with nothing?'

'Him. Dada. The Owd Devil himself.'

'Is that Forbes's intention, to ruin your father?'

'Nah, nah,' Gowry said. 'More it is to give the rest of us a leg up by fetching us all to Scotland, by giving us the opportunity to clear out of Malahide, to better ourselves. I tell you fair and square, Albert, there will not be enough in the brewing of stout to support even one of us before long.'

'And will' – Albert cleared his throat – 'I mean, will Forbes be able to support you all over here?'

'He will be supporting us and we will be supporting him.'

'Was this always his plan?'

'Always,' Gowry lied. 'Since we were kiddies shivering under corn sacks by the light o' the peat fire.'

'Corn sacks?'

'For blankets.'

'Oh!'

'The nuns would come and throw scraps over the wall for us,' Gowry went on, plying his vocation as a tall tale-teller. 'Think of that, Bertie, having to be fed by nuns, though we were Protestants and there were thousands of starving Papes queuing up for the Church's charity.'

'I hadn't realised,' Albert said, 'that things were so bad.'

'Bad!' Gowry exclaimed, not raising his voice. 'They were worse.'

'So being a – what is it?'

'Chauffeur.' Gowry completed the question with its answer, 'Sure and being a chauffeur ain't so bad after all, not when you never saw a motoring vehicle until you were twelve years old.'

It didn't dawn on Albert until later that *he* hadn't seen a petrol-driven motor vehicle until he was almost thirty, mainly because Daimler – or was it Benz? – hadn't invented one prior to that time. He did not disagree with Gowry McCulloch, though, for the talk flowed on like the very stuff of history and one small inaccuracy made no difference and since what he was being told was only what he wanted to hear and to believe.

'And your sisters?' Albert said.

'Will do anything Forbes tells them to.'

'Loyalty, yes,' said Albert. 'I must say I do admire loyalty.'

'She's loyal to him, ain't she?' Gowry asked. 'Your daughter?'

'Sylvie?' Albert did not offer a correction. 'Yes, she loves him.'

'Aye, don't we all love a chap who succeeds against the odds?'

Deceived by the platitude, Bertie nodded agreement and asked, very humbly, if he might order another beer.

Forbes was more vigorous in the morning than in the evening when the rigours of employment had taken their toll and a slackening of mental agility rendered him less able to cope with Sylvie's little tricks and tirades. There was another reason too: he called before noon whenever his schedule allowed because he had begun to wonder if her sexual inventiveness indicated that she was entertaining other men besides himself.

Suspicion kept him from becoming bored with the same old fare, however. Jealousy over imagined infidelities fuelled both his love and his lust and he would question her closely about the handsome minister at St Columba's or the preacher at the Maryhill Home Mission for, at his insistence, Sylvie had relinquished all connection with the Coral Strand in favour of the Church and the clique of holy-rollers who met in the tin hall in Stevenson Street.

Brilliant though he was at mathematical calculations, Forbes knew nothing about psychology and even less about the theological hair-splitting that pitted free will against determinism. Comparisons between his lover and his wife seldom fell in the latter's favour. He regarded Sylvie as far more interesting than Lindsay not in spite but because of her craziness. He even encouraged her to preach bizarre little sermons about God's guiding hand while he lay damp and sated against her, to repeat sentimental poems in his ear while he dressed; to twist and pervert his judgement to the point where he thought her unique and curiously impenetrable in way that his pretty, plain-spoken little wife could never be now that he had succeeded in domesticating her.

He did not understand Sylvie and therefore could not control her. He provided her with every material thing, even loved her after his fashion; yet he remained blind to the fact that she was not like other women and marched to a different drummer.

'What are you doing, sweetheart?'

'Did Dada let you in?'

'I have my own key, remember.'

'Has Dada gone?'

'Yes, he's popped out for a little while.'

'Is Gowry not with you?'

'Gowry has gone with your dada for a glass of refreshment.' She nodded. 'Is it cold this morning?'

'Very cold.'

'I wish it were summer. Do you remember summer, Forbes?'

'Of course I remember summer.'

He crossed the parlour and, slipping round the back of her chair, kissed the top of her head. Morag, the day-maid, had lighted the fire and dusted the room and everything looked perfectly ship-shape. Morag would be in the kitchen now along with Mrs Maddigan, the non-resident cook cum housekeeper, who was the very soul of discretion and wouldn't show her face when he, Forbes, was visiting. Sylvie was clad in a close-fitting camisole under a silk dressing-gown that he had bought her last New Year. In spite of the bitter weather, her little feet were bare. Her hair had been brushed and ribboned, though, and there was nothing slatternly about her appearance.

She said, 'Do you remember what you said last summer?'

June past; a glorious summer afternoon. He had dismissed Gowry and had taken the wheel of the motor and with Sylvie at his side had driven out into the countryside west of the city. She had been in chiffon, he recalled, pale lemon chiffon, cool and fragrant as a marsh flower in the baking heat of the afternoon. They had eaten lunch in the garden of a loch-side hotel, then had puttered along a rutted back road between somnolent trees and fields heavy with ripening barley. In one of those fields he had made love to her. He had wooed her first, murmuring, touching, sleek with perspiration, lying on a plaid rug in the motionless barley field a million miles from anywhere.

The unreality of the setting had obviously fixed the day in her mind, for she referred to it often and seemed to be chiding him because there had been no other like it.

'I remember what we did,' Forbes replied.

'What you said?'

'What did I say?'

'You said you loved me.'

'And I do. I do love you, Sylvie.'

She shook her head. 'It isn't the same. Why isn't it the same?'

He had no answer, no explanation beyond the obvious: it was summer no longer, the streets of Glasgow were locked in freezing fog. It could not be the same now as it had been then, for transcendent moments of happiness could not be recalled, could not be precisely duplicated like the spacing of ordinates.

'No,' Forbes said. 'Perhaps next summer we'll—'

'Will you come to live with me next summer?'

'Oh, Sylvie . . .' He sighed, then said, 'What's *this* you're doing?'

He leaned over her shoulder and studied the photograph she had clipped from the *Glasgow Herald*: the King, the Queen and Princess Louise in court attire. He could not imagine what occasion had brought the three together until, peering at the small print, he saw that it was not a recent photograph but one drawn from files to illustrate an article on naval reform, though what Princess Louise had to do with the Royal Navy, Forbes had no idea.

Together with three large scrapbooks and a pot of paste, other illustrations snipped from newspapers and journals littered the table: the Grevilles' Whitsun party at Reigate; the King and Admiral Fisher riding in a carriage; an oval portrait of Mrs George Keppel who everyone knew was the King's special friend. Court and courtiers, lords and ladies, aristocrats and diplomats, the odd foreign prince or dignitary, Sylvie was obsessed with them. The closet in the hallway was crammed with mutilated copies of the *Sketch*, the *Tatler* and the *London Illustrated News* but Sylvie had no interest in the world at large, only in the artificial glamour of garden parties, court balls, race meetings, yachting regattas, banquets, state openings, fashions and frothy gossip. She spent hours browsing through her collection of scraps or, as now, bringing them up to date. It was, Albert said, a harmless pastime. Forbes agreed, even although he still had enough of the Irishman in him to resent the English monarchy's glittering appeal.

'That's a pretty one,' he said.

He slid his hands from her shoulders and cupped her breasts through gown and camisole.

Sylvie cocked her head and studied the portrait of Alice Keppel for a moment, sighed. 'They say she sleeps with him.'

'I expect she does,' said Forbes.

For a moment or two he had almost forgotten why he had called this morning. Touching her reminded him. He did not have much time. Gowry would be hammering at the door in twenty-five or thirty minutes to remind him that he was expected at Beardmore's. Hastily, he rubbed his palms over Sylvie's nipples and nuzzled his chin against her curls.

'I don't think she sleeps with him. I don't think the King would do that.'

'I wouldn't be so sure, dearest,' Forbes said.

'He is in love with his queen, with Alexandra.'

'Hmm.' Forbes slipped the tips of his fingers under the top of the camisole, stretching the ribbons and lace. 'You're probably right.'

'Why do people make up such nasty stories?'

'I've no idea.'

'It's mischief, that's all. It's wickedness.'

'Yes, of course it is.'

He could feel her ribs rise and fall against his fingertips. Distracted and indecisive, she was at her most vulnerable. All he had to do was tell her what he wanted and she would comply.

Morning meetings lacked the sort of stealth that novelty required, though, a drowned light, a sheet to hide under, silence in the streets. He wanted her, though, and quickly, quickly. He hurried to the door and turned the key. Unbuttoning himself, he returned to the table, lifted her up by the hands and drew her to him. He opened her robe. Her expression was blank. He had seen that expression too often of late, as if she were thinking of someone else. He slipped his hand beneath the camisole, between her legs. Saw her eyelids droop. Felt her surge against him, warm flesh against his cold fingers.

Braced against the table's edge, he pulled her against him and carefully inserted himself into her. He held her poised for a split second then drew her down on to him. She gave her customary little gasp, then, remembering who she was and what he meant to her, lifted her knees and rocked backwards, throwing her weight against his forearms. He entered her, not suddenly: he might be selfish but he was never cruel. She began to move against him, rhythmically at first then frantically. He tightened his buttocks and the long muscles of his thighs. Kneading her belly against him, she held him within her. Holding, holding, until quickly and carelessly he spent. When he struggled to extract himself, he lost balance, fell against her and, still spending, turned her around and around in a brusque little dance.

'Stop, Sylvie,' he gasped. 'Stop, let me . . .'

She refused to release him. She sagged against him, clutching whatever was within her and beseeching it to stay.

He dragged himself from her, angrily hauled up his trousers, tucked in his shirt and, with his back to her, began buttoning, as if modesty would undo what had already been done. When he swung round again, still furious, he saw that she was crouched on all fours, rocking her hips back and forth, back and forth as if she had been suddenly struck by pain.

Astonished, he knelt by her. 'Sylvie? What's wrong? Did I hurt you? Oh, sweetheart, I didn't mean to hurt you.'

The dressing-gown hung about her, hiding her body like a tent. She rocked for a moment more then abruptly sat back on her heels and drew the gown about her.

'There!' she said, smiling. 'That's done.'

'What? What's done?' Forbes frowned, then scowled. He got to his feet. 'Go and wash,' he told her. 'Sylvie, go and wash immediately.'

She looked up at him, smiling dreamily.

'Are you not staying for lunch?' she asked.

'No, damn it. I'm not staying for lunch. Sylvie. Wash.'

'Wash it away. Wash it away. Wash it all away.'

The chant reminded him of Harry's childish crooning. Anger welled up in him once more. Helpless anger. He had no knowledge of how she cleansed herself and the mechanisms that he supposed he knew so well became secret and arcane. He reached down, took her by the arm and lifted her, not roughly.

'Please, sweetheart,' he said. 'We do have to be careful, you know.'

She laughed silently. She looked wicked, then innocent, innocent and wicked by turns. He was helpless now, anger transformed into panic. He caught her hand, led her swiftly across the drawing-room and unlocked the door. He glanced across the hall, glimpsed the servant, Morag, in the kitchen doorway a second before she vanished.

Sylvie skipped beside him, swinging herself on his hand while he steered her to the door of the bathroom and opened it. The light from the marbled window was grey and cold. Brass taps, clinical white enamel, the pedestal, the steely mirror, the copper geyser, the odour of Regina Violet; he felt sickly and unclean pushing her into that chilly, antiseptic room.

'Wash it away. Wash it away. Wash it away,' she chanted gleefully; then, just before he closed the door, wiggled her fingers and showed her teeth once more. 'Bye-bye, dearest. Bye-bye.'

'Sylvie . . .'

The lock clicked loudly.

There was nothing for him to do but wait.

He was still waiting when, twenty minutes later, Gowry arrived to collect him and, ten minutes after that, he left.

The mould loft was enormous. Lindsay never failed to be impressed by it. She loitered on the matting at the top of the stairs and wondered how it would appear from her son's perspective, a vast sea of planks upon which loftmen, draughts-men and carpenters floated like mirages. The air smelled of freshly cut timber, sawdust and chalk, though the floor itself was kept scrupulously clean and there were no loud sounds save the rap of a mallet now and then or the brief, shrill whine of a band saw or planing machine.

It had been almost three years since she had last been here but she remembered most of what Tom had told her about how the floor was prepared for laying-off, how measurements from sheer drawings were chalked or scrived on to the flat black surface. Batten lines for a body plan were already in place and even at this early stage, Lindsay realised that there was something unusual about the shape of the vessel.

Carefully wiping her shoes, Lindsay stepped from the matting and eased her way down the side of the loft. Chalked figures indicated that the length of the vessel was one hundred and forty feet but the beam seemed unusually narrow. Puzzled, she studied the layout intently.

It was not until she glanced up that she noticed that two men were watching her across the breadth of the loft. Tom Calder wore a half-length brown cotton jacket and looked less like a marine engineer than a storekeeper. His companion was dressed in naval uniform. Stepping carefully over the chalk lines, Lindsay made her way towards them.

'Ah, Lindsay,' Tom said. 'I'd like you to meet Lieutenant Commander Geoffrey Paget. Mrs Forbes McCulloch.'

The officer removed his cap, held it down by his trouser-leg, and shook her hand. Although it was cold he wore no topcoat. The two and a half stripes visible on his cuff suggested that he was probably a career officer caught in the limbo where promotions ceased to be automatic. She waited for Tom to explain just what Lieutenant Commander Paget was doing here and where he was based. A naval dockyard had been opened recently at Rosyth on the Forth but she had a feeling, just a feeling, that the officer was not a salt horse, as she had heard them called, but a staffer. Neither Tom nor Geoffrey Paget chose to enlighten her, however, and there was an awkward, almost embarrassed, pause.

At length Tom cleared his throat and said, 'Mrs McCulloch is, in fact, a partner in our company. Quite trustworthy.'

'A partner,' Geoffrey Paget said. 'Really?'

English, well-spoken, with a high, clear voice that hinted at arrogance. Clean-shaven, sharp-featured, hair as fair as her own. Face and hands lightly tanned as if he had recently returned from a Mediterranean tour. She could not decide whether she found him handsome or not – probably not – but she certainly did not find his manner attractive.

'I am not an active partner,' she said. 'I take only a passing interest in what goes on at the yard. My husband—'

'I believe you've met Forbes,' Tom put in.

'Yes, I have.'

Lindsay said, 'Are you here to monitor our Admiralty contract, sir?'

Tom, she noticed, looked pained.

The officer, however, showed no displeasure, simply tilted his head back a little as if to distance himself from her.

'What contract would that be, ma'am?' he enquired.

'The one that my father is engaged upon.'

'Your father, ma'am?'

'Arthur Franklin.'

'Oh, you're one of the family,' Geoffrey Paget said. 'I see.'

'I would hardly be strolling about the mould loft if I wasn't one of the family, sir, now would I?' Lindsay said. 'My grandfather is Owen Franklin and I am a stockholder in the firm. Even by the Admiralty's strict criteria, and having regard to the fact that I'm female, I suppose I *might* be considered — what was it, Tom? — trustworthy?'

'I shouldn't have said that,' Tom admitted. 'My apologies. It's just that, well, I didn't expect to see you here, Lindsay. Got caught off guard a bit.'

'I brought Harry to visit.'

'Harry?' Tom said. 'Where is the wee chap?'

'Grandee took him to look at the boats.'

'Well wrapped up, I hope,' Tom said.

'Well wrapped up,' said Lindsay.

Mention of her family steadied her. Her grandfather had built the floor upon which they stood now and her grandfather had found her 'trustworthy' enough to incorporate into the partnership, her sex notwithstanding. She was just as entitled to be here as anyone, including naval officers.

'Do you have children, Lieutenant?' she asked suddenly.

'No, I'm afraid that I do not.'

'I have two children, two sons,' Lindsay said, as if that were justification enough for her intrusion, a basic sort of accounting that even a naval officer might understand. She assumed that he had a mother and that, even if he did not have a wife — perhaps he did for all she knew – he would be sensible enough to appreciate that the next generation of cadets would have to come from somewhere. She was tempted to press the point but, to her chagrin, Geoffrey Paget had taken Tom by the arm and, excluding her from the conversation, had deliberately turned away.

'Sir?' she said, testily.

He put out his hand, wrist bent. 'One moment, please.'

He spoke to Tom in a low voice. She saw Tom – her ally – glance at her as if he had never seen her before. The word 'trustworthy' rang in her head like a telephone bell, irritating and insistent. She told herself to be calm, not to allow herself to be riled by this display of masculine superiority.

She said, 'If you wish, sir, I will leave.'

'No,' Geoffrey Paget said. 'Wait.'

He turned again, not in the least contrite, and placed himself before her. It was only then that she realised how tall he was, almost as tall as Tom, in fact. He separated his feet as if he were standing on the deck of a flagship, squaring up to an admiral. He still held his hat down by his trouser-leg and Lindsay noticed how he tapped the shiny brim against his knee two, three, four times before he spoke. Behind the officer, Tom raised his eyebrows and shrugged as if to disassociate himself from the official line.

The officer said, 'What has your father told you of what's going on?'

'Not a thing,' Lindsay said. 'All I know, sir, is that he and my husband have both been much occupied in meeting the demands of a naval commission.'

'Did either of them tell you what this commission involves?'

'No, they did not.'

There was no pause, no hesitation. It was, Lindsay imagined, like being interrogated by an advocate in a court of law.

Officer Paget said, 'Do you know what's being laid off on the floor behind you, ma'am?'

'I'm not sufficiently versed in naval architecture to be able to tell from the moulds what sort of vessel we're building.'

'Do you know what it's not?'

'It's not a torpedo-boat or a destroyer,' Lindsay said. 'Or, if it is, it's not like any I've ever seen before.'

'If I tell you . . .' Geoffrey Paget hesitated. 'Will you promise, will you swear, not to discuss the matter with anyone?'

'Who would I discuss . . . ? Yes,' Lindsay said, 'you have my word.'

'Total secrecy, Linnet,' Tom put in.

She inclined away from them and surveyed the battens and scrive lines that were already in place. Towards the top of the loft a team of carpenters were mocking up a portion of the hull in rough frames and sections, a procedure that even she knew was unusual.

She had no doubt at all that the boat was a weapon of war.

'Total secrecy,' Lindsay agreed.

'It's a submarine,' Geoffrey Paget said, 'a brand-new type of submarine.'

And Lindsay, for no reason that she could explain, experienced within her a first faint stirring of fear.

CHAPTER SIXTEEN

Marching with the Times

It did not take Lindsay long to recover an interest in what was going on at Aydon Road and to discover why Lieutenant Commander Paget had been so touchy about her unexpected appearance in the loft.

The answer lay in the echoing corridors of the Admiralty building in Whitehall, where Admiral Sir John Fisher was manoeuvring to impose his will upon the salty old die-hards who resisted his proposals for modernising the navy. They, the salty old die-hards, believed that the legacy of Frobisher and Drake, Raleigh and Nelson, was sufficient to sustain them and that as the British fleet had always been the finest in the world it was bound to remain so by deed of history. Fisher, however, had a weather eye on Germany's growing fleet at Kiel and let it be known that he would seize any excuse to destroy it without formal declaration of war, a threat that naturally caused panic in the arrogant and suspicious Germans as well as the arrogant and suspicious gentlemen of Westminster.

The fact that Jackie Fisher had the ear of the sovereign and, whatever his faults as a diplomat, could not be accused of lacking patriotism, gave him an edge over his detractors. To shake off the complacent torpor that had paralysed the naval authorities for so long, he was granted funds to undertake a rebuilding programme the like of which had never been seen: an immense combination of shipbuilding skills and talents designed to ensure Britain's domination of the seas for a century or more. Armour-plate, guns, warships: the list of orders that went out into the land was astonishing, and Franklin's, that modest little Clydeside firm, was not forgotten.

Under special licence from Vickers, to Franklin's fell the honour of building the prototype of a new class of ocean-going submarine based on designs by the Royal Navy's most experienced architects. That Vickers had apparently been overlooked and the navy's own construction yards similarly bypassed spoke volumes for the First Sea Lord's deviousness. He knew how critical the old curmudgeons would be if the vessel failed to meet standards or, worse, went down with all hands, for there were already far too many senior officers in command positions who regarded sub-marines as flash-in-the-pan. It was just as well to have the thing built up in Scotland by a firm so small and inconsequential that it would make an ideal scapegoat if the design proved faulty or something went horribly wrong on the trials.

Donald and Martin were in the process of finalising the contract. Tom had been heavily involved in preliminary discus-sions and had spent rather too much time in consultation with Royal Navy architects, engineering officers and gunnery experts, all of whom seemed eager to add a wrinkle or frill to the elaborate drawings from which the prototype would be con-structed. She would be propelled on the surface by two massive diesel engines, far larger and more powerful than any ever fitted into a submersible before. She would be ocean-going and fast, carry three guns and a crew of twenty-two and, according to Fisher, would make mincemeat of anything afloat, particularly if it happened to be German.

Even during her first confinement Lindsay had heard some-thing of the war in the Far East, of great sea battles fought between the Russian and Japanese fleets when tactical use of torpedoes had changed the nature of sea warfare during the routs at Vladivostock, Chemulpho and Port Arthur.

If she had been livelier and not burdened by the duties of marriage and motherhood she might have taken a keener interest in what was going on halfway around the world. But by then she was nursing a child, a son, and all her perspectives had altered. Soon after Philip was born a strange new component crept into her thinking: not fear – not exactly fear – but an inescapable nagging feeling that every bullet, every shell, every torpedo fired anywhere would create a resonance that might somehow damage her children. There was nothing supernatural about it, no element of prescience. It stemmed only from physical weakness coupled to Forbes's insistence that she remain buried at home.

Then on a cold January morning, just after she had taken her first step against domestic tyranny, she met Lieutenant Commander Geoffrey Paget and was drawn into the wide world again, a world where fear had a shape, a face, and a uniform, and turned out to be more frightening than anything she could possibly have imagined.

Geoffrey was the only son of an only son. His father had been a small-town banker who had entered the accounts section of the Royal Navy and had attained the exalted position of Cashier at the Chatham dockyard before he was struck down by kidney failure at the age of forty-six.

Geoffrey had been fourteen at the time. Born and raised in civil quarters in the village of Ashercombe and educated at a modest public school near Gillingham, there had never been any question of what would become of him; his destiny was written not in the stars but in the tides. Within months of his father's death he had been enrolled as a cadet at Dartmouth College and his career in the Royal Navy launched.

Geoffrey had known no other life but the navy. His mother – God bless her – continued to live in Ashercombe with her sister and her sister's husband, worthy, well-to-do provision merchants with established naval contracts and a wholesale outlet in

Maidstone. Geoffrey regarded Ashercombe as home, though he spent no more than two or three weeks a year there. He had sailed in many ships to many ports, had served on coastal patrol boats, and, in his mid-twenties, had improved his chances of promotion by undertaking a two-year course in ship construction. It was a circuitous route on to Fisher's staff at the Admiralty but one that in hindsight appeared to have been engineered. After four years in submarines he had become the voice in Jackie Fisher's ear on all matters related to that specialised aspect of warfare.

Geoffrey was no spy, nor was it his brief to act as a technical supervisor; there were other officers better equipped than he for that role. Primarily he was Jackie Fisher's man. The Vickers' licence stipulated that what was being built on Clydeside remain secret and it was to ensure the fulfilment of that clause that Lieutenant Commander Paget was assigned to liaise with the Franklins.

Falling for the wife of a partner was emphatically not part of the detail, particularly as Geoffrey had just broken off a five-year engagement with a certain Miss Elizabeth Altham for the plain and simple reason that he did not love her enough to wish to marry her.

Recently he had come to believe that he did not know what love was; not, that is, until he looked across the mould loft in Aydon Road in the bleak light of a January morning and saw a white-faced little woman in neat but dowdy tailor-made tweeds with a hat that seemed just a shade over-large for her small, pinched, pretty features. Nothing in her manner suggested dowdiness or, for that matter, humility and Geoffrey was too inexperienced with women to realise that resistance was possible let alone necessary.

Lindsay in turn refused to be impressed by the naval officer and apparently had no interest in an Englishman whom she had only just met and who, if she were lucky, she would never have to meet again.

She did meet him again, however.

She met him at Cissie's apartments in Sandyford Avenue less than one week later, not by accident but by design.

By then she had found out a little about Lieutenant Commander Paget, not from her father but from her husband who, it seemed, had dined with the chap at the Barbary, and regarded the English naval officer as a bit of a joke. Lieutenant Commander Paget did not regard Forbes McCulloch as a bit of a joke. He found nothing comical in the slippery Dubliner or in his brother who, for some unimaginable reason, had been brought along to make up the party. He, Geoffrey, had been silenced by the presence of the brother and an evening that should have been devoted to business deteriorated into a bout of hard drinking and soft-voiced boasting.

Geoffrey, therefore, remained less impressed by Mrs McCulloch's husband than by Mrs McCulloch herself.

He rose from the armchair where Cissie had placed him.

'Why, Mrs McCulloch,' he said, 'I did not expect to find you here.'

'Oh! Nor I you, Lieutenant.'

'Lieutenant Commander.'

'My apologies.'

'No, ma'am. *My* apologies. I should not have corrected you.'

'If I am open to correction then you were right to do so.'

'You are not open to correction.'

'Then you're *not* a Lieutenant Commander.'

'Ma'am — yes, I am.'

'Then I stand corrected.'

'Why stand at all, for heaven's sake,' Cissie intervened. 'Sit, the pair of you, and I'll ring for tea.'

After tea and scones had been served by the Calders' maid, Geoffrey relaxed. He had been drilled in social niceties and could balance a teacup and saucer on his knee with the best of them.

'You did not bring your little boy with you today, Mrs McCulloch?'

'No. He is at home with his nurse.'

'I thought perhaps you were one of those mothers who cannot bear to be separated from their children even for an afternoon.'

'Are there such mothers?' Cissie said. 'I'm certainly not one of them. I'm only too relieved to have a breather now and then. Besides, it's only right that a boy should spend time with his grandmother.'

'Is that where Ewan is?' Lindsay said.

'She's taken him shopping, Pansy and she.'

Geoffrey did not seem put out by domestic small talk.

Conversation drifted this way and that, without target or objective.

She watched him. He watched her. They were, even then, wary.

'Are you billeted in Glasgow?'

'I have a room in the Conservative Club.'

'Very grand,' said Cissie.

'Officially I'm on temporary attachment to the staff of Rear Admiral Collings at Rosyth,' Geoffrey said.

Lindsay asked another question, then another. He answered with apparent candour, his replies too skilfully worded to give much away.

Cissie was not insensitive to what was going on, though she was hard put to explain it to her husband later that evening.

'No, no,' Tom said. 'I find it hard to believe that Lindsay would be daft enough to make eyes at a sailor.'

'Some sailor!' Cissie said. 'He's a Lieutenant Commander, as he constantly keeps reminding us.'

'You don't like him?' Tom asked.

'I didn't say that.' Cissie arched a provocative eyebrow. 'I think he's very attractive, if you must know – in a stuffy kind of way.'

'Isn't that what you used to say about me?'

'No, I never thought you attractive – just stuffy. And I was right, Mr Calder,' Cissie informed her husband. 'I was absolutely right.'

'Did she leave with him?' Tom asked.

'Yes.'

'On foot?'

'Well, I didn't see the royal yacht moored outside. Yes, dear, on foot.'

'It doesn't seem quite right,' Tom said.

'What doesn't?'

'I mean, Lindsay's a married woman.'

'But look who she's married to,' Cissie said.

'Even so,' Tom said, 'it isn't proper.'

'Stuffy. I told you so. Stuffy.'

'I wonder what they found to talk about,' Tom said.

'Boats, I expect,' said Cissie.

They had not talked of boats or the building of boats or of the ships that Geoffrey had sailed in or the ports he had visited. They did not discuss the possibility of finding a cab or remark on the fact that he was walking with her and that she seemed quite content to allow him to accompany her through the forlorn dusk of the winter afternoon.

Sandyford Avenue ran into Scotstoun Avenue, Scotstoun Avenue into Kennilworth. Kennilworth in turn rose up past the little mansions of the well-heeled and well-to-do. It did not seem like half past four o'clock but like some unrecorded hour that was neither day nor night, for winter on Clydeside distorted sights, smells and sounds. Leaves shoaled the pavement's edge, dry as tinder in the frost. Frost was already beginning to fall again, sifting down out of a brown foggy air that tasted of horses and coal smoke. Tram-cars clashed on Dumbarton Road, trains rattled along the suburban lines that linked commerce to home comforts; the hoofs of the horses of draymen and merchants, explosions of exhaust from motorised vans and motor-cars and, when they finally reached the tenements at the back of Brunswick Park, the chatter of schoolchildren trailing home for tea.

What did they talk about that first time? Lindsay could not remember. They might have walked in silence for all it mattered.

It was not at all as it had been when she had fallen in love with Forbes. There was no desire for the experience itself, no urgent need to possess. She had learned the lessons of marriage and knew now what love was not. She had no longing to be loved by a naval officer, a stranger from the south. Their affinity had no basis in reality. She did not love Geoffrey Paget, not yet, but in the course of a companionable stroll through suburban streets she realised that she did not love Forbes, that her marriage was, and had been from the first, a sham.

'Is this where you live, Mrs McCulloch?'

'Close by.'

They stopped by the gates of St Anne's Church, the hump of the hill that led over Brunswick Park Road and down to the crescent behind them. Five minutes would see her to her door but tactfully he did not offer to walk her so far. She smiled and offered him her hand. He took it, shook it briefly, tipped his cap. He waited, though, and did not immediately turn away.

A horse-van trundled past, trailing floury white dust; a motor-cab nipped briskly over the cobbles and into Bradley Street.

'I must go,' Lindsay said.

'Of course.'

'Do you know where you are, sir?'

'Yes, I know where I am.'

'If you go down . . .'

'I know where I am,' he said again.

'Thank you for walking me home, Lieutenant Commander.'

'It was my pleasure, Mrs McCulloch.'

'Perhaps we will meet again before you go back to London.'

'I hope that may be the case.'

She sensed that Geoffrey Paget could not make the running no matter how inclined he might be to do so. The friendship could not be rushed. There were decisions to be made, intricate decisions so tiny and imprecise that they were hardly more than gestures. She needed to be confident, to lift herself up, find some of the old Franklin fire, to march with the times. But she was afraid, afraid of what she had discovered about her marriage, what it might mean in the long term and how many times would she have to be together with Geoffrey Paget before she could be sure exactly where she stood in his estimation, if she stood anywhere at all, that is?

She took a few quick steps uphill.

Then stopped. Then turned.

He stood as he had stood in Cissie's drawing-room, feet apart, watching her, waiting perhaps for her decision.

'Geoffrey,' Lindsay heard herself say. 'Do you sing?'

'Sing?' When he laughed he looked quite different. 'No, I don't sing. I've a voice like a crow, I'm afraid.' Then he said, 'I do play the piano, however.'

'Really? The piano?'

'Why do you ask?'

'No reason,' Lindsay said and, swinging away, set off up Brunswick Hill.

'A musical evening?' Arthur said. 'Good God, we haven't had one of those in ages. A musical evening? There's a jolly thought. Might be just what we need to cheer us all up.'

'It won't cheer us up,' said Forbes. 'It'll only unsettle the children.'

'Unsettle them? Why?' said Arthur.

'The noise.'

'Singing isn't a noise.'

'It is to some,' said Gowry, who had invited himself to supper again.

Winn was upstairs putting the children to bed but Blossom was present. She nodded in agreement with her brother.

'I thought,' said Arthur, 'that all you Irish folk were musical.'

'You're obviously confusing us with the Welsh,' said Blossom.

She was a large young woman, broad-shouldered, broad-hipped, her features disconcertingly like those of her mother. She had also inherited Kay's argumentative streak and could turn a chance remark into an argument at the drop of a hat. The informality that Arthur had introduced into the household in respect of Miss Runciman had backfired upon him now. He could not reasonably insist that 'servants' be kept in their place, not when Eleanor was seated at his right hand and not, especially, when Forbes's servants were also relatives. He could not quite accept that Blossom and Winn were actually his nieces and Gowry his nephew.

Cautiously, Arthur said, 'I don't believe I am.'

'It's dancers we are,' said Gowry.

'Not singers,' said Blossom.

'I see,' said Arthur, 'then perhaps you could dance for us.'

Brothers and sister exchanged glances filled with contempt for the poor benighted Scotsman who imagined that he could wheedle them into co-operating.

Lindsay said, 'It need not be a large gathering.'

'It need not be a gathering at all,' said Forbes.

'A few friends, Cissie and Tom,' Arthur said. 'Pappy if he's at home. Donald and Aunt Lilias, of course . . .'

'It sounds to me like a large gathering,' said Blossom.

Lindsay said, 'You are under no obligation to attend.'

'Am I not now?' said Blossom. 'Will we not be invited?'

'Of course you'll be invited,' Arthur said.

'However, you don't have to accept,' said Lindsay.

'I suppose we'll just have to sit upstairs listening to your caterwauling . . .'

'Bloss,' Forbes warned.

Scowling, the woman shovelled beef stew into her mouth.

'I'm thinking I'll go out that evening,' Gowry said.

It was on the tip of Lindsay's tongue to remind him that he

was only a guest in the house and had, in theory at least, a place of his own to go to.

'Winn won't like it,' Blossom said.

'It has nothing to do with us,' Eleanor Runciman said. 'We are servants here and it's up to the master to do as he sees fit.'

'Is it now?' Blossom said. 'Forbes, is it?'

Eleanor said, 'I will cater to the guests downstairs. If you feel you will be inconvenienced by the noise then perhaps you should ask for an evening off.'

'An evening off?' said Blossom. 'What would I do with an evening off?'

'I simply cannot imagine,' said Eleanor.

'If you . . .'

'Bloss,' Forbes said again, and shook his head. He turned to Lindsay. 'I doubt if you're strong enough to put up with a houseful of choristers.'

'Oh, but I am,' Lindsay told him, smiling. 'There's nothing I would like better than to have the whole choir round for a jamboree.'

'What's a jamboree?' said Gowry.

'A sort of musical evening,' Forbes said. 'Dearest, are you sure you know what you're doing?'

'Indeed,' said Lindsay, 'I do.'

'That's settled then,' said Arthur, rubbing his hands.

'When will it be, Mr Arthur?' Eleanor asked.

'Two weeks on Saturday. Time enough?'

'Ample time, Papa.'

'Will you write the invitations, or shall I?' Arthur asked.

'I will,' Lindsay answered and, lifting her knife and fork again, went on eating as if nothing at all had happened.

'He plays the piano?' Cissie said. 'Heavens! I can't imagine him playing the piano. I'd have thought that a banjo would have been more his style.'

'Prejudice,' Lindsay said. 'Rank prejudice.'

'Well, I mean,' said Cissie, 'I can hardly imagine him lugging a Steinway around in his dunnage. Don't all sailors play the banjo, or is it the mandolin?'

'He isn't a rating, Cissie. He's an officer. He has been a serving officer for twenty years.'

'How do you know? Did he tell you? Have you met him again?'

'Papa told me.'

'Did your father tell you what our dear Lieutenant Commander is doing, hanging about Franklin's?'

'It's a state secret, apparently.'

Cissie shrugged her son higher into her arms. They were in Cissie's drawing-room and Ewan, a rather petted little boy, had grown weary of his cousin Harry's antics and had crept up on to his mother's knee. Wrapped in a fine lace shawl, Philip slept on the sofa, well padded and protected with cushions. Winn and the Calders' nursemaid, Jenny, had been allowed a half-hour to take tea in the kitchen and, no doubt, exchange gossip.

'It's the submarine, isn't it?' Cissie said.

'How do you know about the submarine? Did Tom tell you?'

'No, Tom's said not a word. I peeped at his papers.'

'Cissie Franklin!'

'If four hundred common shipwrights know what's going on at Aydon Road why shouldn't the wife of a manager?'

'That isn't the point.'

'I notice that you know what's going on, about the submarine.'

'It's a matter of being trusted with a secret and keeping it.'

'It is a submarine, though, aren't I right?'

Lindsay hesitated. 'Yes.'

'I'm not so simple as I look, you know.'

Cissie detached her son's thumb from his mouth and, as he cuddled into her, tousled his fair hair with her fingertips. On the floor behind the sofa Harry was seated cross-legged, happily imitating the sound of a circular saw and waving his arms in an attempt to induce his 'cousin' to come and play with him again. Philip, very lightly, snored.

'How long,' Cissie said, 'does it take to build a submarine?'

'I'm not sure.'

'Is that also a state secret?'

'Completion date is the twenty-fifth of May.'

'So Lieutenant Paget will be in Glasgow until May, will he?'

'Lieutenant Commander,' Lindsay said.

Cissie laughed. 'Of course, of course. Lieutenant Commander. Will he?'

'I hope he will,' said Lindsay. 'I rather like him.'

'Is he definitely coming to your musical evening?'

'If he's not on duty.'

'If he's not on duty,' said Cissie, wryly. 'He won't be on duty.'

'What makes you say that?'

'Because' – Cissie grinned wickedly – 'I think he rather likes you too.'

Owen had been reluctant to leave the city at that cruel time of year. He'd had a heavy cold before Christmas and a chesty cough that had persisted into the New Year in spite of Dr Hough's best efforts to shift it. It was not Glasgow's gay social whirl that inclined Owen to linger in Harper's Hill but, rather, a stultifying weakness of the spirit and something akin to depression.

'Go abroad. Go to the south of France,' Donald had ranted. 'God Almighty, Pappy, it isn't as if you can't afford it.'

'The King pops off for weeks on end. If it's good enough for Teddy,' Martin had put in, 'it should be good enough for you.'

He did not go abroad. He had never willingly gone abroad, even when Kath was alive. Such trips as there had been were undertaken purely in pursuit of business. He took no pleasure in being far away from home. That said, he had to confess that Strathmore had grown upon him. He felt almost as much at home there as he did in Glasgow. His longing to be in the city, at the centre of things, had waned with the years. He was happy enough to take off for the country with a few old cronies for company or even to be on his own, with Giles to see to his needs. When the lease of the old house came up for renewal he hadn't thought twice about signing for another five years.

He was slightly less than eager to entertain Sir Robert Montgomery Raeburn and his wife, Edith, however. He could not imagine what had got into him back in the late summer when he had promised them a week's board and lodging in the snowy season. It was a promise that could not be broken, though, for Bob Raeburn was president of the Institute of Marine Engineers and Shipbuilders and had been a friend of sorts for many years. Bob Raeburn was also an alpinist of some distinction, addicted to chopping his way up icy gullies and fluted snow-fields with his dear lady wife tagging along on a rope behind him. His name was scrawled all over the registers of the Monte Rosa Hotel in Zermatt and the Nesthorn in the Lotschental, accompanied by comments about bad coffee and bad weather and, now and then, a record of an ascent of a difficult ridge or mention of a 'dawdle' along a mule path eight or nine thousand feet above the valley.

In January, three days before the Raeburns were due, Owen and Giles left for Strathmore. The trip was less arduous than it had once been, for the horse-drawn carriage from Perth to the village had been replaced by a motorised omnibus that took less than an hour, even on the unpaved roads. Although it was bitterly cold in the hills there was no trace of fog and the crystal-clear air and brilliant sunshine seemed to benefit Owen's lungs. Within a day of arrival, he felt better than he had done in weeks.

The Raeburns rolled up in due course, complete with two female servants and a mound of luggage that included hanks of brown rope, several pairs of nailed boots, and two long-handled objects like pick-axes. The couple were amiable and only too delighted to have been invited into the heart of the hills in the off season for hospitality. They dined well, chatted to Owen for an hour and then retired early. They were up and gone next morning before Owen had even opened his eyes and he saw them not until a half-hour after dark when, bone weary, they trailed back into Strathmore in search of tea, hot baths and a bed to lie down on for an hour before dinner.

By the middle of the week Owen felt more like a boarding-house keeper than a country-house host and was bored by the couple's tales of perpendicular ascents and hair-rising descents. He was also irked by Sir Robert's prying into Franklin's private affairs. Owen had been informed what was happening at the yard but he hadn't asked to see the drawings and had no intention of divulging any information whatsoever about the prototype. If Sir Robert was so desperate for information then Owen reckoned that he would do better to milk one of his sources in Whitehall.

For Owen it was not an enjoyable week in spite of the fine weather and the beauty of the Perthshire landscapes under snow.

Each day about noon, he went out with Giles for a walk through the birch trees or up the long slope to the ridge above the moor. He felt old now, even in invigorating weather. His legs seemed quite leaden and he pressed on for the full hour simply because he was reluctant to let Giles see just how debilitated he had become and how badly the chest cold had affected his stamina. His breathing was easier; he could feel sharp, unsatu-rated air going down into him like a healing draught and he would stride out for ten or fifteen minutes as if he were still in his prime. But his prime was long past and he knew that his disinterest in the work in the yard, in what his sons and grandsons were up to, indicated that he had retreated into that phase when only a woolly tangle of old habits kept one going at all. He had done his bit, done his best. Soon he would rest in silence, that white, unforgiving silence which to an active man seemed more terrible than all the pains of hell.

In the afternoons, after lunch, he warmed his feet at the log fire, smelled the scent of pine resin and other woody odours that reminded him of his boyhood in Pemberton's backyard – and slept. He did not dream of Pemberton's yard or Aydon Road, of the vigorous days of his youth, of steam engines, of boilers so perfectly constructed that they might have been works of art. He did not even dream of Kath, for here in Strathmore, where he had made a promise that he had failed to keep, she seemed pleasantly at hand, demanding nothing of him, not grief or longing or responsibility, not even the effort of memory.

The cough wakened him from a deep, death-like sleep. He was stretched out in the wooden-armed lounging chair, feet resting on a stool. He wore a huge, knitted cardigan and heavy corduroy trousers and Giles had draped a shawl about his shoulders to cut off the draughts from the half-open door. It was not the chill that wakened him but the cough, the resurrected cough, the violence of which he had almost forgotten in the week among the hills.

'God!' he exclaimed, wrenching himself forward and pressing his hands to his chest. 'God! What is this?'

A fresh spasm wrenched his throat and ribs. He felt as if the fibres along the top of his diaphragm were being torn like old sailcloth. He drove the air down into his lungs and reared back, coughing, coughing, coughing until he felt his lungs release whatever gummy substance had collected in their sacs and vents. He coughed again and, groping for his handkerchief and holding it to his face, coughed once more, more easily this time. Exhausted, he leaned on the chair's wooden arm and rested, then, unfolding the crumpled handkerchief, he peered into it with vague distaste and saw blood.

One solitary gout of bright red blood.

He blinked, closed the handkerchief in his fist and, even as the door opened, flung the cloth on to the back of the logs in the fireplace. He watched it char and begin to smoulder and then, when Giles touched him on the shoulder, started as if from a reverie.

'Are you all right, sir?' Giles enquired.

The servant was concerned. Giles was old too now; no, not

old but older, his crisp black hair flecked with silver, his sober features wrinkled.

'What? Yes, Giles, I'm fine,' Owen answered. 'Bit of a tickle in the throat, that's all.' He forced himself to sit back, to appear relaxed. He yawned and rubbed a hand across his mouth. 'Might have a dram, though, even if it's on the early side. What do you think?'

'Whisky and soda, sir?'

'Whisky and soda would do very nicely. Pour one for yourself while you're at it.'

Giles nodded and went away.

Owen studied the logs in the fireplace, the blistered remains of the handkerchief. He felt no sense of panic or despair. He looked up at the French doors, at the shadows of the evergreens cleaving the white lawn, the cold, blue-enamelled sky above the trees. No pain, no soreness in his throat or chest, only a slight tenderness just under his gullet. None the less he had been given a sign and burning the evidence would not make it go away. He had hoped that when it came it would come quickly. Apparently, that was not to be. The end promised to be just as hard and lonely as the beginning had been. A long haul to the breakers' yard, Owen, a long haul in prospect.

He sighed and hoisted himself to his feet.

When Giles returned a minute or two later, Owen was standing by the fireplace with one foot on the fender and one elbow on the mantelshelf.

He lifted the tumbler from the silver tray and sniffed it.

'Feeling better now, Mr Owen, are we?' Giles said.

'Much better, thanks,' said Owen and, raising his glass to no one in particular, downed his whisky-soda like a man.

'Didn't expect to see you here,' Albert said. 'Kirby's isn't one of your usual haunts, is it?'

'I've been here a few times,' Gowry said.

'Forbes brought you, I suppose.'

'That he did.'

'Where is he then? Where is his majesty?' Bertie said.

'At home in the bosom of his family,' Gowry said.

'On a Saturday night?'

'Musical evening.'

'Pardon?' said Bertie.

'They're all singing bloody songs around the piano.'

'Sounds delightful. Why aren't you there?'

Gowry created a small, strangulated sound in his throat, leaned an elbow on the bar and picked up his glass. He was drinking whisky, Albert noticed, with a beer chaser. Unfortunately he, Albert, had just purchased a tot of rum and paid for it himself.

'I'm here,' Gowry said, 'because I want a word with you.'

Albert was struck by doubt. 'Concerning Sylvie?'

'Concerning Forbes,' said Gowry. 'I've a message to deliver.'

'Why didn't you come to the house with it?'

'He told me I might find you here.'

'Did he, now?' said Albert. 'What is this mysterious message that you don't want Sylvie to hear? Is he tiring of her already?'

'He's got to go away.'

'Away? Where? For how long?'

'Month, maybe more.' Gowry paused to sip beer. 'Business. You should know how it is with Forbes by now, Bertie. No matter how fond he may be of your daughter, business will always come first.'

'A month?' said Albert. 'Sylvie isn't going to like it. What about our financial arrangements?'

'I'll take care of those.'

'You?'

'Well, who else is Forbes going to trust? His missus?'

'He's cutting us adrift, isn't he?'

'No, he's not cutting you adrift, Bertie. If he was cutting you adrift he wouldn't have sent me here, would he? Money ain't the problem,' Gowry said. 'Sylvie's the problem. Forbes doubts if you can cope with her.'

'Oh, I can cope. I *can* cope. I'm her father after all.'

'No, you're not,' said Gowry 'You're no more her father than I am.'

'Forbes told you, did he?'

'Does her real papa know where she is?'

'He thinks she's still in London.'

'Hasn't he tried to find her?'

'He wrote to the Coral Strand once, so I heard.'

'The Coral Strand?' said Gowry.

'It's a missionary society with offices in Holborn.' Albert shrugged. 'It's amazing that he and she have never bumped into each other. Or him and me, for that matter. I mean, you think Glasgow's a small town but you can go about for years without meeting people you know, or would prefer to avoid.'

'Well, you certainly won't be finding her papa in a place like this.'

'Kirby's isn't his style. Since he married into the family I'm sure he'd just rather forget that Sylvie ever existed.'

'A new leaf,' Gowry said, 'that sort of thing?'

'Exactly,' Albert said. 'Marrying into the family was the best thing he ever did. Sooner or later he'll come in for his share, or she will.'

'She?'

'Owen's granddaughter. Cissie.'

'Cissie!' Gowry grinned. 'Of course: Cissie.'

'You did *know* that Tom Calder was Sylvie's father, didn't you?'

'I told you, no secrets between brothers,' Gowry said, and winked. He made a signal to the barmaid and, a moment later, a fresh tot of rum appeared on the counter in front of Albert Hartnell. 'Now who's going to tell Sylvie that Forbes won't be visiting her for some time to come?'

'I suppose I'll have to,' Albert said. 'Unless . . .'

'You want me to do it, don't you?'

'Would you?'

'Of course I will,' said Gowry.

It seemed that Geoffrey had mastered all forty-eight of Bach's preludes, together with several Beethoven sonatas and dozens of music-hall songs. He played with relaxation that Lindsay could only envy. All passages, from *tranquillo* to *vivace*, lay equally easily under his hands.

He invited Lindsay to play with him but this she could not bring herself to do. She stood idly by, fuming at her timidity, while Matilda Perrino – still unmarried – rubbed hip and elbow with the naval officer and scampered her way through a furious Liszt duet until, laughing and red-cheeked, she was forced to surrender. Matilda's reward was a consoling hug from Geoffrey and much applause from the twenty or so fellow musicians who had gathered in the parlour to listen. Thereafter, the piano was Geoffrey Paget's for the rest of the evening.

Arthur sang, Tom Calder too; it was almost like the old days, except that Martin and Donald were absent, Mercy, pregnant once more, had turned down an invitation, and the room was full of a younger element from the choir; younger, some of them, than Lindsay herself which made her feel that she had grown up rather too quickly.

Blossom had vanished upstairs with a supper tray for Winn who had elected to sulk in the nursery for the whole of the evening. Forbes was out of his depth among choristers and instrumentalists whom he could not dominate or impress. He had gone off too, the Lord knew where. When supper was announced the choir members made a beeline for the tables in the hall. Geoffrey remained at the piano, playing jolly little tunes with a shanty flavour, playing so lightly that the keys seemed to offer no resistance at all.

Lindsay stood by the piano, watching him. He looked up and smiled, raised an eyebrow as if to indicate that he was not embarrassed by his talent. There was no secret to it, no dark discipline. He had, he said, always been keen on music, had taken lessons from an early age and, even now, practised whenever he could.

'I'm rusty, though,' he said.

'Oh, no,' said Lindsay. 'No, you're not.'

'I think the piano flatters me. It's a very fine instrument.'

'Come whenever you're free,' Lindsay heard herself say. 'Come any afternoon and use it, practise upon it. I'll make sure that you are not disturbed.'

'Is that a genuine offer?'

'Absolutely genuine.'

'What will your father say?'

'Papa won't mind in the slightest.'

Geoffrey paused. 'And your husband?'

'Forbes has no say over what goes on in the piano parlour.' She flushed. 'I mean, please come whenever you wish, whenever you have time to spare.'

He continued to play, glancing down at the keyboard for a moment. The tune was sprightly, almost rollicking. She watched the fluid movement of his hands, the left in particular, and felt within her that little niggle of fear again accompanied by a strange sweet narrowing of focus. Then two Brunswick Park sopranos, juggling plates and glasses, appeared giggling in the doorway and silks and velvets filled the corner of Lindsay's eye. She heard Matilda call out, 'I have it. I have something for the lieutenant. No need for you to bother,' and the choirmaster's spinster daughter came scurrying across the parlour carrying a plate heaped with cooked meats with which to entice the bachelor officer.

Geoffrey said, quietly, 'I'm tempted to take you up on it, you know.'

'Please,' Lindsay said, 'please do.'

Then, like the perfect hostess, the perfect wife, she stepped aside to make way for her guest.

Gowry parked the Vauxhall in the lane adjacent to the Mission Hall. Motorised vehicles were still uncommon hereabouts and he feared that he might soon be surrounded by inquisitive urchins keen not merely to gawk but to thieve.

All, however, was quiet.

In spite of his padded leather topcoat, quilted motoring cap and elbow-length gauntlets, he was cold. Freezing air did not affect his patience or his sense of purpose. He had spied on Sylvie before. Had spent several dismal hours on Sunday forenoons loitering by the church to see who talked to her or who accompanied her back to the door of the Mansions. No one ever did. Sylvie did not linger on the pavement outside the church but hopped away like a solitary little bunnikins. Same thing at the Mission Hall: no would-be beau pursued her to press his suit. As far as Gowry could make out, Forbes's fears were groundless.

She emerged on an exuberant wave of song, hesitated only long enough to tie a scarf over her bonnet and punch her little fists into her muff; then she was off, heading north-west along Stevenson Street.

Gowry promptly tugged the ignition rod and cranked the handle. He heard the familiar groan of gases in the valve regulator and prayed that the beast would start first time. Sylvie had already passed out of sight. He cranked again, heard the engine connect and leaped into the driver's seat. He released the brake, guided the Vauxhall slowly out of the lane into Stevenson Street and soon caught up with Sylvie who was skipping along blithe as a lark.

She glanced round only when the Vauxhall came abreast of her.

'Oh,' she said. 'I thought it was Forbes.'

'It isn't Forbes. It's me instead. Get in.'

She clambered on to the running board and alighted beside him. He had kept the engine ticking over and, as soon as Sylvie was secure, eased the motor-car over the broken cobbles.

'Is Forbes not coming then?' Sylvie said.

'Nope,' Gowry said. 'Forbes won't be coming for some time.'

'Has he deserted me?'

'He has to go off to work elsewhere.'

'Where?'

Gowry thought quickly. 'Portsmouth.'

'Is *she* going with him?'

'Nope.'

'I could go with him. I could go to Portsmouth. Wouldn't he like that?'

Gowry opened his mouth, changed his mind: said, 'He's appointed me to look after you while he's away.'

'Will I ever see Forbes again?' Sylvie said.

'Certainly you will. He'll be back before you know it.'

'My dada isn't at home.'

'I know. He's down town, at Kirby's.'

'That's where I first met Forbes,' Sylvie said. 'I might surprise him. I might make a trip down to Portsmouth and surprise him.'

'It costs a lot of money for a railway fare to Portsmouth.'

'You would give me the money.'

'Would I now?' Gowry said. 'Don't be too sure.'

'I like this motor-car. I've been out into the country in it.'

'Sylvie . . .'

'Drive faster.'

'I can't.'

'Why not?'

'Because we're there.'

She made no protest when he accompanied her through the tiny garden and into the close. They went upstairs together. Snowball, Mrs O'Connor's cat, was seated on the stairs. It paid them not the slightest attention. Sylvie unlocked the front door of the apartment. Gowry followed her into the darkened hallway. He expected her to switch on the electric light, but she did not.

She said, 'I do hope he hasn't gone away for good.'

'Don't be so daft, Sylvie,' Gowry said.

'Then I would only have you to look after me.'

'Would that be so bad?'

'Bad enough,' she said.

He did not move. He could hear the rustle of clothes, the topple of her bonnet on to the rug. She was very close to him. She seemed to be moving around him, as if he were a totem pole.

She said, 'Did you go to Kirby's especially to see Albert?'

'Yes, I did.'

'About the money?'

'You're all paid up. Forbes took care of it.'

'Forbes takes care of everything.'

'Nearly everything,' Gowry said.

He started when she caught his hand; he couldn't help himself. He was confident, but not that confident. He would have preferred to see what she was up to, what sort of a dance she supposed she was leading him. He was not in love with her, would never be in love with her. She would never be able to torment him the way she had done his brother. He couldn't blame Forbes for wanting breathing space.

She took his hand in both of hers and stripped off the leather gauntlet.

'What's this you're doing, Sylvie?' Gowry said.

'Making you feel at home.'

He gave her the other hand. She tugged off that glove too.

She took his hand and led it to her neck, slid it down to her chest. She had removed her coat and unbuttoned her blouse and the top of her bodice, not as far as her breasts but enough to let him touch the angular arrangement of bones above them. She pushed herself against him and, on tiptoe, kissed him on the cheek and then on the lips. He reached for her, but she danced away. 'Are you going to stay and tuck me in?' she asked, in a tiny, unprotected voice. 'Are you going to do that for me too, Gowry-Wowry?'

'Sure and I am,' he said.

CHAPTER SEVENTEEN

Just Between Friends

If Forbes had been willing to listen she might have been able to make him believe that her friendship with Geoffrey Paget was just that, a friendship and not an affair. This, though, would have been a lie, or at best a half-truth, for she had been falling in love with Geoffrey almost since the year began. Once momentum had been achieved there was no stopping it and Geoffrey and she were drawn even closer by a need to pretend that they were in fact *not* falling in love. The tedious paraphernalia of discretion, all the rules and regulations that they imposed upon themselves were designed to prevent friends and enemies alike from leaping to what was after all the right conclusion or, to be hair-splittingly accurate, not *quite* the right conclusion.

By tacit agreement they contrived never to be alone except in public places and during Geoffrey's frequent afternoon visits to Brunswick Cresent they were always chaperoned by Miss Runciman or glowering Blossom McCulloch. Blossom was too insensitive to appreciate quite what was taking place under her very nose but Eleanor Runciman could with ease read the signs and signals. Unrequited love, *unrecognised* love, was not the same as an affair of the heart, of course, but it was close enough for the housekeeper to fall in with the fancy that Lindsay and the naval officer were behaving quite properly and that anyone who suggested otherwise knew nothing about loyalty.

Eleanor guarded Lindsay's reputation. Eleanor also contrived to allow the Lieutenant Commander and Mrs McCulloch two or three unsupervised minutes just after he arrived and again just before he left, for in Eleanor's book there was nothing in the rules to prevent a gentleman kissing a lady's hand or bussing her cheek or even placing a friendly arm about her shoulder, provided the limb did not dwell there too long. Eleanor assumed, correctly as it happened, that in those stolen moments Lindsay and Geoffrey would also kiss lip to lip, that he would say something complimentary about her and she would say something flattering about him and, because they were trapped in virtuous necessity, they would be deluded into believing that conducting an affair of the heart was so easy that they need have no fear of its outcome.

Forbes was furious because he could not contrive a reason for denying Paget the house without accusing the officer to his face, nor could he challenge Lindsay who, he knew, would turn him aside by pointing out that Geoffrey Paget was a high-ranking naval officer who had the power to allocate contracts and bring profit to the firm in which he and she were partners. Perhaps he would have been less inclined to harsh judgement if he had not been denying himself the pleasure of Sylvie's company. He missed Sylvie in more ways than he would have believed possible. Gowry's reports brought no comfort. Beneath his anger there lay melancholy and it did not take him long to transfer his guilt and place the blame with Lindsay.

'Did Paget come today, Winn?'

'Yes, at half past two o'clock.'

'What did he do?'

'Played the piano for an hour.'

'Was Lindsay with him?'

'Much of the time, Forbes, yes.'

'And Runciman was there with them?'

'It was Blossom's turn today.'

'What did they do afterwards?'

'Took tea, I think.'

'Together?'

'Yes.'

'Alone?'

'Blossom would never leave them alone.'

'When did Paget leave?'

'About half past four o'clock.'

In course of time Forbes might have lost his temper and bloodied Paget's nose or have capitulated with his conscience and returned to Sylvie, but a piece of unexpected news came down from Harper's Hill and changed everything, not just for Forbes but for everyone.

Lindsay wept into her pillow. Forbes did his best to comfort her. He put an arm about her, rubbed himself against her, caressed her tenderly and poured out the dregs of his boyish charm.

'Didn't you know that Pappy was ailing?' he asked.

'Aunt Lilias assured us it was only the remnants of a winter cold.'

'He stayed up in Strathmore much too long, if you ask me.'

'I think he wanted to hide his illness from us.'

'Why would he do that?'

'So that he could settle all his affairs without interruption.'

'He didn't look so bad, not last time I saw him,' Forbes said.

'I called in a week ago,' Lindsay said. 'He was resting in bed but he came downstairs and joined us for tea. Oh, it's such a shame that he won't live to watch Harry growing up.'

'That's the way of life, sweetheart,' said Forbes. 'He's a tough old fellah, though. He might surprise us all yet. I mean, he might pull through.'

'He's dying, Forbes. Dying. The doctor has told us so.'

'Doctors! Who believes what doctors tell you?'

'Pappy's eighty-two years old.'

'Yes.' Forbes stroked her shoulder. 'I suppose Hough's been around long enough to recognise a dying man when he sees one.'

She brushed his hand away. Her cheeks were pink and tears glistened on her lashes. She leaned against the bed-head. 'You're wondering how much we'll get from him, aren't you?'

'Oh, now, how can you . . .'

'You're wondering how the property will be divided.'

'Pappy's a wealthy man. Linnet. I wouldn't hardly be human if it hadn't crossed my mind. I'm his grandson, remember.'

'And so is Gowry.'

'What?'

'And Winn is surely entitled to a share. And Blossom. *And* all those others back in Ireland that you refuse to discuss.'

'They mean nothing to Pappy. They're strangers. I doubt if Winn and Blossom have clapped eyes on him more than half a dozen times. And the others, pish on the others.'

Lindsay was silent for a moment then she said, 'Why do you never touch me, Forbes? Why do you never tell me that you love me?'

'So that's it?' he said thinly.

'Is there someone else?'

'I don't know what you mean.'

'Do you have another woman, a mistress, that you prefer to me?'

He shifted away from her and leaned against the bolster. 'Who put that notion into your head? Has some one been slandering me? Who was it? Cissie? Pansy? You really shouldn't listen to idle gossip, Linnet.'

'Answer my question.'

He tried to make light of it. 'When, just tell me, would I find time for another woman?'

'When you go out with Gowry.'

'So it's Gowry who's been filling your head with this nonsense.'

'I didn't say that,' Lindsay told him. 'I asked a question,

Forbes, which you haven't answered yet.' She leaned on to her elbow and stared at him. '*Is* there another woman? If you tell me there isn't then I will believe you.'

'There isn't. Jesus, of course there isn't.'

She pursed her lips. 'Then I believe you.'

'I haven't been attentive enough, Linnet. There! I admit it. But that's going to change as soon as you're well again.'

'Forbes, I am *not* ill,' Lindsay said. 'Since Philip was born you haven't come near me. Do you no longer find me attractive?'

He folded his arms across his chest, fists bunched under his armpits. 'Is that why you've encouraged Paget to come creeping round? Because he finds you attractive? Is attention all you want from him, Lindsay? It isn't all he wants from you. God, no: that bloody sailorman's after a lot more than attention.'

'Geoffrey's a friend, that's all.'

'Huh!' Forbes exclaimed. 'I've heard that tale before. God, but you do have a damned nerve, Lindsay, accusing me of taking a lover when you're up to something behind my back. I can guess what goes on here in the afternoons.'

'Nothing goes on.'

'Piano-playing! Bloody piano-playing! Do you take me for a fool?'

Her eyes were glistening again but not with tears. He had riled her at last. He had more to go on, more, as it were, to work with than she had when it came to accusation. He would have to be careful, though, careful not to push Lindsay too far, not with the old man dangling at death's door. He thanked his lucky stars that he had had the sense to break off with Sylvie when he did and wondered what Gowry had been saying or what snatch of conversation Lindsay had overheard. He didn't doubt Gowry's loyalty, only his discretion. He would have a word with Gowry first thing tomorrow morning. And he would not see Sylvie again, at least not until everything had settled down and he was able to gauge just how much Lindsay and his marriage were worth.

He felt a vague tweak of desire for her but the time was not ripe to soothe and pacify his wife in that way, not unless she asked for it; then, charitably, he would salute and do his duty.

She said, 'Geoffrey is not my lover, if that's what you're thinking. If Winn or Blossom have told you that he is, or have even suggested that he might be, then they do not know me – or Geoffrey for that matter – very well. I'm *your* wife, Forbes, for better or for worse, though sometimes it's difficult to remember what that means.'

'Well,' he said, not harshly, 'we're going to have a lot more on our minds than Geoffrey Paget in the next few weeks.'

'Pappy, you mean?'

'Yes, Pappy.' Forbes drew her head down on to his shoulder. 'Poor old fellah. I wonder how long he will last. I hope he doesn't suffer, that's all.'

He held her, patting her gently, until she began to cry again and then, snuggling against him, eventually fell asleep.

Kay said, 'I'm sorry to see you like this, Daddy. I'm just glad I got here in time.'

Owen could no longer rouse himself to speak. He had heard that she was on her way from Dublin, but the conversations that took place around his bed were filtered through a mist of the medicines that the doctor had administered to take away his pain.

If he had been less strong, less stubborn, he might have let go, but he had no control now, no choice but to suffer and be silent. His memories occupied him during his waking hours. Memories smoked within his brain like the coal piles on the flanks of Franklin town, after which he had been named. When he sipped a little of the soup that Lilias or Pansy brought him, for instance, he remembered the soup that old Hugh Pemberton had made all those years ago on the sooty black stove in the back room of the iron yard overlooking the canal. How he had loved the taste of that soup, soup filled with beans and lentils and tasting of the ham bone that Hugh made the stock with, stock that, as day succeeded day, became richer and thicker until you could spread it upon your bread like a marmalade. He had told Kath about the soup. She had laughed and had tried to manufacture it for him but something was missing, some ingredient that could not be duplicated: the hunger of his youth, perhaps.

When he thought of Kath it was as if she were a ghost long gone away from him, gone long before his boyhood had even begun. He too was fading now, the struggle too much for him. He welcomed the effects of the sweetish grass-green liquid that Lilias fed him when the cough denied him sleep. He would be asleep soon enough, asleep like the little boy in the song, asleep in his daddy's arms. He wondered if his daddy would cry when he saw him. If, in the brilliant bright light of reawakening, his daddy would be there to greet him, his mammy too. How old would they be? How old would he be? How would he recognise them when he had never known who they were?

He did not care about the future. He longed to cling to his past, not to have to shed his memories. The ships, the children — he would give anything to be able to carry the past on with him, all its mistakes and regrets intact, for surely he would be man enough to stand before the Lord and defend himself and whatever he had achieved. Memories of the manner of that achievement were coming home now, coming back now, one by one in the grass-green hours after the medicine eased his body into a state that Lilias mistook for sleep.

He had summoned Gammon to Strathmore, old Harrington too. The lawyers had done what he had asked them to do, had offered him efficiency not sympathy, for they were not so far from the end themselves. Then they had gone away and he had been left with Giles, the views of the hills, the worsening cough, breathing that was like breathing nails even before he had left Perthshire for the last time and had journeyed home to wait for the end.

'Is it not better if you sit up, Daddy?' Kay said.

'He no longer has the strength to sit up,' Lilias said.

'Dear God! I can't be doing to see him so reduced.'

'No,' Lilias said, out of his sight. 'No, it's sad, so sad.'

He wanted to tell them it was not sad at all, not so bad as they, in their prime, imagined it to be. But he was too weary and too stubborn to sleep, too restless in his mind to care about them, to give anything of himself to children to whom he had already given everything.

Kay stooped over him.

'Do you not know me?' she whispered, her voice rustling like paper.

He tried to nod, but his head was too light.

'I've come from Ireland to see you.'

He tried again but the thick, soupy substance in his chest choked him. He coughed, weakly now, for there was no blood left to bring up. Lilias appeared, her elongated face; her elongated long fingers held the cotton to his mouth. He let the substance slip from his tongue to his lips, felt her lift it away.

'Forbes is here too,' Kay said. 'Do you not want to talk to Forbes?'

They had all come to bid him farewell. Lilias had eked them into his bedroom, though whether they had come in daylight or in the dark he did not know, for daylight and darkness were all the same to him. Even the halo of the candle that Lilias lit when she sat by him did not seem bright enough to let him see all that he wanted to see. They came, concerned and kindly, to usher him out of their lives. He supposed that he enjoyed their tears, their murmured lamentations, all the little songs they sang to him, rocking on the edge of his bed: Martin and Pansy, Johnny and Ross. Cissie weeping, Mercy too: all his children's children gathered in a solemn rank that he could not see the end of.

'Do you have something to say to Forbes?' Kay whispered.

He had seen Forbes. He had seen Tom. Lindsay with Arthur, his best son, standing by her shoulder. He had seen all the little boys and girls who had been brought to him for the last time but that he could not quite identify by name now, little girls and boys who already existed in a different dimension, who were already so very far away.

Kay touched him urgently. 'Daddy, speak to me.'

Lilias tugged her back.

'For heaven's sake, Kay, leave him be. He can't hear you.'

'He hears me,' Kay said. 'Don't you, Dadda?'

He had forgiven his rebellious daughters long ago. There had never been much difference between them and he understood better than anyone the nature of their folly. Only Arthur, his best son, remembered the squabbles and could not forgive and forget. He should reply to his daughter, tell Kay something. He tried to raise his hand but lost interest before it left the blanket. He was overcome by a need to sleep. Strange. He felt himself growing strong again, very strong in the light of the day. And yet he needed to sleep. Strange. Strange.

'Look, Daddy, Forbes is here. Forbes, speak to . . .'

Her voice faded.

Owen heard nothing but the beat of his heart, then that, too, stopped.

Lindsay was less stricken than she had imagined she would be. Somehow she had always known that Pappy would not be with them for ever. With Nanny she had had, as it were, practice in facing up to the fact of death: perhaps that was the reason why, when the telephone rang in the hallway of the house in Brunswick Crescent and Forbes told her it was all over, she felt nothing but relief. If Pappy had died eight years ago, or ten, then everything that he had once been would have remained and she would have been stunned by his absence and lost without him. But that man had gone long since, had commenced the process of change and separation on the morning when he had divided the partnership among them and had gracefully bowed out.

For days she waited for grief to strike but it did not, not greatly. The funeral was a vast and solemn service at St Anne's. The burial, which Lindsay did not, of course, attend was followed by a luncheon for sixty invited guests in the upstairs room at the Barbary. That in turn was followed by a family dinner at Harper's Hill in the evening and throughout it all there was an air of communal participation, of sharing, that somehow dissipated her grief.

On that evening in Harper's Hill they were as they had once been: the Franklins, their wives and husbands, the whole family together, dining together, chattering, laughing at tales of Pappy's mischief; and the past became all of a piece. Whatever was in Donald, in Arthur, in Lilias and Kay that their children could not share remained hidden. Only the platitudes held true: Pappy would have loved it, Pappy would have had fun, Pappy would have urged them to eat more, drink more, to sing a song or two to please him; which is just what they did, all of them, unforced, ungrudgingly, singing all the songs, sad and jolly, that Owen in his lifetime had loved.

Later that night in bed, Forbes made love to her, fast and greedy and demanding love, a charmless act to which Lindsay yielded because, in her imagination, she was not with Forbes at all.

Four days later Geoffrey turned up at the door in Brunswick Crescent and Lindsay in person admitted him to the house.

'I didn't quite know what to do,' Geoffrey began. 'I attended the service, of course, but I wasn't sure whether to write or not. I was at rather a loss, to be truthful. I didn't want you to think, Lindsay, that I didn't care.'

'I know,' she said. 'I know that.'

'It seemed wrong to impose at such a time.'

'I'm glad to see you,' she said.

'Truly?' Geoffrey said. 'I'm not intruding?'

'Of course not,' Lindsay said.

'I know from what you've told me that he meant a great deal to you.'

'Not just to me,' Lindsay said.

'That much was apparent from the turnout at church. I've never seen such a vast gathering,' Geoffrey said. 'Thousands. More, I believe, than turned out for Admiral Hattersfield's funeral last year at Devonport.'

Lindsay laughed. 'Pappy would have been flattered to hear it.'

'You don't seem particularly – how do I put this? – upset.'

'No, I'm not,' Lindsay said. 'My grandfather was eighty-two years old, you know. All the stuff and nonsense that's talked about aged people – he had a good innings, that sort of thing – turns out not to be stuff and nonsense at all. It's true. He *did* have a good innings. How can I regret that Pappy has gone when he left so much of himself behind, so much that was good.'

'Well,' Geoffrey said, 'I'd still like to offer my condolences.'

'Thank you,' Lindsay said.

'I – I won't stay.'

'No, please do,' Lindsay said.

He looked around the parlour, at the half-drawn curtains that signified a family in mourning, at the deep slats of April sunlight that caught and held fine motes of dust above the Indian carpet, at the piano, the bright fire in the grate.

'Is Miss Runciman not with us?' he asked.

'She has gone out this afternoon with my father.'

'With your father?'

'To buy linen, bed linen.'

'They shop together?'

'Why not?' Lindsay said. 'What's so shocking about that? I may not be terribly affected by what's happened but my father certainly is. Miss Runciman will persuade him to take her to tea in one of the warehouses and will listen to him prattle on about my grandfather and his sister, Kay. Eleanor will offer him comfort. It may not seem proper to you, but Eleanor

Runciman is more than just a housekeeper; she is also a very good friend.'

'Ah, well, I do know something about friendship,' Geoffrey said.

'I don't think my father and Eleanor Runciman have ever kissed, though,' Lindsay said. 'Perhaps they will one day.'

'Will it matter whether they do or not?'

'Probably not,' Lindsay said. 'She loves him, I think, and he's very fond of her and that's all that counts in the long run.'

'If you were in Miss Runciman's position would that be enough for you?'

'No,' Lindsay said.

'No?'

'I should want to be kissed.'

'Like this?' he said.

'Yes,' Lindsay said, 'just like that,' and drew back only a moment before Blossom flung open the door and Aunt Kay stalked into the room.

'Is that the chap Winn's been telling me about?' Kay said. 'Is that the chap who's trying to steal her away from you?'

'I wouldn't go that far,' Forbes told his mother. 'Myself, I think Paget's just out for a bit of a lark.'

'Then you're more of a fool than I took you for.'

'Linnet won't give in to him,' Forbes said. 'She knows where her best interests lie – and that's right here with me.'

'If she's had her head turned by this sailor,' Kay said, 'she won't know or care where her best interests lie. There's no reasoning with a woman when she thinks she's fallen in love.'

'Mother, for God's sake,' Forbes said, 'you're making a mountain out of a molehill. Lindsay would never abandon the children and I'm damned sure friend Paget won't want to sail off into the sunset with another man's brats in tow. Besides – if you'll excuse me – it's really none of your concern.'

'Aye, but it is, son,' Kay said. 'It's very much my concern.'

'You're still determined to come back to Glasgow?'

'Of course I am.'

'What's stopping you?' Forbes said. 'I have ample room for you here.'

'She'll not be abandoning the others,' Winn said.

'She'll abandon Dadda quick enough,' Blossom said, 'but she'll not let the children stay behind unless they want to.'

'Well, I can't take them all in,' Forbes said. 'One more — Charlie, say, or Rena — but no more. I mean, if you want to move the lot to Glasgow I've funds enough to provide them with board and lodging for a week or two and perhaps I might even be able to find them jobs but you can't expect me to provide for them all indefinitely.'

'Charlie won't leave,' Winn said.

'And Babs is for marrying, soon as she can,' said Blossom.

'And young Peter,' Kay put in, 'is his father's boy.'

'Peter's what age?' said Forbes.

'Seventeen,' said Blossom.

'He's gone into the brewery,' said Winn. 'The brewery will be his.'

'How bad are things financially?' Forbes asked.

'Worse than ever,' Kay told him.

They were seated in the downstairs drawing-room, huddled about the elegant fireplace as if they were peasants unused to spacious interiors. Daniel McCulloch's house in Malahide was not much smaller than the Franklins' house in Brunswick Park but neglect and lack of cash had given it a ramshackle air.

'Is Dadda still involved with the Fellowship?' Forbes enquired.

'He is *supporting* the Fellowship just about single-handed. There is nothing I can say to stop him throwing good money after bad,' Kay said. 'He would be having us all working for the blessed Fellowship if he could manage it. He won't even employ a hand now who doesn't subscribe to the Fellowship of Erin.

Catholic or Protestant, that has never been an issue with your daddy. It has always been the fight, the struggle, the *politics* of it that's consumed him. I tell you, son,' Kay went on, 'I wish he had been addicted to drink instead of politics. I could have coped with the drink better than I can with the Fellowship.'

'I take it,' Forbes said, 'he still has the horses?'

'A few,' Kay said. 'I don't object to the horses. You can understand an Irishman's love of horseflesh. But the other thing, the Fellowship of Erin thing, that's beyond my comprehension.'

'Is Peter with him in this too?' said Forbes.

'Aye, and Charlie,' Kay said. 'It's too late. We've lost them already.'

Leaning forward in her chair, Blossom patted her brother's knee. 'You are well out of it, Forbes. The best thing Mam ever did was getting you out of it before you were old enough to be snared.'

'Didn't you know what Dadda was like before you ran off with him?' Forbes asked.

'God now, and how could I know? He didn't talk about politics. He talked about love. It was never love, though, not with him. Marrying me was just another form of politics. Oh, he was charm itself in those early days, as decent a man on the surface as you could ever hope to meet. How was I to know that he would be spending half his time with the horses and half his time with the Fellowship, though it didn't call itself that in those days, and that there would be precious little left for me?'

'If he had devoted as much time and effort to the brewery as he put into the Fellowship then we would all of us be dressed up like lords and ladies and be living in fine houses in Grafton Street,' Winn said.

'I doubt that,' Forbes said. 'Dadda was lazy to begin with. He needed an excuse for doing as little as possible and the Fellowship provided it. It's not politics, believe me, not real genuine politics.'

'Thanks to God you're not like him,' Winn said, patting her

brother's knee in turn. 'It's a fine thing you've done, Forbes, making so much of yourself that you can take on the burden for the rest of us.'

'Not all,' said Forbes hastily. 'You and Mam, but not all of them.'

'You mustn't let this foolish nonsense with the sailor and your wife distract you,' Kay said. 'It will be a flirtation and it will blow itself out when he goes back to sea and he finds some other man's wife to have his fun with.'

Forbes kept his doubts to himself. 'Paget's a shore officer. He works under Fisher, the First Sea Lord, and has the ear of the purchasing and commissioning committees. In other words, Mam, I can't punch the bastard's nose and get away with it, not if I want to keep navy contracts rolling in.'

'I understand that,' Kay said impatiently. 'But with your grandfather gone, there will surely be more opportunity for you to make your mark.'

'Perhaps,' Forbes said. 'We'll have to await the reading of Pappy's will to find out how the firm's been divided and just how much will come to us.'

'Us?' said Winn.

'Lindsay and me,' Forbes said.

'Lindsay's a bitch out of hell to put you through this, Forbes. I mean the stuff with the sailor,' Blossom said. 'I can't think what she could want from marriage more than you have given her.'

'Selfish.' Winn nodded. 'That's what she is, born selfish. It's not for me to speak ill of the dead but that old man has much to answer for.'

'He did not spoil *us*, did he?' Blossom said.

'He did not care what happened to us,' said Winn. 'When I look at poor Gowry in his uniform, I could weep. He should have been a gentleman, not a motoring-car driver.'

Aware that her daughters were leading the conversation on to very thin ice, Kay intervened. 'Lindsay's as flighty as her father but she has a mind of her own, so let her have her fling until you find out what's gone to her, then, son, you can rein her in again.'

'Rein her in?' said Forbes. 'How?'

'Give her something to think about besides making eyes at sailors.'

'What, for instance?' Forbes asked.

'More babies,' his mother told him.

'Lots more babies,' said Blossom.

'Really?' Forbes said. 'Will that do it?'

'Aye, son,' his mother assured him. 'That will do it, every time.'

The disposal of Owen Franklin's assets was undoubtedly complicated by the diversity of his holdings but Pappy had spent the best part of a week with Messrs Harrington and Gammon up at Strathmore revising earlier wills and drafting fresh instructions which, with the lawyers' aid, left everything nicely cut and dried. Even after payment of death duties there was a considerable sum left in addition to principal property.

The effect of Owen's death on Franklin's was almost indetectable. He had had the foresight to make clear separation between personal and partnership holdings some years ago and had retained only a portion of interest in the family firm. It was, however, this portion that excited Forbes's interest, for he was still, more than ever, hungry for recognition and the power that went with it. Lindsay, however, had no expectation of gain and was soon rather bored by the more formal part of the proceedings.

Outside, a sharp late April sun shone on the terraces above Kelvingrove. From her chair in the drawing-room, where the reading was taking place, Lindsay could just make out the leaves beginning to unfurl on the tops of the trees. She felt oddly relaxed and unthreatened now that her grandfather was no longer present. He seemed to be everywhere, though, yet nowhere.

The house on Harper's Hill would not change greatly. Giles would be replaced by a younger man, Cook might decide to retire and, in course of time, most of the bedrooms would become empty, for her cousins were already going out into the world to marry and bear children and establish homes of their own. To Martin's children, and Mercy's, to Harry and Philip and little Ewan Calder, Pappy would not even be a memory. On the oceans of the world, however, in distant ports and in harbours tucked into the great brown rivers that ran through faraway continents, the boats that Pappy had built would endure. Some day, perhaps, she would see the *Covenant* or the *Commonwealth*, the *Liberty* or the *Cormorant* nosing up the Clyde again and would point it out to Harry or Philip and tell him that her grandfather had built it and hope that her sons would understand just what his legacy meant to them all.

Meanwhile, the disposal of Pappy's assets continued.

Harper's Hill went to Donald. Cash sums equal to the value of the property went to Arthur and Kay. Pensions were left for Owen's cook and housekeeper. The trusty Giles received a lump sum sufficient to allow him to retire in comfort. The lease on the Perthshire retreat had been terminated by payment of a year's rent and personal items brought down from Strathmore were now stored in Harper's Hill. Objects of sentimental worth, in addition to books, paintings and private papers, would be divided between the three surviving children, each of whom might have what he or she wished; any disagreements to be settled by Mr Harrington.

By her side, Lindsay felt her husband stiffen.

'As to the partnership, the shareholding of a sixth of the sixty-fourth part has been transferred by previous deed to Mr Thomas Calder, my grand son-in-law, whereby interest, right and property passes . . .'

'Good God!' Forbes murmured. 'Calder got it.'

'. . . subject to registration, and on the same and several conditions which I held before the execution hereof, I, the said testator, do hereby assign . . .'

Lindsay glanced across the library. Tom sat motionless, apparently unmoved by the announcement that he had just become a partner in Franklin & Sons and would from now on share not only in its decisions but in its profits.

'. . . in which case,' Mr Harrington concluded, 'there being no questions or objections relating to this reading of the will of the deceased Owen Franklin, I declare the reading duly concluded.' He closed the leather folder on his documents and, with a little sigh, set his small, moist hand upon it like a seal.

'Bastard!' Forbes hissed beneath his breath. 'Bastard, bastard, bastard!' Then, throwing all pretence of courtesy to the winds, shot out of his chair and hurriedly left the room.

'This,' Gowry said, 'is not a good idea. For a start she isn't expecting you.'

'What does that have to do with any bloody thing?' Forbes shouted. 'Are you trying to warn me that she might be in bed with somebody else?'

'No, no, no, no,' said Gowry placatingly. 'I just mean that you've ignored her for months and now you're turning up a fair bit less than sober.'

'I'm bloody sober enough,' Forbes said. 'Sober enough to do what I feel like doing. Jesus! I've paid for the bloody privilege, haven't I?'

'That you have, that you have.'

'Wait here.'

'I think,' Gowry said, 'I should be coming up with you.'

'What the devil for?'

'Sylvie's used to seeing me these days. Let me go first. Let me tell her you're back from — where was it? — from Portsmouth.'

'Sod off, Gowry. Bloody sod off.'

'I'm not trying to stop you. I just want to go with you.'

'Why?'

'To make sure you don't break your neck on the stairs.'

'Hah!' Forbes said sarcastically. 'Always got my best interests at heart, haven't you? Sometimes I think I should have left you to rot in bloody Malahide.'

'Sometimes I think you should have,' said Gowry, but his brother had already gone charging through the iron gate and across the strip of lawn that led to the back door of the Mansions. Peeling off his gauntlets and unbuttoning his coat, Gowry followed him anxiously.

They had been drinking – at least Forbes had – for the best part of the afternoon. What Gowry couldn't grasp, though, was just what Forbes had expected to gain from his grandfather's will or why the fact that Tom Calder had been admitted to a full partnership in Franklin's had riled him beyond reason. It seemed to Gowry just the sort of thing that the old buffer *would* do, given that he had always been generous and loyal to those who were loyal to him. My God, Gowry thought, how ambition could gnaw away at you and spoil you to the point of destruction. What was it that Reverend Staveacre, vicar of the church at Malahide, kept saying? *Ambition may be as innocent as hunger: equally it may become the last infirmity of noble minds.* Well, there had never been anything noble about the McCullochs and any polish Forbes had acquired while growing up surely wasn't much more than skin deep.

There had been no sign of Albert at Kirby's and Gowry rather hoped that there would be nobody at home in the Mansions. If Sylvie did happen to be out he knew that she would only have toddled down to a prayer meeting or, if there was nothing doing at the Mission, might have skipped into the Salvation Army Hall in Canal Street in the hope of finding some comfort and joy. On the other hand, Gowry thought, she was probably sitting up in the parlour with her scrapbooks around her, her nightdress hanging off her bones, like some wicked little fairground fortune-teller who took on clients on the side.

Baby, baby, he thought, no, no, don't try to tell him tonight.

He tugged at his brother's sleeve.

'Hold on,' he said. 'At least have the decency to knock.'

Forbes shook off the restraining hand. 'Have you got one?'

'Got what?'

'A key?'

'I have, as a matter of fact. The one you gave me.'

'Use it then, for Christ's sake.'

Gowry opened the outer door and, blocking Forbes's path, called out in a loud voice, 'Sylvie, Sylvie. Guess who's here?' Silence: all the doors off the hall were closed and, for a moment, it seemed that the apartment was deserted. Gowry stuck out a hand, switched on the electrical light.

'*Sylvie?*' Forbes roared. '*Where are you?*'

'She'll be in the drawing-room,' Gowry said, 'if she's anywhere.'

Forbes pushed his brother aside, flew across the hall and flung open the door to the parlour. Gowry followed. To his dismay Sylvie was seated at the oval table, paste-pot, scissors and scraps before her, a pile of newspapers on the carpet by the side of her chair. A coal fire blazed in the hearth and the tall lamp in the corner of the room was lit. The scene, Gowry thought, was almost cosy; or would have been if Sylvie had been a child with a father and mother comfortably ensconced in armchairs nearby. When he was alone with her he was oblivious to her pathos but now, with Forbes present, he felt nothing but pity for the abandoned girl.

She looked up and said, 'Ah, Forbes! There you are,' as if he had never been further from her than the room next door.

Her composure brought Forbes up short. He reeled towards her and braced himself against the sofa. 'Where's Albert?'

'Out. Did you have a nice trip?'

'Trip?'

'I thought you might have written.' Sylvie snipped around a portrait head of some bearded duke or other, trimmed off the shreds, and put the scrap into a shallow wicker basket before her on the table. 'Would you care for some tea?'

'No, I wouldn't care for some tea,' Forbes said.

'Gowry?'

'No, thanks all the same,' Gowry said.

He loitered nervously by the door. She *was* wearing a nightdress, one of the long flowing ones with a floral pattern and lace at the throat and cuffs. She wore a robe over it, however, and a tiny little muslin cap over her hair and looked nothing like a gypsy fortune-teller; more, he thought, like someone convalescing from an illness.

Forbes said, 'Aren't you surprised to see me?'

'I knew you would come back.'

'Did you now?' Forbes emerged from behind the sofa, rounded the table, thrust a hand under her armpit and yanked her to her feet. He planted a kiss on her mouth while she hung limply, caught between chair and the table. 'Is that what you thought I'd come back for, sweetheart?'

When he released her she seated herself demurely on the chair again, folding the robe and nightdress under her thin thighs. She reached for the paste brush. Forbes gripped her arm, turned her around and kissed her again, even more violently than before.

Gowry looked down at the carpet.

Then he heard her say, 'I knew you would come when Gowry told you.'

'Told me?' Forbes said. 'Told me what?'

'About the baby?'

Gowry's head jerked up and he heard himself say, in perfect unison with his brother, 'What baby?'

'My baby?'

'Your baby?' Forbes laughed uncertainly. 'You haven't got a baby.'

'I will have soon.'

'You're — *what?*'

'It is nesting inside me right now.'

Gowry had his hands spread, shoulders raised, even before Forbes spun round to confront him.

'Did you know about this?' Forbes shouted. 'Did you know about this and didn't have the guts to tell me?'

'I had no idea – I don't know what – first I've heard . . .'

'Now, now, Gowry-Wowry.' Sylvie tilted her head and flashed him such a coy and castigating look that Gowry felt the hair on the nape of his neck rise.

'Now, now, now, you know I told you ages ago.'

'She's – she never – Forbes, I swear, I didn't . . .'

'I feel sure it will be a girl, a little girl just like me.'

Forbes slapped his palms flat upon the tabletop and, leaning forward like an orator, addressed her soberly. 'I see. Yes, I see. And when is this baby due, Sylvie, tell me that? When will it be born?'

'She,' Sylvie said. She sucked her lip, considering. 'August. In August.'

'In August,' Forbes said quietly. 'And it's going to be a little girl, just like the Duchess of Athlone's, am I right?'

'It won't be the duchess's baby, it will be ours, yours and mine.'

'August,' Forbes said, even more quietly. He glanced round at Gowry whose hands remained spread in a gesture of helpless ignorance. 'Did the doctor tell you it would be born in August, Sylvie?'

'I do not like doctors.'

'Bertie, your dada, does he know about the baby yet?' Forbes asked.

Forbes was almost in control of himself now, Gowry realised, the drink purged from his system. He, himself, he was trembling inside. He would have been trembling outside too if he had not had the sense to disguise his fear. He leaned against the wall, pretending to be nothing more than an observer. He could see the crooked shape of his brother's back, though, and Sylvie's face, half hidden by his brother's shoulder, her expression so guileless that he almost began to wonder if she were telling the truth.

'Dada will be at our wedding,' Sylvie said. 'I want Dada to give me away.'

'So you *haven't* told Bertie and you *haven't* visited a doctor,' Forbes said. 'In other words, you're behaving like the stupid little bitch you've always been. Do you really believe I'm going to leave my wife and children and marry you just because you've got yourself knocked up, because you *say* you've got yourself knocked up?'

'Forbes . . .' Gowry began.

'Shut your mouth,' Forbes told him. 'Do you, Sylvie? Do you think for one minute I'm going to take your bloody word for it?'

'She's inside me. Here. Already here.'

'*You liar!*' Forbes shouted. '*You sodding little liar!*' Stepping back, he addressed Gowry. 'Did you know about this?'

'Not me,' said Gowry.

Forbes returned to Sylvie. 'So it's in there, is it? You're what — four, five months gone. All right. Show me. Go on, show me.'

She did not understand. She glanced at Gowry. He shrugged.

Forbes said, 'It's got to be showing by now, honey, so let's see it.'

'For God's sake, Forbes,' Gowry protested.

'Shut up,' Forbes said. 'I know what I'm doing. Go ahead, take it off, Sylvie, or lift it up. Let's see your wonderful big belly.'

Willingly, far too willingly, she slid from the chair and took a few paces into the centre of the room. She seemed, Gowry thought, remarkably confident, her smile complacent. She took off the robe and tossed it behind her. He watched it swirl in the light from the lamp and fall softly to the patterned carpet. There should have been music, he thought, something Egyptian or Turkish-sounding to lend her performance weight. She pressed her knees together, caught the hem of her nightgown and jerkily lifted it. She looked so thin, so white at that moment that Gowry wondered what Forbes had ever seen in her.

She lifted the garment until it covered her face. Her body was frail, starved and, Gowry thought, somehow unfinished. Slowly and deliberately she pirouetted and, from under the nightgown, said, 'Can you see, my darling? Can you see it now?' The swelling was graceful, the prettiest part of her. It sloped from below her breasts, curved down in a soft line and dipped into the shadow of her thighs. He had seen her naked before but never like this, never so exposed, yet pride in her condition removed every vestige of sexuality from the display. She lowered the nightgown, let it waft about her shoulders. She patted the swelling with both hands and giggled. 'See. I told you so, Forbes.'

'I see *nothing*.' Forbes danced with rage, with the truth of the evidence before his eyes. 'I see nothing. I see *fat*, that's all. You're *fat*, Sylvie. Fat like a bloody pig. Like a *sow*. *Fat!* Fat! FAT!'

Gowry had sympathy for his brother. He wanted to tell Sylvie to cover herself, to sit down and discuss the matter like a normal human being, except that she was no more normal than Forbes was, or he was himself. He felt ugly with the shame of what he saw and yet he remained afraid that she would tell on him, confess to Forbes what they – what he and she – had done.

He watched two fat tears course down Sylvie's cheeks.

'Marry you?' Forbes ranted. 'Marry a bitch like you? I wouldn't be marrying you if you were the last bloody woman on the face of the earth, not if you were carrying ten babies in that fat belly of yours. My wife, my wife is my *wife*, Sylvie. She's worth a thousand of you. Jesus! Do you think I want a trollop like you sitting at *my* supper table, sharing *my* bed, meeting *my* mother, talking to *my* friends.'

'I thought you loved me.'

'Hah! Who could love a daft little cow like you? Oh, aye, sweetheart, you're daft all right. You're soft in the head, mad as a bloody hatter.'

'I thought you wanted to marry me.'

'*Marry you!* I wanted to *bed* you and' – he sucked in a shuddering breath that lifted his chest high – 'and I've done that. You've nothing left, Sylvie, nothing left to offer me, especially that, that *thing* you think is mine.'

Her tears ran in two straight lines that met only at the point of her chin. She uttered no sound, not a breath or whisper. At least she has that much sense, Gowry thought, that much dignity. He regretted having slept with her, not because she'd disappointed him but because he couldn't step back past their frantic intimacies and pretend to be her friend. He could not even pretend that he cared for her, daft as she was. He had closed off love through selfishness and hated the emotional impotence that was all that was left of it.

Sylvie pulled the gown down and seated herself at the table again.

She did not throw herself forward, scatter the scraps, spill the paste, topple the scissors. She simply sat there, narrow shoulders slumped, and let the tears fall silently into her lap.

'F-Forbes, I d-don't think she understands,' Gowry stammered.

'Oh, she understands all right,' Forbes said. 'For the first time in her life, she understands. Now come on, let's get out of here before I choke.'

Pivoting, he stalked out of the apartment, Gowry trailing at his heels.

And never saw Sylvie again.

CHAPTER EIGHTEEN

The Deciding Factor

The wonders of the warship were many and varied. Lindsay had taken several tours of such vessels with her father and her admiration for the mechanical marvels of the big boats had not lessened even when she learned more about their construction. Of the prototype submarine in the slip at Aydon Road she knew little or nothing, however, for the secrets of the navy's latest 'box of tricks' were jealously guarded.

Franklin's workers refused to talk about it even in bars crowded with men to whom the latest commission at Stephens or Fairfields or Connells held more than passing interest, for they were proud that they had been chosen to participate in forefront development and enjoyed taunting their rivals by singing dumb about what lay behind the specially rigged sail sheets that hid the Aydon Road vessel from prying eyes.

By the first day of May the steel shell was packed with a mass of pipes, cables, tanks and gauges so complex that even Tom Calder, armed with the plans, had a problem relating one part to another. Tours of the prototype were not only forbidden but were well-nigh impossible and neither Tom nor her father would have dared to invite Lindsay to go below. Lieutenant Commander Paget, however, had more authority, and late one May afternoon he collected Lindsay from Brunswick Crescent in a motorised taxi-cab and drove off with her into the softly falling rain. Peering from the front windows of the house, Winn and Blossom were outraged. As soon as the motor vehicle passed out of sight behind the trees, they loped into the piano parlour where Eleanor Runciman was seated by the fireplace casually embroidering a pillow slip.

'He's taken her with him.'

'In a hired motoring car.'

'Hmm,' Eleanor purred.

'Where have they gone?'

'What's he going to do to her?'

'Will they be back before Forbes comes home?'

'Why won't you tell us? Is it — bad?'

Eleanor glanced up from her needle which, in fact, was only a prop in her performance and had added hardly more than four stitches to the design.

'Secret,' she said. 'State secret,' and tapped the side of her nose with her forefinger. 'I am sworn to tell no one.'

'Not even us?' said Blossom.

'Not even you, my dear,' said Eleanor, and returned to the work in hand.

In the taxi-cab Geoffrey took off his cap before he kissed her. He did not care that they were in plain sight of the driver and, for once, did not dictate to himself a castigatory memo. He acted on an impulse that had been nurtured throughout a fortnight's sojourn in Rosyth and a week of tedious meetings in London.

During this time he had thought of Lindsay constantly, even while seated at table with Jackie Fisher and Sir Edward Moncur, chairman of the Navy Estimates Board, gentlemen upon whose good opinion his future depended. Lindsay had accompanied him along the marble corridors of Admiralty House, had been with him in his room in his club, on his strolls across St James's Park; on the night train, at the breakfast bar at Waverley railway station, on the quays and docksides of Rosyth; had been with him while he shaved in the morning and when he bathed before dinner, even when he addressed the crew who would take over the D-Class prototype and the storemen who would stock her for her sea trials.

He could hardly believe that she was with him now in body as well as spirit and experienced immense relief when she returned his kiss, rubbed it lightly upon his upper lip. She tasted of lemon, he thought, like a fragrant Italian gin. She put her hand down by her side and clasped his fingers.

'I missed you,' she said.

He knew he would have to go soon, would have to leave her, not just for a week or two but for months, perhaps years; yet he felt steady, oddly steady, just having her hand to hold.

'And I you,' he said.

'How long do we have?' Lindsay asked.

'An hour is all I can spare, I'm sorry.'

'No. I mean, how long . . .'

'A week or so, that's all.'

'But you will be back, won't you?'

'For the launch and then the trials, yes,' Geoffrey said.

He had told himself that he only wished to be her friend, to strike up a friendship that was as close to platonic as possible, but he knew now that he had been deceiving himself all along and that if she had not been another man's wife he would have found a means of possessing her completely. He had never been an opportunist, though, and reluctantly he drew away.

Lindsay said, 'Will you write to me, Geoffrey?'

'Is that wise?'

'Perhaps it's better to be just a little unwise than totally foolish.'

He nodded: 'Yes, I'll write.'

Outlined against the window's smudges of spring rain, Geoffrey's features were almost too clean cut, too regular. She saw control there, tautness, the angular discipline of the jawline. She knew so little about him: of his wishes and desires she had no knowledge at all. There would be so much to discover in the months of separation. Next time they met, whenever that might be, there would surely be unity, a kind of harmony, for although they had loved without loving and had nothing but tender memories to share, next time they would not be strangers to the notion of being in love.

The taxi-cab prowled among the tenements that guarded Aydon Road and, forty minutes before shift-change, drew to a halt in front of the office block. Lieutenant Commander Paget gave Mrs Lindsay McCulloch his hand.

But only to help her alight.

Gowry said, 'Look, I really don't have much time. I have to pick up his lordship at half past five o'clock.'

'Kind of you to spare us any time at all,' said Bertie sarcastically. 'Does he know you're meeting me?'

'Sure and he does. He sent me,' Gowry said.

'Why didn't he come himself?'

'In case you brought Sylvie with you.'

'So he really doesn't want to see Sylvie ever again?'

'That is about the size of it,' Gowry said. 'Talking of size, how is she?'

'Showing.'

'Have you called in a doctor?'

'She won't have it. It's her child, she says, and she'll not have anyone fiddling with it.'

'That isn't right,' Gowry said.

'I know it isn't,' Albert said. 'If only Forbes would come to the house and talk to her, I'm sure she'd listen to him.'

'Perhaps she'll listen to me.'

'Only Forbes. She's never listened to anyone but Forbes.'

'What are they saying about her down at the Mission Hall?'

'She's stopped going. In fact, she's stopped going out altogether.'

'That isn't right either.'

'What am I supposed to do about it?' Albert said testily. 'I didn't knock her up. I haven't left her in the lurch.'

'Not exactly in the lurch,' Gowry said. 'There will be some sort of financial arrangement. Something to keep you going.'

'Did he tell you to say that?'

'He's not *that* callous, Bertie,' Gowry said. 'He'll pay rent on the apartment for two years, then, if Sylvie hasn't found a husband by that time, the arrangement will be reviewed.'

'That's fine as far as it goes,' Albert said. 'But what are we supposed to live on in the meantime? I'm not fit to work and I'm damned if I'm going back to begging on the streets.'

'You were never a beggar,' Gowry said.

'As close as you care to imagine. I couldn't have done it without Sylvie and I'm not dragging her back to that existence, not now she's almost a mother.'

'Fifty shillings a week.'

'Insufficient.'

'Sixty, that's as far as Forbes'll go.'

'Three quid a week' – Albert pulled a face – 'won't go far enough.'

'Three quid a week and a roof over your head,' Gowry said. 'Good God, man, thousands of Clydesiders would jump at an offer like that.'

'I'll have to let the servants go.'

'Aww!' said Gowry.

'Make it a fiver?'

'No.'

Albert shifted his buttocks on the massive arm of the lock-gate.

Gowry and he had arranged to meet on the towpath of the canal at the bottom end of Wordsworth Street. At that hour of the afternoon the path was almost deserted and there was little enough traffic on the canal these days, only an occasional horse-drawn barge or a puffer nosing across country. Albert wore a flannel donkey jacket and a knitted cardigan over a collarless shirt. He hadn't shaved and the stubble on his jowls was frost white. He looked shabby, Gowry thought, like a man on the road to becoming a liability.

Albert said, 'Forbes isn't the only fish in the sea, you know.'

'What the hell is that supposed to mean?'

'She's not entirely dependent on him.'

'Who is she dependent on then?' said Gowry. 'You?'

'She still has a papa,' Bertie said. 'He might be very interested in what's befell his daughter. I'm sure he'd be willing to shoulder some of the burden if only he knew what sort of plight she was in.'

Gowry swore and got to his feet.

The surface of the canal was smoored with rain, hardly rain at all, really, just a pinkish sort of haze that held the city's smoke within it, along with tints of early summer. The nap of Gowry's tunic was pearled with moisture and a little bead or two gathered on the brim of his hat, like sweat.

For a moment there was no sound but the splash of water in the sluice of the lock and the distant clanking of tram-cars from the direction of Maryhill depot. Then Albert said, 'I mean, your brother's not the only rich man of my acquaintance, not the only one who's feathered his nest through marriage.'

Gowry swore again, walked four or five paces along the towpath and returned. He put his hands on his hips. He said stiffly, 'I take it you're referring to Tom Calder? Has she been in touch with Calder?'

'She wants nothing to do with him.'

'What makes you think Sylvie will agree to taking money from him?'

'She doesn't have to agree.' Albert put his arms behind him and leaned back a little. 'In fact, if I play it right Sylvie needn't know anything about it. Like – what – an anonymous bene-factor?'

'Calder won't fall for that. He'll want to see her.'

'Oh, that can be arranged too, I'm sure.'

Gowry dug his hands into his trouser pockets and had another little stroll to himself. He turned, walked, returned, said, 'It's a good one, Bertie, that I will admit. Play Calder against Forbes. Blackmail them both.'

'I thought you'd like it,' Albert said.

'I don't suppose it matters that you might ruin two marriages or, at best, bring a whole lot of misery to two ladies who've done nothing to harm you.'

'I have Sylvie to think of,' Albert stated.

'Calder will pay up,' Gowry said, 'but Forbes might not.'

'Forbes might not? Really? Forbes might not? Oh, how I'd like to be a fly on the wall when Tom Calder and your precious brother come face to face. Do you suppose for one minute that Calder will let Forbes keep his mucky little secret intact? He'll pay, of course he will – Tom Calder, I mean – but he'll make damned sure that Forbes pays too.'

'Aren't you forgetting one thing?' Gowry said.

'What's that then?'

'The baby.'

'Baby?'

'Sylvie's baby,' Gowry said. 'In four months or so there's going to be a real live baby squawking in your ear.'

'I'm not scared of babies. I learned a lot about babies from my dear departed wife, though we never had none of our own. I raised Sylvie, didn't I?'

'Sure and look at the hash you made of that.' Gowry clamped a hand to Albert Hartnell's shoulder. The wall of the lock loomed behind him, dark brown water swirling below. 'Still, it's not for me to judge, is it? Poor cow never had much of a chance, however you look at it. She isn't quite right in the head, Bertie, I suppose you've realised that?'

'She's just – just her own person.'

'She's got a little screw loose, Bertie. She needs a lot of care and attention.'

'He promised he'd look after us.'

'He will. He will,' Gowry said. 'But he won't be blackmailed into marrying her, if that's what's on your mind. Take it from me: I know my brother, he's capable of anything when he's crossed.'

'I was under the impression he cared for her.'

'I think he does, or at least he did,' Gowry said. 'It could have gone happily on for years and years if only she'd had the savvy to let well alone. She tried to trap him, Bertie. She tried to trap him with the oldest trick in the book and I'm not entirely sure that you didn't put her up to it.'

'Now, now, now, no need for that.'

'All right. I'll give you the benefit. None the less,' Gowry said, 'I'd advise you not to tamper with the Franklins.'

'Your brother ain't a Franklin, nor is Tom Calder.'

'Not to tamper with that family in any shape or form,' Gowry said. 'My brother will do what's right by her.'

'Like marry her?'

'Rot! That's rot – and you know it. Sylvie might have feathers for brains, Bertie, but you certainly haven't. Marriage was never on. *Never*. He'll see her right as far as money goes, but don't expect any more from Forbes than he's prepared to give. And don't – you hear me? – *don't* drag Calder or anyone else from the family into this mess.'

'I thought you liked my plan.'

'Maybe I do, maybe I don't,' Gowry said. 'But I've been around long enough to realise that the best-laid schemes have a way of going wrong, especially if you're dealing with my brother.'

'Is that a threat?'

'No, it's a warning, Bertie. And you would do well to heed it.'

Albert grunted and, getting to his feet, stepped away from the arm of the lock-gate. He had no qualms about Gowry McCulloch. But behind Gowry stood the Dubliner, the smooth-tongued snake who – as he, Albert, saw it – had corrupted them all. He hated those smart young men who claimed the world for themselves. He hated them with a smouldering hatred fired more by jealousy than justice, a weak-kneed, impotent sort of hatred that crushed him and kept him in his place.

'Sixty shillings a week,' Gowry said.

'Rent paid?'

'Rent paid,' Gowry said. 'And get her to a doctor or, if she really won't wear that, fetch in a midwife to give her the once-over. If there's one thing I don't want, it's for Sylvie to lose this child.'

Surprised, Albert said, 'The child? What do you care about the child?'

Gowry grinned. 'Spare a minute to think about it, Bertie.'

After a pause, Albert said, 'Don't tell me you're setting up the kiddie as protection against your brother?'

'Got it in one, Bert,' Gowry said, and, still grinning, went off towards the bottom end of Wordsworth Street where he had parked the motor-car.

Lindsay's tour of the submarine both excited and depressed her. A team from Vickers-Martin were fitting a wicked-looking machine-gun on the bow quarter, for on submarines, so Geoffrey informed her, the weapons, along with everything else, were installed before launching. The Vickers' crew was being assisted by several of Franklin's metal workers supervised by George Crush. Geoffrey had instructed her to wear a tight-fitting skirt, shoes with low heels and to put her hair up into a knot and cover it with a scarf and as she was helped up the scaffolding and led to the conning tower Lindsay was conscious of the men's eyes upon her. She did not know what awaited her within the fish-shaped hull or if she would be alone down there with Geoffrey and, if so, what speculations that would give rise to and what sort of twisted story might wend back to Forbes before the day was done.

She should have known better. The claustrophobic chambers

at the foot of the iron ladder were crowded. There were men everywhere: men kneeling, men lying on their backs, men in overalls, men stripped almost naked. In the operating-room steering cables were being adjusted and it was all Geoffrey could do to find sufficient room to point out the gauges and explain their functions. The engines too were all in place and Lindsay inhaled the odours of oil and sweat mingled with a throat-catching whiff of chlorine from the accumulators. A submarine was no place for a woman, she realised. The word that sprang into her mind was 'foetal' as she inched after Geoffrey along the plating to inspect the tiny saloon where the sailors would sleep during off-watches. Franklin's joiners were busy assembling bunks. The rapping of hammers seemed to vibrate throughout the vessel and Lindsay was soon headachy and rather breathless. She was proud of the Franklin's workforce, however, for it was plain that it was not just the prospect of wages that kept them hard at it but the satisfaction of creating something intricate and complex by the exercise of their skills.

She was relieved when, after twenty minutes below, Geoffrey guided her up out of the glare of the electric lanterns and into hazy sunlight. She shook her head to clear it and looked at the greeny-brown coil of the Clyde and thought of the open sea and the depths to which that skinny fish-shaped shell would descend, carrying with it all the ingenuity of which men were capable, backed by human lives.

'Do you ever think what might happen if a piece of equipment fails?'

'Too much to do making sure that it doesn't,' Geoffrey said.

'How many in the crew?'

'In this craft, two officers and twenty men. That's a hefty complement for a submarine but we need a large crew to operate such a powerful vessel.' Reading her concern, he said, 'Cruising underwater isn't as bad as you might imagine, not nearly as bad as chasing through a rough sea in a rocky old destroyer.'

'Will you be on board during the trials?'

'Yes, certainly.'

'Who else — besides the crew, I mean?'

'Two naval inspection officers, plus three from the yard.'

'My father?'

'I doubt it. Tom Calder probably, and a couple of engineers.'

'Geoffrey?'

'Hmm?'

'Is she safe?'

'As houses,' Geoffrey said.

On the ride back to Brunswick Park in the taxi-cab, he made no attempt to kiss her, for which Lindsay — in a way — was glad.

Baby Philip was greedy that evening. He suckled on her breast with a petulance that suggested punishment. Harry, on the other hand, was quieter than usual and contented himself by building elaborate constructions on the tabletop with his collection of wooden alphabet bricks. Lindsay watched him out of a corner of her eye and wondered if he had inherited the Franklins' aptitude for thoroughness and if, in twenty or thirty years' time, he would be designing and building ships too and, if so, what sort of ships they would be: great liners that would slip smoothly across the Atlantic in three or four days perhaps, or warships so swift and deadly that nothing that sailed in or upon the seven seas would be safe from their guns.

The rain had drifted away and the evening sky had taken on a shimmering brilliance that filled the rooms to the front of the house. In the dining-room the table had been set and dinner would be served as soon as she had finished feeding Philip. With her baby at her breast and Harry in sight, Lindsay felt more relaxed. Winn had gone off in a huff because she, Lindsay, would not say where she had been that afternoon. In fact, she had returned home before Forbes and had spent a few minutes with her father in the parlour discussing the prototype's place in the navy's programme of modernisation and what it might mean to Franklin's future, then she had gone up to the nursery.

Winn had been on to her at once, quizzing, interrogating, probing. There would be more of the same from Forbes, no doubt, an inquisition that she would just have to endure. She had nothing to hide, everything to hide: kisses and state secrets, the effervescent sensation that being in love endowed her with, and the confidence to keep such inspiring secrets to herself.

Forbes would probably make love to her tonight. He usually did when he thought she was avoiding him. He would take her with angry determination, no longer expecting her to give him pleasure or admit that he was pleasing her, thrusting himself into her with all the force of a pugilist, as if she were an opponent from whom he must wrest a victory. She would match his energy stroke for stroke, though, lifting herself rhythmically against him while dwelling only on the spasmodic sensations that he wrung from her, sensations that she had learned to enjoy even although she knew that his purpose was pragmatic, not to give and take love but to teach her a lesson in obedience, and render her pregnant once more.

Geoffrey would soon be gone. At least for a time they would become letter-lovers, their kisses replaced by tenderness of another kind, less satisfying but in its way more tangible. Forbes had simply failed to realise that babies protected her, rendered her more mother than wife. Another baby, another child, would only increase her happiness and strengthen her position, for no matter how many sisters and brothers Forbes imported she would never allow herself to become a prisoner in her own home again.

Pappy Owen had given her a measure of independence and for that she was grateful, but in hindsight she resented his ill-considered match-making, the fact that he had thrown Forbes and her together to heal old wounds, the wounds of a former generation. She missed Pappy, his joviality, his appetite for life, but he had been replaced by others, particularly by her children.

They were her family now, her centre, her future. They were the deciding factor, if only Forbes would realise it, that kept her from taking Geoffrey Paget as her lover or of running off with him to live in scandal and in sin.

She watched Harry place one brick precariously upon another and heard Philip sigh as he removed his mouth from her nipple.

'Hello,' said a voice from the landing. 'Anyone home?'

Harry looked up. He cupped his little fists over the tower of bricks and held them, squeezing down, as the nursery door opened and Gowry put his head around it.

'Oh, sorry,' he said. 'I'll come back when you've done.'

'It's all right.' Lindsay turned the chair and covered her breast with a square of cotton cloth known as a Mother's Modesty. 'Come in if you wish. If you're looking for Winn, though, she isn't here. I believe she's in the kitchen with Blossom.'

'I'm not looking for Winn,' Gowry said. 'I'm looking for you.'

'Me?' said Lindsay, surprised.

'You, and this lump,' Gowry said. Harry, abandoning his tower, raced across the floor and threw himself against his uncle's legs. Gowry stooped and lifted the little boy into his arms. 'I've never been up here before.' He swung Harry down to his hip and round again as if he were as weightless as a straw doll. 'It's nice and quiet.' He tucked Harry under one arm and pulled out a nursery chair. He placed it at a discreet angle and seated himself upon it, Harry on his knee.

The boy chattered, 'I builded a steeple, Uncle Gowry. See, I builded a steeple.'

Gowry gave his attention to the bricks on the table, nodding. 'So you have, sure and you have,' he said. 'That's a marvellous bit of architecture, Harry, but if I let you go will you be tiptoeing over there and make sure it doesn't fall down.'

'Won't fall down.'

'Well, it looks a wee bit shaky to me.'

'Archy – archy . . .'

'Archy-teck-ture,' said Gowry. 'It means a building.'

'My building.'

'Yes, your building. Go and look after it. Add some more.'

Harry slid from his uncle's knee and returned to the table. He clambered on to a chair and stared hard at the bricks. 'Archy-teck-ture,' he said, frowning, as if the nature of the word had changed the concept of construction for him. 'Archy-teck-ture,' then he lifted a coloured block and with exaggerated care placed it on top of the column.

Philip, meanwhile, returned to the breast.

'What do you want, Gowry?' Lindsay said. 'Did Forbes send you?'

'I do have a mind of my own, you know,' Gowry said. 'Forbes doesn't know where I am.' He looked around. 'So this is where the kiddies live, is it? Got everything they need, I see.'

'Winn could have told you that.'

'You can't always be trusting what others tell you. Him, for instance.' He nodded at Philip, hidden in the crook of Lindsay's arm. 'How long will he be feeding off you?'

'I thought you would know that, given all those sisters and brothers.'

'I didn't pay enough attention when I was a boy at home.'

'He will have milk for another month or two, until he's fully weaned.'

'Is it sore?'

'Gowry!'

'Well, is it?'

'I'm tender, if you must know. But, no, it's not painful.'

'Good,' Gowry said, with an odd little nod of the head. 'That's good.'

He sat silent for a moment, contemplating the crown of the baby's head, then he said, 'Supposing you – I mean, supposing a woman has no milk to give, what happens then?'

'A wet nurse is employed.'

'Yes, I've heard about those.'

'Or a milk formula can be purchased from the chemist's suitable for even small babies,' Lindsay said. 'Why are you asking *me* these questions, Gowry? Surely Winn or Blossom would have been able to answer them.'

'I don't want them to know I'm interested in babies.'

'Why are you interested in babies?'

'In the lodging where I live there's a girl, a young girl. She's been left in the lurch in – well – a delicate condition. I feel sorry for her.'

'Do you mean that she's pregnant?'

Gowry nodded.

'Is it yours?' Lindsay said. 'Are you the father?'

He looked startled, then shocked. 'God, no! She's not my sweetheart. No, no, it couldn't be mine, not mine.'

'I take it the father's absconded?'

'Yes, and I feel sorry for her.' Gowry shrugged. 'I only have to sleep there, thanks to God, but those further down the ladder have to live there. Families. Singles. This girl, she's a single. I'm not sure what she's going to do.'

'There are places she can go. Charities.'

'I don't think she'd be doing that.'

'She could go back to her parents.'

'They'd never take her in. Anyhow, I think she's an orphan.'

'Are you making this up?' Lindsay said.

He grinned. 'No. It's all true, I swear it is.'

Lindsay looked down at her son who, at last, seemed to have had his fill. His lips had slipped from her teat and his eyes were closed. She glanced at Harry who, in spite of his uncle's presence, had become absorbed in play again. He wrestled with hands and arms to keep the pile of bricks upright while balancing another on the top. Disaster, Lindsay reckoned, was inevitable.

Gowry said, 'That's not why I came up here, really.'

'Why did you come?'

'I've something to tell you.'

'What's that?'

'My mam, she's planning to stay in Glasgow for the whole summer.'

'Does Forbes know?' Lindsay asked. 'Of course he does. Who will look after your father while she's away?'

'He can look after himself,' Gowry said. 'Anyhow, I thought you might like a wee bit of a warning and I know Forbes won't say anything.'

Lindsay was wary of Gowry. She suspected some trick or ruse but could not imagine what purpose would be served by it. She did not like her Aunt Kay, but she could hardly refuse to have her in the house. She would, however, issue due warning to her father who might choose to take a holiday just to escape, two or three weeks in a good hotel down the coast, after the submarine was launched and trials completed. Two or three weeks with Miss Runciman to look after him and provide him with company: would that be considered outrageous? Lindsay wondered. Given their ages, probably not. If they weren't too far off she might take the children down for a week or so, without Winn and, needless to say, without Forbes. Tom and Cissie might come too and Lilias and Uncle Donald; like old times it would be, happy times in the Bruce Hotel, only with a whole new cast of sand-babies.

Gowry got to his feet. 'You won't say anything, will you? I mean, you won't say anything to Forbes, or to Winn and Bloss?'

'About what?' said Lindsay. 'Your mother – or this girl of yours?'

'Either,' Gowry said.

'No, I won't say anything,' Lindsay promised.

He watched her button her blouse and then came closer. He looked down at the child drowsing in her arms. 'May I hold him?'

Lindsay felt a curious little squinch of apprehension. Gowry looked so tall, standing over her, and the uniform made him menacing.

'Just for a minute,' Gowry said, 'let me hold him.'

Forbes had never taken either of his babies into his arms. Even now it was all he could bring himself to do to allow Harry to clamber on to his knee for a few minutes at a time. She arranged the shawl about Philip's legs and feet then very carefully transferred the sleepy child to the Irishman's arms.

In spite of the uniform, Gowry was not awkward, not nervous. When Philip sighed and nestled against him, he uttered a crooning sound, and with the tip of his little finger brushed away a fleck of milk from the baby's bottom lip.

He looked up at Lindsay, grinning broadly.

'That's fine, isn't it now?' he murmured. 'Sure and isn't that fine?'

'Indeed, it is,' said Lindsay.

Once before, on the Niger, Tom had feared for his life. He had been alone on the river, alone that is without Britons around him and only two gruff French agents for company. It had rained with tropical force most of the night and the currents had become so strong that the launch in which he had been travelling had lost power and had swung back and across the basin, broadside to the walls of cocoa-brown water. There was danger, but not an excess of it; what had really frightened him had been the smell of the floodwater, of Africa, a sudden awareness of his isolation and an uncharacteristic dread that he was being punished for daring to be there at all.

On the days of the submarine's trials there was no turbulence on the surface of the Gareloch, not a breath of wind, not a ripple on the shingle shore, and the moorland hills that flanked the upper waters of the firth were as still as painted scenery against a deep blue August sky; yet Tom was frightened, more frightened than he had ever been on the swirling flood currents of the Niger. He had attended several trials on the sheltered stretch of water that branched off the Clyde estuary. Measured miles and testing grounds for paddle steamers were here and the piers at

Cree, Mambeg and Clynder had a familiarity that should have been calming. Nothing could calm Tom that hot August week, however, for an irrational fear had corroded his common sense.

Royal Naval observers manned the pier at Cree. It was a stubby, high-sided construction that nosed into water deep enough to accommodate the salvage vessel, *Kettledrum*, which had been brought up all the way from Sheerness to assist in the trials. Tom had already spent three hot glaring days on the deck of the *Kettledrum* watching the *Snark*, as the prototype was now called, being sealed and lowered to a depth of sixty-nine feet without crew or observers on board, sealed, lowered and raised again to ensure that the hull was absolutely watertight. She crossed this first hurdle with flying colours and as Commander Coles, chief naval observer, remarked, had 'come up drier than she had gone down'.

But Tom was fretful and impatient. He knew that the hull would withstand pressure down to one hundred and fifty feet and he was uncommonly aggrieved at the navy's thoroughness. On the first manned trials, the *Snark* was given a good surface run, a little sniff of the wind, as it were, though there was no wind, not a breath. Results were not recorded; the official trials for speed and manoeuvrability, above and below water, would take place later in the week.

The navy's high brass were lodged in a hotel in Helensburgh and ferried round to Cree each morning, but Tom went home to Glasgow each evening to take a late supper with his wife, kiss his little boy, to lie down to sleep in his own bed with dread growling in his brain like an overture. There were several aspects to his anxiety. One which he shared with all Franklin's partners was a fear that the submarine would fail to meet the requirements of the Admiralty's commissioning body and that the vessel would prove 'unacceptable'.

On paper the *Snark* was a perfect fighting machine, sleek, supple and fast, an ocean-going monster with a strike-range far in excess of anything that the Royal Navy so far possessed. On paper she represented a feat of advanced engineering and — on paper — she could not fail to satisfy. But a rejected submarine had no market whatsoever, was fit only for the scrap heap; if the navy did turn her down then Franklin's financial loss would be considerable if not ruinous and he, Tom, would have to bear a lion's share of the blame.

Tom's other anxieties were much more personal: fear of the unknown, of the underside of the sea, of pressures he could calculate mathematically but could not imagine, of tensile strengths and submergence limits, and darkness, the suffocating darkness that might turn the graceful metal shell into a tomb. He was afraid, desperately afraid, of going down in her.

But on Thursday, come what may, he would have to do just that.

It was early, far too early, so early in fact that dawn was still little more than a pearly promise in the eastern sky. Ewan was fast asleep in the room to the rear of the apartment, clothes thrown off, his little limbs spread out across the sheet for coolness.

In the kitchen, Cissie fussed with a frying-pan, breaking eggs and sliding ham into a clean, sizzling pool of fat. She wore a thin cotton dressing-gown over her nightdress and had stuck her bare feet into a pair of Tom's old carpet slippers. At that moment she reminded him of his Aunt Sarah who had raised him after his mother's final illness, and his mood lightened at the realisation that Cissie was not so very different from any one of the thousands of women across Clydeside who would be cooking breakfast and packing their husbands off to work. Cissie was a good wife, an attentive wife, a loving wife: Tom regretted that he could not explain what troubled him, not without seeming like a coward.

He had a suspicion that Cissie had guessed the reason for his brooding silences, and this morning she too was quiet. He missed her prattle, her small talk, the sharing of inconsequentialities. She plonked a second fried egg on to a clean tea-plate and put it down beside him.

'Eat,' she said.

Tom was already dressed in his suit, shaved, groomed, ready for the long day ahead. He looked at the eggs, at the crimson slices of ham, and felt his throat close. He lifted his teacup and tried to sip the hot sugary liquid without gagging.

'You're not being shot at dawn, Tom Calder,' Cissie said. 'Stop behaving as if this is your last meal on earth.' She spoke over her shoulder from her stance in front of the gas stove, a green and black object that occupied a cupboard left of the sinks. The kitchen was spacious. Jenny, the maid, kept it spotless.

Cissie went on, 'You built the blessed boat. If you can't be sure that it's watertight then who can?'

'It's not that,' said Tom, abashed.

She carried her plate to the table and sat opposite him. The window was behind her, the blind drawn up. Pale light illuminated her head and shoulders and she looked cool and soft. He did not want to leave her, did not want to run the risk that he would not return, that the sea would claim him and transform poor Cissie into a grieving widow.

'Yes, it is,' Cissie said. 'You can't fool me, Tom, you're frightened of going underwater, aren't you?'

He managed to nod.

'How deep is the Gareloch?' she asked.

'We test at a hundred feet.'

'I mean, how deep is the loch?'

Tom swallowed. 'Deep.'

'Theory and practice,' Cissie said. 'Theory and practice; you just can't have one without the other. Don't start with the "what-ifs". I had quite enough of those from my father and brothers.' She looked, he thought, a lot less soft than she had done a minute ago. She frowned, freckles glowing. 'I'm not having it, Tom Calder. I'm not going to let you worry over nothing. Now eat that egg and hurry up or you'll miss the train, and that would never do. Eat.'

Alarmed and oddly amused, Tom ate.

She was right, of course. There was nothing much to be afraid of. The *Snark* was his responsibility as much as anyone else's. If he was reluctant to accept responsibility what hope was there for the programme in future? She wasn't made of paper; she wouldn't crumple under pressure. Every gram of steel had been checked for flaws; every rivet, every cable, every hinge, every valve double-checked. Experts had built her engines and boilers, the fuelling systems were infallible, the ballast tanks and air-supply intakes had been adapted by no less a person than Arthur Franklin. He would be safer inside the *Snark* than on the train to Helensburgh.

'See, you see,' Cissie said, as if she could read his thoughts. 'I'm right, aren't I? She's just another boat, really, even if she does run underwater.'

'That's true,' Tom said.

'I'm not worried. Why should you be worried?' Cissie said, then, with mock severity, 'Now, sit up straight and finish your breakfast.'

'Like a good boy?' Tom said.

'Like a good boy,' said Cissie.

Ten minutes later, feeling better, Tom stepped out into daylight and headed west for the railway station. Above him in the window bay of the handsome sandstone tenement, Cissie waved and blew kisses until he turned the corner out of sight.

And then she wept.

The commander of the *Snark* was Captain John Bridges. He had been deputy in charge of submarines at Devonport for the best part of five years and had fought shoulder to shoulder with Geoffrey in the war of red tape. He had been instructed to select a crew of experienced submariners and had spent the best part of a fortnight prior to launch familiarising himself with the *Snark*'s operating systems. The crew, based at Rosyth, had been brought over only after the submarine had taken to the water, and had nursed her downriver under cover of darkness to the test berth at Cree.

The *Snark* was a powerful vessel brimful of innovations. Captain Bridges very much looked forward to taking her on her first sea-going voyage to Gibraltar as well as steering her through gunnery and torpedo trials and mock attacks that would surely prove her value as a fighting machine. He had no doubt at all that she would perform well in the flat calm of the Gareloch and would live up to all expectations.

Three Royal Navy observers would be taken on board for the first submergence run, together with three 'workers' from the shipyard. Captain Bridges had met with Arthur Franklin and Thomas Calder several times but the third member of the shipbuilders' party was a stranger to him. He was not well pleased at being distracted from his preparations by the young man's questions and curtly took himself off.

'What the devil are *you* doing here?' Arthur said.

'I wangled an invitation,' Forbes said. 'I'm a partner, after all, and this is too good an opportunity to miss.'

'Why wasn't I told? More to the point, why wasn't I consulted?' Arthur said. 'I knew nothing of this. Precisely what did you do to "wangle" yourself on board the *Snark* during secret trials?'

'I asked our friend here,' Forbes said. 'Didn't I, Geoffrey?'

Geoffrey Paget nodded, rather bleakly.

'And he could hardly refuse,' Forbes said. 'Could he?'

They were gathered on the pier above the submarine. She was already fuelled and the smell of oil hung heavy over the water. Four or five small craft flitted on the firth far away and the long, splinter-like shape of a paddle-wheeler, wafting blue smoke, passed across the narrow mouth of the Gareloch. It was quiet, very quiet in the sun-stunned morning light. Even the gulls were lazily propped on weedy posts or along the ridge of the gear-shed that backed the pier.

Outward, three or four hundred yards off, two small launches and the ugly bulk of the *Kettledrum* were easing into positions clear of the marker buoys, and most of the activity on the *Snark* was taking place within the hull.

The navy observers were not so much aloof as preoccupied. Divided by rank and station into three teams, each of which would conduct a series of specific tests and accurately record the results. Commander Coles, a former engineer and very important person, had chosen the *Kettledrum* as his vantage point. If he were sceptical about the *Snark*'s capabilities he gave no sign of it. He said little to any of the officers, not even to Geoffrey Paget who was an old adversary from the boardrooms of Whitehall.

The whiff of autocratic tensions and service politics was strong in the air, like the smell of baking seaweed, but Tom was oblivious to it. He experienced a flash of annoyance at Forbes's unexpected appearance, however, at his brother-in-law's gall in begging a trip in the Royal Navy's prize possession. It occurred to him that Forbes might have employed a form of blackmail to persuade Paget to invite him on board and – just before fear closed in again – wondered if Cissie's conjectures were correct and Lindsay, the model wife, really had embarked on an affair with the English officer.

Tom noticed the smirk on Forbes's lips, his swagger as he went towards the ladders. Then it was his turn to go forward and he became encased in icy fear again, cut off by the sure and certain knowledge that he would soon be dead and Cissie, poor Cissie, would be left to mourn alone.

He walked stiffly to the ladder and forced himself to descend.

There was no motion on the deck, not even tidal sway. The piles of the pier loomed above him, the water already deep. He pushed himself clumsily through the hatch, and looked up despairingly at the oval of sky above just before it vanished, sheared off by metal. Then he stopped breathing for a time, suspended, as he was ushered forward into the diving station. He was free to go where he wished, to take notes and make recordings against which the accuracy of the naval observers' reports could be checked. Arthur had already gone back into the engine-room and Forbes, trailing Geoffrey Paget like a fox, had vanished into the forward control-room. Sweating, Tom pressed himself against the ladder, unable to bring himself to move.

The *Snark* shuddered, the lights flickered, and the engines thundered.

Tom felt the pressure of sound, not water, pressing upon him. He had heard all this before, of course, had endured it with grim satisfaction while the craft had been tethered to the shore. But he was at sea now, or the next best thing, the Gareloch opening unseen around him.

He clung to the steel ladder and stared at the depth indicator over the crewman's shoulder. Sense told him it would be five or ten minutes before the *Snark* was ready to dive. At the moment she was running light, ballast tanks empty. First she would travel a short distance awash, the bridge lookout replaced by the periscope, then she would submerge to periscope depth and finally to full submersion and, with only the compass to hold her on course, would descend to a depth of sixty feet.

He tried to fix on that, on sixty feet.

The rating at the wheel tapped the gauge, turned and grinned at him. 'Fine morning for a trip on the Skylark, sir?'

'Yes,' Tom got out thickly. 'V-very fine.'

'Not a thing to worry about, sir. She's sweet as a nut, she is.'

The glass on the gauges was still unsmeared. Everything around him was shining and new, glossy with fresh paint. He tried to make himself listen to the engines, to interpret changes in pitch and tone as she picked up speed. He tried to visualise her route, the short, button-hooked shape of the cruising run, past familiar hills and friendly piers, but all he could think of were the depths beneath his feet, the dark and waiting depths. He was blanking out, not swooning, simply blanking out.

Geoffrey Paget came swarming up towards him, Forbes on his heels.

In spite of his height, the Lieutenant Commander moved with the grace of a tea-dancer, slipping past crew members at their stations.

Forbes was less nimble, less careful. He seemed almost to be scurrying, as if he had found his hole at last, a burrow-like tube narrow and straight enough to contain his ambition. He should, Tom thought, be fired out like a torpedo, sent back the way he had come to explode harmlessly on a distant shore, lost in a puff of smoke, or not go up at all, just lie there, a dud rusting on the shingle.

Geoffrey touched his shoulder. 'All right, Tom?'

'All right, thanks.'

The officer and his leech moved forward.

Tom knew that he should follow them, pretend to assist Arthur Franklin or at least observe the navy's observers. He could not move, though. He was limp with the effort of sustaining dread. He wanted nothing but to put the trial behind him. He heard the sound of voices crackling through the tubes, the scramble upstairs as the deck hamper was removed. He thought he smelled fresh air again as the hamper was dropped, then heard the clang of the conning tower and the squeak of the wheels and conduit valves as the *Snark* was finally sealed for submersion. He clung tightly to the ladder, watching the gauge.

'First time under, sir?'

'It – it is.'

'You'll hardly notice a thing.'

He doubted that. He knew more about the *Snark* than any ordinary seaman, except the captain. What was disturbingly novel was the sensation of being carried underwater, the claustrophobic pressure of being taken down, deliberately, intentionally, voluntarily drowned. The crackle of voices, more distinct: a command. He glimpsed Paget and Forbes against a bulkhead ahead of him, the smooth broadcloth of a navy observer's uniform. Soon water would be allowed to pour into the ballast tanks and the greater part of the vessel's capacity to float would be destroyed.

She would, in effect, be sunk.

'Here we go now, sir,' the sailor said, very quietly.

The man's voice was lost as the engines were switched over and a strange, cold, creaking closed around him, more sensation than sound. The arrow on the big, moon-faced dial began to ascend, counting off feet. The angle of the ladder altered. A hose behind him hissed. Trimming, she's being trimmed fore and aft, Tom told himself, ashamed of his incapacity, his crippled intelligence. Declination: two degrees. Declination: easing back to one and a quarter. He could still summon up figures and facts, the algebraic equations that had flickered off the point of his pencil in the drawing office at Aydon Road. Was she underwater yet? Was she groping forward under the surface of the loch? No, she was still gliding, gliding down on an almost imperceptible declivity.

Tom closed his eyes and swallowed dryly as the vessel that he had helped the Franklins build sank with hardly a trace.

'Are you as concerned as I am, dear?' Cissie asked. 'About the trials, I mean.'

'I'm not concerned at all,' Lindsay said, truthfully.

'Forbes won't be on board, of course.'

'Knowing Forbes, he probably will be,' Lindsay said. 'He went off early this morning with a smile on his face; very unusual, I assure you. I've a feeling he's hoping to persuade the powers-that-be to allow him to participate in one of the submergence tests.'

'Why?'

'He finds the prospect exciting.'

'Exciting!' Cissie shook her head. 'Tom's worried. Tom's frightened.'

'Surely Tom doesn't consider the *Snark* unsafe?'

'No, of course he doesn't consider her unsafe. It's just that he's been nursing this — what? — presentiment for weeks now. I think the delay in beginning the trials had something to do with it.'

'The Navy Board caused the delay. The *Snark*'s been lying in Aydon Road for weeks while experts from the navy have been crawling all over her, suggesting "modifications". No wonder Tom's nervous.'

'I don't understand any of it,' said Cissie. 'Tom doesn't talk much about his work and I feel it's intrusive to ask questions. I suppose shipbuilding's all anyone ever talks about in your house.'

'There isn't much talk about anything in our house these days,' said Lindsay. 'Aunt Kay has the unhappy knack of killing conversation.'

'How long will she be with you?'

'I have no idea,' said Lindsay. 'According to Gowry she might not go back to Dublin at all.'

'Really?' Cissie busied herself with the teapot, did the honours for her cousin, set the pot down again, lifted her cup in both hands and looked across the little table at Lindsay. She hesitated. 'Do you think Kay's here to keep an eye on you, by any chance? To make sure you behave?'

'Behave? What do you mean?'

'Because of — you know.'

'No, I do not know, Cissie. Explain yourself.'

'I mean' — Cissie's plump cheeks glowed — 'I mean, well, there have been rumours about you and, well, Lieutenant Commander Paget.'

'Ah!' said Lindsay.

'He's very keen on you, that much is obvious.'

'He *is* keen on me,' Lindsay admitted.

'And are you — you know, with him?'

'I'm in love with him, if that's what you mean.'

'Good Lord!'

'Come now, Cissie, don't pretend you're shocked. You threw us together in the first place, if you recall, right here in this very room.'

'I'm not taking the blame for . . .'

'Blame? Who said anything about blame?'

'Aren't you miserable?' Cissie blurted out.

'Of course I'm not miserable,' Lindsay said.

'Are you and he . . . Oh, no!' A pause: '*Are* you?'

'Cissie, I'm married to Forbes McCulloch, in case you've forgotten.'

'But you don't, you don't *belong* to him, do you?' Cissie said.

'I most certainly do not "belong" to him,' Lindsay said. 'But I do not belong to Geoffrey Paget either.'

'I thought you said you loved him; Geoffrey, I mean.'

'I do.'

'But . . .'

'He is not my lover, Cissie, if that's what you're driving at. He's not my lover and never will be.'

Flame-cheeked with embarrassment, Cissie set down her cup, and confessed: 'That's what Tom said.'

'Have Tom and you been discussing my private affairs?'

'Well, it has been rather obvious, hasn't it?' Cissie settled in her chair, sensing that the awkward part of the conversation was behind her. 'I mean, you've made no secret of your – *not* your affair; I don't know what to call it.'

'Friendship.'

'I thought you said it was love.'

'Cissie, stop all this fiddle-faddle.'

'Yes, I'm sorry. You're right, dear. Even if I am your cousin I've no right to pry into your aff—business. You thought you were in love with Forbes once, didn't you?'

'So did you.'

'I'm so glad I got over it.'

'Do you still think I stole Forbes from you?' Lindsay asked.

'Stole? No, not exactly. Forbes simply preferred you to me. I didn't have enough to offer him, I suppose. Look at me. I'm no oil-painting, am I? But, do you know, I'm rather glad I'm not? Tom likes me the way I am and I'm not liable to have handsome naval officers throwing themselves at *me*.'

'What if one did?' said Lindsay.

'I'd soon send him packing.'

'Even if he loved you, or if you loved him?'

'I can't imagine it,' Cissie said. 'In any case I wouldn't let it happen. I wouldn't betray Tom, not for anyone.'

'Yes,' Lindsay said, 'but that's because you love Tom.'

'I do,' said Cissie without irony or embarrassment. 'I do, very much.'

Lindsay nodded. How could she grudge Cissie her happiness? Now and then, though, she regretted that she had not encouraged Tom Calder's interest; had, as it were, let him slip. She would not hurt her cousin for all the tea in China by bringing it up now. Besides, they had both moved on, had grown up. The selfish passion she had once felt for Forbes McCulloch had been partly competitive, genuine at the time but not enduring, the marriage itself less a mistake than a misjudgement.

Cissie, innocent and contented, would only be baffled by the nature of her relationship with Forbes, by its unrefined intimacy. Cissie could not possibly understand how she, Lindsay, could satisfy her sexual needs with one man while she professed to love another. It was, perhaps, the ultimate deceit, the ultimate revenge, though Lindsay did not regard it as such. What she did with her body was one thing, what she did with her heart quite another, which was too modern a concept for Cissie ever to grasp.

Cissie said, 'You're not, I mean, you're not planning to do anything rash, Lindsay, are you?'

Lindsay guessed what was coming. 'What, for instance?'

'Like running off with Geoffrey Paget.'

Lindsay laughed. 'Running off *where* with Geoffrey? To sea?'

'If you don't love Forbes any more,' Cissie said, 'and you do love Geoffrey Paget . . . I mean, there is such a thing as divorce.'

'One needs grounds for divorce,' said Lindsay, 'and not caring much for one's husband would not, I imagine, be sufficient for the court. Besides which, I will never desert my children.'

'I think that's very wise, very admirable.'

'Do you?'

'A romance,' Cissie said, 'not an affair.'

'There's nothing romantic about it,' said Lindsay curtly. 'I didn't ask for it to happen. I wasn't on the lookout for another chap. It isn't a flirtation, Cissie. I care about Geoffrey and I believe he cares for me. The feeling is both comforting and uncomfortable at one and the same time.'

'Perhaps it's just as well he's going away.'

'No,' Lindsay said. 'No.'

Cissie, nonplussed, said, 'Well, at least you're keeping your feet firmly on the ground. I'm glad of that – for the children's sake.'

Eleanor Runciman had volunteered to accompany Lindsay to Sandyford Avenue that afternoon. Philip had been left behind with Winn, for hot weather and strong sunlight did not agree with him and he had been a little out of sorts for a day or two. Eleanor, too, was anxious about the submarine's trials. She was still Arthur's confidante and knew how much importance attached to the results. She had offered to take the two boys, Harry and Ewan, out to visit the Victoria Park, a far piece for little legs, but Lindsay had no doubt that they would be sustained by the purchase of ice-cream along the way and a glass of lemonade when they got there. She wished now that she had gone with them, for she was beginning to find Cissie's remarks just a little irksome, and the parlour stuffy.

In the hallway, the clock chimed the half-hour; half-past three o'clock. Though Cissie's apartments were spotless, sunlight slanting through the bay window found a few loose motes of dust and expanded them into a pale silvery ribbon. Beyond, the red sandstone facade of the tenements on the other side of the avenue, flattened by sunlight, seemed to exist in only one dimension.

Cissie had just reached for the hot-water jug to refresh the teapot when the doorbell rang. The cousins glanced at each other in mild bewilderment.

'The boys are back early,' Cissie said.

'Perhaps it's too hot for them,' said Lindsay, frowning.

They listened to the padding of the maid's shoes on the carpet of the hall, heard the outer door open and the strange sifting emptiness of the tiled close; voices, low voices, not gruff or grumbling but very light and airy, almost blithesome in the flocculent air of the August afternoon.

A moment later Jenny, the day-maid, came into the parlour and said in a puzzled tone, 'There's someone here to see you, ma'am.'

'Who is it, Jenny?'

'I don't know, ma'am. She says her name is McCulloch, Mrs Forbes McCulloch.' And before the servant had finished speaking, little Sylvie Calder waddled past her and, smiling, entered the room.

CHAPTER NINETEEN

Night Without End

It was half past eight o'clock before Tom got home. Cissie was in the dining-room and looked as if she had been sitting there for hours, rehearsing not anger or even patience but a deliberate meditative calm. He assumed that she had been concerned for him and that the lucid little occupations of motherhood had not kept her from fretting after all.

'Did it go well, dear?' she asked as soon as he appeared.

'It went very well,' Tom informed her. 'Very well indeed.'

He moved across the room, cupped her face in his hands and kissed her, as if it were she, not he, who had been in peril that day.

'Tom, have you been drinking?'

'I had a brandy at the Coventry.'

'The Coventry?'

'The hotel in Helensburgh.'

'With Forbes?' Cissie said.

'Forbes was there too, yes. He went down with us on the first run.'

'Geoffrey arranged it, I suppose?'

'He did.'

'And you?' Cissie remained motionless at the dining-table. 'Was it as bad as you imagined it would be, Tom?'

He grinned and made light of it. 'Worse.'

'At least you survived,' Cissie said solemnly.

'Fortunately, yes.'

He removed his jacket and unfastened his collar. He was still clammy with the aftermath of the morning's ordeal. In fact, he had consumed two light ales as well as a brandy. Six naval officers had been present at the drinks party and unless he had misinterpreted Commander Coles's compliments, it seemed probable that the *Snark* would be accepted and commissioned and that more Admiralty contracts would come Franklin's way. Reason enough for celebration: if he'd been slightly less eager to tell his tale to Cissie he might have lingered at the party instead of catching the early evening train home.

He seated himself at the table and took Cissie's hand. 'I've been a pig for the past week or two, dearest. Please forgive me?'

'You had every right to be nervous. There's nothing to forgive.'

Tom placed his hands behind his head and rocked placidly on the dining chair. It was late in the evening now. Sunlight had cooled to pale blue shadow and ridges of pink and gold cloud lofted high above the rooftops. He would not be required to attend the speed tests at the Gareloch tomorrow, thank the Lord. Peter Holt would cover them.

'I really was terrified,' he said. 'But in a queer way I enjoyed it. She really is a superb machine. She slid down smoothly and surfaced without a hiccup. Sixty feet below the surface and you'd hardly have known you were underwater at all. Captain Bridges really knows his onions, of course. Talking of onions, darling, what's for supper?'

Cissie said, 'Your daughter called this afternoon.'

The legs of the chair came down with a thump. 'My daughter?'

Cissie watched him closely. 'Your daughter Sylvie.'

'Good God! I didn't even know she was back in Glasgow.'

'When did you last see her?' Cissie asked.

'Oh, not for years. Five years at least. I wrote to her care of the Coral Strand offices but my letters were returned unopened. I thought — I don't know what I thought — that she had found a niche for herself in London.'

'You didn't try very hard to find her, did you, Tom?'

'I suppose I didn't, really.'

'Apparently she didn't go to London at all. She never left Glasgow.'

'What?' said Tom again. 'But why didn't she—'

'She's expecting a child.'

'Sylvie married? That's excellent. What does her husband—'

'She isn't married,' Cissie said.

'I see,' Tom said. 'I see. But where's Albert? Where's her stepfather?'

'She claims he abandoned her,' Cissie said.

'Is it — is it Albert's child? *Could* it be his child?'

'It isn't his child,' Cissie said, white-faced.

'Who then? Who is he? If he thinks—'

'It's Forbes McCulloch.'

'Surely you're mistaken.' Tom was bewildered. 'Forbes? Our Forbes?'

'Lindsay's husband, yes.'

'Absolute nonsense!' Tom protested. 'Sylvie doesn't know McCulloch. She's never even met the man.'

'I'm afraid she has, Tom. She claims to have known him since he was a student. She met him at some drinking club in Glasgow which he used to frequent quite regularly. She claims that Forbes promised to marry her.'

'She's making it up.' He got unsteadily to his feet. He knew that Cissie was telling the truth but he continued to protest, to deny the cold, hard fact that Sylvie had come back into his life. 'My daughter's always been a bit fanciful. It's my fault, I suppose. My fault, yes. I shouldn't have let her go off without a word. My only excuse is that her mother cheated and deceived me and I took it out on Sylvie. I wanted rid of her.' He heaved in a breath. 'But this story she told you — no, that's a lie. It must be a lie. I'll bet that Albert's behind it. He'll be after money again. Forbes! How could Forbes *possibly* be the father of her child? Sylvie's lying, she *must* be lying.'

'Lindsay believed her. Lindsay thinks she's telling the truth.'

He opened his mouth, sucked air. 'Lindsay?'

Cissie nodded mournfully. She was close to tears now, afraid of a past that Tom never talked about, of what might be revealed now that his daughter had returned and how it would affect her husband and her marriage.

'Do you mean to say that Lindsay was here when Sylvie called?'

Cissie nodded again and softly began to cry. He sat down and reached for her hand.

'Poor Lindsay,' he said. 'Poor, poor Lindsay.'

Cissie sniffed. 'What are you going to do?'

'What *can* I do, dearest? Lindsay isn't *my* wife.'

'About your daughter, I mean. She's convinced, utterly convinced that Forbes intends to divorce Lindsay and marry her instead.'

'How can she possibly believe that?'

'Because he told her so. Because he promised.'

'Bastard!' Tom spat the word out. 'I'd like to go over to Brunswick Park right now and kill that little bastard.'

'Oh, Tom, no.'

'No,' he said. 'No, of course I won't.'

'You'll have to help her. Sylvie, I mean.'

'How far is she gone?' Tom asked.

'She's due soon to judge by the size of her.'

'How has she supported herself all these years?'

'Forbes has been keeping her as his – his mistress.'

'Where?'

'She refused to tell us,' Cissie answered.

'Forbes will know where to find her.' Tom released his wife's hand, got to his feet and reached for his jacket. 'I'm going over to Brunswick Park.'

'Please, Tom, don't. Not tonight.'

'Cissie, I have to. You said yourself . . .'

'Tomorrow, yes, but not tonight, Tom. Please.'

'Why not do it now? Why not?'

'Because I want you to stay here with me.'

He was flooded with guilt and anger. He had laboured hard for security and, to achieve it, he had let Sylvie slip from him. He had seized his chance for happiness and had never regretted it. Cissie was everything that Dorothy had never been. What they said about blood and water was untrue: he cared less about Sylvie than he did about Cissie, or Lindsay for that matter. Cissie was right. He was too angry to confront Forbes McCulloch tonight. Tomorrow he would try to track down Albert Hartnell and wring the whole, sorry story from him. He seated himself once more. He did not understand the circles that fate had drawn around him, could not read the pattern, the grand design. Perhaps, like the *Snark*, the whole of life was nothing but an accumulation of separate bits and pieces that teetered on the edge of breakdown and disaster but that somehow mysteriously continued to function.

He beckoned Cissie to him and took her on to his knee.

He held her loosely, head against his chest, and stroked her hair.

'I don't want you to leave me, dearest,' she said.

'I won't.'

'Not ever?'

'Not ever,' Tom Calder said.

Keeping the secret to herself proved the easiest thing in the world. Cissie had promised to tell no one except Tom what had occurred and Lindsay had urged her cousin to dissuade Tom from rushing over to Brunswick Park that night. For the girl, for Sylvie, Lindsay felt only a thin, irritating pity. She too had obviously been taken in by Forbes's callous charm, the charm that made no distinctions between them, that dictated that one became lover and one wife by a process not of adaptation or by choice but solely to satisfy his whim. Sylvie's illusions were pathetic. She had swallowed all Forbes's lies without question and had become enchanted by them.

From the moment the drawing-room door had opened and the girl had entered, belly thrust out before her, a jaunty summer hat perched on her golden curls, Lindsay had recognised not a rival but a nemesis. She had glimpsed the girl in the Kelvingrove seven or eight years ago when Tom, Cissie and she had first come together to experiment with flirtation. She had seen her again at the launch of the *Hashitaka* when Forbes had become agitated and had dragged her away from the rail. She had had no inkling then that the silly child was Tom Calder's daughter or Forbes's mistress or that the same silly, shadowy child would one day become her saviour.

She had felt no animosity, hardly even surprise when Miss Sylvie Calder had introduced herself and, with a gaiety that was anything but infectious, had accepted a chair at Cissie's tea-table and helped herself to a scone. She had drunk tea, had eaten buttered tea-bread, had explained herself and her situation, had issued her ultimatum and within a half-hour had gone off again, waddling out of the apartment shortly before Miss Runciman had brought the children back from the park. It had all been very genteel, very civilised. At first Lindsay had experienced no jealousy, no sense of outrage at having been systematically deceived by her husband for so many years. Instead, she had felt strangely liberated from the constraints that marriage to Forbes had placed upon her, as if she, like Pappy, had finally found a purpose in adversity.

Geoffrey: she thought at once of Geoffrey. The time-honoured tradition of tit-for-tat meant that she was free now to become Geoffrey's lover or, if she wished, his wife. Given the circumstances, the court would surely support a petition for divorce without quibble. Suddenly she was in a position to be shot of Forbes, not just Forbes but the whole McCulloch clan – Winn, Blossom, Gowry, even Aunt Kay – in one fell swoop, to shake them out of her life and her father's life and send them packing back to where they belonged.

It would be a wonderful revenge, a triumph as thoroughly demeaning as any that Forbes could possibly devise – except that she would never be able to bring herself to go through with it. She had to pull back, not to protect Forbes or save face for the Franklins but for Tom's sake; Sylvie was Tom's daughter and Cissie was Tom's wife and all three would be terribly damaged by the scandal of a prolonged and public divorce.

White-faced and shocked, Cissie had stammered, 'Do you believe her?'

'Of course I believe her,' Lindsay had answered.

'Oh, God! Oh, dear God! I wish Pappy were still with us,' Cissie had said, wringing her plump hands. 'Pappy would know what to do.'

'Are you implying that I don't know what to do?'

'You?' Cissie had said. 'But you're – you're the wife.'

'That isn't a fatal condition, Cissie, or one that precludes me from making my own decisions. As it so happens, I do know what to do.'

'What?'

'You'll see,' Lindsay had answered. 'Wait a little while, dearest, then, believe me, you'll see.'

Forbes had come home late, long after his mother and sisters had gone to bed. Lindsay had taken herself upstairs to the nursery after supper to give Philip his nightly feed then she had gone directly into the master bedroom to make ready.

Below, in the piano parlour, Eleanor waited for Mr Arthur.

He had been tempted by naval hospitality and had dined with the officers at the Coventry. It had been a jovial party and, as it happened, not at all awkward. Lieutenant Commander Paget had been present at the start of the proceedings but he had been called away to answer the telephone and, after making apologies to Commander Coles, had left the company soon after.

Much as he liked the English officer Arthur had not been sorry to see him go. He was aware of the delicate relationship that existed between his daughter and Geoffrey Paget – how could he not be? – but he was prepared to take Eleanor's word for it that there was nothing sinister in the friendship and that when Geoffrey left Glasgow in a week's time that would be an end of it. Even so, the tension between Forbes and Geoffrey Paget had been palpable throughout the day and Arthur could not entirely relax until Paget had gone.

Forbes and he had travelled home together on the last train. He had to put up with the young man's infernal, slightly tipsy, bragging about the superiority of the *Snark* over anything that the Germans had built, as if he, Forbes, had contributed more to the building of the underwater craft than the settling of contracts for basic materials and a few specialised castings. They changed trains at Dalmuir, disembarked on the deserted platform at Partick West and walked home from there.

The air had cooled but a long afterglow lingered in the western sky, mingling with the smoke from Clydeside furnaces and the faint, feeble glare from those yards that were fortunate enough to be operating a night shift. Tram-cars heading along Dumbarton Road to the depot threw out quick, clicking echoes that pealed away down sober side streets and rose tentatively into the heights of Brunswick Park. The trees in the little piece of park were motionless in the papery light of the gas lamps by the time Arthur and his son-in-law reached home and it seemed that the whole of the crescent was already fast asleep.

Any rapport that had existed between Arthur and his son-in-law dwindled as they climbed the steps to the front door. Neither man dared ring the doorbell for fear of waking the children and Forbes was first to find his key. He let himself in first, turned, muttered, 'Goodnight,' and headed off up the staircase to his portion of the house. Relieved that the long, arduous day was finally over, Arthur opened the door of the parlour and peeped in.

'Ah, Eleanor,' he said, '*you're* still up, I see.'

'I am, Mr Arthur,' Eleanor answered him. 'Unfortunately, I am.'

Forbes went first to the lavatory and relieved himself. The walk from the station had cleared his head, leaving pleasant memories of the long day on the sea loch, the stimulation of travelling underwater and the triumph of browbeating Paget and forcing him to retreat. He was sure he had got his message over and that Paget had left the party early because he was too cowardly to stay for dinner.

He paused on the landing, glanced up into the gloomy well of the nursery floor where, all snug and secure, his children slept. Then he opened the door of the master bedroom and stepped, unsuspectingly, inside.

Lindsay had been drowsing over the Blackwood edition of Conrad's *Typhoon*, but as soon as she heard the scrape of Forbes's key in the front door she snapped awake. Suddenly beset by nerves, she dropped the book to the carpet and for a moment became so agitated that she could hardly breathe. She rocked forward in the chair, clenched her fists into her lap and willed herself not to dissolve in tears. She thought of Geoffrey, of Geoffrey's voice on the telephone, so placid and soothing and unsurprised. Geoffrey would take over. Geoffrey would take command just as she had asked him to.

The lavatory flushed. She listened to the deluge of water pouring from the cistern above the pedestal. Door opening. Door closing. She forced herself upright in the chair and willed herself to appear unruffled. Cold and calculating, that's how she must be, like Forbes, just like Forbes.

She groped for the book, found and opened it.

Forbes entered the bedroom.

'Lindsay! he exclaimed. 'I thought you'd be in bed by now.'

Sun and sea air had revitalised his tan. His hair was tousled, his dark eyes somnolent. He looked young, almost boyish with his jacket slung across his shoulder and his shirt sleeves unfastened. For a split second Lindsay questioned if this handsome young man, image of the boy she had once loved, could ever betray her. She wanted to cry out, to hold out her arms, have him comfort her as if she were still an innocent and unlettered in the ways of the world.

'What the hell are you doing dressed up?' Forbes said.

'Waiting for you.'

'Waiting for . . .' He grinned, uncertainly. 'Are we going somewhere, then?'

'I am,' Lindsay said.

Her voice was remarkably firm. She had rehearsed it, planned it with the meticulousness of an engineer setting out a project. All she had to do now was square up to him and carry it through. She closed the novel and balanced it on the crocodile-hide portmanteau that Eleanor had packed for her. The portmanteau contained her vanity case, shoes, a summer hat, underclothing, nightgowns, ribbons and stockings, a blouse, a travelling skirt, two summer dresses and a useful coat in *peau-de-soie*: everything she needed, in fact, tucked neatly into an oblong of crocodile hide no larger than a footstool.

'*You* are? You are what?' Forbes said.

'I'm leaving you.'

'You're *what*?' He threw up a hand. 'What's this you're telling me? Don't you know what a day I've had? For God's sake, Linnet, I haven't the patience for any of your idiotic nonsense, not tonight.' He thumped down on the side of the bed, hands cupping thighs, elbows cocked. He glowered at her, guilt and uncertainty undercutting anger.

He said, 'Take that bloody coat off and put that bag away.'

She turned her wrist and consulted the gold bracelet watch that her papa had given her. She said, 'At midnight, in approximately fifteen minutes, Forbes, you will be rid of me for good and all.'

'Rid of you? What the – what does *that* mean?'

'Free to go to Sylvie or, if you wish, to bring Sylvie here to live.'

'Ssssss . . . Sylvie?'

'Once you explain the situation I'm sure your family will have no objection. I expect you'll require the services of a midwife very soon, unless your mother feels she can cope with the birth herself. Winn – well, having another infant to care for won't make much difference to Winn, will it?'

'What the holy hell are you talking about?' He got to his feet, not suddenly but sluggishly, as if a giant hand were pushing against him. 'What the holy hell does Tom Calder's – does this woman have to do with me?'

'Please don't raise your voice, Forbes, you'll waken the children.' He was vertical at last, hands clasping thighs, elbows cocked. Like a thin veneer of transparent varnish laid over pine, his tan had lost its shine. 'I don't think you want to waken the children, do you, Forbes?' Lindsay continued. 'I don't think you want to waken anyone. I mean, surely it would be better if you had a good night's sleep before you decide what you're going to tell them. By the by, was it a difficult day on the Gareloch? You look rather tired.'

'You're going away with Paget, aren't you?'

'That,' Lindsay said, 'is irrelevant.'

'Irrelevant! My wife running off with a bloody sailor isn't irrelevant!'

'I'm not running off with anyone, Forbes. I'm leaving you. That's all there is to it. I'm simply clearing the decks before your new wife arrives.'

'New wife? What are you *raving* about?'

'Tom Calder's daughter. Tom, I expect, will have something to say about it, of course. He may be none too keen on you taking her in; though as you've already taken her in, in a manner of speaking, I personally see no harm in it.'

'Oh, Jesus! *Jesus!*' He sat down again, head in hands. 'Don't go, Lindsay. Please, don't go. I'll . . .' He peered from the tops of his eyes, a wary gesture that cast doubt upon his sincerity. 'I'll take care of it. I promise I'll take care of it.'

'I see,' Lindsay said. 'How will you do that, Forbes? Do you intend to keep the poor girl in the background, to preserve her for your amusement a little while longer? As a matter of interest, how long *have* you been keeping her?'

He shook his head, rotating it between his hands. 'Not long.'

'How long is "not long"? A year, two years? Three, perhaps? Since our marriage, or *before* our marriage? I hope that taking time off to teach me my wifely duties didn't inconvenience you.' Lindsay paused. 'I take it you don't deny that Sylvie Calder is your mistress?'

'No, but I didn't know she was Tom Calder's daughter when I . . .'

'Would it have made any difference?'

'Probably not.'

'Is it your child she's carrying?'

'Of course.'

Denial had switched to contrition, contrition to defiance: at least, Lindsay thought, he's still man enough to try to brazen it out.

He said, 'Who told you she was expecting? Gowry?'

'She told me herself.'

'You mean she came here?'

'She turned up at Cissie's where I just happened to be taking tea.'

'Bitch!' Forbes said, shaking his head. 'Stupid little bitch! What did she hope to gain by bothering Cissie? Money, I suppose.'

'No,' Lindsay said. 'I don't think she's interested in money.'

'Shows how well you know her.'

'I think,' Lindsay said, 'she's interested in having you for a husband.'

'I told her' – he shook his head again – 'months ago, I told her she couldn't ever have me. I never made promises I couldn't keep. I looked after her, gave her everything, her and her bloody dada, both.'

'Albert Hartnell?'

'Yes, bloody Albert Hartnell. I wouldn't be surprised if this was another of his tricks to squeeze money—'

'I told you, Forbes, it *isn't* about money,' Lindsay said.

'Then it's nasty,' Forbes said. 'Then it's revenge.'

'She wants you to marry her, to have a proper father for her child.'

'She's not right in the head, you know,' Forbes said. 'Don't tell me you're going to allow a lunatic to wreck our marriage?'

Impatiently, not ostentatiously, Lindsay glanced at her watch again.

'I'm leaving in five minutes, Forbes. If you've anything else to tell me please be quick about it.'

'Christ, you're serious, aren't you?'

'Of course I am.'

'What's your father going to say to it?'

'He'll understand.'

'What about the children?'

'Philip will thrive well enough on milk formula and Papa will see to it that Harry is entertained.' She got to her feet. 'I'm not going far, Forbes, and I will be back, you know.'

'Yes,' he said, almost smugly. 'Sure and you will.'

'By which time I expect you to have moved out or, if you prefer it, to have reached an agreement with my father.'

'An agreement? What sort of agreement?'

'To purchase his share of the house.'

'*What?*' Forbes shouted loudly enough to make the light fittings ring. 'What the hell's this you've cooked up now?'

'I can't be sure, of course,' Lindsay said, 'but I imagine my father will be looking for full cash payment from you before he signs anything.'

'I don't *have* that kind of ready money,' Forbes shouted.

'Think what you'll save when Sylvie's living here. No more rent to pay on your second home in St Mungo's Mansions, for a start. Admittedly you will have to raise a substantial amount of capital rather quickly but perhaps your mother will help with a loan.'

'You leave my mam out of this.'

Lindsay reached for the handle of the portmanteau. 'I don't think we can leave anyone out of it, really, Forbes, do you?'

He darted forward, caught her arm, drew her upright. His grip was brutal but when she stared at his fist he slackened it. He did not, however, let go.

'You don't mean any of it, Lindsay,' he said. 'You're just trying to scare me, aren't you? You won't leave. I know you, you won't leave the kiddies, or your papa, or your precious Miss Runciman. You don't want a scandal any more than I do. Give me a day, a couple of days to straighten everything out and I guarantee that you won't be bothered by Sylvie Calder ever again.'

'I'm not bothered by Sylvie Calder now,' Lindsay said. 'To tell you the truth, Forbes, I'm not even particularly "bothered" by you. As for Harry and Philip, I'm not abandoning them. Odd as it may seem, I love them very much and I certainly won't be leaving them for long. As soon as I've consulted a lawyer . . .'

'Lawyer? Divorce, do you mean?'

'Until we're legally divorced, how can you possibly marry Sylvie?'

'Oh, no, no, Lindsay, that's the last thing I want.'

'What *do* you want, Forbes?'

'I want *you*, darling. I want *you*. Here. With me.'

'As it was before?'

'Yes, exactly as it was before.'

Lindsay allowed his answer to hang in silence for a moment then she separated herself from him with a shrug of the shoulder.

'That's what I thought,' she said.

She lifted the portmanteau and tugged open the bedroom door. She swung the bag into her arms and hurried downstairs.

He pursued her.

She heard his breathless shout of 'Lindsay, Lindsay,' change to an urgent whisper. 'Lindsay, for God's sake, Lindsay, listen to me, talk to me,' then she was in the hallway, heading for the front door. A strip of light at the bottom of the parlour door indicated that Papa and Eleanor were probably listening. She resisted the temptation to call out goodbye. She felt jubilant and determined and, at one and the same time, bleak and melancholy. She made it to the door and pulled it open before Forbes snared her with an arm about her waist.

It was, she realised, in danger of degenerating into farce, his conniving nature and appealing charm reduced to bullying. He raised his fist. It hovered turnip-shaped and pale above her face. Forbes's face, white too, was twisted less by rage than frustration. He still could not believe that she would defy him, would leave against his will.

She clutched the portmanteau firmly, prepared to drive the edge up into his stomach, to sacrifice her dignity too just to be free of him.

Abruptly, he released her.

She followed her husband's gaze, looked down the steep steps to the pavement's edge where a motorised taxi-cab waited, engine puttering, big boggle-eyed headlamps flickering.

Geoffrey was in uniform, looking very neat and self-con-tained, one foot on the bottom step and a hand on the railing. As she came down the steps towards him he held out his hand, and she took it. He relieved her of the portmanteau and, without so much as a glance at Forbes, ushered her across the pavement and into the taxi-cab.

He climbed in beside her and closed the door.

'Are you all right?' he asked.

'I'm fine,' said Lindsay. 'Really, I'm fine.'

'Where to now, sir?' the cabby enquired.

'The Central Hotel,' said Geoffrey.

From the top step Forbes watched the taxi-cab gather speed. He was still convinced it would only swing once around the park before it returned and Lindsay would come back into the house and tell it him that it had all been a dreadful mistake and beg his forgiveness. The cab, however, did not loop around the park. It went on across the top of Fingleton Street, swept away along the long curve of Brunswick Crescent and swiftly passed out of sight.

Forbes did not move. He remained stock-still on the top step.

He was still sure that the boggle-eyed headlamps would reappear at any moment and the vehicle return.

Then he heard his father-in-law say, 'She's gone, Forbes. Can't you see that she's gone?'

He swung round. Arthur Franklin and the Runciman woman were observing him from within the hallway. There was no breath of wind in the streets yet Forbes felt as if he were being sucked into the hallway on a great wild rush of air. Arthur reached out to him. He thrust his father-in-law aside and, staggering from wall to wall, blundered towards the staircase.

He fell to his knees.

Lifting his head, he peered into the gloom of the upper floors.

He opened his mouth and howled: 'Mam. Mammy, help me.'

And a moment later, still struggling into their dressing-gowns, his mother and sisters came tumbling down the stairs.

*　　*　　*

Bludgeoned by sea air and exhaustion, Tom fell asleep as soon as his head touched the pillow. He slept for the best part of two hours and did not stir when Cissie crept in beside him, drew back the top blanket and adjusted the sheets.

For once, she did not put her arms about him and hold him close. She lay on her back, listening to his snores. She had left the curtains parted and the blind raised to let in whatever air there was and she could make out a shaft of moonlight lying like cool water across the foot of the bed.

Tom's snoring ceased.

He turned on an elbow and then on to his back. He eased his hands out from under the sheet and placed them cautiously behind his head.

Looking up, Cissie could make out his profile in the half-darkness, etched by a glimmer of moonlight. She heard him sigh a shuddering sigh and knew that he was wide awake and that sleep would not easily return to his busy, bothered brain.

'Can't you sleep, Tom?'

'No.' He paused. 'I will have to do something about it, you know. I can't just pretend that nothing's happened. I'll have to take care of her now.'

Cissie eased herself against him, gently laid an arm across his stomach and drew herself supportively against his flank.

'I know, dear,' she said. 'I know.'

The Central Hotel by the railway station in the heart of the city was busy even at that late hour. Last trains from the south had recently arrived and porters and receptionists were attending to weary travellers, checking them in and escorting them to their rooms. There was still activity in the kitchens and in the huge ground-floor dining-room waiters were briskly setting up for breakfast.

Geoffrey had been fortunate to obtain a room on short notice. August was a prime month for tourist traffic and

Glasgow a popular staging post for the Highlands where, in a few days' time, the grouse-shooting season would begin. He guided Lindsay to the oak-fronted desk in the foyer and waited politely while a colonel type, with waxed moustaches and a tweed suit so new that it creaked, fussed over security for his guns. Behind him, sheltering among potted palms, his lady loitered; no Rosie O'Grady this but a woman of such elegant and affected ennui that she could be nothing but his wife. She studied Geoffrey with a cold predatory gaze for a moment, then, meeting Lindsay's eye, smirked knowingly.

Lindsay felt her cheeks grow hot. She was used to hotels, to mixing with wealthy and sophisticated people but there was something in the woman's vulpine smile that brought home the magnitude of what she had done. She had cut herself off from respectability, from the tangible securities of marriage. She had run off with a man who was not her husband and was here, at midnight, in a hotel with him. She had no idea how the lady knew that Geoffrey and she were not husband and wife, but know she did, as surely as if she, Lindsay, had been branded on the forehead with a scarlet letter or sported the tattered red shawl of a woman of the streets.

She took Geoffrey's arm and hung on to him while he confirmed the telephone booking with a balding, middle-aged clerk.

'How long will madam being staying, sir?' the clerk asked.

The question caught Geoffrey off guard. He turned to Lindsay and raised an enquiring eyebrow.

Lindsay heard herself say, 'Three nights, possibly longer.'

'Is that suitable?' Geoffrey said.

'That is suitable, sir,' said the clerk.

He presented the register, swivelled it round towards Lindsay, pointed out the pen and ink-stand.

Geoffrey took a half pace backward and allowed Lindsay to sign her name and, in the space allotted for address, simply 'Brunswick Park'. The clerk did not bat an eyelid. He blotted the entry assiduously and simultaneously raised a hand and snapped his fingers. A bell-boy came running out of nowhere and wrested Lindsay's portmanteau from Geoffrey's grasp.

'One-o-seven,' the clerk said. 'Will madam be requiring breakfast to be served in her room?'

'I'll – no, I'll come down, thank you.'

'Very good, madam,' said the clerk. 'Very good,' and with a jerk of the head indicated to the bell-boy that he should make himself scarce until the lady was ready to be escorted upstairs.

Many men of her acquaintance had mistresses. Aunt Lilias could probably rhyme them off. Some, indeed, were famous for flouting convention; others so discreet that no one, not even Aunt Lilias, could be sure if gossip about them was true or false. Whispers would soon accumulate around her name. It was unrealistic to suppose that her desertion would remain secret for long. There would be no core to it, no substance, of course, no validity to the rumours that Geoffrey Paget and she had become shameless lovers and that Forbes, poor Forbes, was the partner who had been wronged.

Had it been like this for Forbes and Sylvie Calder, she wondered; like this, without the awkwardness? Had they spent many nights together in hotel beds before Forbes had set the girl up in a place of her own? Forbes had often been 'out of town' on shipyard business. She tried to recall episodes and incidents that might give her husband's duplicity shape and form, something to bolster her flagging confidence and ease her guilt; but Forbes seemed far, far away and Sylvie, in Lindsay's thoughts, hardly existed at all.

She was suddenly very, very tired.

She longed for Geoffrey to go now, to leave her to sleep alone and unafraid in a big, not quite dark room as she had done when she was a child.

It was not that she did not love Geoffrey or that she wasn't grateful for what he had done for her. She was wary of the situation that she had created, however, of the burden of temptation and weight of responsibility that she had placed on Geoffrey's shoulders.

For a moment, a hideous moment, she even began to question Geoffrey's integrity and wonder if perhaps he was just another seducer, more sinister and subtle and devious than other men, but just like them, just like Forbes.

'I – I must go up, Geoffrey,' she said.

'Of course.'

He kissed her cheek briefly, touched her arm, stepped back.

The colonel and his predatory wife had gone but Lindsay could still recall the penetration of that vulpine glance, so cynical and sophisticated.

'At what time will you breakfast?' Geoffrey said.

'Eight thirty,' Lindsay answered.

'And then what will you do?'

She hadn't thought of that, hadn't faced up to the long formless days that would follow her desertion, days in which others would make the running and she, the instigator, the renegade, would be robbed of volition and, by her own actions, would spin off into a kind of limbo.

'I'll join you for breakfast, if I may,' Geoffrey said.

'Don't you have to report to someone? I mean – the trials?'

'One of the advantages of my position is that I am answerable to no one this side of Trafalgar Square.' Though she did not quite believe him, Lindsay was comforted. He said, 'Rest if you can. I'll see you in the morning.'

'Geoffrey,' she said. 'Thank you. Thank you with all my heart.'

'No need for thanks,' he said gruffly. 'No need at all.'

Then, after giving the desk clerk an ostentatious salute that the fellow would surely remember, he stepped out through the polished swing doors and left Lindsay to follow the bell-boy up the carpeted staircase to her room.

✻   ✻   ✻

After an hour of argument, recrimination and what passed for debate, it seemed that Forbes could not have cared less what became of Sylvie Calder or of his wife. He had been beaten down by the clamour around him, defeated by sheer exhaustion and rendered numb by the several nips of whisky that his sisters had pressed upon him for therapeutic purposes. Perhaps his sisters' treatment had been the right one, for the red roaring rage that had possessed him after Lindsay had left with Geoffrey Paget had burned itself out completely and he sprawled in the room's only armchair, all undone, listening with brooding indifference to the pointless conversations that ebbed and flowed about him.

'It was your plan, was it not?' his mother was saying. 'All part of your plan to be rid of us. Well, Arthur, I'll tell you this, you'll not be getting rid of us so easily as all that.'

'How,' Eleanor Runciman said, 'could it be Mr Arthur's "plan" when none of us knew until this afternoon what your precious son had been up to behind everyone's back?'

'I really can't understand what she's doing here, Mam,' said Blossom. 'She ain't no kin to any of us.'

'Shouldn't be allowed to open her mouth,' said Winn.

'I've more right to be here than you have, miss,' Eleanor said. 'If Mr Arthur asks me to make myself scarce then I will, but I am not dancing to your tune, oh no. I have raised Lindsay since she was—'

'Yes, yes, yes, we've heard all that before,' Winn interrupted. 'But nothing you have to say is going to help my brother get his wife back.'

'Might I be pointing out, Arthur,' Kay said, 'that it wasn't you who brought Forbes here. It was Pappy, rest his soul, and he wouldn't have let any of this happen if he'd still been alive.'

'I don't see how Pappy could have prevented it,' Arthur said, 'any more than I could have prevented it. I mean to say, Pappy couldn't stop you, you and your sister, running off with your lovers thirty-odd years ago.'

'I knew, I *knew* it would come down to that,' Kay

screeched. 'You still blame me for what happened to your wife, don't you?'

'Don't be ridiculous, Kay,' Arthur said. 'I am merely drawing an analogy. If you pause to consider . . .'

'Pause to consider what?' Kay said. 'Whatever I did was done for poor Helen. She was dying, and we all knew it. Everyone, it seems, except you. Besides, I didn't abandon husband and children to sneak off with some sailor.'

'She did not sneak off with anyone,' Eleanor said.

'Oh, no?' Blossom said. 'Then who was that in the taxi-cab, I ask you? Lord bleedin' Nelson?'

'I think,' Arthur said, 'we are drifting from the point.'

'Point? What point is that?' Kay said. 'The point that you're going to make money out of us by using this tragedy to your own advantage.'

Eleanor leaped in. 'How dare you say that.'

'Shut that woman up, Arthur.'

'Eleanor has every right to speak her mind,' Arthur said.

'She's a housekeeper, that's all she is, a servant.'

'And what, tell me, are you, Winifred?' Arthur said.

'I'm — I'm your niece. I'm Forbes's sister.'

'How dare you even suggest that Mr Arthur is at all interested in money at a time like this,' Eleanor waded in. 'The matter to be decided has nothing whatsoever to do with money.'

'Hasn't it?' said Blossom. 'What *does* it have to do with, then?'

'A baby. A child.' Eleanor glanced at her master who nodded agreement. 'All this jawing about what's going to happen to the house, what's going to become of *you*, and not a thought about the poor girl who's carrying *his* baby.'

'Hasn't been proved. Hasn't been proved,' Winn shrilled. 'Only got her word for it and none of us has seen her yet. She'll have to be put on the spot before we decide anything, won't she, Mam?'

'She will, she will,' Kay agreed, but mutedly.

'Do you think it's *not* his baby?' Arthur said.

'Look at him,' said Eleanor. 'Not a word of denial out of him.'

'Forbes,' Blossom instructed her brother, 'say something.'

He peered at them from under half-closed lids, surveyed them as if they were strangers or, at best, merchants in the metal market with whom he was forced to negotiate against his will. He stirred leadenly, hoisted himself up and reached for the whisky glass that was balanced on the piano stool. He swirled the liquid in the glass, drank it in a swallow and pushed himself out of the chair.

'I'm going to bed,' he said.

'You can't,' Winn told him.

'I damned well can,' said Forbes.

'You can't, not with nothing settled yet,' said Blossom.

'It isn't up to us right now,' Forbes said. 'It's up to Lindsay. Whatever you might think of her, she isn't daft. She'll make up her own mind what she wants to do. Once we find that out, we can start again.'

'Surely you're not going to allow *her* to call the tune,' said Blossom.

'He does not have much choice,' said Eleanor.

'Mam, are you going to let her talk about our Forbes like that?'

Kay shook her head. 'Unfortunately, girls, she's right. It isn't up to us to make the next move. It's up to her, to Lindsay.'

'What if she wants a' – Winn's voice dropped – 'a divorce?'

'Who could blame her?' Eleanor Runciman said.

'If she wants a divorce,' Arthur said, 'then you *will* have to leave my house. It wouldn't be proper for you to stay here during court proceedings. I mean, I couldn't possibly condone that course of action.'

'Or,' Kay said, 'you could sell Forbes the house.'

'I could,' Arthur said. 'I may.'

'Forbes, what do you have to say for yourself?' Blossom asked.

'I told you, I'm going to my bed.'

'Wait,' Eleanor said. 'There is one thing we have to decide tonight.'

'And what might that be, dear?' said Arthur.

'Who's going to take care of Sylvie Calder in the meantime?'

'Her father, surely,' Blossom said. 'She's his responsibility.'

'No,' Forbes said. 'She's my responsibility.' He opened the parlour door and leaned against it, resting brow and shoulder against the woodwork. 'Sylvie will not be a problem. I'll take care of Sylvie.'

'You will?' said Winn.

'But how?' said Blossom.

'In the best way I know how,' Forbes said and with a final nod, weary but unrepentant, took himself off to bed.

CHAPTER TWENTY

For Ever and a Day

The search for orders and the laying down of several new keels had continued while the *Snark* had been under construction and during the long delay before her trials. On that Friday morning in August the yard was buzzing. Big saws carving up timber for new cradles, hammermen rapping on the hull of a torpedo-boat destroyer, caulkers pitching the deck of a high-powered diesel launch slated to go into service with the coastguard in mid-September; the air dry, dry and faintly sulphurous with the threat of thunder.

George Crush was seated in the upstairs lavatory in the general office block when, not long after half past eight, he heard shouting in the corridor and, lowering his newspaper, identified Tom Calder's unmistakable baritone raised not just in enquiry but in anger.

'Where is he? Where is the little bastard?'

For a moment George wondered what he might have done that would rouse the wrath of such a patient man and, leaning forward, hastily checked the bolt on the inside of the lavatory door.

'Forbes, Forbes. I know you're here. It's no use hiding.'

'Ooooooow!' George whistled softly. 'That's the way of it, is it?' and immediately began fumbling with his trousers and braces.

Behind the pebble-glass door of his office at the corridor's end, Forbes also heard Tom's shout but, unlike George, he wasn't mystified. He had known that Calder would come for him sooner or later and as he had no wish to have his mother and sisters around when the confrontation occurred, had left Brunswick Park early that morning, without a word to anyone. There had been no sign of Gowry and the Vauxhall was locked in the garage behind the house so Forbes had walked downhill through the oppressive and unnatural heat.

He had purchased a mug of tea and a sausage sandwich from a stall at the corner of Scott Street and, like a beggar or a waif, had breakfasted standing up. He had had no sleep at all but, all things considered, felt well enough, apart from a slight headache. He was calm, that was the main thing. He might have lost control of the situation temporarily but he was confident that Lindsay would come crawling back to him once Sylvie was out of the way. He had drunk a second cup of tea and then, with the headache waning, had walked on to Aydon Road and had gone directly upstairs to his office to await the inevitable.

The pebble-glass door crashed open.

'I'm not hiding, Tom,' Forbes said.

It had not been Tom's intention to lose his temper. He could not recall the last time it had happened. Even when Dorothy had brazenly confessed her sins he had experienced only helpless inferiority and had tried to be understanding and reasonable. Rationality had always been his downfall. It was not until he had kissed Ewan and Cissie goodbye that blind red rage overwhelmed him.

The coppery sky, dry heat, the metallic taste of smoke compressed by thunderheads had, it seemed, contrived to release him from self-lacerating passivity.

'Where is she, Forbes? I want to know where she is.'

'Ask Arthur.'

'I've asked Arthur. I spoke to Arthur on the telephone not ten minutes ago. He doesn't know where she is.'

'She went off with her sailor, with Paget.'

'I don't mean your wife, damn it. I mean my daughter.'

'Why should I tell you where Sylvie is? You abandoned her.'

'That,' Tom said, 'is it.'

'What are you going to do?' Forbes said. 'Have her back? Take her over? Incorporate her into your wonderful new family, her and the baby? Don't be bloody ridiculous. She *hates* you. She would *die* before she'd let you take charge.'

'Then why did she come to my house, not yours?'

'Vengeance,' Forbes said, shrugging. 'Malice. How the hell do I know what goes on in Sylvie's head? She's muddled. No, she's cracked. Deranged. Sure and she even believed I'd marry her if she just managed to get herself knocked up. Which she did, of course, which she did.'

'She came to me for help.'

'She came to your house only to make trouble,' Forbes said, 'otherwise she'd still be there. Am I not right?'

'Are you going to marry her?'

Forbes laughed. 'Don't tell me she got it from you? I always thought she got it from her mother – her crazy streak, I mean. Marry her, marry Sylvie? Jesus, Tom, you're as daft as she is if you think I'm going to sacrifice my career and my family just to marry your daughter.'

'What happened to Albert?'

'Nothing. He got paid. He still gets paid.'

'Where is she, damn it? Where have you put her?'

Forbes shook his head. 'It's too late to saddle the white charger, Tom. Too late to gallop to the rescue. Anyhow, I'll fix it.'

'Fix it? Fix what?'

'Everything,' Forbes said. 'Lindsay, too.'

'How,' Tom said, thickly, 'are you going to fix it?'

'Sylvie?' Forbes said. 'Buy her off. Money's all she's after, all she's ever been after. I think that's why we hit it off so well. Right now, with a kiddie on the way, other daft ideas may be rattling around in her head, but she'll see reason quickly enough when there's an offer on the table. And if she won't see reason then Albert certainly will.'

'And Lindsay, how will you fix it with Lindsay?'

'I don't have to,' Forbes said. 'Lindsay will come back of her own accord once she thinks she's taught me a lesson.'

Tom nodded too. He hitched a trouser-leg, seated himself on the edge of the desk and folded his arms. He regarded Forbes benignly – rational, reasonable and apparently relieved that his young partner had everything under control.

'I see,' Tom said. 'I see.'

Pressed to the wall by the pebble-glass door, ear cocked, George Crush was puzzled by the sudden silence. He knew that Forbes had a mistress, of course – Forbes had been unable to resist bragging about her – but he itched for more information about Calder's daughter, and prissy Lindsay Franklin and her sailorman lover. He hugged himself with anticipation, delighted that the Franklins' close-knit family was unravelling at last.

A moment later he was diving for cover as the pebble-glass door of the office exploded in a shower of glass and young Forbes McCulloch, like some dumb drag-weight, was left hanging in the broken frame.

Before George could right himself, Forbes was yanked back through the splintered space. He reappeared almost at once as Tom Calder hurled him against the door for a second time.

'*Where is she, Forbes?*' Tom was shouting. '*What the hell have you done with her, you bastard?*'

George had no inclination to rush to Forbes's aid or pit himself against Calder. He scrambled to get to his feet but then the door whanged open and more chips of broken glass showered over him and he elected instead to crawl into the nearest corner, hug his knees to his chest and make himself too small to be noticed. He winced as Forbes landed on the boards in front of him, winced again when Tom Calder followed, pouncing out of the light like some great cat or gigantic stick insect.

Blood trickled from Forbes's nose and he was too winded to retaliate or even defend himself properly. Down the corridor doors were swinging open, heads appearing: Martin Franklin, Ross, Johnny too. Tom ignored them and continued to beat Forbes about the face with an unclenched fist.

'*Where — is — she — Forbes? Tell — me — where — she — is.*'

He knelt and pinned Forbes to the floor.

'*Where's my daughter? What have you done to her?*'

To George's horror Forbes spat into Tom Calder's face.

'Sod off!' Forbes said, squinting through pain. 'I'm telling you nothing. You'll get nothing out of me.' Then almost with an air of detachment Tom grabbed Forbes by the shoulders and began to beat his head rhythmically upon the floorboards, intent, it seemed, on killing him.

'*Where — is — she? Where — is — she? Where . . .*'

'I know where she is,' George croaked.

Starched white linen tablecloths, heavy silver services and waiters who seemed to glide about on oiled castors lent the breakfast-room in the Central Hotel a certain tranquillity in spite of bustling activity in the wings.

Breakfast for two at a corner table was a novelty that restored Lindsay's spirits and, for a time at least, reduced her guilt about leaving her children. Gradually she yielded to Geoffrey's reassuring voice and gentlemanly good manners. He was effortlessly pleasant and appeared to have all the time in the world to devote to her. Different, so different from Forbes. He asked how well she had slept, how she felt. He even offered to take her back to Brunswick Park if she had changed her mind.

Lindsay shook her head. 'It wasn't just a gesture, Geoffrey.'

'No, I didn't think it was,' he said. 'You will go back at some point, though, will you not?'

'To see the children, yes.'

'And your husband?'

'I don't much care if I never see Forbes again.'

'Did you have no clue that he was seeing another woman?'

'None.'

'It must have been a frightful shock.'

'Oddly,' Lindsay said, 'I think I rather expected it, though not that he had taken up with Tom Calder's daughter.'

'I gather it began some time ago.'

'Years ago apparently, before Forbes and I were even married.'

'Perhaps it wasn't entirely a coincidence,' Geoffrey suggested.

Lindsay had eaten porridge, kippers, a little scrambled egg and several slices of crisp toast spread with fresh butter and marmalade, washed down with black coffee. She was pleasantly full and her guilt had diminished and she felt more clear-eyed and clear-headed than she had done in months. The illicit pleasure of being with Geoffrey was stimulating. She watched him light a cigarette, watched smoke curl from the matchstick, saw him inhale, shake out the match and place it gently in an ashtray. He exhaled and smiled at her through the dispersing smoke.

She had dressed with care, had arranged her hair, touched her face with powder, her lips with rouge: enough, just enough, to let him know that she did not take him for granted.

'Not a coincidence: what do you mean?' Lindsay said.

'If your husband had a choice – which apparently he had – he chose you over this other girl. Doesn't that indicate something other than coincidence?'

'Geoffrey, don't tell me you're arguing Forbes's case for him?'

'I wouldn't dare,' said Geoffrey. 'It's a fair question, though.'

'It's not a comedy of manners, Geoffrey, not a matter of misplaced affections or mistaken identities. The girl's pregnant.'

Lindsay paused. 'Are you asking if Forbes loved me more than he loved her? The answer's remarkably simple: I had money and poor Sylvie Calder did not. I had sound family connections and Sylvie Calder had none. Even so, she obviously offered him something that I could not and that's why he took up with her without a thought for me or how it would affect our marriage.'

'He didn't choose to marry the girl, however.'

'Of course he didn't.'

'And he will not marry her now?'

'No.'

'Are you sure, Lindsay?'

'Absolutely sure.'

Geoffrey blew smoke, wafted it away from her with the flat of his hand. His cuffs, Lindsay noticed, were fastened with silver links rubbed to a fine patina that all but obliterated the monogram. She wondered if the links had once belonged to his father and provided a connection with home, if they were symbols of the sailor's life, the traveller's life where everything had to be compact and functional, nothing superfluous. Would she ever attain that degree of intimacy with him, she wondered, become so necessary that he would not leave her behind no matter how far he travelled?

'Did the fact that Forbes was your cousin make any difference?'

'None.' Lindsay did not resent his inquisitiveness. 'Forbes had lived all his life in Ireland. We were strangers when we first met, old enough by then to . . .' She experienced a twinge of suspicion, then of surprise. 'Geoffrey, are you asking why I chose to marry him?'

'Probably.'

'My grandfather threw us together.'

'I don't think that's good enough,' Geoffrey said mildly.

Now she understood: he was probing, gently probing to discover if she still loved Forbes, if all those fine confused feelings had really been swept away or if some spark of attraction still remained between them. How could she answer him? How could she tell him that she had been driven by a physical desire that had transcended common sense and that had even survived the tedium of courtship. How could she possibly admit that she still took pleasure in Forbes's love-making? How could she separate sex from love in a way that Geoffrey would understand, would not misconstrue? She wanted Geoffrey's arms about her but she did not feel for him the clamouring ache, the infuriating and insistent demand of the blood that Forbes had once roused in her and perhaps still did.

'Do you feel that way about me?' Geoffrey said.

If she said *Yes* then Geoffrey would fight for her. If she said *Yes*, he would take it as a signal that all was up with her marriage: Geoffrey was sure enough of himself to assume responsibility for another man's children but another man's wife, however, might never be his. If she said *No*, however, he might slip away from her to avoid a commitment that could never be fulfilled and she would lose his love and friendship for ever.

The risks, the dangers were considerable.

It took courage for Lindsay to accept them.

'No, Geoffrey,' she heard herself say. 'No, I do not.'

'At least you're honest, Lindsay.'

'How could I be anything else after what you've done for me?'

'I've done nothing,' he said.

'You've asked for nothing, if that's what you mean.'

'I'm in love with you, Lindsay, but that doesn't give me the right to ask anything of you, not even that you love me in turn.'

'If I do go back to Forbes . . .'

'You will,' Geoffrey said. 'You should.'

'Will you still love me then?'

'No,' he said, 'that's not the real issue, darling. The real issue is will you still love me? I can't answer that question for you.'

'And I can't answer it either.'

'Then we'll just have to wait and see,' Geoffrey said.

'Do you mean it?'

'Of course I do.' He put down the cigarette and glanced at his wristlet watch. 'Listen, I'm not abandoning you, Lindsay, but I will have to show my face at the Gareloch some time this morning. I'd take you with me but that really wouldn't be advisable under the circumstances.'

'No. It wouldn't fit in with my plan.'

'Plan?'

'Oh, yes,' Lindsay said. 'I'm not entirely lacking in female wiles, Geoffrey. I spent a good deal of time last night thinking it out.'

'What do you intend to do?'

She smiled at him and touched his hand.

'Go straight to Harper's Hill,' Lindsay said, 'and talk to my Aunt Lilias.'

'Will she help you?'

'Oh, yes,' Lindsay said. 'I'm absolutely sure she will.'

Martin was delegated to come after him, to calm him down and find out what had started the row. At that moment Tom did not care who knew about his private affairs or even what the outcome would be for the partnership and his future in it. He had assaulted a Franklin. He had bloodied the nose of a managerial colleague in front of witnesses, and if George Crush hadn't spoken out he might have gone on to commit murder. He should be ashamed of his behaviour but he was not. His blood was still on fire and he had no particular patience with Martin, although he did acknowledge that his brother-in-law had every right to ask for and every reason to be told the truth.

He allowed Martin to steer him into the office and give him a hand towel from the bottom drawer to wrap round his broken knuckles.

'What the devil was *that* all about?' Martin said.

'Why don't you ask your precious cousin?'

'Be easy, Tom. Be easy. I'm asking you,' Martin said. 'Besides,

Forbes has already gone. As soon as you let him go, he picked himself up and charged off down the main staircase with George Crush scuttling in his wake.'

Tom wiped bloody spittle from his face with the hand towel. 'All right,' he said. 'All right.'

'Does it have to do with Lindsay?' Martin asked.

'Lindsay? What makes you think it has to do with Lindsay?'

'You were were keen on her once. I thought perhaps . . .'

Tom gave a little grunt, not quite laughter. 'I didn't realise it had been so obvious. No, it doesn't have to do with Lindsay, although she is involved.' He looked straight at his brother-in-law, at the broad Franklin features, the honest blue eyes. 'I've a grown daughter, did you know that?'

'Yes. We all know that.'

'Apparently she's been Forbes McCulloch's mistress for the past five or six years, and now he's got her pregnant. That's it.'

Martin was silent for half a second. He absorbed the information slowly, frowning, his jaw set. He was too mature to feign embarrassment.

At length, he said, 'Does Lindsay know?'

'Yes, Lindsay knows.'

'Will she – I mean, will she leave him because of it?'

'She's already gone. She left Brunswick Park late last night.'

Martin nodded, frowning. 'Divorce, I suppose, is inevitable.'

'Is that all that concerns you, Martin? A possible scandal?'

'No, no, no, of course not. Sorry, Tom, your daughter must be your first concern. Have you seen her yet?'

'Not yet. I didn't know where he had put her until five minutes ago.'

'Is that what the fight was about?'

'I lost my temper. I shouldn't have lost my temper.'

'God!' Martin said. 'If it had been me – I mean, if he had done that to my daughter I think I'd have killed him. He was never right for Lindsay, you know. He should never have been brought into our family. He should have been left in Ireland where he belongs. Pappy has a great deal to answer for. Pappy and Aunt Kay too. It's not as if we needed new blood. Hah! New blood, listen to me! Bad blood, that's what it is. Bad blood all along. Did he tell you where to find her?'

'George did.'

'Crush? My God! Crush knew, and you didn't?' Martin placed an arm about Tom's shoulder. 'That's rotten, just rotten.'

Tom did not shake him off. He was relieved that the secret was out. He could leave the Franklins to sort out their own affairs now, arrange the family pow-wow by which Lindsay's 'fate', and Forbes McCulloch's too, would be decided, as if nothing were more important than family honour and family pride. It was Arthur who had told him what had happened at Brunswick Park, who had telephoned him early that morning just before he'd left home. For a second Tom was tempted to inform Martin that Lindsay had not just walked out on her husband but had walked out on the arm of Lieutenant Commander Geoffrey Paget, the Admiralty's purchasing officer.

No, he would leave Arthur to impart that tasty bit of news.

Sylvie was his only concern right now.

'Where is your daughter?' Martin said. 'Where's he been keeping her?'

'St Mungo's Mansions, at the very end of Maryhill Road.'

'You must go there, Tom. Find her. Make sure she's – I say, do you think that's where Forbes has gone shooting off to?'

'I doubt it,' Tom answered. 'Somehow I very much doubt it.'

He ran across the yard with George trailing behind him. He was drenched in sweat and the front of his shirt and jacket were soiled. His head pounded, his heart too, a gigantic throbbing that seemed to pulse all through him right down to his feet. He felt as if he had been wired to an electrical outlet and pounded with a high voltage charge. But he was not out of control yet, not quite out of control. He ran diagonally across the square behind the office block, swung into the lane behind the paint store and headed for the stables where the big Clydesdale dray horses were kept and, in a separate building, the firm's vans and motor-cars.

The stink of horse manure and petrol hung over the cobbled forecourt where Donald Franklin's Lanchester was being washed by two young apprentices clad in a new style of dark blue overalls. They looked up, startled, when Forbes suddenly appeared in the yard.

'Where is he?' Forbes snapped. 'Where's my brother?'

'B-b-brother, sir?'

'Are you a bloody idiot? My brother, Gowry McCulloch. I'm looking for my brother. I want my brother out here. Now.'

'Gowry isnae here, Mr McCulloch.'

'Where is he then, damn it?'

'Dunno, Mr McCulloch. He hasnae been seen here all mornin'. We just thought he was wi' you, like he usually is.'

Suddenly all the energy left him. Crushed by Gowry's absence, he felt as if he had charged into a blank brick wall. He had directed himself at Gowry, at telling Gowry what to do to solve the problem, how to execute the master plan that would fix everything for all of them. Now Gowry was missing and he had lost his ally, his tool.

He slithered on the ribbons of soapy water that trickled from the motor-car and snaked away through the ruts made by the hoofs of countless horses in the years before his arrival in Glasgow, in the good old days of Pappy Franklin's reign. The Lanchester glinted in the coppery light. Two young apprentice boys gawked at him as if he were a spectre. Then George, sawing like a war-horse, stumped into the yard and began to yell apologies into his ear.

'I'm sorry, son. I'm sorry, Forbes. I should never have opened my trap. I mean, I thought – I thought he was going to do for you. I thought he was . . .'

'George. Shut. Up.'

'Honest to God, Forbes, I thought he was for murdering you.'

'Perhaps,' Forbes said, 'perhaps you should have let him.'

He gave a little shiver as shock crept into his bones. He felt in danger of passing out or, worse, of doing something so rash that it would finish him for ever. The apprentices watched, the water hose splashed on the cobbles, and George, still gasping for breath, ran out of apologies.

Lindsay had left him, he had been without sleep for thirty hours, and he was sore and bleeding: almost overcome by the stench of the stable yard and the din of industry around him, he felt himself waver.

'Can you start that machine?' Forbes snapped.

'What's that, Mr McCulloch?'

'That machine, the motor-car. Can you start it?'

'Aye, sir, but . . .'

'Start it then.'

'But Mr McCulloch, it's Mr Franklin's motor-car.'

'Start it, just start it.'

He pushed through a wave of exhaustion, telling himself that to act without Gowry would be dangerous, that he must not be there when it happened. The boys cranked the handle at the front of the machine. Forbes heaved himself into the driving seat and waited for the engine to fire. He felt the shudder, the jerk and jounce of the big combustion engine and waited, quite patiently now, for the drive chain to engage.

George, by the running board, said, 'Where are you going, Forbes? At least tell me where you're going.'

'To look for Gowry,' Forbes answered, then, fumbling for a low gear, steered his uncle's motor-car away from the stables and out into Aydon Road.

'I thought it would be you,' Sylvie said. 'I didn't really expect him to come himself. I did what you told me to do, but it did not do one bit of good, did it?'

'That depends,' Gowry said.

'It doesn't depend on Forbes, though.'

Already the conversation was becoming horribly slewed, but then, Gowry thought, everything about the situation was already horribly slewed.

Sylvie said, 'If we had been depending on Forbes he would have called round last night, wouldn't he not now? I must say, Gowry, you do take me for a fool sometimes. I enjoyed it, though, I enjoyed telling them. It was fun, in its way, even if it did me no good in the long run.'

She tied the ribbons of her sun-bonnet with tiny, butterfly movements. Her hands looked tinier than ever and her skin was almost translucent. She seemed to be all stomach, swollen up in front, reduced everywhere else. When she moved, however, she wasn't clumsy. Even her flat-heeled gait had about it, Gowry thought, a certain daintiness that housed and protected her appeal.

She said, 'Did Forbes send you to punish me?'

'Nope. He doesn't want to punish you, Sylvie.'

'What *will* he do, Gowry-Wowry, now he has lost me?'

'Sylvie, I've no idea,' Gowry lied. 'Why don't you forget about Forbes?'

She patted her stomach. 'How can I?'

'It might not be his, you know,' Gowry said.

'It's not your baby.' She pouted. 'It's Forbes's baby.'

'What makes you so certain?' Gowry asked.

'I *know* it is. I *feel* it is.'

'Well,' Gowry said, 'I suppose that's as good an answer as any.'

'It's the only answer you will ever get, dearest,' Sylvie said. 'Are you taking me out for the day? You promised you would and, as you can see' – she pirouetted slowly before him – 'I'm all ready.'

'Sure and I'm taking you out,' Gowry said. 'Where's Albert?'

'Still sleeping, sleeping it off.'

'You didn't tell him what happened yesterday, did you?'

'He would not have understood.' She pirouetted again, lazily, her arms stuck out like rudimentary wings. 'The wife was not so very upset. I had tea with them, with *both* wives. Perhaps they knew all along, about me, I mean, and that's why they weren't surprised to see me.'

'They didn't know about you.'

'She didn't know about the baby? You didn't tell her about the baby?'

'No,' Gowry said. 'I thought it would be more conclusive if you told her.'

'Oh, it was,' said Sylvie. 'Absolutely positively conclusive. Did she give him what-for when he got home last night?'

'She walked out on him.'

'Did she now?'

Realising his error at once, Gowry reached lightly for her arm. 'Now, Sylvie, don't go getting your hopes up. She'll be back in a day or two.'

'And he won't leave her?'

'Never,' Gowry said. 'I think you know that already.'

She nodded, large movements of her little, bonneted head.

'Is that why you sent me to my papa's wife's house? To see for myself?'

'Yes, and to let them see you,' Gowry said.

'To let them know I exist,' she said.

'That's it,' said Gowry. 'Now, if you're ready, we had better be pushing along before Albert wakes up and blames us for his sore head.'

She giggled. 'Very well, dearest. If we are leaving at once perhaps you would be good enough to carry King Edward down to the motor-car for me.'

'King Edward?' Gowry said.

Indicating a bulky, brown-paper-wrapped package on the table, Sylvie said, 'My royal scrapbooks. I want to take them with me.'

'But why?' he asked.

'In case I don't come back,' she said.

The sound was like a drum inside his head. He opened his eyes. Shoals of pure black tadpoles swam through pond light until they were consumed by two or three large red flashes that may or may not have been carp.

Albert burped, swallowed and sat up in bed.

The sour taste of Irish rye whiskey in his mouth reminded him of the night before and he wondered how he had got from Kirby's to the nether end of Maryhill Road. His last recollection was of tumbling downstairs at the club and falling full length into the lane.

Sliding his stained shirt sleeves up, he peered at his elbows and confirmed that they were heavily bruised. He put his head in his hands, groaned and listened to the remorseless thud, thump, thud, thump of the big steam hammer that reverberated inside his skull.

'Sylvie?' he shouted: no shout at all, a dry crackle. 'Syl-veee?'

There was no answer. There seldom was. She did not run to do his bidding like a dutiful daughter. As she kept reminding him, she was not his real daughter at all and if he wanted a servant to dance attendance upon him then he had better scratch up the money to employ one now that Morag and the cook had been dismissed. He missed the ministrations of a good obedient woman in the mornings more than he missed hugs and cuddles at night.

Now, in the sick, sour, stenchy state of the monumentally hung-over he needed his wife, his good, true, loyal and devoted wife, his Florence, to cradle and cosset him. But Florence was gone, never to return, and soon he would have no one to turn to, for Sylvie would be occupied with baby, baby, baby as soon as the poor wee bastard popped into the cruel, cruel world.

'Sylvie, sweetheart, please stop that noise.'

The thudding continued unabated.

Albert rolled out of bed.

He was trouserless, drawerless and practically shirtless too, for the garment was ripped from collar to midriff and stained with — something; not blood, thank God, not blood. Still examining his fragile frame, he crabbed to the bedroom door and went out into the hall, heading for the water closet.

It was only when he reached the hallway that he realised that the unremitting racket was definitely emanating from somewhere outside his head. He glanced towards the drawing-room and mumbled, 'Sylvie?' while, more by instinct than neural command, his feet swung him towards the apartment's big main door.

'All right, all right, I'm coming, I'm coming.'

He opened the door and squinted into the dismal light of the landing.

'You?' he said. 'You?'

'Where is she, Albert?'

'Through the — in the — what are *you* doing here, Tom Calder?' He swung round, his head floating before him like a punctured balloon. He blinked, and peered at the drawing-room door, then, rolling his eyes, at the door of Sylvie's bedroom. 'Is she — I mean, did she send for you? She isn't having — hasn't had . . .'

'The baby?' Tom stepped past him, looking round too. 'For God's sake, Albert, don't tell me you're drunk at a time like this? Where is she?'

'In the . . . on the . . . I don't know,' said Albert, helplessly. 'I haven't been too well myself lately.'

'Out of my damned way.'

Tom strode across the hall and flung open the drawing-room door. He studied the room from the threshold for a moment or two, then, cutting a series of diagonals across the hall, flung open the doors to the kitchen, the bedrooms and, finally, the lavatory.

One hand laid against his cheek like a man with toothache, Albert watched Tom complete the inspection.

'She isn't in the apartment. Where is she, Albert? Did McCulloch come for her? Did Forbes take her away?'

'McCulloch?'

'Forbes McCulloch, the person who's been paying your rent.'

'Oh, yes. Forbes. No, he wouldn't come for her. He abandoned her.'

'What do you mean?'

'Wants no more to do with her since she got — you know.'

'Is it not his child?'

Albert raised his other hand, pressed it hard against his other cheek, causing his moustache to flick out at the ends like torpedo fins. He groaned once more, low and crooning. 'Yes, yes, it's his child. There's no doubt of that. I had nothing to do with it. Had to happen sooner or later, nature being what it is, had to happen. How did you . . .'

'Find out? Sylvie called on my wife yesterday afternoon.'

'Your wife?' For a moment it seemed that Albert had forgotten about Tom Calder's marriage, then he said, 'To the Franklin girl, yes, right, of course. You married the Franklin girl.'

'Sylvie told my wife everything.'

'And your wife told you?'

'Of course she told me. What's more, Sylvie showed herself to Lindsay McCulloch and told both of them the whole sad, sordid story. Don't tell me that you didn't know? I thought you'd sent her to ask for money?'

'Money? Me? No, not me. No.' Alarm at the unjust accusation awakened Albert's wits. 'Wait,' he said. 'I have to go to the lavatory. Back in a mo'.'

In the clean, cool, tiled room Albert relieved himself. He bathed his face with tap water and washed out his mouth. He drank half a tumbler of water slowly and then, a little revived if not exactly refreshed, returned to the hall.

Tom was in the drawing-room, looking down into the street.

The sky had a funny tinge to it, whisky-coloured, sour. Even from the heights of the Mansions you could see no distance at all.

Albert stared bleakly at the window, waiting for Tom Calder to make the next move which, with any luck, might even be an offer of financial assistance.

Tom turned.

'Are you lying to me, Albert? Do you really not know where Sylvie is?'

'Would I lie to—no, I don't. I really do not.'

Still clad only in the torn shirt, he seated himself on the arm of the sofa and modestly tucked the shirt-tails into his lap. He told himself that he had negotiated with Tom Calder too many times in the past to be intimidated and he was confident that paternal sentiment would leave Sylvie's father vulnerable to the right kind of persuasion.

It did not occur to him that Tom Calder too had changed.

'When did you see her last?' Tom asked.

'Yesterday, in the forenoon.'

'Here?'

'Yes, here. I left about noon to go into the city on business.'

'Drinking business, I suppose,' Tom said. 'Was Sylvie here when you got back last night?'

'I think — yes, I'm sure she was. Tucked up in bed.'

'You don't know, do you, Albert?' Tom did not await an answer. 'How long has she known Forbes McCulloch?'

'If you mean how long has she been his — his sweetheart, five years going on six. I didn't approve of the arrangement and all I can say is, thank God her mother, that Florence isn't alive to see what's befallen her daughter. Yes, I say daughter, Tom; although she wasn't, she seemed like it, and Florence and I both thought of her as our flesh, our own dear child.' He placed a finger to the corner of his eye and brushed at an invisible tear. 'Since McCulloch abandoned her things have been very bad for us. She, the dear girl, knows how worried I've been about making ends meet what with the baby coming and all, and how I've not been well. I mean, she wouldn't stoop, would not humiliate herself by begging Forbes to give her money. She wanted to go to you, to take you into her confidence. She knew you'd understand, that you'd see us right until we got straightened out and back on our feet. But I said no. No, I said. Tom's got a life of his own and a wife of his own and a house of his own and he doesn't want to be bothered with you. But' — Albert paused for breath, sighed, gestured with an open palm — 'obviously she didn't heed my advice. Swallowed her pride, not for her sake, for my sake, my sake and the baby's.'

Tom listened patiently and apparently without scepticism to the harangue. He listened without moving from his stance by the window, his arms folded, long chin tucked down almost to his breastbone.

Albert watched for a sign, any sign — a quiver of the lip, a clenching of the fingers, a quick moist flutter of the eyelids — that he was making headway, getting through, but Tom's expression was remarkably unrevealing.

'So,' Albert said, 'will you help her, Tom? She's been a foolish girl, a wicked girl, she's aware of that, she's ready to admit it, but she has no one else to turn to now, no one else who will stand by her in her time of need, and you, after all, are her papa.'

'Where is she, Albert? She's more than eight months pregnant. Where is she?'

It was the one question that Tom had no right to ask, the one question to which he, Albert Hartnell, could not fudge an answer, a question that nullified all that had gone before and wasted the long heart-rending, hypocritical speech that had been the one and only card in his hand.

He covered his eyes to hide his tears.

'Oh, Tom,' he said, sincerely. 'Oh, Tom, I wish to God I knew.'

*   *   *

Gowry drove for a little over an hour. Even at speed the motion of the Vauxhall generated no cooling breeze. The air seemed almost abrasive, stinging his cheekbones and brow. He followed the route that Forbes and he had driven one afternoon not long after his brother's break-up with Sylvie. They had talked about it then in a general sort of way and before he'd had any reason to take Forbes's suggestion seriously.

She bounced beside him, knees spread under the summer dress, one fist on the padded rim of the panel, the other hand held not to her bonnet but to her stomach as if to keep in place whatever nestled within her.

Fifteen miles out the road narrowed and dipped into the valley under the ridge of the Ottershaw Hills and the twin rivers that watered the plain became visible. The sky to the west was marked by a long, flat plain of matt black cloud that lay motionless behind the mountains.

Inside his flapping leather overcoat Gowry sweated.

He wished that she would ask him where he was taking her. Her trust in him made him feel bad.

They passed farm wagons laden with late hay or, for all he knew, straw from the first-cut crops of the autumn season. They passed a miller's van grinding down the hill into the village, then two carts and, scattered along the grassy verge, a skitter of eight or ten bullocks in the care of a man and a boy.

Gowry braked, slowed to a point where he could hear the engine spluttering and smell the brassy stench of the radiator coming up to the boil.

As the motor crawled past, Sylvie waved and called out, 'Don't be frighted. Don't be frighted,' not to the boy or the man but to the dung-smeared and panicky cattle. 'It's only a motoring car, our motoring car.'

Gowry steered to the bottom of the hill and turned left towards the loch.

✳   ✳   ✳

'I take it you've heard the news?' Kay said as soon as her sister-in-law was shown into the drawing-room.

'Of course I have heard the news,' Lilias retorted. 'Do you think I would be visiting at this hour of the morning if I hadn't heard the news?' She paused and composed herself for the half lie. 'Martin called me on the telephone and I cancelled my appointments and came round straight away.'

'Do you want tea?'

'No, Kay, I do not want tea. I want an explanation as to what's going on.'

'Desertion,' Kay McCulloch said. 'Plain and simple. There's your explanation. She's run off with her sailor boy.'

'That isn't the story I heard,' Lilias said.

She seated herself on the sofa and glanced at the portrait of her long-dead sister-in-law that hung over the empty fireplace. It had been years, in fact, since she had been in this room in her brother's house, for she had never been a frequent visitor to Brunswick Park. In spite of her agitation the portrait caught and held her attention; she had forgotten just how pretty Lindsay's mother had been in her youth.

Kay said, 'I'm not sure he'll want to take her back.'

Lilias gave herself a little shake. 'Pardon?'

'Forbes: I'm not sure he'll have her back.'

Lilias had heard rumours about Lieutenant Commander Paget's interest in her niece but, having met the fellow, found it difficult to cast him in the role of seducer. It was fortunate, however, that Martin had had the foresight to call her on the telephone and tell her what had occurred at the yard and to confirm Lindsay's version of events, otherwise she might have been tempted to give some credence to Kay's threat.

Kay said, 'He might: just to avoid a public scandal, he might.'

'A public scandal?' Lilias said.

'A divorce would be all over the newspapers.'

Lilias gave a ragged little laugh. 'Ah, I see. Forbes is willing to forgive and forget out of a sense of family duty. How noble of him. What, may I enquire, would Forbes's case stand upon?'

'Desertion. She walked off with another man.'

Even Lilias was flabbergasted at the woman's effrontery, the conviction that her son was the wronged party and her ability not merely to twist the facts to suit that view but to accept her version as absolute and incontestable.

'Lieutenant Commander Paget?'

'That's the man,' said Kay, nodding. 'Her lover.'

'Kay.' Lilias chose her words with care. 'I feel that I should warn you to be careful in what you say. There is such as a thing as slander, you know.'

'Walked out of this house on his arm and hasn't been seen since.'

'What — twelve hours ago?'

Flat denial, Kay's defence, would not stand up for long. Apparently it hadn't dawned on her sister-in-law that she, Lilias, had already heard the whole story and that Forbes McCulloch's scandalous affair with poor Tom Calder's daughter was swiftly becoming common knowledge.

'Is . . .' Lilias paused. 'Is Forbes at work?'

'Of course he is,' Kay said indignantly. 'He's not going to squander valuable time trailing after her, is he? It's up to her to come back to him.'

'I see,' said Lilias. 'And to ask his forgiveness?'

'He's a generous boy. He might do it.'

'Is that what you would advise him to do, Kay?'

'It isn't up to me. He's a grown man now.'

'Not too old to heed his mother's advice, surely?' Lilias said.

She had lost her awe of the McCullochs long ago. She had nothing but scorn for them and knew that if she set her mind to it she could shred her sister-in-law's arguments and grind them down as finely as a pound of Scotch beef. It was, Lilias saw, not ignorance or deviousness but a mad kind of egotism that protected Kay and her kin against reality. She wondered at the nature of the man – a man she had never met – who stood in the shadow of this woman, who had fathered sons and daughters upon her and who, by the immutable laws of nature, must have had some sort of influence upon their lives.

'I will be telling Forbes,' Kay said, 'to do what's right.'

'Right for whom?' said Lilias.

'For the family.'

'To follow his conscience?' Lilias said. 'Is that what you mean?'

Instinct made Kay wary but not wary enough to avoid the trap. She stiffened her shoulders, straightened her spine and endeavoured to appear both hurt and haughty. 'Aye, that is what I mean.'

'And the child?'

'He would not be wanting the children to be without a mother.'

'Or a father?' Lilias said.

The foxy eye was suddenly as sharp and glittering as a shard of glass. Her head twitched and her lips were sucked in against her teeth. She squinted up malevolently at her tall and elegant sister-in-law as Lilias got to her feet.

'Or a father?' Lilias said again.

'Forbes isn't the father. That creature is lying.'

'That creature?' Lilias said. 'Well, eventually it will be for a court to decide whether she's lying or not.'

'Court, what court?' Kay said.

'Oh, come now, Kay, surely you don't think my niece is going to remain married to an adulterer?'

'She's the adulterer.'

'Is she?' Lilias said. 'On what evidence?'

'On the evidence of that sailorman.'

'Well,' Lilias said, almost too airily, 'I doubt if a counter-claim will carry much weight when it comes to arranging the financial settlement; but you never can tell with the law, can you? Meanwhile, our Mr Harrington or one of his colleagues will draft a petition for judicial separation so that proceedings may get under way. Lindsay will probably be anxious to have charge of the children – her children, I mean – and be free of her obligations to Forbes. She will, of course, expect to be maintained here in the family house on terms not dissimilar to those under which your son has been keeping Miss Sylvie Calder: rent paid and livings provided, that is. If those terms do not prove satisfactory, or if Forbes wishes to marry again in the near future, then we will progress immediately to a full petition for divorce, in which case the newspapermen will have a great deal of fun and the Franklins' business may very well suffer some setback.'

Kay listened with her mouth open.

'As to his position in the firm, the partnership,' Lilias concluded, 'that is not a matter than can be settled at once. Besides, it's something for the men to discuss and decide upon.'

'How?' Kay began: she swallowed. 'How did we fall to talking about the end of my son's marriage? Lindsay hasn't been gone but twelve hours; you said so yourself. Nobody knows where she is, what she feels about any of this. She's with her sailor . . .' Abruptly Kay jerked upright, scowling. 'Oh! So that's it!' she exclaimed. 'You *want* Lindsay to marry this sailor, don't you, so that Franklin's will have more pull with the navy contractors?'

'Don't,' Lilias said, 'be ridiculous.'

'Forbes will have something to say about that.'

'No doubt he will,' said Lilias. 'However, I have said *my* piece, Kay, and I'm going home now.'

'Hah!' Kay said. 'It'll be a different story when she turns up, you'll see.'

Lilias could not resist. 'Sylvie Calder, do you mean?'

'I mean Lindsay. She won't agree to any of this divorce nonsense.'

'Will she not?' Lilias said. 'Oh, I think she might, my dear, given that it was her idea in the first place. By the way, she has "turned up" as you put it, not that she was ever really lost.'

'What? Where is she?'

'At Harper's Hill, of course,' Lilias said, 'waiting to join me for lunch.'

They sat idly for a while on the shore of the loch under a jumble of elephant-grey boulders. Behind and around them conifers released a resinous smell in the sultry noon heat. The loch was not large enough to attract boatmen and there were no fishermen casting from the shore at that hour on a weekday.

The couple by the loch side did not speak. There seemed to be nothing left for them to say.

Sylvie sat back, the crown of the sun-bonnet crushed against the rocks, her legs stuck out before her. Even she was perspiring now, a light film of sweat on her upper lip and forehead. Folded passively on her stomach, her hands moved with the rhythm of her breathing. Propped on an elbow at her side, Gowry studied her cautiously. From across the tops of the trees, where the ridge broke to the north, came a faint mutter of thunder. Gowry raised his head and listened for a moment, then he said, 'You can still be rid of it, Sylvie.'

'It's too late,' she said.

'No, it isn't,' Gowry said.

He had taken off the leather overcoat and had left it in the Vauxhall. The motor-car was parked at the end of a rough track fifty or sixty yards away behind the rock step. He leaned closer, and lowered his voice.

'You can still be rid of it if you want to,' he said. 'I know a way.'

'What way would that be?'

'The way the girls do it in the part of Ireland where I come from.'

'Drowning. It's drowning,' Sylvie said. 'Isn't it?'

'Hmm,' Gowry murmured. 'It never fails.'

'She hasn't arrived yet. How can we drown her if she hasn't arrived?'

'You walk out into the water and stand there,' Gowry said. 'Stand there for – oh, five or ten minutes.'

Sylvie turned her head just an inch. 'That won't do it.'

'It will, you know. I've seen it happen.'

'Where?'

'In Malahide, in Ireland.'

'They must be very strange people in Malahide.'

'Oh, I see,' Gowry said. 'No, no, it isn't the drowning that does it, it's the cold. The cold does it. The cold causes them not to breathe any more.'

Her cool grey eyes were upon him. 'And then what happens to them?'

'They pop out.'

'Under the water?' Sylvie said.

'Under the water,' Gowry said. 'It's painless. You won't even notice it. You don't even have to look. It just happens.'

'Does not.'

'Does too,' said Gowry.

She turned her head again and looked at her feet, then, lifting herself away from the rock, stared at the glassy water.

'Do you think,' she said, 'I should try?'

'I dunno,' said Gowry. 'It's up to you.'

'Does it always work?'

'Always.'

'Gowry, do you want me to try?'

Sweat ran down the sides of his face. He did not dare wipe it away. She wasn't looking at him, though, she was looking at the water.

'I think,' Gowry said, 'that Forbes might want you to try.'

'Did he tell you that?'

'Yes. Yes, he did.'

'It would be all right without the baby, wouldn't it?' Sylvie said. 'I mean, it would be all as right as rain again without the baby. He would come back and it would just be the same as it was before.'

'Hmm.'

She glanced at him quickly. 'What about his wife? She'd know about the baby. She would think badly of me. I wouldn't want her to think badly of me.'

He wanted to ask why Lindsay's opinion mattered but Sylvie had a blank expression on her face now, neither anxious nor eager.

Along the edge of the loch a dipper hopped, leaving no ripple.

Gowry said, 'She wouldn't care what had happened to the baby.'

Sylvie removed one hand from the mound of her stomach, bent the elbow, braced the wrist. She still didn't look at him.

'I'll do it if you tell me to, Gowry,' she said.

'Forbes . . .'

'No, Gowry. If you tell me to, I'll do it.'

'All right,' he whispered. 'Do it.'

She pushed herself up on her arm, rolled on to one knee and hoisted herself to her feet. The dipper flew off, skimming low along the edge of the loch. The loch reminded Gowry of oil, a great slick of black diesel, brown only in the sunless shallows where the stones were. He watched her stoop and take off her shoes and waddle down to the water's edge.

Out beyond the brown rim the water swiftly became black.

He longed for her to give him a second chance, to glance back, swing round, say in that bright, bewildered voice of hers, 'Gowry, are you sure?'

She did not turn round. She knew what he wanted her to do, what Forbes required of her. Barefoot and bare-legged, she walked straight into the loch. She did not lift her skirts. He watched them fill with air then water, saw them settle around her first like petals then like weed. He was hardly breathing now. Any slight sound might break into the spell that Sylvie laboured under. Oh, yes, laboured under! How much of a joke is that right now, Gowry? he thought, as he watched her wade ankle-deep, knee-deep, out through the brown shallows.

She waded on, her arms raised, struggling against the weight of her skirts, the weight of the water. She stopped. She stared straight ahead of her at the wall of conifers on the further shore. The sun bonnet had slipped back on its ribbon and hung on her curls. She placed her hands on the surface of the water, palms down, fingers spread. She seemed to be thinking, to be contemplating something, Gowry could not imagine what. The waterline was slick and black around her distended stomach. One step and she would be gone. One step, he thought, one tiny step. He felt sweat all over his body, chill as ice.

She seemed to be waiting, not afraid, but lost without his instruction.

Gowry got quietly to his feet, never taking his eyes from her.

She paddled her palms gently on the surface of water.

He saw ripples spread out across the loch in thin steely lines and heard them lap on the brown stones in the shallows; then he closed his eyes and said, 'Sylvie, come back here,' just as she disappeared.

CHAPTER TWENTY-ONE

The Piper's Tune

By mid-afternoon the streets of Glasgow were awash and most of its citizens sheltering indoors or splashing along the pavements under the ineffectual protection of umbrellas and oilskin capes. The storm, it seemed, did not have the good manners to move on but rumbled and spluttered unseen behind the rain that poured unrelentingly out of formless clouds.

In Aydon Road Franklin's crews had been pulled off the hulls, for the ladders had become dangerously slippery and there was still in the black sky traces of the lightning that had raked the west of Scotland for an hour or more. In Sandyford, in Cissie's apartment, mistress and day-maid cowered in the small back bedroom while Ewan, normally so timid, leaped up and down on the bed and yelled with delight at every ear-splitting thunderclap and nerve-tingling lightning flash. In Harper's Hill, over the remains of a late lunch, Lindsay and her aunt were far too busy plotting strategy to be distracted by mere weather. When rain came sweeping over Kelvingrove and struck the big front windows, though, they did pause for a moment before continuing their discussion in raised voices. At the first peal of thunder, Pansy, not even trying to be brave, vanished downstairs to join the younger servants skulking in the pantry.

In Brunswick Crescent the inhabitants had scattered themselves throughout the house for reasons other than fear of a natural phenomenon. When Forbes had returned home he had stepped straight into a blazing row with his mother and sisters and had borne the brunt of their fury and frustration. He had been in no mood to back down, however, and in the heat of the moment had screamed at them to go to hell, or back to Malahide, or do what the hell they wanted, and had blamed them for the predicament in which he, the favoured son, now found himself.

The Lanchester, Uncle Donald Franklin's pride and joy, remained parked in the lane behind the crescent where Forbes had dumped it after a fruitless search for his brother. First he had driven to Gowry's lodgings, then, close to opening time, to Kirby's. Finally, in desperation, he had steered the awkward machine the length of Maryhill Road to tour side streets and back streets in the vicinity of St Mungo's Mansions in search of the yellow Vauxhall. At one point he had even been tempted to jettison the Lanchester and race upstairs to the tenement flat, but something – caution perhaps, not conscience – had checked him and he had driven away again, fast and furious, before frustration overwhelmed common sense.

With thunder pealing overhead and lightning sizzling among spires and chimney-pots, Forbes had headed back to Brunswick Park. He knew that he was beaten, that Gowry had eluded him; Gowry might be anywhere, trolling about in the Vauxhall or back by now in the stable yard at Aydon Road listening to the apprentice boys' tales of mystery and woe. There lurked in Forbes, however, a faint flicker of hope that his brother had taken things into his own hands and that, out of loyalty, had gone to do what he, Forbes, dared not.

Then he had stepped into the shouting match in the drawing-room and had learned of Lindsay's intentions and been told just what his mother really thought of him and how by his shenanigans he had ruined his sisters' prospects.

There was no moral disapproval in the family's revisionist view of his worth, only fury at how he had let *them* down, how his wayward behaviour had affected *them* and damaged *their* future; not a word about Sylvie, not a thought for what had propelled him into Sylvie Calder's arms, what *he* needed, what *he* wanted that neither Franklins nor McCullochs could provide. Then, when thunder broke over the house and Philip started shrieking upstairs in the nursery, he lost patience completely and stalked off into the piano parlour from whose narrow rear window he could look down into the lane.

After a time Philip stopped shrieking and rested his head against Eleanor's bony shoulder. She had prudently removed her cameo brooch and hair-pins and had brought down from the nursery — snatched from under Winn's nose — a knitted blanket which, though not required for warmth, offered the child softness and security. She had wrapped him in it before she had lifted him from his cot and, steering Harry before her, had taken both children down from the nursery to her small bedroom two floors below.

Miss Runciman was not disturbed by freak weather but she was concerned by its effect on the children, particularly on Harry who was old enough to be aware that something unusual had happened downstairs. With disarming lack of guile he had asked where his mother was and why Winn was crying and why Grandma McCulloch shouted so loudly at Blossom after Great-aunt Lilias had gone away, questions that Eleanor had done her best to answer in a manner that would not alarm him.

She had brought a jug of hot chocolate up from the kitchen and a small bowl filled with cream, and to entertain Harry and soothe Philip, she fed each of them turn and turn about with spoonfuls while the thunder crept closer and the arguments downstairs grew louder and more intrusive. At some point Forbes must have returned home; Eleanor could make out his voice, not sinuous now, but sharp and violent. Soon thunder drowned out the voices and Philip snuggled, whimpering, against her while Harry, fascinated by the force of the rainstorm, stood on tiptoe at the little window and peered down into the lane where Donald Franklin's motor-car, hood down and panelled windows wide open, appeared to be filling up with water, like a bathtub.

'Oh!' Harry said. 'Oh-oooh!'

Eleanor said, 'Someone's been very careless, Harry, haven't they?'

'Papa,' Harry said, with a little sigh. 'It was Papa.'

Cradling Philip in her arms, Eleanor made a few more tours of the bedroom before she laid him on her bed to sleep. She sat by him, stroking his silky hair while lightning petered out and the thunder prowled off into the distance. There were no sounds from below, the voices had ceased. She heard a door slam and another open. She heard feet upon the stairs and another door, on the floor above this time, open and close.

Elbows propped on the windowsill, Harry was oblivious to everything except the silver rods of rain that shot out of the sky, the torrents of white water discharged by overloaded eaves and the rivers of mud that covered the cobbles of the lane. Eleanor watched him fondly from the corner of her eye; Lindsay's child, Arthur's grandson, as bright and lively and curious as any Franklin.

Then Harry turned to her and said, 'It's Uncle Gowry. Uncle Gowry's come home early too.'

Going to the window, Eleanor saw that the little boy had told her the truth and together they watched Gowry brake the Vauxhall, climb down from the driver's seat and unlock the padlock on the garage doors. He was drenched, drenched to the very skin, but he did not seem to care.

He hauled open the doors, then, glancing round, stopped what he was doing as Forbes emerged from the gate at the rear of the house and crossed the lane towards him.

'Papa,' Harry said, almost beneath his breath.

'Yes, dear — Papa,' said Eleanor Runciman and, frowning, watched the brothers' curious meeting in the rain.

'Look at you,' Forbes said. 'A drowned rat's got nothing on you, boy. Where have you been with my motoring car then? Sylvie's?'

'Aye, Sylvie's.'

'Don't go telling me she's dropped the kiddie?'

'No, she hasn't dropped the kiddie,' Gowry said. 'Do you like standing here in your shirt sleeves getting soaked or will you be going inside?'

'I wouldn't be going inside, not if I were you,' Forbes said. 'Mam's on the rampage and I'm sick of the sound of her whining. Tell you what, why don't we step into the garage here and have a wee bit of a chat?'

'Why don't we do just that,' said Gowry.

They moved through the doorway into the gloom. The brick-built mews still reeked of horses, though it had been twenty years at least since a horse had been stabled there. Rain hissed on the sloping slate roof and Gowry shivered a little and pulled the leather overcoat more tightly around him.

Forbes said, 'So, you went to see Sylvie, did you?'

'I did,' Gowry said.

'And?'

'There is no "and", Forbes. We went for a drive, that's all.'

'A drive in the country?'

'Yes.'

Forbes's face was white in the trick of the half light, almost skull-like, Gowry thought. He was clad only in a waistcoat and collarless shirt and the smart serge trousers that he wore to the office. He did not seem to feel the chill that had come into the air now that the rain had begun to take effect. Gowry folded his arms tightly across his chest. He wanted only to be somewhere warm, somewhere dry, out of all this.

'Did you take her to the loch?' Forbes said.

'Yes.'

'Did she go willingly?'

Gowry shrugged. 'A day in the country; yes.'

'Did she tell you that she'd seen my wife yesterday? I mean,' Forbes said edgily, 'that she'd called on my sister-in-law, on Cissie Calder, that it was two birds with the one stone. Lindsay was there too, taking' – he paused – 'taking tea. And then there was Sylvie with her belly sticking out and a story to tell them.' Again, he paused. 'She's ruined it for me, the bitch. Ruined everything. Lindsay's left me and she's even talking about divorce.'

There was a whining note in his brother's voice that Gowry had never detected before. He wondered if what Forbes had said about Mam were true, if any of this was exactly true; if, perhaps, it was not the Irish version, Forbes's version. He kept his mouth shut, though, said nothing about his affair with Sylvie. It was something that Forbes did not need to know and, with luck, would never know; how he, Gowry, had colluded in the end game, how he had rounded it off by a simple act of betrayal.

All he wanted now was to be finished with it, to climb out of the servant's uniform once and for all and to be slave to no man, least of all his brother.

He knew the question Forbes wanted to ask, though, how all the rest of it, the cat-footed, soft-footed, self-justifying approach was only fear of what the answer would be and the consequence of it.

He lacked Forbes's ruthlessness, his viciousness.

He had discovered that much about himself that very forenoon.

'You see where I am?' Forbes said.

'You'll get her back,' Gowry said. 'Lindsay I mean – which is more than can be said for Sylvie.'

'Is she – did you . . .'

'She did it herself,' Gowry said.

'What? She . . .'

'She walked into the loch,' Gowry said. 'I didn't have to push

464

her. I just had to tell her that was what you wanted her to do, that was your wish, your will for her, and she walked out into the water of her own accord.'

'And – what did you do?'

'I watched,' Gowry said.

'God! She always was a stupid little cow but I didn't think . . .'

'And then I told her what *I* wanted her to do,' Gowry said.

'What do you mean?'

'I told her to come back. I told her *I* wanted her to come back.' He shook his head, ruefully. 'I left it too late, though, almost too late. She'd have gone through with it if I'd just left her alone. That's what got to me. I never thought she would actually go through with it.'

'You mean Sylvie's dead?'

'Of course Sylvie isn't dead,' said Gowry. 'Do you think I'd be standing here now if I'd let her go through with it? All I had to do to put a stop to it was tell her that I really wanted her to come back.'

'She isn't dead then?'

'Then I had to prove it,' Gowry said. 'I had to go out for her. I had to go out into the deep water and bring her back in. Christ, Forbes, she would have done it, if I hadn't stopped her.'

'Done it for me.'

'Done it because nobody ever, *ever* told her to come back to them.'

'So,' Forbes said, 'you've turned on me too, have you?'

'Turned on you?' Gowry said.

'How am I going to get Lindsay back now when Sylvie's still . . .'

'That's your pigeon, Forbes, not mine,' Gowry said. 'I'm going home.'

'Home?'

'To Ireland, to bloody Ireland, to Dublin or maybe to Belfast,' Gowry said, 'and I'm taking Sylvie with me.'

'She won't go, she won't leave *me*.'

'She will, Forbes. She left you this forenoon.'

'Ireland!' Forbes said. 'What the hell will you do in Ireland?'

'Work,' Forbes said. 'Work in a brewery, in a motor garage, something, anything to keep body and soul together. My body, my soul – and my wife's.'

'You'll marry her?' Forbes said. 'You'll marry her with my baby inside her? God, you must be desperate to have her. Listen, why don't we—'

'Talk about it?' Gowry said. 'I've talked enough, Forbes. I've listened to you long enough. I'm sick, *sick* of your talk. Know what, you almost talked me into murder and I would have had to live with that for the rest of my life. I'd rather live with Sylvie, thank you very much.'

He moved suddenly, pushing Forbes aside.

He hauled open the garage door and stepped out into the lane.

The rain had eased, though only a little, and water ran in torrents still from rhones and eaves and rooftops, and the lane behind the house was like a river, carrying away the summer dust.

'Gowry,' Forbes shouted. 'Goddamn you, Gowry, you can't go like this. Listen to me, listen to me.'

Already halfway down the lane, Gowry raised a fist.

'Don't worry, Forbes, I'll post you back the uniform,' he shouted, then, digging his hands into his pockets, trudged on around the corner and out of his brother's sight.

'Hold on, Kay,' Arthur said. 'It isn't a sinking ship, you know. You don't all have to leave just because of Forbes.'

'Because of Forbes?' his sister said. 'Because of you, more like.'

'Me?' Arthur said. 'What have I done?'

'You never made us welcome.'

'That,' said Eleanor Runciman, 'is very unfair.'

'I was always led to believe that blood was thicker than water, Arthur,' Kay said, 'but not in this household, it seems.'

'If you're implying that Eleanor . . .'

'Gentlemen do not address a housekeeper by her Christian name.'

'I do,' Arthur said. 'In this house, I do.'

'Well, it isn't right,' Kay said. 'And this isn't the sort of lax atmosphere in which I want my girls to grow up — so we're leaving, all three of us.'

'When?' Eleanor said. 'If, that is, I may be permitted to enquire.'

'It's none of your concern,' Kay said.

'I will have to engage new staff as soon as possible.'

'That's up to Forbes,' Kay said. 'My girls work for him, not you.'

'I suppose that's true,' Arthur said. 'He isn't leaving with you, I take it?'

'Forbes leave? This is his home,' Kay said. 'It may no longer be his wife's home but it is his home and it will remain so unless you take it into your head to throw him out, too.'

'Kay, I am not asking you to leave,' Arthur said, with a sigh. 'In fact, I thought you might prefer to stay on and offer your support.'

'Support, support to whom?'

'Your son,' said Eleanor.

'This woman,' Kay said peevishly, 'should not be here while we discuss our private business.'

'Stay where you are, Eleanor,' Arthur said. 'I may be in need of your advice in a moment or two.'

'Advice about what?' said Kay.

'How to proceed,' said Arthur.

'Proceed?'

'It seems clear,' Arthur said, 'that you are leaving because you do not wish to be involved in any sort of scandal.'

'Scandal? I'm not afraid of scandal,' Kay said.

'Then why,' Arthur said, '*are* you leaving?'

'Because Forbes told them to go,' Eleanor put in.

'That, miss, is a downright lie,' Kay snapped.

'First Gowry and now you,' Eleanor said. 'I saw him dismiss Gowry this afternoon. He has, I believe, already gone. I may only be a humble housekeeper, Mrs McCulloch, but I have been with the Franklins long enough to take everything that happens in this family very seriously. I heard your argument. No, I was not eavesdropping; the voices were all over the house. I could not help but hear them. Forbes wants Lindsay back, does he not?'

'That has nothing to do with it, nothing at all,' said Kay.

Arthur was seated on the piano stool, elbow resting on the lid, not at all put out by the prospect of his sister's departure or by Eleanor's interventions.

He said, 'Nothing to do with it! Of course it has.' He drummed his fingers on the polished wood. 'As for there being no scandal, Kay, of course there's a scandal. It's a scandal that Forbes fathered a child on another woman, not just any woman, but the daughter of a colleague.'

'Forbes married too young,' Kay said. 'He never had time to sow his wild oats. You pushed him too hard, Donald and you. You forced him into marriage.'

'What utter nonsense!' Arthur exclaimed.

'You even denied him a place of his own. That's all that Forbes ever wanted, a place of his own. But you wouldn't let your precious daughter go. No, you had to have her by you to make up for what happened to Margaret.'

Arthur sucked his under lip. If he was hurt by his sister's remark he gave no sign of it. 'I'm sorry if that's what you think, Kay,' he said, 'but I'm no longer prepared to spend my life listening out for the piper's tune.'

'The what? What are you talking about?'

'Those days are past. I'm tired of yearning for what I never had or what might have been. I've survived thus far and I will survive a few more years yet, God willing, and I will give my support to Lindsay whatever she chooses to do.'

'Even if she chooses to share a bed with some sailor?'

'If Lindsay decides to remain with Forbes, or if she decides to divorce him,' Arthur went on evenly, 'I will support her.'

'And her lover, her officer?' Kay persisted.

'If she loves Geoffrey Paget I will not stand in the way of a divorce,' Arthur said. 'However, you have turned the issue on its head. You were always good at that, Kay, much cleverer at that than any of us boys ever gave you credit for. It's not my daughter who is to blame for this current mess, it's your son. You will not face that fact, will you? You cannot bring yourself to admit that Forbes has let you down.'

'He was — Forbes was . . .'

'Wrong,' Arthur said. 'He was wrong, Kay, admit it.'

'She never loved him,' Kay said.

'If you mean Lindsay,' Arthur said, 'that remains to be seen.'

'*If* she comes back to him?' Kay said.

'Or if she does not,' said Arthur. 'Meanwhile, I have no wish to be blamed for anything that's happened here. If you feel it's best to leave and allow Forbes to sort out his own troubles then that is your decision, not mine.'

'Wishy-washy, Arthur. You always were wishy-washy.'

He got to his feet and gave the lid of the piano a firm little rap with his knuckles, a sign of temper that only Eleanor recognised.

'When are you leaving us, Kay?' he asked.

'Tomorrow morning, first thing.'

'Well, thank God for that,' said Arthur.

Tom had given Albert Hartnell two five pound notes with the promise of another when he, Albert, let him know that Sylvie had returned to the Mansions. He had been tempted to wait in the apartment until his daughter appeared but he had no idea how long that might be. Besides, he found the place so depressing and Albert so lachrymose that he had left after a half-hour to catch a tram-car back into Glasgow and a train from there to Partick West.

As he trekked towards Aydon Road under looming black clouds, he found himself thinking of Lindsay, the changes that Forbes had wrought in her and how those changes had been reversed by her friendship with Geoffrey Paget. He would hardly blame her if she did run off with the naval officer, though he did not think she would. Yesterday, just yesterday, he had been on and under the Gareloch inside the *Snark* and his fears had been for his safety; how trivial and remote those fears seemed now. It wasn't sudden death or headline disasters that took you down but the unexpected intrusions of the past, those little claws of shame and contrition that tore at your stability.

Thunder boomed over Anniesland and sent echoes chasing like gigantic billiard balls down Crow Road. Lightning flickered above the tenements and the first great pattering drops of rain spotted the pavements. Pedestrians quickened their steps and carters whipped their horses into a trot as the rain came slicing down. Tom turned up his collar and loped towards the shelter of Franklin's office block and the consolations of the drawing-board. For the time being, he did not know what else to do but return to work and await word from Albert or from Sylvie, a message, he knew, that might never arrive.

At half past six o'clock Tom packed up and went home. The streets still ran with rainwater but the sky had cleared and little blinks of sunshine and faint patches of blue were visible across the river. He had heard no more about the morning's unfortunate incident, for Forbes, apparently, had left the yard and had not been seen since; nor had there been a message from St Mungo's Mansions. The first thing Tom saw when he let himself in to the hallway of the Sandyford apartment, however, was luggage: two large suitcases, a carpet-cloth valise and a big hat-box tied with twine. His first thought was that Cissie, like

Lindsay, had decided to leave home, that he had somehow driven her away.

He flung open the drawing-room door.

'Hello, Papa,' Sylvie said. 'I'm so glad you weren't late. We could not have waited for you if you had been late.'

He could think of nothing, nothing at all to say. It had been so long since he had seen her that he had almost forgotten what she looked like. He had cherished a vague idealised image of her in his mind, like a tiny tinted miniature locked behind scratched glass. Now she was here, perched on his armchair, with Gowry McCulloch standing awkwardly behind her and Cissie seated across the carpet. He felt tears thicken in his throat at the sight of his lost daughter, that chance child, the changeling whom he had traded away.

He glanced at Cissie and said, 'Where's Ewan?'

'The maid's taken him out for just a little while,' Cissie said.

Sylvie said, 'I didn't know until yesterday that I had a brother.'

'Half-brother,' Gowry McCulloch corrected her gently.

'A half-brother then. I am going to have a sister for him, or will she be — what will she be, Gowry?'

'I'll have to work that one out,' Gowry said. He glanced at Tom. 'I thought you might want — I've brought her to say goodbye.'

'We're going to Ireland on the night boat, Papa,' Sylvie said. 'Gowry, baby and me. We are sailing off to Ireland in search of better weather. She will be a little Irish colleen and Gowry will teach her to dance when she is old enough or, if she has a voice, she will learn to sing Irish songs.'

Her hair was coarser, not so golden, and quite bedraggled under her flowered bonnet. In spite of her prattle, she was a child no more. The shape of the child within her was so vast that it seemed to consume even his memory of Sylvie. He was tempted to throw himself on his knees, take her into his arms and beg her forgiveness for all the harm that he had done to her. But the man behind the chair – not Forbes but Gowry – seemed so stern and protective that Tom could not bring himself to approach her too closely. Instead, he aligned himself with Cissie, positioning himself by her chair; plump, freckled, plain, loving Cissie who was his protection against the past and his promise for the future.

'Is your brother behind this abrupt departure?' he asked Gowry. 'Are you doing it for his sake?'

'No, I'm doing it for her sake,' Gowry McCulloch said.

'I came back, you see.' Sylvie twisted round and glanced up, smiling, at the man behind her. 'Gowry fetched me back. Gowry says he will marry me, and I will be his for ever.'

'I hope,' Tom said, cautiously, 'that's how it will be.'

'That's how it will be,' Gowry said.

'I suppose you'll need money?' Tom said.

'I have money,' Gowry said.

'Did Forbes . . .'

'No, my money, my own money,' Gowry said. 'There is one thing you can do for us, though.'

'Albert needs looking after,' Sylvie said. 'Dada needs looking after until we are settled and he can catch the boat and come to Ireland and stay with us. Will you buy him a boat ticket when the time comes?'

'Of course I will,' Tom said. 'I'll make sure that Albert doesn't starve.'

'Or drink himself to death,' said Gowry.

'Dada is very upset to see me go, but baby won't wait and Gowry says we had better go at once.'

'We're leaving nothing behind,' Gowry said. 'I mean nothing.'

'Why are you doing this, Gowry?' Tom heard himself ask.

'Because he loves her, of course,' Cissie said. 'Is that not so?'

'Yes,' Sylvie answered for him. 'Gowry loves me.'

'It's high time someone did,' said Gowry.

*   *   *

It was, after all, a half-life or no real life at all and by the weekend Lindsay was sure that it would not end in tears, not her tears at any rate.

She still loved Geoffrey and in more propitious circumstances would have been happy to be his wife. But the truth was that she loved him lightly, admiringly, and, because she was a Franklin, she could not bring herself to swoop into an affair without a thought for the consequences.

She had, she knew, used Geoffrey, exploiting his reticence and natural decency, secure in the knowledge that he would never threaten her as Forbes threatened her and that, no matter how sometimes she might wish it so, he would never demand from her a dark, tempestuous, tormented passion. That, perhaps, was their true and mutual bond, source of their trust, the mainspring of a love that would tick away as quick and constant as a little watch, and that Lindsay would feel within her, against her heart, wherever he or she might be.

The trials were over and he must leave soon.

The *Snark* would cruise down the west coast to Barrow-in-Furness for Vickers-Martin to test her guns, then on to Devonport for a thorough testing of her torpedoes against mock targets. Then probably across to Gibraltar for crew training before she joined the fleet somewhere. Geoffrey would not sail with her: no doubt the First Sea Lord had other plans for him. The D-class prototype would not be rejected, however, Geoffrey was certain of that. Delivery payments would be forthcoming by the month's end and unless he missed his guess (and here he lied, even to Lindsay he lied) more contracts for undersea vessels would come Franklin's way in the future.

He would leave on Monday morning on the early train.

Lindsay had seen little enough of Geoffrey during her 'holiday' in the Central Hotel, for she had been planning too, planning how to return home again. There had been messages from Eleanor, a telephone call from her father, cheerful news from Brunswick Crescent, trips up and down to Harper's

Hill to consult her aunt and uncle, to be hugged sympathetically by Martin and patronised by Pansy, and to pick up every scrap of news from every possible source. She had even made time to meet her children in Kelvingrove late on Saturday forenoon, after the McCullochs had fled.

The air had been fresh after the thunderstorm, a breeze shook the wet leaves on the trees along the river, and Miss Runciman, as they strolled the walks behind the perambulator, had told her with palpable glee that Forbes had been devastated by his mother's threatened departure although he had instigated it and knew it was the only way to get Lindsay back. Soon after Forbes had left for work, therefore, Kay, Blossom and Winn had swept off, bag and baggage, and to all intents and purposes, literally as well as figuratively, Forbes would return to an empty house with no one to boss or bully or provide a target for his wrath.

After lunch at the Hill, Lindsay left Miss Runciman and the children with Aunt Lilias and went to call on Cissie and Tom at Sandyford. There she learned that Sylvie and Gowry had also left for Ireland and that Forbes, apparently searching not for his wife or his mistress but for his brother, had dropped in at Sandyford on his way to the yard. He had been so agitated and contrite that, astonishingly, he had wept into Cissie's shoulder over porridge and toast and had told her, with something approaching sincerity, that he had always considered her to be the best of his cousins and the only one he could trust.

Tom had been disgusted, or just this side of it, by the outburst and had refused to share a ride to work in the big, damp Lanchester that Forbes claimed to have borrowed to make his desperate rounds.

'You will go back to him, won't you?' Cissie said. 'I mean, dearest, you *must* go back to him, for in spite of all he has done, he *is* your husband and he cannot live without you.'

'Oh, I doubt that,' Lindsay said. 'I think Forbes would manage very well without me.'

'But what would he do? I mean, you're so — so close.'

It was not what Forbes would do without her that troubled Lindsay but what he would do with her. She feared that he would somehow re-knit the marriage to suit him, that his anxiety would quickly be forgotten and another girl, another woman, brought in to replace Sylvie. He would justify it by telling himself that he was too much of a man to be content with one woman and that he needed complexity, variety and spice. He would surely be more cautious next time too and appear to accommodate himself to marriage until his lies had taken root and he could safely renege on all his promises once more. In a word, Lindsay thought, how could she ever trust him again?

'Close?' she replied to wide-eyed Cissie. 'Yes, I suppose we are.'

'There's a special meeting of the partners on Monday morning,' Tom said. 'We're examining ways of acquiring more capital with a view to increasing our capacity. If your friend Paget's to be believed we might be in for a period of expansion, and we'll need to be ready for it.'

'Will — will anything be said about . . .'

'I hope not,' Tom said, 'but I think it rather depends on you.'

'On me?' said Lindsay, surprised.

'On whether you'll be there in person, or whether you will not.'

She was tempted to give him an answer. Tom Calder was after all her friend too, a chap she should perhaps have married. Different worlds, different times, different projections: there was no crystal ball, no writing in the stars to tell you what to do for the best. You had only your heart to listen to and, perhaps, your head. Tom, she realised, had tactfully reminded her that Franklin's was her destiny, Harry and Philip her future; a future that sometimes seemed to stretch into a dazzling infinity of possibilities and at other times to be as preordained as the passing of the seasons and the rising of the tides.

She would not go off with Geoffrey, of course, would not run away from her responsibilities. But she would not tell Tom that, or Forbes. She would keep her decision a secret for just a little while longer.

'Do you not think,' Lindsay said, 'that it rather depends on Forbes?'

'On Forbes?' said Cissie.

'On whether he accepts my offer,' Lindsay said, 'or whether he does not.'

'What offer?' Cissie said.

'Four sixty-fourths, Forbes,' Lindsay said. 'A transfer of four sixty-fourths from your share of the partnership into my name.'

'That can't be done,' Forbes said.

'Indeed it can. All it requires is the agreement of a majority of the partners and that, given the circumstances, will certainly be forthcoming,' Lindsay said. 'According to Mr Harrington there's no legal impediment to the transfer of shares between existing partners. He will draft the document and the board will nod it through.'

'You have been busy, haven't you?' Forbes said. 'Who put this idea into you head? Paget, was it? Is this what passes for pillow talk between you?'

He was sprawled on the sofa in the ground-floor drawing-room, legs crossed and hands behind his head. He did not appear to be at all distraught. Cissie, no doubt, would have been disappointed to find him so recovered but it came as no surprise to Lindsay. In fact, she would have been disappointed if he had been anything other than his sly, old arrogant self, for she had learned how to deal with that aspect of his character and had no wish to alter it. For this reason she had warned him of her arrival and had made sure that Eleanor, Arthur and the children would all remain at Harper's Hill.

Although Forbes had dressed with care, he could not quite manage to hide the bruised shadows under his eyes, or the wariness in them, and beneath the wariness she sensed an unusual fragility. He was, she realised, unsure of her, vastly and manifestly unsure.

'It was Paget, wasn't it?' Forbes said. 'He put you up to this, didn't he?'

'No,' Lindsay said, and left it at that.

Forbes smiled, and dandled his foot in mid-air. 'Where is your sailor boy right now? Is he waiting outside in a motor-cab to cart you back to his bed?'

'No,' said Lindsay again.

'You're staying in a hotel, aren't you?'

'I am.'

'How long are you going to remain there?' Forbes asked. 'I mean, sweetheart, haven't you got everything you want by now? I mean, you've got rid of my mother, my sisters, probably even my brother. You've got me all to yourself at last. Isn't that enough for you?'

'How much did you have to pay Gowry to take her away?'

Silence for a moment: 'I didn't know he had taken her away.'

'Well, he has,' Lindsay said. 'He's taken her to Ireland, I believe, where the baby will be born.'

'Really? So that's where old Gowry-Wowry's disappeared to, is it?' Forbes said. 'Who told you?'

'Tom. They called on Tom and Cissie before they left.'

'Scrounging the price of the fares, I expect.' He shook his head. 'I might have guessed it. Bloody Gowry just wanted Sylvie for himself. God knows why!'

'For the same reasons as you wanted her, probably,' Lindsay said.

'For your information I gave her up ages ago,' Forbes said. 'Haven't clapped eyes on her in months. So Gowry meant what he said, did he?'

'Good for Gowry,' Lindsay said.

Forbes brought his arms from behind his head. 'I didn't pay him to run off with her, you know. I didn't know he'd skedaddled until this very minute. I've been looking for the bugger for half the day.' He cocked his head. 'Did you have anything to do with this, Linnet? Did you shell out, too?'

'No.'

'All right,' Forbes said. 'That's my brother gone. You've cleared my family out good and proper, Lindsay. Isn't that enough for you? Do you have to ruin me financially as well?'

'That isn't my intention, Forbes.'

'What is your intention then?' Forbes said. 'To have more to spend pampering your sailor boy?'

Lindsay did not deny his allegation. She wanted him to believe his own insinuations, to convince himself that she was no better than he was, that one black did make a white. She felt disloyal to Geoffrey and yet – the little ticking mainspring within her was working well – she felt so close to him that she was almost sorry for Forbes who had nothing left to cling to now except the hope that she would allow him back into her life.

Forbes would never understand how she cared for Geoffrey or what there was between them. How could Forbes possibly know that without the knowledge that Geoffrey believed in her, even loved her, she would not have presumed to push him so far? She had not taken up with Geoffrey just to punish Forbes for his callous infidelity, however, for that long, ragged betrayal meant less to her than anyone, even Forbes, might imagine. What she did now she did out of pride, Franklin pride, to correct the mistakes that Pappy had made and to set her own course for the future for herself and her sons and, perhaps, for their sons too.

'Those are my terms, Forbes,' she said. 'Take them or leave them.'

'Terms. You're my wife, Lindsay. You don't make terms. No matter what you think I've done, *you* don't make the terms of our marriage.'

'In that case,' Lindsay said, rising, 'we will leave it to the lawyers.'

'What? Old Harrington?'

'To the court.'

'I see,' Forbes said tightly. 'It's a nice little threat, Linnet, a nice little bit of blackmail, but it isn't going to wash, not with me.'

'That's what Geoffrey said you'd say.'

'Did he now?'

'That's what he hoped you say.'

'Did he?'

'He predicted that you would take profit over marriage.'

'You're lying to me, Lindsay. He said nothing of the kind.'

'Oh, but he did,' said Lindsay. 'Do try to understand, Forbes, that I don't particularly wish to come back and live with you. I'd prefer a new life with Geoffrey Paget – and make no mistake, I have that choice – but I do have the children to consider and for that reason I'm prepared—'

'You'll never get the children.'

'I already have the children.'

'What? Jesus!' He looked up at the ceiling, wariness finally tinged with panic. She glimpsed in him now something of what Cissie had seen; not tears, not contrition but the bizarre vulnerability of a man trapped by his own hubris. 'Where are they? What have you done with the boys?'

'They're perfectly safe,' Lindsay said. 'They will always be perfectly safe with me, Forbes. Besides, what do you want with them? Are there not plenty more to come, here or in Ireland?'

'Bitch!' he said, without much rancour.

'I want the transfer of four points from the sixty-fourth part of your stake in Franklin's,' Lindsay said calmly. 'I do not want to ruin you or deprive you of income. You will continue to share in annual profits and take a salary, and you will still be a partner, of course, very much a partner.'

'But you'll have the lion's share?'

'Yes.'

'Do you really believe that all I care about is money?'

'No, I think you care more about power.'

'I didn't marry you for your money, Linnet.'

'Why did you marry me, Forbes?'

'Because I thought you'd make a good wife.'

'How disappointed you must be,' Lindsay said. 'I suppose that a good wife would be satisfied with an apology, some show or sign of remorse from her husband, an assurance that he really loved her and that no one else mattered.'

'I do love you, Linnet, you know that.'

'Do I?' Lindsay said. 'No, Forbes, I don't think I do.'

'What are you going to do with the kiddies?'

'Nothing. Eleanor and my father will bring them home shortly and put them to bed,' Lindsay said. 'By your definition I may not be a good wife, Forbes, but I'm not wicked enough to use the children against you. All I want is a larger share of the partnership just in case you decide that the next girl you take up with is worth the sacrifice of your home and family.'

'God, that's calculating.'

Lindsay felt her resolve beginning to crack. She strove to bear in mind that she had Geoffrey behind her and a legion of new possibilities, that she did not need Forbes now or require him to bend to her will. It could not be a contest, a struggle between equals. She had never quite grasped the fact before that what had made Pappy, Donald, her father and her cousins too, so different, was that they were males, born with the knowledge of how to compete without compromise. She, like most decent women, lacked that knowledge, that instinct.

'I have to be calculating, Forbes,' she said, 'otherwise you may take me for a soft mark again.'

'You were never a soft mark, Linnet,' Forbes said.

'And Sylvie Calder, what was she?'

'How the hell can I answer that one?' Forbes said. 'If I tell you she was just a bit of fun you'll think even less of me than you do now. And if I tell you I really cared for her . . .'

'Did you?'

'At first, yes. I did. I cared for her quite a lot.' He made as if to rise, to reach for her, but Lindsay stepped quickly away. 'I didn't care for her the way I cared for you. No, that's not just sweet talk, Linnet, that's the truth.'

'You just got tired of her and wanted a change, is that it?'

'She wanted me to marry her.'

'Ah, I see. That was never part of the bargain, was it?'

'I had no bargain with Sylvie,' Forbes said. 'I had an understanding, I suppose, an arrangement that I thought she understood perfectly well. But no, no, no, she had to have me all to herself.'

'What was your understanding with me, Forbes? Do you remember?'

'Oh, God! Not the love, honour and obey song-and-dance, Linnet. You're not going to warble that old tune, are you? You knew what you were getting into when you married me.'

'No, Forbes, I did not,' Lindsay said. 'But *you* thought *you* did.'

'Is Paget really waiting outside for you?'

'No.'

'Stay then. See the children. We'll all have supper together.'

'Geoffrey's waiting for me at my hotel.'

'My God! First you tell me you want terms, you *demand* bloody terms for what I did, then you waltz out of here and into bed with your sailor boy.'

'I'm beginning to think you don't want me back. Is the price too high, Forbes, is that it?' Lindsay made towards the door. 'I must go. I've no wish to keep Geoffrey waiting.'

Forbes got to his feet. 'He's leaving for London on Monday, or did he neglect to mention that interesting little fact?'

'I know perfectly well he's leaving on Monday,' Lindsay said.

'What will you do then, sweetheart?' Forbes said.

'Go with him, perhaps,' said Lindsay.

'Never! You'll never leave the boys, or the firm, or your father.' He straightened and fashioned the swaggering little gesture that she both loved and hated. 'Or me,' he said. 'Or me.'

'Well, Forbes,' Lindsay said, 'I hope you're willing to take the chance.'

And then she left.

Sunday would be their last day together. She did not know when she would see him again or if she would ever see him again but, oddly, she took on trust Geoffrey's assurances that they would meet as often as his duties allowed and that, with luck, he would be back in Scotland before the year was out.

In the morning, after breakfast, they attended church together, sat together, sang together in the strange echoing surroundings of the old Tron Kirk, unrecognised in the packed congregation. After lunch, they went walking, not in Kelvingrove but on Glasgow Green where Lindsay had never been before. She tried to imagine how difficult it must be for Sylvie Calder, a stranger in a new country, but she could not hold her concern for the girl in mind for long. Although she was content to be with Geoffrey, there was in her an odd impatience, as if she had merely stolen time out from the front line and that reality lay not here but elsewhere.

Geoffrey was very understanding. He did not press her, did not attempt to push his way into her other life.

She had told him of her meeting with Forbes, of the 'terms' she had offered her husband and his reluctance to accept them. She did not have to explain to Geoffrey why she needed terms at all, for he had always understood that what she felt for him was infinitely more complicated than what he felt for her and that her marriage was not over until her husband chose to end it. There were, he knew, no measured miles, no marker buoys, no gauges to record what proportion of their relationship was love and what necessity, or just where selfishness planed into friendship. He had, however, become part of her life, an important part, and that, for the time being, was enough for both of them.

✳   ✳   ✳

It came as no great surprise when Forbes capitulated.

Perhaps there should have been a meeting, a confrontation between the two men in Lindsay's life, but there was not.

When she returned to the hotel to dress for dinner she found a printed message on a silver tray on the dressing-table in her room, a simple, two-word message relayed through her father.

It said: '*Forbes accepts.*'

And that was when the pain began.

Rationally she had always known that she could not have all that she wanted, a past with Forbes and a future with Geoffrey. Choice not compromise was the reality that she had tried to avoid. She had leaned on Forbes finally, as she had leaned on Geoffrey, and now she must pay for it.

She lay on the bed in her hotel room and wept quietly for a quarter of an hour, weakened by the tensions of the past few days and by the knowledge that she would have to begin rebuilding her life to the pattern that had been handed her. And she wanted Geoffrey, wanted Geoffrey desperately, to justify her love by having him hold her naked in his arms. With an intensity that shook her to the core of her being, she wanted the future that Geoffrey offered, its mystery, its novelty. She wanted Geoffrey to be her love, her lover and her saviour. And yet she also wanted Forbes, her children, the ruined marriage that must be rebuilt, the opportunity that her grandfather had offered her to fulfil a role in the closed little world of the Franklin family.

Now the decision had been made.

She supposed that she might still back out, throw everything to the winds, but even as the thought crossed her mind she discarded it.

Tomorrow morning, early, Geoffrey and she must say goodbye.

There was, however, always tonight.

When the old-fashioned horse-drawn hansom rolled up to the kerb, Sergeant Corbett immediately leaped out of the office doorway with more alacrity than seemed right in a man of his years.

He had obviously been watching out for her and was quick to take the portmanteau from the hold and offer her a hand down the step.

'Am I expected, Sergeant?' Lindsay asked.

'Aye, Mr Forbes told me to look out for you.'

'And I'm late,' said Lindsay.

'Been away, Mrs McCulloch, have you?' Sergeant Corbett asked as he lugged the portmanteau towards the door. 'Bit of a holiday, was it?'

'Bit of a holiday, yes,' Lindsay answered. 'A day or two, that's all. I came directly from the railway station.'

'Like me to keep the case in my cubby while you're upstairs?'

'If you would, Sergeant, thank you.'

Even the commissionaire seemed unsure. She wondered what tales had been circulating around the yard, what sort of gossip George Crush had managed to generate. It hardly mattered. In a week or two it would all blow over and some other sensation, small or large, would take its place.

She stood in the foyer looking up at the staircase.

She had a thin little ache within her, not entirely unpleasant, and an empty feeling in the region of her heart that would not be filled until the first letter arrived from the south.

She had told the sergeant the truth, or part of it; she had come from the railway station. She had seen Geoffrey off on the London train at half past eight o'clock. He had been at his smartest, in uniform, cap squared, his baggage, worn and rather salt-stained, on the porter's barrow at his side. He did not, Lindsay noted, travel as lightly as she had imagined he would.

They had kissed in the corridor of the hotel.

They'd kissed again, almost without touching, on the railway platform. He had boarded the train at the last possible moment, just as great white plumes of steam had rolled back from the locomotive and the guard's whistle had shrilled. Lindsay shed no tears: she had nothing left to weep for. Geoffrey hadn't moved inside but leaned casually in the compartment window, glancing this way and that – then at her. Then at her. Smiling at her. Trim and reassuring, and satisfied.

'Write to me, darling,' Geoffrey said.

'I will,' she'd told him, as couplings clanked and the carriages began to draw tightly away. 'I will.'

She hadn't walked after the train. She'd stayed where she was, motionless, until the curve of the track carried him out of sight. She'd felt very alone, however, when she returned to the hotel to settle her bill and collect the portmanteau; very alone in the hansom too, clipping through the Glasgow streets in soft August sunlight, alone yet not alone, sad yet not sad, somehow oddly eager to arrive at where she belonged.

She hesitated. She knew what awaited her upstairs, the curious faces of men who were her partners, not just in shipbuilding but in life, her father and uncle, cousin Martin, Tom Calder too, and Forbes, her husband.

She went quickly upstairs and along the corridor, opened the door of the boardroom and stepped inside. It looked almost as it had done that day eight years ago when she had nervously attended her first management meeting, the panorama of the Clyde, lean and brown and sinewy, spread in the window, berths and sheds and jib cranes scattered untidily on the shores. She could smell tobacco and mingled with it the distinctive odour of the river and its industries that still brought a lift of pride to her heart.

Donald was seated at the head of the table, Mr Harrington by his side. Her father and Tom had their heads together discussing a diagram that Tom had drawn on his pad. Martin, arms folded, was watching the door, ready to greet her with a cheerful nod and a wink. And Forbes, grim and anxious, was over by the window, his shoulders resting against the glass. When he saw her, his expression changed and he could not quite disguise the relief in his eyes.

'There you are,' he said gruffly. 'It's about time too.'

'Ah, Lindsay,' Uncle Donald said. 'I'm so glad you could come.'

She lingered, at a loss, at the table's end.

How would they regard her now? Would they admire or condemn her for wresting power from her husband, for forgiving him his transgressions only at a price? Did they, perhaps, wonder what she had been up to all day yesterday, and all night too perhaps, with the First Lord's right-hand man?

Well, Lindsay thought, as she pulled out a chair at the table, they'll just have to wonder, won't they, for I'm not going to tell them.

'Gentlemen,' she said, smiling, 'don't you think it's time we began?'